KU-752-291

Acknowledgements

Thanks are due to Amira Ghazalla for rescuing me from ignorance too many times to mention, to Charlotte Horton for Cairo and Upper Egypt in 1997, to Maureen O'Farrell for Enta 'Omri and Cairo 1998.

In Luxor, 1997 and 1999, to Hassan Elaraby of Zalat Alabaster of Luxor, for his hospitality, his name, the germ of an idea and the look in his eye, to his nephew Ahmed the scarab maker, to Abu Nagarr for taking me places and showing me things. To Anwar in Aswan, for the mimosa.

To Umm Khalthoum (RIP) and Khaled for the singing, Laura Lloyd for the walks in the Old City, Tracey for the dancing nights and the Saudi rhythms, the Sufis at Al Ghouri, Mohammed and the staff of the Lotus Hotel for my moonlit desk on the roof, Ottavio for 'Chateau Champoleon', Madame Shenouda.

In England to Sgt Matthew Foley for listening and steering me right, to Tom Porteous for joining in, to Peter, Jennifer and Candida Blaker for hospitality at a vital time, to Cellmark Diagnostics for information on DNA testing, to Susan Swift, David Flusfeder, Derek Johns, Sam North, Linda Shaughnessy and the staff of AP Watt, Rebecca Lloyd, Philip Gwyn Jones, Karen Duffy, and Yvette Cowles at Flamingo, and Yvette's dancers across the country, John Warr of Warr's Harley-Davidson. Louis Adomakoh and Clare Brennan, of course. Roger Willis and Andy Shokks. Younus for correcting my Arabic, Ali for his necklace. Elizabeth Jane Howard, Beryl Bainbridge, Julie Myerson, Terence Blacker, Louis de Bernières for encouragement from further down the line. John Walsh for his amusement. Also Francesca Brill, Sandra Yarwood and Brad and Damon of Natural Nylon for their commitment to *Baby Love* the film, and the judges of the Orange Prize 1998 for the mixed honour of being longlisted.

Louisa Young

lives in London with her daughter. This is her second novel; her first was the highly acclaimed *Baby Love*. She is currently working on the third book of the Evangeline trilogy.

From the reviews for *Baby Love*:

'Engaging, wise-cracking, likeable, brilliantly sustained . . . funny, humane and utterly readable, full of insights about the way we are.' *Good Housekeeping*

'A tough, dextrous first novel.' Emily Ormond, *Guardian*

'*Baby Love* is as rich and improbable as a tale told by Scheherezade . . . intelligent, funny and tough.'
Jane Shilling, *The Times*

'Funny and scary . . . with a memorably David Lynch-style take on Shepherd's Bush . . . in writing honestly and unsentimentally, Young celebrates the unequivocal nature of parental love with verve and style.'
Julie Myerson, *Mail on Sunday*

'Must-read book of the month is Louisa Young's *Baby Love*, a story that manages to do the impossible: blend a promiscuous mix of single motherhood, belly dancing, psychotic boyfriends and motorbikes into a stylishly literate thriller.' *Marie Claire*

'Wry, perky, entertaining . . . ludicrously far-fetched but very enjoyable, packed with interesting facts about the history of belly-dancing and touching descriptions of mother-child love.' Christina Patterson, *Observer*

BY THE SAME AUTHOR:

A Great Task of Happiness: the Life of Kathleen Scott
Baby Love

Visit the Website: www.louisayoung.demon.co.uk
Email: angeline@louisayoung.demon.co.uk

LOUISA YOUNG

desiring cairo

Flamingo
An Imprint of HarperCollins*Publishers*

f l a m i n g o	The term 'Original' signifies publication direct into paperback with no preceding British hardback edition.
ORIGINAL	The Flamingo Original series publishes fine writing at an affordable price at the point of first publication.

Flamingo
an imprint of HarperCollins*Publishers*
77–85 Fulham Palace Road,
Hammersmith, London w6 8jb

www.fireandwater.com

First published in Great Britain by Flamingo 1999
9 8 7 6 5 4 3 2 1

Copyright © Louisa Young 1999

Louisa Young asserts the moral right to
be identified as the author of this work

Photograph of the author © Rupert Horrox

A catalogue record for this book
is available from the British Library

ISBN 0 00 655189 0

Set in Postscript Linotype Sabon
Typeset by Rowland Phototypesetting Ltd,
Bury St Edmunds, Suffolk

Printed in England by Clays Ltd, St Ives plc

for Isabel Adomakoh Young, the lovely daughter

CONTENTS

'I do believe that, with all its drawbacks, Egypt is the most interesting and convenient country that a lady can travel over.'

Eliot Warburton, 1845

one

Hakim

When Hakim ibn Ismail el Araby turned up on my doorstep, trailing clouds of chaos in his wake, I naturally assumed that the anonymous letters had something to do with him. Not that they were from him – like the rest of his family, the boy could haggle in ten languages and convert currencies, to his own advantage, faster than I could find a calculator, but writing in English was not one of his accomplishments. No, I rather thought they might be to him.

'I don't know if this is for you,' I said, over the breakfast table on the morning after his arrival. There we were, the three of us: Hakim and Lily tucking into boiled eggs and toast, and me making coffee, washing up, wiping surfaces, fetching the post. I don't normally make breakfast for young men who turn up out of the blue, but I do boil eggs for Lily. It makes me feel that I am giving her security, which she needs.

'My letter?' he said. 'You open, so you can read.'

I had already seen what it said. I was thinking all the obvious things – considering the nice-quality white envelope (no name, just my address), the perfectly ordinary looking office-type typing, the perfectly ordinary Mount Pleasant postmark (just one of London's main and busiest post offices). And inside a perfectly ordinary-looking piece of white

A4 paper, food of a million photocopiers and printers, with 'You killed my love' typed on it.

'It says "You killed my love",' I said.

'Strange for letter,' he said. 'Not mine, I think. Who do you love?'

'Not my love. The person who wrote the letter's love. I think.'

'Their love for you? Or what?' he said.

'I don't think so. Nobody loves me.'

'I love you,' said Lily. 'You know I do. I love you up to the moon and back again. Don't tell porkies.'

Lily my five-year-old daughter loves me. Big-eyed little-mouthed fat-cheeked clever-browed Lily. I basked in that for a moment. I'll never be used to it, unimpressed by it. Then I ran through the other love-contenders. Neil my lawyer friend doesn't love me any more. Harry . . . Harry who was my love . . . well (as the Shangri-Las sang) I called it love . . . Harry doesn't write letters like that. And we're on terms now, we speak, we have dismantled our melodrama, more or less. And my mum and dad love me. I didn't think it was them either. Though I had killed their love, in a way.

There's something you should know straight off. My sister died. She was pillion on my motorcycle, pregnant, claiming that she needed rescuing from her then boyfriend who she said was violent . . . Lily is – was – hers. Mine now. It's a long story and it has given me enough pain and grief over the years, and since everything settled a year and a half ago I do not want to drag over it.

I have grown up into a very private and anti-social person, what with my terrible experiences and my exciting past life. I was seriously fantasising about moving to the country when Hakim appeared. In fact I believe I was looking at a clutch of estate agents' details at the very moment my doorbell rang. It was September the eighth. Lily had started school that week. I wasn't worried about her, because she had been going to nursery for years, and we'd done the preview days where she goes in for a few hours before lunch and I hold her hand a bit. We'd bought a duffel coat though it was too warm for it; her Teletubby came to the gates with us although he wasn't allowed to stay.

So. Mid-morning, September the eighth. Nine days after Princess Diana was killed, two days after her funeral. You can probably imagine why I had been hiding my head under a cushion for a week. Young mothers dead in car crashes upset me no end. Cover their faces, and all that, when they die young. And cover my face too. Deep in the sand.

Watching (because no, I didn't join in) the national grievathon made me want to spit. This happens every day. Every day death turns people inside out, and when they get themselves right side out again they don't fit any more. Every day grief craps in the corners of someone's mind, somewhere where they can't find it, and if they can they can never get rid of the smell. To see it all writ so large and so sentimental for someone who we only saw on television, made me, what, angry. Resentful. I wasn't proud of that. Part of me would have liked to unite with the nation – truly. I get lonely out here, being a curmudgeon and an eccentric. But I kept wanting to shout at them. I've lost to death, I know what it is – and this is not your loss. Haven't you any grief of your own?

And for her children it's just motherlessness. Motherless children. Like so many.

Anyway. That morning. The doorbell rang. I answered it. There stood a young man in beautifully cut but unavoidably vulgar white clothes, with a dark overcoat which didn't really know what to do with itself slung over his shoulders. Or perhaps it was his shoulders which didn't know what to do with an overcoat. He looked too young for his clothes, his hair too short. Beside him was a large suitcase. He had a

3

small teardrop-shaped *aya* of the Qur'an in gold hanging on a chain round his neck, but I didn't need that to tell me he was Egyptian. There is something about that country, and it was all over him. Furthermore I knew his face.

He smiled a little nervously, the look at odds with his flashy clothes. '*Salaam alekum*,' he said. 'Madame Angelina? Good morning. Hello.'

I got the impression that he wasn't sure which greeting was the correct one for the circumstances. Not knowing quite what the circumstances were myself, I wasn't able to help him.

'*We alekum elsalaam*,' I replied automatically.

'Amira Amar,' he said quietly. Amira Amar means Princess Moon. Amar means beautiful, as well. It is a name some people used to call me when I stayed? lived? when I was in Egypt, ten years ago. After I ran away from Harry because he threw the chair out of the window at me because he thought I knew that my sister was a prostitute and didn't care, whereas in fact I hadn't a clue. I ended up in Egypt because it was somewhere I could work. I stayed there because that is what Egypt is like.

I was a belly dancer.

God, it seems strange even now to use the past tense. If I *was* a belly dancer, then what am I now? I am now ... a single mother, only the child is not mine. Oh well – she's mine, damn right she is, but it was only a year and a half ago that Janie's ex-boyfriend Jim decided to claim her as his, and gave us all a bit of a runaround until it turned out that he wasn't her father after all. So I live with the tiny yet fundamental fear that any Tom, Dick or Harry (and yes it might have been Harry) that my sister shagged in the course of her professional engagements (though she didn't shag Harry professionally – no, that was personal. As far as I know. Though of course she's not here to tell me. Harry said he

was drunk and thought it was me. God save us) . . . any Tom,
Dick or Harry might turn up and claim her, and have a claim.

So, I am an ex-belly dancer with a slightly gammy leg from
breaking it in three places in the accident which killed Janie.
(See how cool I am? I say the accident killed her, not that I
killed her. Two years ago I would have said I killed her. Now
that I know things about her that I could kill her for, I am
more forgiving of myself.)

So, I am an ex-belly dancer with a gammy leg and a beautiful child and a dead sister. I know a little about Arab social
history and culture – particularly through the dancing and
costume – and I earn a living as some kind of small-scale but
specific expert on that. I don't call myself an expert. The
first thing you learn about anything worth knowing anything
about is that you know nothing. Know about Arab culture?
It would take you seven hundred brains and seven thousand
years. But I wrote a book on belly dancing, and a few editors
and journalists know my phone number, and nobody else
whose number they have knows anything about belly dancing, so I am cast. And I write about other things, and teach
sometimes, and do some editing sometimes for some of the
magazines I've written for. Once I was costume consultant
on a TV series of *The Arabian Nights*. It's not like when I
used to jet off to Jordan to dance at weddings. But that's not
necessarily a bad thing.

What else? I try to lead a quiet life because I think that is
best for Lily. Every now and then I yearn for Egypt, and for
love, and for the beautiful clear sense of being right in my
skin, right in the world, that I used to get when I was dancing.
But though I am a bust-up dancer, and know what I have
lost, I don't like to think of myself as broken. So I carry on
as normal: working, taking Lily to school, seeing friends. Lily
is quite enough joy and glory, so I don't resent my stationary
existence. I love and cherish it. It seems safe. Or did, until

5

Jim came threatening it, and Ben Cooper the Bent Copper started blackmailing me and forcing me into the path of Eddie Bates, bastard, gangster, criminal mastermind and sexual obsessive. I describe him lightly, because he is the most frightening thing I have ever known.

But that's over. He's in prison. It's safe again.

I do keep a list of the men who I hope are not my child's father: Eddie Bates, Ben Cooper, Harry. Not necessarily in that order.

And so that is me, and I still live up in the clouds in my top floor flat in Shepherds Bush, and on my doorstep holding out his arms and hands and calling me a name from long ago, the name of someone who I certainly am not any more, stands – oh my God, it's one of Abu Nil's boys. It can't be the big one, Sa'id. Then . . . it must be Hakim. Hakim el Araby. Last seen in Luxor in 1987. Hakim, the sweet little scamp from the alabaster family at Thebes.

two

Luxor

'Hakim,' I said.

'Sister,' he cried, and grinned at me and poured a flood of the beautiful language over me, the precise meaning of much of which passed me by, though the spirit was clear. He was delighted to see me, he was amazed to find me home, what a long time it had been, and how was my health, *Alhamdulillah*, praise to God, and that of my father and mother, and so on, and so forth.

I invited him to step inside and take coffee. For a moment I wondered if he was old enough to drink coffee. He must have been ten when I saw him last, and here he was, grown up. Sort of. He refused the entrance and the coffee twice and I almost laughed. Here he is with his suitcase, straight from the airport, so recently left Egypt that I can smell the aroma of apple tobacco on his clothes, and his courtesy will hardly let him admit that he is here, and presumably for a reason.

'Come in, come in,' I said, and pulled his suitcase inside the door and led him to the kitchen where I found myself making *ahwa turky* – coffee stewed up the Egyptian way in my old *tanaka* – instead of a nice pot of espresso as I normally do. *Ahwa turky* made with Lavazza – it wasn't bad, actually.

He sat gingerly at my kitchen table and, as you do, looked around, taking stock of me and my life. I had no idea what

7

he made of it. I hadn't seen him since 1987, in Luxor; he'd been a kid, drawing pictures in the dust, playing football in the street, chasing scorpions, escaping his big brother. There were plans to send them to school in Cairo, and they didn't want to go. Presumably he had gone – he looked provincial, but not that provincial. More Cairene than Luxori. If I could still pick up those nice distinctions.

His father, now, his father I knew. Well, used to know, when I was there. It's a bore, this language thing. I could find my way round a newspaper or a novel in Arabic, with a dictionary; I could converse and grow fond and build a friendship, but maintain it? Write? Correspond? No. So there was a man, Ismail el Araby, known in the village way as Abu Sa'id, father of Sa'id. I used to call him Abu Nil, for some reason. Father of the Nile. He was one of the kindest I ever knew, with a face as brown and smooth and fissured as a kabanos, and a sneaky sense of humour, and two handsome sons, and secrets, who I liked enormously, but the friendship died. Killed by circumstance and illiteracy. My illiteracy. I had put it down as one of those magically unlikely friendships, of its time and of its place, like a Bob Dylan ballad, complete.

And now here's his boy, here in my flat.

There's no telling what my flat would mean to Hakim. My piles of fruit and laundry and newspapers, Lily's dolls on the sofa all seated in a row reading picture books, the late roses from Mum's garden dropping petals all over everywhere, the bag of empties waiting to be taken to the bottle bank. Would he be thinking me profligate, sluttish, what? I had a sudden and sharp resurgence of a feeling I often had in Cairo; an awareness of incomprehension, of the impossibility of complete comprehension: 'I do not know what all these people know; I have not learned what they all learned, they share something that I cannot share.' There were times when I hadn't a clue. Everybody laughing, and me bemused. Everybody

worried, and I could not, could not, using all my experience
and intelligence and imagination, work out why. Just humans,
bred in different habits. Before and after the marvels of the
individual, over and under all our common humanity, there
is this thing. We are different. It delighted me far more often
than it alarmed me, even in a world so very . . . different,
shall we say . . . for women. But it was always there. I was
a foreigner, I could not truly understand. I was not at home.
And for a moment, watching Hakim looking at my kitchen,
I felt a sudden cold flurry of not being at home.

But of course this flurry was not mine, it was his. I was
right in my territory; he was the one who was . . .

'Hakim, have you been to England before?'

In the tiny moment that I waited for his answer, I realised
he was wondering whether to lie to me. Why would he want
to do that?

'No,' he said. He looked so damn young. Silky, like a boy
who doesn't shave yet. Chicken-boned.

'What are you doing here?' I asked, in a completely friendly
way, of course. He took his coffee, smiled broadly, ignored
the question and offered me a cigarette. Marlboro. Of course.
The flash Egyptians always smoked Marlboro, while the
amazed foreigners puffed away on Cleopatra 100s at about
half a piastre a packet. Hakim, evidently, is baby flash. I
refused the fag, and opened the window. He made no 'oh
would you rather I didn't' noises. It didn't matter. Lily, with
her smoke-susceptible eczema and sweet delicate little lungs,
wouldn't be home for several hours. The doctor said I
shouldn't let anyone smoke in the flat at all, since the asthma
scare, but . . . oh God. Is he young enough for me to tell
him not to smoke? It's hard to tell an Egyptian anyway:
so inhospitable, so northern health-obsessive. Maybe later.
Anyway the window was open. The distant hum of the A40
filtered vertiginously up, up and past to diffuse in the clouds.

'You look well,' he said.

'*Alhamdulillah*,' I replied. Praise to God.

He started to speak in Arabic again, and I stopped him.

'My Arabic is not good,' I said.

'It was,' he said.

'It's been many years. I'm out of practice.' I learnt my Arabic initially from love songs. While I danced I soaked up all sorts of useful vocabulary: *Habibi, kefaya, enta 'omri* – my darling, enough, you are my life. *Elli shuftu abl ma teshoufak enaya*, what I saw before my eyes saw you ... It did get broader after that, but ... it was a long time ago.

'It's OK. My English is better. You have a husband?'

'No.'

He looked at the dolls. Their names are Tulip, Liner, Rose, Rosie and Rosabel.

'Just a child,' I said.

I wasn't actually prepared to go through a delicate dance around his sensibilities about this. I don't explain the whole story to people. It's too long, too private, too complicated, and, dare I say it, too boring for me to witness their stock reactions of amazement, shock, sympathy, incomprehension, in reaction to the weirdnesses that underpin my life. That *are* my life. And Lily's. It's not their business. If and when it becomes their business, I tell them. But very few new people need to know the whole story. Anyway I'm fifteen years older than him.

He raised an eyebrow.

'Child, no husband,' I said. 'That's right.'

'Divorced?'

If we had been in Egypt, I would have said yes, or said that the husband was dead, just to make life easier; here, I may not tell the whole truth, but I don't need to lie for comfort or protection.

'No,' I said. 'Never married.' Well, it was true. Janie never was married to Lily's father, whoever he was. And I have never been married.

Pity crept over his face, and incomprehension, and concern, and distaste, all at once, like the rainbow colours of oil skimming over water.

'It's different here, Hakim,' I said. 'It's no shame. No dishonour. If anything, the dishonour is to a man who leaves a woman and child. There is no dishonour to the woman.' If only that were quite true, I thought. But if I was going to educate him in Western ways, I was bloody well going to educate him in the ways of rational London post-feminism, not in those of hypocritical Tory backbenchers. He looked utterly unconvinced.

'How is your father?' I asked, realising that I hadn't asked before just at the moment that it suited me to change the subject. 'Is he well?'

Hakim narrowed his pale eyes and murmured something I didn't catch. This was wrong. The reply should have been a firm and grateful *Alhamdulillah*. I looked questioningly at him. He flashed me another little smile and said: 'I have a present for you', then with a laugh he went to the hall and began to unpack his suitcase, laying small piles of very tidy clothing all over the floor, as carefully as a stream of ants. I peered round the door at him. 'Give me one moment!' he cried.

I went back to my coffee. A minute or two later he came in with a small package. It was wrapped in white tissue and looked fluffy and light, but when I took it from him it was heavy. I laid it on the table to unwrap it. When the crisp, clean paper fell aside, there lay a small blue globe; a smooth, hard, polished ball of lapis lazuli, the shape and texture of a tiny cannonball. Its shades of colour shifted a little: murkier islands, paler seas. Flecks of gold streamed across it like clouds. It looked like the world.

I picked it up, felt its weight and gazed at it until its surface began to move and drift of its own accord, whereupon I uttered some absolutely genuine expressions of delight, and sat down with it balanced on my palm. It nestled. A world of my own. I liked it very much.

After three hours, during which time Hakim drank five cups of coffee, smoked eight cigarettes, read two Arabic newspapers and asked me a great many shyly phrased questions about my personal life, and I made five pots of coffee, put on a wash, cleared breakfast, washed up, changed Lily's sheets and accepted three phone calls from my friend Brigid about exactly how many of her children were coming to spend the night on Friday, I decided that lunch, out, would be a good idea. The suitcase stayed. I live in the last flat at the very end of the balcony on the seventh floor. Even with the lift (and I use the stairs. Good for my not-so-good leg) it would have been a drag to move it. And he still hadn't told me his plans.

Finances being tight, and hospitable urges being still quite strong, we went to the Serbian café and had toasted cheese sandwiches. I wondered if he was rich. He looked it . . . sort of. Balls of lapis are rarely cheap. But he's so young. And a little gold proves nothing. That golden Qur'anic verse might be all he has in the world.

'So why are you here, Hakim?' I said, open, brazen, and verging on impatient. Arab languor will take its time, and there's no rushing it, but this was my time too, London time, Western time, modern time. I had things to do, important things. Thinking about Lily, for example, or watering my flowerpots, or hanging the washing over the radiators, or seriously considering getting a job now she was at school. Seriously considering which was my duty; working the absurd hours required by any interesting job or being available to my small child when she needed me. Seriously considering having a word with our lovely new government about it. I couldn't sit about all day making him coffee, anyway. If only on principle.

Then an image flew across my memory: his father's grave face as he passed me a dish of water into the darkness of the room, the courtyard dazzling white behind him as he pushed the heavy weighted mosquito nets aside. Abu Sa'id, bringing the water himself, cool water, every hour or so, for the four days that Nadia was sick. West Bank Luxor, 1987. Abu Sa'id, sitting on the doorstep of his own room at night, staring out into his white courtyard, keeping watch for us, the English girls, who lay in his bed. Sometimes he sat till dawn, sometimes he disappeared silently during the night, and emerged at midday from his son's room, where he had been lying on a mat.

To begin with I had thought there were no women in the house, only Abu Sa'id and Sa'id and Hakim. One reason why I liked Abu Sa'id so much was that he seemed alone, like me, and unlike everybody else in Egypt, who came arrayed and entangled with uncles and wives and cousins and brothers. Then after a day or two I noticed a tall silent figure, who slipped out of sight when she saw me, like a fish in dark waters. I asked young Sa'id who she was, and he shrugged, as if to say she's nothing. A servant, I assumed, and counted his manners against him.

Abu Sa'id never told me what happened to his family, if he ever had one. Never spoke to me of the boys' mother. We just sat on the step, drinking *karkadeh*, the tart crimson tea made from hibiscus flowers, smoking, listening to music on his old Roberts radio, listening for Nadia to wake. He would play his *ney* for me, and sometimes I would dance a bit, imagining myself a snake in the Nile to the serpentine warp of the flute, and he would break off and tell me to sit down, with an old person's laugh at a young person's foolish pleasures, though he wasn't so old. Fifty, perhaps. Once he played me a tape of Yaseen el Touhami, the Sufi poet, and rapidly translated his improvisations for me. El Touhamy never goes anywhere to be recorded. If you want to record him, you have to go where he is. And they do – to the mosques and the moulids, to the streets. We can have recordings if we want, in our poor necrophiliac way, but he and life and creation are doing their living business. I loved that. I wanted to be elevated enough to refuse to listen to him on tape. Wanted to share the purity of his creative transcendence. But alas I am not a Sufi, I am a mere London girl. And I was enchanted by the sound of him reproduced and preserved on the slightly stretched tape, crackling slightly on the banks of the Nile, with the palms black against the rose and gold of the beautiful sphinx-shaped cliffs behind Qurnah, to the west, and Abu Sa'id murmuring the words for me, a low and clarificatory counterpoint to the rhythms. He spoke beautiful English, too, though he didn't write it.

Abu Sa'id, his kindness. I wondered that he had sent Hakim alone, without getting in touch.

Hakim was looking into his thick dark coffee, twiddling his spoon and making an irritating little clinking sound. He looked about ten, like when I'd first met him. He lifted only his ambiguous eyes to answer my question.

'I will tell you,' he said. 'I will tell you, but now I cannot tell you. For now I need just your trust.'

Oh?

I looked.

'I will stay just for one week,' he said.

'In London?' I asked, but I knew what he meant.

'In your house. Please? Then all will just become clear in the fullness of time.'

I was sad that he had sensed unwelcome from me, though I knew I was giving it off. I was ashamed. You cannot be unwelcoming to an Arab. There is something so wrong about it. What churls we are, we English, with our privacy and our territory and our cold cold hearts. In Egypt when men speak to you on the streets what they say is 'Welcome'. There are signs in the streets of Hakim's home town saying 'Smile you are in Luxor'. Yes I know it's for the tourists but even so. When I think of the kindness, the generosity, the hospitality of people I knew – and hardly knew – in Egypt, let alone of Hakim's father . . . Shame.

'You must stay as long as you need,' I said, and I meant it.

three

Talking about Gary Cooper

The sitting room is also the kitchen, and I wasn't putting him in there, so I had the choice: put him in Lily's room, in which case she would be in with me, and probably in my bed; or put him in my study, in which case I would *have* to get a job because I certainly wouldn't be doing any work at home. I don't want a job. I don't want Lily back in my bed, I've only just got her out of it.

I put him in Lily's room. She was narked at the idea, initially. Wouldn't you be? Finish your first day at big school, and what do you find but your normally very territory-protective mother has moved a man into your bedroom. I told her about him as we walked back from school. She was on 'Mummy there's a guinea pig can we have a guinea pig please please can we have a guinea pig' and I took the opportunity to mention the new living creature that we already had.

'I don't want a man, I want a guinea pig!'

'He's more a boy than a man,' I said, hoping to endear him to her. 'And he's quite like a guinea pig. He has lovely silky hair.'

'A boy? You said a man.'

I still hadn't decided quite which I thought him. A boy, of course, would be easier. I could mother him.

'How old is he?' she wanted to know.

'I think he's about nineteen.'

'That's a grown-up,' she said, disappointedly.

'Wait till you see him.'

'Is he going to live with us?'

'Just for a little while,' I said.

'Will he be my daddy?'

The way they come at you. Out of nowhere. She doesn't mention daddies for months on end and then, matter-of-fact as you like, something like that.

'No honey, he won't.'

'But daddies are the men that live with children.'

'Not only, love. Some daddies live with children and some don't, and some men that live with children are daddies and some aren't, but Hakim isn't in our family, no – he's just coming to stay, like Brigid's boys do, and Caitlin. Just for a bit.'

'But we don't know him.'

'I know him, love.' Sort of. 'I knew him in Egypt before you were born.'

'Mummy you're very clever.'

'Oh good. Why?'

'You know so many things I don't know.'

My heart filled with joy at her sweet absurdity. Such are the everyday pleasantries of my life.

She started coughing the moment she walked through the door.

'Lily, hon, this is Hakim, Hakim, this is Lily.'

She took one look at him and then she started to curl. Curled her face into my stomach, her arms around my waist, her feet around her legs, her mouth into a simper, her eyelashes into a flutter. Oh, it's going to be like that, is it. The last one was cousin Max, on my father's side: six foot one of teenage Liverpudlian love-god, with long yellow hair and a playful disposition. He gave her a piggyback and she just went around saying 'Max Max Max' for a week.

'Hello, Lily,' said Hakim encouragingly.

'Hello,' she whispered, and then pulled me down and started hissing in my ear like a ferocious little boiler.

'What?' I said, trying to edge my head away from her and get the words into focus. 'What?'

She was telling me that he *could* sleep in her bed and if he wanted he could have one of her teddies, not old brown teddy but one of the others, the one with the pink pyjamas. Pushover.

And that is how we all came to be sitting around the breakfast table reading anonymous letters.

Hakim denied all knowledge. I had no knowledge. But then that is how it's meant to be with anonymous letters. I didn't like it.

Then there were three calls where whoever it was said nothing at all, just left the line hanging open. The first time it was only a few minutes, the second about ten, and the third nearly quarter of an hour. I 1471ed them, but of course they'd been blocked. So I called BT to get them to do something about it. But it didn't happen again. I tried to file it under irritating, but I couldn't quite.

Then it was chased out of my mind by a call from Harry, saying could he come round. Harry worried me more than the letter. These uncommunicative communications were new, and external, unknown. Harry is deep in me.

Harry is a half-settled negotiation, a half-healed wound.

You need to know a bit more about Harry, other than that he was my darling, for years, years ago.

I had of course wondered how he came to be a policeman after so many years of being a bit wide and a bit flash, automotive man with his fully-powered V8 Pontiacs and his James Dean jeans. We'd been sitting on the deckchairs on the balcony outside the flat, a few days after Jim's claim to Lily had crashed and burned. The fallout was fairly spectacular, what with Eddie Bates being arrested, Ben Cooper the Bent Copper getting his comeuppance, Harry turning out to be a policeman, and Jim turning out not to be Lily's father after all.

I realise that I'm still not mentioning it. The offensive thing. The other things I found out. The bit I hate and have not . . . OK. These are the things:

a) My sister never told me she was a prostitute.
b) She made pornographic films using religious accoutrements, specifically clothing more usually worn by devout Muslim women for reasons of modesty, and used in these works of art bits of film of me dancing.
c) She pretended to be me in order to sell sex to men who had admired me in performance.

I don't like to think about these things.

I recall sitting there with my feet up on the balcony wall, bandaged up from my dashing getaway after Eddie abducted me and . . . well, anyway there we were, in the evening sun, drinking beers from the bottle, admiring the sunset over the A40 and watching Lily and Brigid's children careering about on their bicycles up and down the balcony, waiting for Mrs Krickic next door to come out and tell them to slow down a bit because they were disturbing her budgies. Harry and I circling each other in the fallout, coming round, making up, moving on . . . who knows.

'So why did you become a policeman, Harry?' I asked.

He looked very sheepish. Having been undercover, I suppose he wasn't accustomed to talking about it. I suppose. I don't know. What do undercover people do or feel? What do I know about undercover? But he's not very accustomed to talking anyway. Joking, yes. Charming, yes, in his tall, laconic way. But not talking. I used to like it: I could read anything I wanted into his handsome silences, and did. But now I'm older and I'm not so insecure, and I like to know what's going on.

'Um,' he said.

I waited encouragingly.

'Well actually,' he said, and looked a little puzzled, and then sort of took a breath, and almost laughed a little. He shot me a glance, sideways. This is what he has always done when preparing to confide. It pleased me that he still did it. Made me feel that I knew him. Made me feel secure, at one with the world. A bit.

'OK,' he said. 'Because of *High Noon*.'

I was silenced for a moment.

I began to hum, 'Do not forsake me, oh my darling,' without realising I was doing it.

'Well, you asked,' he said.

High Noon. Where Sheriff Gary Cooper had to deal with the bad guys even though he had a ticket out of town with the lovely Quaker girl who didn't believe in violence, and none of the cowardly townsfolk would help him, so he did it alone.

'*High Noon*,' I mused.

'I wanted to do the right thing,' he said. 'That's all.'

He seemed so uncomfortable admitting that he had some notion of morality, and that it had made him do something, that I didn't push him. I think he was truly embarrassed. Identifying with Gary Cooper.

But certainly it changed my view of him. From black leather to white stetson, just like that. The bastard cross of Marlon Brando and DelBoy turns out to be Gary Cooper.

Of course all this coincided terribly conveniently with my own sweeping gavotte through life. Here was the peripatetic biking belly dancer grounded and mature with a bad leg and a baby; here was the bad man turned good and willing to consider that he might be said baby's father. 'I want to do the blood test,' he'd said, on the evening of the day of come-uppance. And, 'I want to see her. And you.' And 'I want you to change the birth certificate. Even if it's only to Father Unknown.'

But who knows what they want? And who knows whether it'll make them happy? As I can't remember which country singer (in a white hat) sang: 'Some of God's greatest gifts are unanswered prayers.'

All I wanted was peace and quiet. I wanted to sit on the bench in the playground with my boots in the dust and the fag ends and the dead plane leaves, and watch Lily climb ropes. I wanted to bathe her and tuck her in and read *Thumbelina* to her. I wanted to watch her eat, and to make myself a cheese sandwich in the evening knowing she was asleep in the next room, not scratching her eczema (I wanted her eczema gone). I wanted it to be how it was before Jim and Eddie Bates and Ben started to upturn our lives with their blackmail and lies and obsessions; how it was in the gilded imaginary quotidian past. I didn't want to upturn it even further with the very serious, very real question of her dad. In other words, I wanted to bury my head in the sand. And I did.

But then, sitting on the balcony that night, talking about Gary Cooper, Harry said: 'Part of it, you know, is . . .'

'Is what?' I said.

'Lily,' he said.

'What about her?'

'What I said that night.' He didn't have to say what night. We knew what night. The night that chaos dissolved.

'Mm,' I said.

'The blood test,' he reminded me, gently.

'Mmm.'

I knew he was right, within his rights. I knew it was fair. I knew, rationally, that I didn't have a leg to stand on. I knew that I probably couldn't stop him doing it anyway. But my heart cried out against it. Cried and wept. Why? Fear, I suppose. Simple fear.

'I can't do it, Harry,' I said, knowing as I said it what a daft and pathetic thing it was to say.

'It's not you that'd do it,' he said. 'You don't have to do anything. I'd just get it done, and then I'd tell you, and we'd . . . we'd take it from there.' We hadn't a clue, then, either of us, of the practicalities. Let alone the repercussions. (Nice word, repercussion. Re-percussion. There's a verb: percuss, to strike so as to shake. Well there you go.)

'Shut up,' I said.

He was looking at me, quite kindly, twiddling the empty beer bottle in his big skinny hands, leaning forward a little.

'How long for?' he asked.

'How long what?'

'How long shall I shut up for? I mean, I can see you probably need a bit of time, having just had Jim breathing down your neck being the bad father, and maybe a father is not what you want right now, but, well, the question's been asked now, hasn't it? So how long, do you think, before you'll want to know? Because you're going to want to.'

'I don't want to know.'

'No, but you will.'

'Don't patronise me, Harry. I don't want to know. It's a positive act of not wanting. I actively want not to know. I desire ignorance.'

'Why? Are you scared?'

'No I'm fucking not. Don't give me that crap.'

'Why not? I'm scared. I'd think it was incredibly scary.'

'I like things as they are. That's all. Harry –'

'What?'

'Please can we leave it.'

'Yes,' he said. 'But for how long?'

'Oh for God's . . .' Well. OK. Buy time. 'Fifty years,' I said, rather idiotically.

'It might be worth pointing out, Angel, that you aren't the only person involved in this,' he said.

'I'm sorry?' I replied, cold suddenly, and deadly courteous.

'Lily . . .' he began, poor fool, but he did no more than begin before I bit him off: 'Do you think that I'm not aware of that?' I snapped. 'Do you think that every single thing I do isn't for her wellbeing? Do you imagine that I ever for one moment stop considering what's best for her? Do you think I don't *know*? My whole fucking life for nearly four years has been based on what she wants and what she needs and I do not need you muscling in and telling me that I need to take her into consideration. I *do* take her into consideration. I do every bloody thing that is ever done for that child including protecting her, when she needs it, from people she doesn't know who think they have something to do with her. If I'd told her Jim was her father how do you think she would feel now? Now that he's decided that oh no, he isn't after all, silly me it's just my wife fancied having a kid. Who her father is and what happens about that is an incredibly bloody serious issue and if I'm not up to thinking about it and controlling what happens about it then it is not to happen, that's all. The damage it could do her is immeasurable. And it's down to me. I decide when and how. And I say no. No.'

So I was ranting. Harry has never been impressed by my ranting.

'It's not just Lily,' he said, calmly. If anything he was even more unflappable now. Unpercussable.

'What?'

'It's not just Lily.'

'Oh. So, what. It's you. You need to know. You feel odd. You want to know.'

'Yes,' he said.

I looked him a look.

'It's not unreasonable,' he said.

'It's not possible,' I said, in only half-fake disbelief. The nerve of him.

'Yes it is.'

'No it's not.'

'You can't say that.'

'Just did,' I retorted, maturely.

'Angel,' he said. 'I don't want to . . . but you can't control it. It's not just you. It's the truth – you'll have to face it. You can't just boss it around.'

'I can have a damn good try.'

'Why do you have to be in charge of everything?'

'Because I am. Aren't I? Who else is?'

'You could let someone help you.'

'This is getting a little clichéd, Harry. I get plenty of help, thank you, so you needn't bother offering. I really don't think you'd be much use, frankly.'

'Yes I would.'

'You. Yeah. Very likely. Teach her to drive and check the gap on a sparkplug, babysit and embarrass my boyfriends when we get home. I don't need it.'

'You don't know what a father might give . . .'

'You don't know whether you're her father.'

'I know. It doesn't make it any easier. She's asleep in there and . . . Let me find out. Let me try.'

'No. Or – OK, yes. Try this. You're her father, you want to give her what she needs. What she needs right now is a period of calm after a period of upset. She needs it as much as I do. She also needs me to have a period of calm after a period of upset. I'm not confusing our needs here, I'm recognising that they are the same. That's what she wants, what she needs. You can give that to her. Will you?'

I couldn't read his face at all. His expression was remote – his Mongolian face, I used to call it. Narrowed eyes and inscrutable and handsome.

'Yes,' he said. 'How long a period of calm?'

I could have kicked him. 'I don't know,' I said.

'Amazing!' he murmured.

'What?'

'Something you don't know!'

'Don't be like that.'

'I'm not being like that,' he said. 'I have no intention of being like that. OK, tell me how long within three months, or I'll enquire again. And if you need anything, ring me. I'm assuming,' he said, 'that you're keeping me hanging on, not counting me out.'

My oh my, is he a different man in this white hat. What kind of a comment is that from an emotional illiterate?

I gave him a rather pathetic smile, and he left. Since then, we'd maintained a quiet and sparse rapprochement. During Eddie's trial, which came up gratifyingly quickly, I didn't see much of him. He wasn't directly involved himself – undercover, see – but he kept me posted. If there is one thing I should be grateful to Harry for, it is that he managed to see Eddie put away without my having to give evidence, without my role in the drama coming out. Eddie was guilty of quite enough other things – mister-bigging it for gangs of drug dealers and smugglers and pornography and God knows what. Kidnapping little old me and attacking me was peanuts to his real career, and didn't come up in court, which was just as well.

I didn't go to the trial. Didn't follow it in the papers. It was enough for me that the drama was over. Harry it was that told me the verdict and the sentence. Guilty, fifteen years. I was happy. It was over.

Happy? I was over the fucking moon. I love safety. Safety and calm make me sing and dance. I bless every morning when nothing happens. Dullness and boredom do not exist in a life where activity has been motorbikes flying out of control and sisters dying and babies being orphaned and madmen imprisoning you and bastards claiming paternity of your child. I don't ask for much. Just for nothing much to happen ever again. Maybe a few little quiet ordinary things. A calm ordinary little love affair, or an everyday kind of marriage. Some job or something. Don't talk to me of self-fulfilment. I've survived; so has Lily. This is my achievement.

After that Harry had spent six months in Arizona on some exchange training thing, sending us postcards of giant jack-rabbits in cowboy clothes, and views of downtown Tucson by night. His calls, on his return, had been infrequent, and they were a fly in the calm ointment of our reconstituted lives.

He was out there, and I couldn't tell whether the big thing that he was was ever going to happen. Maybe he had just gone away. Then again he might reappear, any time, wanting things. Wanting to know. I'd been through it before with Jim, Janie's ex, in the days when we believed him to be Lily's father; been through that knowledge that someone outside of you can turn your life upside down and claim that which you treasure above all. And I'd been through it in a different way with Ben Cooper the Bent Copper, when he was blackmailing me to spy on Eddie Bates. I know what it is like when someone has power over your life. It's bloody horrible.

The one thing that Harry didn't mention again was his suggestion, at the end of That Day, when I said was knackered and going to bed, that he come with me.

* * *

I rang him back. He wanted to meet. It seemed to me like a tiny nasty echo of when Jim had reappeared, wanting to meet, wanting to see Lily, wanting to take her from me. How soon before the lawyers' letters start up again? At the same time I recognised the absurdity: this was Harry, who had been my Harry, Harry who wasn't a bad bloke, Harry who now wore a white hat, Harry who wasn't even definitely her father. And I knew I couldn't avoid it forever, because he was right, you cannot avoid what exists. This question existed, no doubt about it. I knew that all I'd said to him that night on the balcony was untenable. A father is a father – if he is then he is. I'd even agreed that about Jim.

So I agreed to meet him the next day. He wanted to make it the evening, I said no, lunch is easier, Lily will be at school. How much they have to learn.

four

Hakim's Business, Harry's News

After the first day, spent drinking coffee and reading Arabic newspapers, Hakim had expanded his repertoire to drinking coffee, reading Arabic newspapers and making and receiving telephone calls. He had a mobile phone, of which he was proud. By day three he wanted an *A to Z*. However he doesn't read English too well. This was obviously going to make life a bit of a problem for him, and for me by default. He decided that the simplest thing would be for me to teach him. I thought it would be far easier if I just showed him where Somerset House was on the map, and wrote out CHARING CROSS in big letters so he could tell when he'd reached the right station. I instructed him in English, he wrote it down in Arabic. I didn't want to think about it actually. 'You killed my love' was on my mind. I didn't want it to be. I know the form. You ignore anonymous letters, you put odd phone calls down to the vagaries of the system. You have better things to worry about. And I do. I have Harry.

But it was on my mind. Latching on to that which is always on my mind. Because I did . . . kill. Janie. And however much you may know, reasonably, and accept everybody else's convictions, there is always . . . It's always there. However much an accident is an accident. The sense of responsibility. Guilt at surviving when she didn't. Helplessness at not having preserved your parents from it. Whatever she may have done makes little difference to that, and the punishment that I had, in losing my fitness to dance, makes little difference either. It matters, but it makes little difference.

I couldn't think what the letter was to do with. But it had touched a nerve. A ganglion actually. So it wasn't till Hakim had left that I wondered what he was going to do at Somerset House.

When he got back, five hours later, I made him a cup of coffee and asked him.

'Nothing,' he said. He looked angry, almost tearful. 'Nothing. What can I do? I don't know your writing. I was lost. It's OK, I ask in shops and everybody speaks Arabic. I get home. But I found nothing. Somerset House is just the wrong place.'

Of course it was. Somerset House is always the wrong place. You think it's the right place because it was in Sherlock Holmes or something, but the right place is now in Preston, or care of a privatised company in New Malden. Poor lost foreigner. I remembered my first days in Cairo, days of lonely chaos before I discovered the bar on the roof of the Odeon, and the flat in the block on Champoleon Street – Château Champoleon, as Orlando the Colombian political correspondent next door called it in his camp Latino/Tennessee accent. Orlando it was taught me never to say America when I meant the United States. There is a brilliant blind chaotic excitement to a new city, an alien city. But God there is some loneliness too. When there's too much going on out there, too much cardamom and donkey shit and Arabic, too many Mercedes and veils and babies, and you can't face it, so you stay in your cheap cockroachy room saying it's only wise to in the heat of the day, or the danger of the evening, pretending that you're taking the opportunity to catch up on Proust, but really you're just building up loneliness and boredom to the point when you have to explode. It's like the internal combustion engine. Suck squeeze bang blow: Suck in loneliness, squeeze it with boredom until BANG! you are blown out on to the streets of the alien city, and thank God for it. Whereupon you suck in strangeness, squeeze it with fascination till BANG! the top of your head blows off with the excitement of it all and blows you into the next strange and fascinating experience. (I was very much a biker in those days, hence the imagery. Orlando liked the image, said it was just like Hegel, thesis, antithesis and synthesis, only in fourtime instead of a waltz, 'But it's all dancing,' he said. Orlando was a gas.)

I don't know what London is like to a stranger. I should imagine horrible. Cold, unfriendly, cliquey, snitty, incomprehensible. And grey, and strange, and wet, and cold. Light when it should be dark; dark when it should be light. And expensive. And big. But people come here, people stay here, whole peoples come and live and settle. No thanks to the welcome we give them, that's for sure. Poor Hakim.

'I'm sorry,' I said. 'I should have helped you. I'll come down with you tomorrow morning.'

'Thank you,' says Hakim.

'*Shukran afwan*,' said Lily, grinning, waiting for approbation.

'Bravo,' said Hakim. She went pink with pleasure, and he smiled and pinched her cheek, and she smiled and pinched his and said, 'Chubby chops', and he said, 'What is chubby chops?', and generally they were carrying on like love's young dream.

'So what is it you're trying to find out about?' I asked.

Hakim went very quiet.

I pointed out to him that if I was to find out for him where he was to go I needed to know what he wanted to find out when he got there. For a while he wouldn't say. Then: 'If someone is dead or married.' Nothing more. This was irritating, but Lily needed her tea and if something's not happening you can't force it. So I fed her and washed her and did all those small yet vital services that prove love and build love and give love's object a chance of being well-adjusted in the future. (Interesting those people who claim to care deeply for their children yet leave the actual caring to someone else. It used to be one word, care, what you do and how you feel. Now it is two, and you can feel it yet never do it, or do it yet never feel it.)

'Who's dead?' she wanted to know. 'Who's married?' She's very interested in death and marriage. Wants me to get married, sometimes. Has proposed to me herself, actually. Best offer I ever had.

The next day brought the next letter. The envelope sat there like a toad on the doormat. Lily ran to pick it up; I stopped her. I picked it up quickly, read it quickly: 'You did it and I mind.'

I didn't like it. Incomprehensible letters making nebulous accusations against I wasn't sure who were actually a worse incursion into my *enderun* (it's a Turkish word. It means that which is within, private, domestic) than Hakim turning up and being mysterious all over the shop. Or were they? Well that's the problem, isn't it. They could be. They have the potential. But by their very nature, you don't know.

I believe I may have mentioned before my slightly obsessively protective attitude to my gaff. I don't like things coming in and upsetting me. I like being quiet and safe and calm. I believe this to be beneficial to my child. I live every day with the sole intention of giving her enough calm security to outweigh the drama and weirdness of her birth. A kid snatched at birth from the jaws of death, while the fangs sank into her mother, is a kid who can soak up a lot of calmness.

31

Whether or not she knows it. My God, after five years it still shocks me. Pulled from the jaws of death and her mother's womb simultaneously.

So now I protect Lily by protecting our home and, as my perceptive Egyptian friend Zeinab and my perceptive Irish friend Brigid have both pointed out, my body. And my heart. There had been signs of a little loosening up: letting Hakim stay, fantasising about maybe finding myself a man. But the potential of these letters sat in the base of the back of my mind, crying out to me.

I gave Hakim a little lecture on the bus (St Catherine's House, it turned out, was the place). At home he was cavalier if courteous, operating all the assumptions of a man who expects a woman to wait on him. Out in the world he found it easier to be a child with me, and hence it was easier for me to mother him.

'Hakim,' I said, once we were settled on the 94. 'Lily has bad lungs and I would appreciate it if you didn't smoke in the flat. Also you drink too much coffee, it makes you manic and nervous. And please tell me now what you want to find out about who.'

We were sitting on the top of the bus, right up at the front because Hakim wanted to see the sights. Willing as I was to point out Shepherds Bush roundabout, Notting Hill tube station and the great dome of Whiteleys in the distance, I was more interested in getting to the point. To my dismay he started to cry. I put my arm round his shoulder and patted him, murmuring kind things in Arabic, the things Zeinab murmurs to her boys when they fall over.

'I bring badness to you,' he said, sniffing. 'I bring badness to your house.'

'Well just tell me what it's all about, and then we can sort it out.'

'I can't tell you,' he said.

'Yes you can. Open your mouth and speak.'

'I can't. I can't. Too much badness.'

'Come on,' I said. 'Come on, just tell me. You can't keep it to yourself, it won't make it better. Just tell me.'

'I can't.'

I was getting bored.

'Why not?' I said.

'Too much badness.'

'Tell me why you can't tell me. It's not fair to bring badness to my house and not tell me what it is. Tell me something. Tell me why you can't tell me.'

He stared out of the window at Holland Park Avenue unfolding before us, and the overlong branches of the plane trees slapped at the window as if at our faces. 'I am in shame,' he murmured.

'Hakim,' I said, in the bad mother voice that brings Lily to heel. 'Stop it. Tell me.'

He turned his face round to me, tears still sitting in his eyes, and said, 'It is family, Angelina. Family.'

'Not Abu Sa'id,' I exclaimed.

'Not the father,' he said. And then, with that slight shift of musculature that denotes the making of a decision, he said, 'Mother.'

For a moment I thought he was calling me mother. Then I realised no, he's just saying it.

Mother.

'Mother?' I repeated, intelligently.

He leaned forward and rested his forehead against the glass.

'I have a mother,' he whispered.

'Ah,' I murmured.

He leaned.

'And?' I suggested.

He leaned back. 'I have a mother.'

33

There's nothing you can do really but sit it out.

I sat.

'An English mother,' he murmured.

'English mother!'

I was surprised. I was very surprised. All I had known was absent mother, gone mother, unspoken-about mother, maybe dead mother, maybe shamed mother. English mother, though, was something new.

'English mother gone back to England. I want her. I look for her. Please don't tell my brother or my father.'

Not bothering to point out how unlikely it was that I would happen to be talking to either of them, I just goggled at him.

'But Hakim, that's good! Finding a mother isn't – yes, it might be complicated and everything but it's basically a good thing to do. It's ... and English! So you're half English! Blimey! ... but why did she ... I mean, tell me the story ...'

I was rather pleased to see a boy so distraught at disobeying his parent. It seemed so old-fashioned, so honourable, so decent and right and endearing. And I was sorry for him, and I was excited about it, and relieved that it wasn't something horrible. Also I know, as adult to adult, that Abu Sa'id is not an unreasonable man, and would probably, I thought, forgive his son for his natural curiosity and desire for his mother. But then – I'm not family. And I'm not Egyptian. And I'm not him. I cannot know where his limits are.

'I don't know the story,' he said. 'I was small. Five years. Sa'id was ten years. He never talked of her. Never. My father said nothing. Never. Not to talk of her, not allowed. When I cried for mama, there was Mariam.'

'Who's Mariam?' I asked.

'The woman in my father's house. Second wife. New mama. The sad woman nobody love.' I remembered the woman who moved like a fish, and hid from me. His wife. The woman in his house. I remembered his unwonted kindness to two English girls. A clear picture sprang up of a man heart-broken by a deserting wife, who still loved her enough to be kind to her countrywomen for her sake. And two bereft boys being foul to a substitute mother. And that poor woman, whom nobody loved. I was nearly in tears myself.

'And you want to find her.'

'Yes.'

'What will you do when you find her?'

'I will ... ask her why she left. See if she is a good woman or bad. See what is my English me.'

Well, you can't fault that.

'I'll help you, then,' I said.

He smiled at me. I found myself thinking 'You big softy', and I wasn't sure if I meant myself or him.

I took one look at the endless shelves of huge volumes in the high institutional halls of the Public Search Room and decided to leave Hakim to it. But of course I couldn't.

'What was her maiden name?' I said. Hakim tried and tried to pronounce it but the sounds just didn't work in his mouth.

We got it in the end. Tomlinson (I think. Could be Tompkinson). It only took another half-hour to find that in 1984 she had married a man called Stephen John Lockwood, in London.

I'd arranged to meet Harry in a sandwich shop in Strutton Ground, near Scotland Yard. I had toasted cheese and salami with gherkins, and he sneered slightly at my choice. He had a cappuccino with his ham roll, and I sneered slightly at that. I don't think men should drink frothy things with chocolate on top. So it wasn't great even before we started.

'Well, to put your mind at rest, I didn't drag you here to talk about Lily,' he said, straight off. I was so pleasantly surprised that I almost forgave him for sneering at my sandwich, but then I got pissed off again about his power to relieve

35

me by saying he wasn't going to mention that which I thought he had no business mentioning anyway.

'Good,' I said, more briskly than I might have. 'So what is it?' Oh shit, I thought, it's all going wrong. I don't want not to get on with him. Oh bugger. (Not bugger, mummy, bother.)

'I thought you might like an update on Ben Cooper and your friend Eddie,' he said, rising to the mood of the occasion. Eddie is no friend of mine and Harry knows it.

'Thank you,' I said. 'Yes, I would.'

'Well,' said Harry, 'as you know, Ben has been evading the police inquiry into his misdemeanours by claiming ill health.' I did know. The slimy bastard had got a psychiatrist to say that the stress of having to account for himself might drive him to suicide. (Eddie Bates had tried a similar ploy – they'd said he wasn't well enough to stand trial, but he'd had to, in the end.) Cooper had kept it up for over a year now. And because he hasn't had his fair hearing yet, he can't be sacked, so he's still sitting about on sick leave, on full pay, the slug, and I'm still sitting about wondering whether I'm going to be called to help put him away. Which I would be happy to do, because he was at least in part responsible for my sister's downfall. Because he was in business with her making the nasty little videos, and because he was the one who, when Eddie Bates saw me dance and wanted me, arranged for Janie to wear my costumes, masquerade as me, and sell herself, as me, to him.

Even as I write it a damp toad settles again in my belly. For Janie, for Eddie, and for my own shame.

'Well now his lawyers are saying that it was too long ago,' Harry was saying, 'and the case should be dropped.'

My jaw dropped to match.

'Surely not,' I said. 'I don't believe it. He can't get away with it. I . . .' Mouthing like a goldfish. Pointless.

'Well no, he probably won't,' said Harry. 'But he might.'

'Anyway that's not all,' he said. I looked up.

'Um,' he said.

'Yes?'

He looked tired and sad.

'Eddie Bates is dead,' he said.

It all stood still for a moment.

And another. Then . . .

'Sorry?' I said.

'Eddie Bates is dead,' he repeated.

I couldn't quite breathe. My eyes started flickering around and I felt myself shaking. To my horror I felt I was going to cry. I heard Harry's voice.

'Angel? Angel?'

I shook myself and came back to myself. Back to myself but different.

'Dead,' I said.

'Dead,' he said.

I reached for a cigarette but there weren't any. I don't smoke any more. Harry reached over to the next table and helped himself to one from the packet belonging to the man sitting there. 'Thank you,' he said to him, in a voice that brooked no denial, and he lit it with the man's lighter, and gave it to me.

'Dead,' I said.

'Yes,' he said.

My face was screwed up and I tried to untangle it. It wouldn't go. We sat there in silence for a few minutes. Then Harry said: 'Forgive an indelicate question, Angeline, but why the fuck do you mind so much?'

I couldn't answer. Not only because I couldn't speak, but because I didn't know, and if I had known I couldn't have told Harry anyway.

My enemy is dead. I should be singing and dancing my

delight. If I was made safe by his imprisonment, how much safer am I now?

More minutes of silence.

'What did he die of?' I asked.

More silence, maintained this time by Harry. Then:

'He hasn't been well.'

Oh.

'How not well? Not well of what?' You see, I couldn't speak.

'Um,' said Harry.

Into my state of shock came a sliver of . . . not fear, but . . . awareness.

'What?'

He sighed. 'I didn't tell you because I thought it would just . . . go away. I thought he'd get better.'

'What?' I said. 'Was it what he was talking about before the trial? What was it?'

I could just about register how difficult Harry was finding this, but I no longer let him get away with not saying things. We are way past the silent understandings, or more often misunderstandings, of our optimistic youth. In theory, at least.

'You know when he was arrested,' said Harry, 'he had a head wound.' I did know. I had inflicted it on him. I had hit him on the head with a poker when he was trying to jump me. Harry knew that. I had told him in the confusion of the end of the day of comeuppance. I seem to remember he had said, 'Attagirl'. Anyway, some such unpolicemanly expression of approval.

Harry was not looking at me. 'He has been suffering ever since from dizzy spells. That's one thing his lawyers put up when they were trying to delay the trial. He's continued to have them inside. Last week a new inmate arrived, who for reasons best known to himself took the first opportunity he could to punch Eddie's lights out. Two days later Eddie was found dead on the floor of his cell. They haven't done the post-mortem yet but it looks like a fractured skull.'

Now my skin was burning up.

'He may have fallen,' said Harry.

I took a drag on the cigarette and started coughing. Harry took the stub from my fingers and put it out.

'So did I kill him?' I asked.

'He never said in court what had caused his initial head injuries,' Harry continued, conversationally. 'That was one reason why the application wasn't accepted. The doctors agreed that he was not in the best nick, but he just said he'd fallen, and the damage wasn't consistent with that, so they couldn't accept it.'

I stared down at my plate. A gherkin had fallen out of my sandwich. I picked it up and ate it, and a huge sadness washed over me. Why do only mad psychotic scumbags love me, and is that love?

'You didn't kill him, legally or otherwise. But you did something,' he said.

'Yes I did.'

Bad people around me die, but I don't kill them, but I do something. Oh for God's sake. Janie wasn't bad. Not bad. Not like Eddie.

'When's the funeral?' I asked.

Harry was shocked. 'You're not going to go?' he said. Aghast.

'Yes,' I said.

'Why? Why the fuck?'

'To see that he's really dead,' I said. 'Because . . . because I thought it was over with the court case, and it wasn't, and I want to make sure it's over now.'

His face was amazed but kind. 'There you go again,' he said. 'You want to do something absurd and ridiculous and stupid, but you've got a completely good understandable reason for it.'

'Oh,' I said. 'Is that what I do?'

'Yes,' he said. 'You should be a lawyer.'

Is that good or bad?

'But it doesn't mean you're right,' he said.

'Right about what?'

'About going to the funeral.'

'You think I shouldn't?'

'I think it unwise,' said Harry.

'I'm sure you do,' I said.

'I'll think about it,' he said.

'About what?'

'Whether to tell you where it is,' he said.

'There you go again,' I said, a little pointedly.

'What?'

'Telling me what to do. Acting like you're in charge.'

'I dare say,' he said, unmoved. Only one step beyond his admirable unflappability lies his bossy pain-in-the-arse stubbornness. It reminded me of how he'd been when I first met Eddie, through him; when he warned me off making friends with him, not knowing that I was only doing so because Ben was making me. It reminded me of how jealous he'd been then, when he'd thought I didn't know Eddie was a villain, when he'd thought that I fancied him. Harry protecting me for my own good, keeping things from me because I couldn't be trusted to behave sensibly. Harry being a patronising sexist git. Harry watching over me, looking out for me, still caring what happens to me. Knowing me.

I would like to be able to take Harry's concern for me and appreciate it. I would like to be able to maintain my independence without having to spit in his eye. I would like to think that I can rise above daily tribulation and problems of communication to a superior level of transcendent human understanding, but I can't.

'Then I'll find out from somebody else,' I said, in a very slightly nyaaah nyaah voice.

'Who?' he said.

'I'll ring . . .' I said, in one of those sentences that you begin, hoping that you'll find an end for it by the time you get there, but I didn't. Who would I ring? We didn't exactly have friends in common. His wife! I'd track down his wife.

His wife.

You killed my love.

You did, and I mind.

Oh.

Well perhaps his wife would ring me. Perhaps in fact she has been ringing me.

'Tell me,' I said to Harry. 'Do people who send anonymous letters ever get violent, generally? Is that the sort of thing that happens. Do you know?'

Harry looked tired. 'What?' he said. 'What a . . .'

It suddenly hit me like a hammer. Eddie's dead. His wife thinks I killed him. I burst into tears, stared at Harry in horror, and hurtled to the back of the café in search of the ladies. Only there wasn't one. The sandwich shop man gave me a handful of paper napkins from a chrome dispenser and turned me round again. The napkins soaked up nothing; just smeared and redistributed. Harry was standing up, wobbly through my tears, tall and a little menacing as he unfolded himself from behind the café table. I remembered his father telling me how he used to stop fights just by unfolding himself out of the squad car and being exceptionally tall. Young miscreants would simply stop toughing each other up and gaze in amazement as more and more of the length of the copper unfolded. He's six foot seven. Harry's a shrimp in comparison, a mere six foot four. I forgot for years that Harry's father was police. So strange. I daresay it helped to get Harry in, despite his past. Though he was never convicted of anything. Nor charged with much, come to think of it. Perhaps his father helped with that too. Not consciously, not on purpose.

The miscreant in me folded.

I was still crying.

'Come on, lover girl,' he said. 'I'll get you a cab.' He looked disgusted. I remembered when he'd told me he was disgusted one time before. Over Janie. When he thought I'd known, and I hadn't.

He took my elbow and walked me into the bright street. I could see reflections of Petty France on the teardrops that shook on my lower lashes. Like a hall of mirrors, a ball of mercury. Like the chrome rims of the surgeons' lights as they pored over my leg, and I gazed desperately into the distorted reflections of my joints and ligaments, yellow and scarlet and black, trying to see what the hell they were doing inside me. Discomfiting and weird reflections. Harry hailed a cab.

Lover girl?

'Remember,' I said, 'you were wrong last time. Don't jump to conclusions.'

'Wheee,' he said, his face hard. 'Wheeeee, splat.'

five

Next

I can't afford to take a cab all the way to Shepherds Bush so I got out at the top of Whitehall and took the bus. The cabbie tried to get stroppy about it but I told him that if he thought the quickest way to Shepherds Bush from Victoria Street was via Trafalgar Square he must be used to passengers walking out on him. At the bus stop I wondered whether Hakim had got home all right, and whether I would be on time to pick up Lily. On the number 12 I wondered whether Sarah Tomlinson el Araby Lockwood would be in London still, in the phone book perhaps, even. At Piccadilly Circus I wondered why London Transport had changed the system so that instead of getting a 12 all the way through you had to change to a 94 at Marble Arch or Oxford Circus. At Oxford Circus I wondered why you wait for half an hour and then three come along at once. Then on Bayswater Road, having wondered every damn boring other thing available, I started to wonder why I was so upset at Eddie Bates being dead. It wasn't just that I may have contributed. Or that his wife seemed to think I had. There was something personal. And I came up with some fairly unwelcome reasons.

1) Although he was a scumbag of the worst order, he had expressed a fairly devoted devotion to me, and I liked

that, even from a scumbag of the worst order. Which makes me something of a scumbag.

2) Although he was a scumbag of the worst order he had an enormous amount of passion in him. Energy, enthusiasm, life force. He was a big, pulsating character. And it's a shock to think of that gone. Pff, just gone.

3) There's an animal thing, a . . .

OK, I can't

OK.

When Eddie jumped on me, and I hit him with the poker and knocked him out

This is quite hard to explain because I don't know why I did it. And I don't know how I did it.

So there he was, with his

I can't describe this. He's dead.

OK. I fucked him then, while he was unconscious. I was as surprised as you are that it was physically possible. I was more surprised that I wanted to do it. I didn't know I wanted to do it. I still find it hard to believe that I did do it. But I did.

I can only suppose that for some reason I still don't understand I wanted to have sex with him, but I didn't want him to have sex with me. Because I hated him and despised him. I am absolutely not happy with the fact that I fancied him. Not happy at all.

Silly word, fancied. From 'fantasy', I imagine. I fantasied him. And then I realised him.

So there is some animal thing, about a man you've had sex with (even though he didn't have it with you) being dead. And there's something about him being unconscious then, and dead now. Horizontal.

So there I am, quasi-necrophiliac, fancier of scumbags, flattered by a scumbag's attentions. Just how I like to see myself.

Let alone about having contributed to his death. Let alone his wife.

I got off at Shepherds Bush Green and got to Lily's school in good time. Just seeing her, love flowed through me, drenching and drowning the poison, flushing it through. You can feel warmth and cleanness in your veins. Palpable goodness, inside you, displacing and unmanning the badness and the shame. Simplicity clearing confusion. Redeemed by love. It happens. All the time.

I bought her a choc ice and we went to the park to chase squirrels.

When we got home Hakim was sitting at the kitchen table with all the telephone books, looking sad.

'There is just one Sarah in London, is not her,' he said.

I expressed doubt. He showed me how he had identified the S section of the book, and found Sarah's Hair Fashion Studio in Lower Norwood, and told me that he had rung, but they hadn't been his mother. I found myself thinking that I really ought to look after him better, and said that after I'd put Lily to bed I would help him. During tea he let her wear his Qur'anic verse pendant, so she ran to put on two of her tiaras and her plastic glittery Cinderella slippers. He didn't know the story so she told him, then he had to be the prince and I had to be the Ugly Sisters and she was – as she is most days anyway, when she's not being a baby animal of some description – Cinderella. When the time came for them to live happily ever after she almost burst with joy. Then he told her the story of Rhodopis, the girl with the rose-red slippers who married Pharaoh Amasis five hundred years before Christ. When I tucked her up later she announced that Hakim was her boyfriend, and could he live with us forever. Probably not, I said. We could marry him, she said, then he would.

She wanted him to come and tell her *Ali Baba and the Forty Thieves,* and he did, including all the boiling oil and dismemberment of corpses, which I had been keeping from her.

When Lily the love fountain was asleep, I was at risk again. Eddie lurked, alive or dead. Spooking me with his ... he threatened and hurt me, I hated him, I fucked him, he's dead. That handsome, thrilling, madcap fellow; that dangerous violent psychotic liar.

Luckily Hakim wanted to cook my dinner. My gratitude was immense. Not for the meal – it was pretty much on the same level as Lily wanting to cook my dinner. Very sweet, hopeless, and more work for me than if I'd done it myself. But for the distraction. After half an hour or so of him being very confused by the contents of my kitchen (the garlic press delighted him), I taught him how to make pasta with sauce out of a pot. He had bought a couple of beers too, which was a relief for me because I am very bad at judging whether the Muslim I am sitting with is a drinking Muslim or not, and I hate to get it wrong. There are clues: if a man has a prayer mark on his forehead, a permanent bruise from the frequency and energy of his devotional prostrations, then I do not offer. If a woman is veiled, I do not offer. But here in London, where so many people are out of kilter with what they would be doing if they were at home, who is to know what to do? Many, many are the nebulous rules, the adjustable rules, the friable rules. I was once warned fair and square to have nothing to do with any man who drinks alcohol and reads the Qur'an: OK to do one or the other, but not both, because hypocrisy is the great sin. I was young and firm and unforgiving in those days, and I took that rule to heart; nowadays I'm a little gentler. Weaker. My standards have slipped. Anyway I am pleased that Hakim takes out his mat and prays in Lily's bedroom, and I am pleased that he is willing to crack a beer with me and gossip, and with his

youth and sweetness keep madcap monsters from my mental
door.

'So, is Sa'id married yet?' I asked, flinging around for a
subject, as we sat down to eat.

Hakim looked surprised at the suggestion. 'Oh no,' he said.

'But he's, what, twenty-five?'

'No one is married now at twenty-five,' he said. He peered
at his beer and looked less than completely happy.

'No one?' I was surprised. Shagging about was definitely
not on in Upper Egypt in my day, and not much in Cairo
either, and where there is no shagging about there tends to
be early marriage. Or some other arrangement.

Hakim screwed up his eyes and ran his fingers over his
forehead, pressing above his eyebrows as if to dislodge something stuck inside. 'No one,' he said crossly.

'Don't be cross with me about it,' I said mildly.

He looked up. 'Not cross with you,' he said, heartfelt,
fearful of giving offence. 'Of course not with you.'

He held my gaze, eye to eye, steady. It made me realise
how seldom he caught my eye, let alone held it.

'Things are strange to me here,' he said. 'At home you are
tourist and the tourist, perhaps you know, is number one. And
number two and number three and number four and so on. In
Luxor for thousands of years we have been guardians of our
palaces and graves, and people – you – have come to visit, and
have brought money for the people who tend to visitors.'

It was one of those moments which make me want a cigarette. When someone starts to talk.

'Let me tell you,' he said. 'During the Gulf War, when I
was quite small. Not so small. After the houses where the
people lived were knocked down and the big hotels all built,
and the tourism schools teach that the tourist is always right;
after they build the walls to hide the villages because the
village isn't so pretty, so they build the walls not the drains,

anyway. Then there was the bombardment of Baghdad and the tourists don't come, and everyone is scared, because so much is ... spent for the people who will come. Just before the bombardment of Baghdad, when everything was just so ... you know ... I went with a visitor from Cairo to the grave of Thutmosis, in the valley of the kings, I think you know the one. There is a metal steps up the cliff, and climbing, and a pit, and steps down inside. My friend's great-uncle was a guard in this grave. It is shaped like an egg, pale cheese colour with black pictograms, beautiful. The king made it hard to find, and now you just go every day.

'You know photographs are not allowed in these graves without a pass. The flash destroys the picture. Too much light, too many people. One time, this day, four tourists come in and just start to take photographs with flash. The old man, the guard, says to them no photograph. All he can say in English, in French, in German (except also "Welcome Luxor"). He says it, in English, in French, in German. The tourists take no notice. He stands in front of them, in front of the pictograms. Then one tourist knocks him down. We came in next – me small boy and the lady visitor, the friend of my mother. The old man is on the floor, blood ... the tourist taking photographs. The lady visitor picks him up, the tourist police come, fuss and bother, no one saw but everybody knows the old man is telling truth.'

'So what happened?'

'The old man was made to apologise.'

He looked at me straight, to see what I thought.

'Luxor is a beautiful place but it is not good,' he said. 'No one is married before thirty because they have not enough money. Business is good for us but even for Sa'id to make enough money for himself to marry will take time. All the money is spent for him going to university, to Sorbonne, business studies – he did only one year, said he knew more than the professors, then economics. But everybody else is leaving school and not going to university. People come by so rich, tourists, Egyptians, Saudi, Europeans. And we are rich, my family. My father employs people. Sa'id does business with Cairo for him. We sell abroad, in Khan el-Khalili, we have the shop in Luxor and the *fabrique* on the West Bank. But Sa'id cannot marry. How is it for the poorer people? Wages are not good. The richness does not travel from the rich people to the poor. The poor people live in places that are built without permission and then the officials say they will knock them down and they will have nowhere to live. In Qurnah because the old village is just among the graves of the Nobles they are always trying to knock it down. They send in tanks, the village people come out with sticks. Just to show that they *are* people, who *can* hold sticks, not just some bit of litter. And now they build New Qurnah, and we are all to leave and go there.'

This was making me sad.

'It's the same everywhere, to one degree or another,' I mumbled. Like that's any comfort. But I have no sophisticated analysis of these situations. I just feel sad, and sometimes want to punch someone for not making the world a fair and just place. A reaction which has hardly changed since I was Lily's age. Janie used to say there was no point because you can't punch God. We stopped talking to him, though. Remained silent during 'Onward Christian Soldiers', and hoped he'd take the hint.

'Many people at home are very unhappy,' he said finally. 'Things happen you don't hear about here. The last years . . . But Egypt doesn't make a big noise of it to the world because they don't want the world to stop to come. And it's just Egyptian people, so the world doesn't mind.'

Of course I knew what he was talking about. Those single paragraphs you read in the sidebars of the foreign pages: four policemen killed in an ambush at Naqquada; train shot at, suspects, fundamentalists, reports say. Like any one of a thousand problems, that only flick our conciousnesses when they happen in places where we've been on holiday. If I lived in Qurnah I could never leave. The Nile before you, five thousand miles of Sahara at your back, ancient Thebes the bones of your home.

Hakim was looking at me. I couldn't remember the last thing he'd said.

'I make coffee,' he said, and did.

Oh yes. It was, 'It's just Egyptian people, so nobody cares.'

Then Zeinab rang. What with one thing and another I hadn't spoken to her since Hakim's appearance, so I told her about him. Or as much as I could with him in the room. He gestured me furiously not to mention his mother, so I didn't. She wanted to come and see him, to welcome him and to check him out. Of course I'd told her about Abu Sa'id, over the years. We decided she should come at the weekend, and bring the boys. Then Brigid rang, was I still on for tomorrow. Yes indeed I was. How many of them? Three boys and Caitlin. All night? Fine. They could go on the lilos on the floor in my room, in with me and Lily. Squashy!

Perhaps a midnight feast might be in order. It'll be Friday after all. Hakim announced his intention to go to the mosque. Then my mother rang, saying would we come for lunch on Sunday; then Harry rang, saying he was sorry he rushed me off like that, and was I all right, and I lied that yes I was, and we had an awkward pause, and said well all right then, 'bye then.

And then Hakim and I sat down with the phone books and I showed him how we needed to look for Tomlinsons or Lockwoods rather than Sarahs, and after a long and interesting chain of calls I was able to give Hakim a piece of paper with two phone numbers on it. 'There you go,' I said. 'Your mother. She's a lecturer at a university by the sea. It's about an hour away. She teaches Arabic.'

six

Tell Mama

I think there's only one other thing I haven't mentioned. Deep in the upholstery of the saggy old red armchair I keep in my study there is a very large sum of money. It is Janie's ill-gotten gains from her career in pornography. I hid it there just over a year ago, having found it in a last tea-chest of her things that Mum had redeemed from the attic but not been able to face looking at. I hid the money in the hope that it would go away, because I didn't want to face the ethical and emotional problems that it brought with it. Of course at the same time I didn't want it to go away, too. It is a very large sum of money and I am after all a single mother of uncertain employment living in a council block, albeit in a separate kingdom on the most distant and salubrious storey of a pretty nice one. I haven't counted it.

Mum asked me once, months later, what had been in the chest. I didn't tell her, about the money or about the jewellery or about the peculiarly nasty pornographic videos. I think I said: 'Oh, nothing, just some clothes and stuff.'

We don't talk enough in our family. We're so quietly convinced that we're doing all right that we don't discuss it. We're all so rational that nothing needs to be said. And yet when I think what I have in my heart that I haven't ever mentioned . . . Janie's death, obviously. Not the fact of it but the niceties of the feelings it produced. Nobody ever blamed me for it, except myself. So I never had a chance to justify myself, defend myself, except to myself. I would have welcomed a judgement by a jury of my peers. Because you know it could have been my fault. There could have been greasy dead leaves or a manhole cover that I should have avoided. I could have been riding like a fool, or over-excited, or not paying attention. Over-accelerating on that dangerous corner, misjudging the surface, slipping gear. But the parents assumed that I wasn't. Assumed. No proof. Then when the police had no doubts about it, that was proof enough for everybody. Everybody except me.

Of course it wasn't my fault that the car came up inside us on the turn. But then I didn't see it. I didn't avoid it. I couldn't accelerate away, escape from the bend I was committed to. I wasn't skilful enough. In the same circumstances I would never expect somebody else to have been able to. But it wasn't somebody else, it was me. I never told Mum and Dad that I blamed myself for my lack of skill. The fact is I was – would be still, if I still rode – a perfectly skilful rider, experienced, calm, patient, swift to react, observant at all times. But not skilful enough.

Of course it was in their interests for me not to be to blame. If I had been they would have lost two daughters. Unless of course they would have been able to forgive me.

Anyway, easier for them to assume there had never been a fault, than to face it and forgive it. And do I blame them for that? No.

The other thing, of course, is Janie's career. About which they know nothing and will know nothing. All our lives our parents protect us and then suddenly one day we're protecting them.

Janie, Janie, Janie. Janie's money, Janie's death, Janie's career. Not to mention Janie's memory, and all that Janie was to me before ... well exactly, before when? Before she died? Before I discovered she was a lying treacherous whore, who prostituted my very identity? We have to go back further ... but I don't know how far back, because I don't know when it all started, and damn it I can't ask her. Not for dates, not for clarification, for denial, for explanation, for apology. How can I get her off my back when she's not here?

I was woken on Friday by the call to prayer, which didn't half take me back.

I was dreaming that I was in Cairo, a clear, intense dream of something absolutely ordinary, of its time, but its time was ten years – no, nine years ago. I was dreaming of going home after work, as I did five or six nights a week. Heading home to Château Champoleon through the dusty, colourless dawn after a night dancing on the Nile boats or in the clubs. In the back of a cab, rhythms sweeping through my blood, my flesh warm and my muscles soft and my brain transcendent from hours of dancing. I could have danced all night – hell, I *did* dance all night. Every night.

In my dream I had been at the Niagara, which was run in those days by a lady of uncertain age who modelled herself on late-nineteenth-century French lesbians, with claret-coloured velvet and frogging and a cigarette holder. She liked me because I was English. 'I most like the English,' she would say. 'Most of all like.' 'Don't mock me,' I'd reply. 'I've read Naguib Mahfouz. I know you hate me.' 'Who's that?' she would say, even though he was terribly famous and soon to win the Nobel prize for literature and have a café named after himself in Khan el-Khalili. 'Oh, just some tuppenny ha'penny little novelist,' I'd say, and she'd say 'Novelist? What is?' and then she'd snort, and say, '*Une danseuse doit être illiterée.*'

In my dream I was walking to my building and thinking

53

about her and revelling in the near-emptiness of the streets. Only at this time of night are the streets finally empty, empty of all but the pattering footsteps of the jackals that come in from the desert in the heart of the night to eat the garbage, and leave empty plastic bags whirling like tumbleweed down Champoleon Street. For a moment, at 4.53 or thereabouts, the streets are empty, but even as you think it, there are people mysteriously starting to do their mysterious jobs in holes and alleyways. The first *fuul* stand is starting to set up, ready to sell breakfast. A degree of rattling can be heard behind the closed doors of the cafés. Dogs are barking.

I dreamed I stopped off up on the roof of the Odeon for a soothing bowl of *omali* before bed. I dreamed of the terracotta bowl, the baked sultanas and nuts and milk, the softened, pudding-baked bread, the hot sweet smell of it, the best of the new day before I collapse at the end of the old one. Five a.m., and the pre-dawn muezzin calls the *fajr*: 'It is better to pray than to sleep,' and me thinking, as you do at five a.m., 'It is better to sleep than to do anything else in the world.' I dreamed I passed Mohammed, the *bauwab*, fast asleep on the stone bench at the foot of the monumental beige granite staircase, by Cecil B de Mille out of Ramses the Great. Walked up so as not to rouse the whole Château with the clanking and wheezing of the ancient lift. I woke up just as, in my dream, I fell into bed. Curiously, the muezzin continued.

It was Hakim, celebrating Friday by teaching Lily the call to prayer in the kitchen. She had *Allah u Akbar* perfectly, and a bit more, but then he sang her something including *Bismillah*, in the name of God, which made her giggle because she calls her navel her bizz. Because when she was smaller her granddad used to blow raspberries on her tummy, making a Bzzz noise. She was explaining this to Hakim. He was giggling too because *bizz* is the Arabic for tit, and he wasn't sure if I knew. I felt a surge of love for both of them, for

Egypt, for life, and decided to make pancakes in celebration, before I remembered that Lily now went to a school where she had to be on time.

By the time I returned from taking her, the post had arrived. There was another letter. It said: 'He was the best of men, he was the worst of men, but with that man to be alive was very heaven.' Irrelevantly, the first thing I thought was what an irritating name Carton was for a romantic antihero, evoking as it does cardboard boxes of long-life apple juice, though no doubt it didn't then. Empty cardboard boxes, actually. And Sydney Carton was not an empty cardboard box. The pitfalls that lie in wait for authors, years down the line ... My next thought was that if all she wanted to do was send me semi-poetic notes and paraphrases then I didn't necessarily mind that much. But.

I tried to remember anything that Eddie had ever said about his wife, and realised that he had never mentioned her to me. So how did I know about her? Through Harry? Maybe, when he was warning me off Eddie, when he thought Eddie and I were about to develop into love's young dream. Or maybe through Fergus Droyle, my crime correspondent buddy, who I'd asked about Eddie right at the beginning. I had the idea that she lived in Monaco. Well, if so she's not there now.

Does she mean me harm? 'You did, and I mind.' She might do. And she knows where I live, as they say. She could, if she wanted, come and visit. This wasn't a pleasant idea. I wasn't exactly scared, but I wasn't keen. As you wouldn't be. It seemed it might be a good idea to have a word with her. Pre-empt her. Fergus would be the logical place to start, if I wanted to track her down. Except ...

I didn't want to ask him. I'd sworn him to secrecy and told him, finally, some of what went on with Eddie and me, and the poor man had gone mauve as his desire to use the story fought with his friendship for me and respect for my privacy.

Later, after the trial, he'd written a piece about Eddie, and had rung me, but I'd refused to say anything. I didn't want to try his loyalty any further by bringing the subject up again. Specially when Eddie was so topical, having died. Some things you should not expect a journalist to bear. It would be unkind.

She would presumably be at the funeral. But I didn't really want to go to the funeral. He was dead and that was that. Also I thought Harry might be there, out of courtesy as one of the men who nicked him (or as his former employee, if he was still keeping that persona going), and I was sorry that Harry had witnessed the hysteria of my immediate response to the news of his death. I seem to have a little bug that jumps out to wind Harry up. It seemed a good idea to avoid further opportunities for it. And no, I didn't want any wild graveside scenes with a vengeful Mrs Bates.

But I did want to locate her. If only to feel better equipped. Fergus or Harry, which would be worse?

Hakim leaned over my shoulder.

'Evangelina,' he said. 'May we ring my mother?'

He's started to say 'may' because Lily corrects him when he says 'can'. Actually she's having quite a good effect on his grammar, but it's a little alarming for me to hear echoed back so precisely what I say to her.

I half wanted to confide in Hakim about the letters but decided that it would be a complicated and useless exercise, so I desisted. One issue at a time, girl. Let's put off the ones that matter most to me. There's a sensible approach.

First we rang the home number. 'Hi, this is Sarah, you can leave a message and we'll get back to you, or you can send a fax, after the beep.' Relaxed, not warm not cold, middle-class, southern. She sounded nice. I held out hope, but I kept quiet about it. I didn't want to influence Hakim.

I hung up, and told him it was a machine, and did he want

me to leave a message, or to leave one himself, or what.

He paused for a second, then picked up the receiver and pressed last number redial (another trick he'd learnt from Lily, who uses it to ring Caitlin after I've been talking to Brigid). I watched his face as he heard his mother's voice. Expressionless, it just grew softer and softer. I thought he might melt away completely, so I offered him my hand as something solid to hold. He took it and gripped it, and hung up the phone.

'If she is not a good mother,' he said, 'I want you to be my mother. The English mother.'

I kissed him on the forehead and narrowly stopped myself from telling him that I would do anything in the world for him.

'May we ring the other number?' he said.

I called directory enquiries, got the number of the university, called the switchboard, got the extension, called the extension.

'Hello, Sarah Tomlinson,' said the same voice.

I had decided to do it on a wing and a prayer. I could not have worked out a script and stuck to it. This is what came out.

'Hello, Sarah, my name's Evangeline Gower, I'm a friend of Ismail.'

'Ismail?' she said.

'El Araby,' I said.

She was quiet. I heard voices in the background.

'If this isn't a good time I can . . .' I said.

'No,' she said. 'No. One moment.' She spoke at the other end, and then came on the line again. 'What's it about?' she said.

'Hakim and Sa'id,' I said. I could almost hear her heart-rate change.

'What about them?' she said, her voice completely different, narrow-throated, nervous, tense.

'Hakim is in London,' I said.

'Oh my God,' she breathed, and spoke again to the voices in the background. I could hear them retreat, and a click, some shuffling, and some breathing, and then, 'Is he with you?'

'Beside me, yes.'

'Oh my God,' she whispered, again, and she began to cry, very softly. Hakim was all eyes.

'What's she saying?' he asked. 'What?' I held my hand up, mouthed 'wait'.

She carried on crying. I spoke to her: 'Listen – do you want to ring him back? Can you take down a number? Otherwise . . . he wants to see you, you know. He wants to talk. Take my number, and if you don't ring he'll ring you tonight. OK?'

She didn't sound negative. I gave her the number and I thought she got it down. She was still crying. 'I don't want to leave you like this,' I said.

'I don't even know who you are,' she snapped suddenly, through the tears. 'Who are you anyway?'

'Evangeline Gower, friend of the family,' I said.

'Family,' she said. She sighed. 'I'll ring in a couple of hours,' she said. 'Tell him . . . is he well?'

'Very well,' I said.

'Tell him . . . say I'm not sorry he's here.'

'OK,' I said.

''Bye.'

''Bye.'

I put the phone down and said, 'She's not sorry you're here, she said to say so. She'll ring back.'

'*Alhamdullillah*,' he said, four times, and smiled, and went to Lily's room, where if I put my ear to the door I could hear him saying *el fateha*, the opening of the Qur'an.

* * *

I tried to do some work: an article about an exhibition of Orientalist paintings that was coming up in Birmingham. The exhibition wasn't open yet and there was some doubt about which paintings were going to be in it, because of some insurance problems. Doubt hung over, among others, an extremely famous and interesting pair with all sorts of splendid and evocative anecdotes attached. One, fairly innocent, harem scene had originally been painted as a cover for the other, more erotic, work, of which it was an almost exact copy, except that the harem ladies were covered up in various cunning ways. The main houri, for example, was sitting with her legs wide because she was holding a great platter with a watermelon on it, rather than displaying herself; another was adjusting her scarf rather than her nipple. The cover lived in the same frame, on top of the naughty picture, and the owner could remove it for selected guests, after dinner, and thus preserve both his pleasures and his reputation. The two paintings had been separated over the years and were now to be reunited. Or not. I was going to have to write two articles, so that they had something to use whatever the outcome. I wrote an introduction that would do for both versions, then admitted that I was not concentrating and rang Fergus.

'Fergus, Evangeline,' I said, in my brisk talking-to-people-in-offices voice.

'Evangeline darlin',' he said, emphasising the Irish. 'What can I do for you?' This made me feel bad because of not having been able to do anything for him on recent occasions, but I don't think he did it on purpose.

'Mrs Bates,' I said. Fergus fancies himself utterly ruled by deadlines and important busyness; he appreciates you getting to the point.

'Oh my God, would you get out of my hair with that,' he said, which was not the response I'd been expecting.

'What do you mean?'

'I've had it up to high dough with that woman,' he said (at least that's what I thought he said – I assumed it was something to do with bread rising; later he told me no, it's high do, as in do re mi, as in top C, when you're singing). 'She's off her flaming trolley, in fact if she and her trolley were ever intimately connected I'd have my doubts. Serious doubts. I can understand a widow woman being upset but she is the most abysmal specimen of a . . . why?'

It never takes him long to get to why.

'I think she's been writing me letters.'

'Does she think you killed her husband?'

'Well yes she does, actually.'

'Join the club, darling. We're a flaming conspiracy, evidently. I killed him, by writing that article, which apparently affected his heart. Every policeman you ever saw killed him, by being a policeman, which was contrary to what he liked. The jury killed him, separately and together, by finding him guilty when he would have preferred not. The prison warders killed him; the prison doctors killed him, the judge killed him and chopped him up into little pieces and left him out for the birds. How did you kill him then? By being the object of his unrequited desires?'

'I suppose so . . . God, Fergus, that's a relief.'

'Did you think it was only you? So did I, till I got to gossiping. You should get out more. You know Harry killed him too, and Ben Cooper, only no one's told him yet that everybody else did too because they like to see him suffer. What has she done to you then? Letters? Phone calls?'

My journalist filter went up.

'Are you going to be writing about this?'

'I'll just say "a girl he admired". Nothing to identify you. Promise.'

'Oh Fergus . . .'

'Please. For colour. There's no sex in it so far. Please.'

I thought for a moment. I did quite want to give him something, because he's a friend and he's helped me in the past. I did also want very much to keep my nose clean.

'I tell you what,' I said.

'What,' he said.

For a second I was about to say 'I'm not telling you'. That's Lily's great joke: 'You know what?' 'What?' 'I'm not telling you.'

'I think . . . let me think about it.' I was thinking that perhaps I wanted to see her first, clear the air, then I thought no, if she's feeling that way about so many people I don't need to. She's not going to firebomb the lot of us.

'Is anyone taking it seriously? Has she made any threats at all?' (This Irishness is contagious. I don't know if it's my dad's Liverpool Irish blood coming out in me but whenever I talk to an Irish person I start using their accent. It makes Brigid, Cork-born and bred, piss herself laughing.)

'Not to my knowledge. I think they're all taking it with a pinch of salt. I was exaggerating a little bit, you know. I don't think she's been pestering the judge. The woman may have some sense. Have you met her? She's a funny woman and that's for sure.'

'What's she like?' I realised I had a clear picture of her as being a bit like the Queen, but younger. Respectable, pretty, pearls, elegant in a dull way. Grace Kelly. Handbag. Why? Because she lived in Monaco? Because Eddie had classy taste and modern art?

'Oh, she's basic gangster Euro-trash, a Marbella queen. Army father, boarding school, home counties, ran wild, ex-model, still wearing the make-up that was in style when she was young and gorgeous, and her heyday hairdo. Brigitte Bardot without the class. White stilettos, shiny eye-shadow. Permatan. Permapissed, as well. Drinks like a Mexican maggot. When Eddie started ignoring her she took to astrology and small dogs. And possibly younger men, but she's always been crazy about Eddie. And terrified of him. Flaming lunatic, basically. There's a lot of them around.'

Oh.

'What's her name?'

'Didn't your boyfriend tell you, then?'

I hung up on him.

He rang back ten seconds later, apologising profusely.

'OK,' he said. 'OK, you mean it. I'm sorry. Her name's Chrissie. She's born Christine Louise Evans, then Chrissie de Lisle, no less, and for no reason other than sheer pretension, in her salad days, and now she goes as Christina Bates. So we'll speak on Monday, will we, or over the weekend?'

'Yeah. No promises. Would you let me know if anything else . . . you know . . .'

'My darling, I'm gossip central on Mrs Bates. Short of anyone blowing a fuse and trying to sue, I don't think anything's going to happen except more of the same. And you know what our friends in the Bill are like, till the stalking law comes in they can't move on this stuff till she's pouring petrol through your letterbox. But I don't think she will. She's an old bat exorcising her sad old life, if you ask me. Ignore her and she'll go away.'

'Thanks, Fergus. I'll speak to you.'

'Indeed you will,' he said.

It occurred to me as I hung up that Fergus didn't know I'd hit Eddie on the head with the poker, and that I didn't know if Mrs Bates knew or not. And I didn't know if she'd been visiting him in prison, and I didn't know when the funeral was. Which I wanted to know, even though I didn't want to go. So I rang back and asked him. Yes she had, she'd been regularly, and there had been something of a rapprochement between them; and next Tuesday, 11 a.m., at Southgate. The same cemetery where Janie is buried.

I was relieved by our conversation, but not that relieved.
Then I ate a bowl of cornflakes and went to get Lily.

When we got back from the park Hakim was standing in the middle of the kitchen with stars in his eyes.

'I speak to her,' he said. 'I go tomorrow. I want to tell you.' Then he grabbed my face and kissed me, grabbed Lily's and kissed her, then disappeared into the bathroom, presumably to wash off our touch because moments later he reappeared and then disappeared again, out the front door, crying, 'I go to mosque.'

Lily looked bemused.

'His mother,' I explained. 'He hasn't seen his mother for fifteen years, and tomorrow he's going to see her. After fifteen years.'

She gazed after him. 'So will I see my father after fifteen years?' she said.

Childish logic. I sat on the floor and drew her to me.

'Oh, darling, I don't know,' I said.

She wouldn't sit with me. 'Well you should know,' she said. 'You know everything else.' Then she looked at me, and then she went into my room and sat silently on the bed.

For a moment I was dumbstruck. Then I followed her in.

'I wanted to go into my room,' she said in a tiny voice, 'but it's not really mine.'

I sat by her. 'Sweetheart?' I said.

'I don't want to cry,' she said.

'You don't have to,' I said. 'You can if you want.'

'I feel bad but I haven't done anything bad.'

There are times when you feel completely bloody useless.

'Sometimes bad things happen to us even if we're good,' I said. 'What's making you feel bad? Do you know?'

'It's too difficult to explain,' she said. Her lower lip was sticking out, just a tiny bit. The tears stayed in her eyes. Full and curved. Their shape echoed the shape of her cheeks.

'Well what's it about? Just tell me the subject. You don't have to explain it all.'

'I don't want to,' she said.

'Why not?'

'I want you to know already,' she whispered.

And of course I did know. There was only one thing about her that I'd ever claimed not to know, that I'd ever claimed not to understand. Or rather – that I'd ever known was there, but not talked about, not shared, not dealt with. There was such closeness between us that I knew if she would choose an orange or an apple, if she wanted a bath or not, what story she wanted at night out of twenty to pick from. I always knew which hand she'd hidden the coin in. I knew every damn thing about her, and I knew this.

'OK,' I said. 'I'll find him.'

When she looked up at me I swear her eyes were twice the size they had been. She grinned like a maniac.

'You do know! You do know!' she yelled.

'I know what you want, darling. I don't know where he is or when we can find him . . .'

'But you know I want him!'

That was all she needed. God, she was happy. I felt so small that I hadn't admitted I knew it all along. To myself, quite apart from her. Going to bed that night she was telling herself a story. 'Well a daddy might be in the zoo, but only if he had other children, because he wouldn't go to the zoo if he didn't have a child with him, so a lost daddy wouldn't go there, unless he was a zookeeper MUMMY! IS MY DADDY A ZOOKEEPER?'

'Not that I know of.'

'It's quite funny you not knowing things,' she said, with an echo of Harry. I kissed her and we did the rituals: 'I love you up to the moon and back again'; 'I love you too, now shut up and go to sleep'; 'Will you scratch my back?' 'No I won't.' 'But it was worth a try, wasn't it Mummy?' 'Yes now shut up and go to sleep'; and then I went and rang Harry.

Because frankly, out of the choice I had, he was the best.

He was out. I didn't leave a message. Anyway then Brigid and Caitlin and the boys appeared bearing sleeping bags, and Lily got out of bed, and the lilos had to be blown up and the whole thing turned into a hoopla of considerable proportions. Around ten I gave up and left them to it, and went to watch the news. It was all about the dead princess and her boyfriend. ('It was her own fault,' said Lily. 'She was a mummy. Why didn't she have her seat-belt on?')

Halfway through Hakim came in and said: 'He's no good that man. No good for Egypt. Rich as ten thousand men. And he did not look after your princess. In Egypt they say your government killed them because they hate Islam and want no Muslim man in your royal family. I say bollocks.' At the same time as I was amused by his finding so soon the grosser end of our lovely language, and pronouncing it like the young bull he so reminded me of, I could see the sincerity of his distaste.

seven

Brighton

The next day, Saturday, there were two letters. One contained a razor blade, the other a poem.

> Distracting is the foliage of my pasture
> The mouth of my girl is a lotus bud
> Her breasts are mandrake apples
> Her arms are vines
> Her eyes are fixed like berries
> Her brow a snare of willow
> And I the wild goose!
> My beak snips her hair for bait,
> As worms for bait in the trap.

I knew this poem. Not that it's famous, out of its field. It's from an ancient papyrus. It's, I don't know, three thousand years old. I didn't like it – I'd never liked it. Hair as worms, bait in a trap. Ugly. Violent. Fixed berries, vines, snares. It speaks to me of desire and resentment – a bad combination.

And a razor blade.

How very unpleasant.

Each one gave me a cold shudder. I didn't know, actually, which was nastier.

I burnt the poem and broke the blade in half with a pair of pliers, then wrapped it in cotton wool, soaked the package in baby oil and threw it in the rubbish, which I then took out on to the balcony and dropped – plop! – into the wheelie bin seven storeys below. I'm pretty ritualistic on occasion.

'What are you doing?' asked the children, interested in any new form of inexplicable behaviour from a grown-up. I was stymied for a moment – what *was* I doing? Frightening off baddies? (Didn't want to admit to the presence of baddies in case it frightened them.) Nothing? (They wouldn't fall for that.) I concentrated on the razor blade, and turned it into a small lecture on domestic safety and what to do with any sharp object, disposal thereof. It worked.

I thought again about protection. There would be absolutely no point taking this to the police. And – well, there is nobody whose business it is to protect me. I am the protector round here. This is my lot, chosen by me and ordained by circumstance. Price of freedom, nature of my generation.

Of course I could talk to Harry about it.

But I won't. I'll talk to Mrs Bates. I also rang one of those telephone insurance companies and arranged household cover, which was very unlike me.

Worms for bait in the trap. Ugh.

Put it away. Now the children are hungry – feed them. First things first.

I made pancakes for everybody for breakfast. After waiting for Brigid to come and take her offspring away, and for Zeinab and her two younger boys to arrive, which they did in the middle of the pancakes so I had to make more, Hakim, Lily, Zeinab, Omar, Hassan, and I all piled into the small car and headed for Brighton, where Hakim was to meet his mother and we were to lie about on the beach in the sweet Indian summer, eating chips from The Meeting Place and breathing in ozone and vinegar, one of life's most beautiful smell combinations. Hakim quivered all the way down the M23, and Lily held his hand. 'It's all right,' she told him helpfully. 'Mummies are very nice and kind. It's their job.'

It was hot, and the fumes and rancid pizza smell of London fell away from us as we piled out on the seafront at noon. Hakim wanted to look at the sea before meeting her. Then he wanted to pray. He was erratic in his praying, but fervent. It was time for *zohr*, midday prayer, and meeting his mother, well . . . He did his abolitions, as he called them. I pictured him washing in a smidgeon of sand, like Bedouins do in the desert. He prayed there on the beach, prostrating himself among a few late prostrate sunbathers, an Arab of the north in the wrong kind of desert. The sunbathers looked upside down beside him. I left the children throwing pebbles at the West Pier with Zeinab, and drove Hakim up the hill to his mother's address.

It was a sweet house. Low eaves, tall staring yellow daisies in the garden, peeking windows facing out to sea, green door, wellies in the porch. I half-expected Mrs Tiggywinkle. It seemed a very long way from Qurnah.

'Please knock,' said Hakim.

'*You* knock,' said I. 'It's your mother.'

He knocked. His poor eyes, his sweet nose, his bumfluff sideburns. As the door was answered he stared across to me in naked terror.

I stood aside, and noted a smallish woman, late forties, dark tunic and trouser type ensemble, chestnut hair not naturally so, and a small gold necklace with a pendant of a hieroglyphic cartouche. Perhaps the disposition to wear culturally significant jewellery is genetic: Hakim's *aya*, her cartouche. Her face was almost as scared as Hakim's.

I made to go but Hakim grabbed me.

'Mama,' he said, 'this is Evangeline, my friend, may she stay?'

I tried to look as if I wasn't his sugar mummy.

Sarah stared at him. They had the same chin.

She moved aside and we went in. Hakim went and stood in front of her and took both her hands in his and bent his head forward, almost as if worshipping at her. Then he gave a package. 'It is not the best present from son to mother but it comes . . .'

'Thank you,' she said, and opened it, and stared at it. Then she went and made a pot of tea. We could hear her sniffing in the kitchen. Every now and then she peeked round the kitchen door and stared at him. It was the most extraordinary scene I have ever witnessed. I actually couldn't bear to look at either of them. Too intense. I feared for my retinas, and looked at the present instead, a small plaster box, in the shape of Nut, the sky goddess, on all fours as she always is. Inside the lid you could see her belly and breasts, spattered with stars, the moon, and the sun at the meeting of her thighs. The bottom of the box was Geb, the earth, her lover. According to the legend the world came to be when her father, Shu, came and separated her body from Geb's. Shu still holds the earth and the sky apart; he is the air. We live between separated lovers, breathing in jealousy. She gives birth to the sun every morning. The Milky Way is milk spilled from her breast. When Lily is pretending to be a baby animal she pretends to breastfeed from me because she thinks it is such a lovely idea. It used almost to break my heart but no longer.

It was a lovely thing. It reminded me of the ceiling in that beautiful side chapel at the temple of Hathor at Dendara. I wondered if it was a replica of something old, but now wasn't the time to ask.

Sarah liked it, but she liked Hakim more.

'How is your father?' she said.

'They don't know I am here,' he said.

She poured him tea but he didn't touch it.

'I'll tell you everything,' she said. 'Every little thing. It would be a shame now to hate each other.'

'No way José,' he said. She was puzzled, but she didn't laugh. He didn't mean her to. He didn't know it was a joke phrase.

'Oh my boy,' she said. 'Oh my little boy.'

And he was. There was no question now but that he was a boy. His vestiges of adulthood fell away in her presence. I swear he was getting shorter by the minute. She was sitting in an armchair, and he left his own seat and went over to sit on the floor by her. He took her hand, and leaned his head against her knee, and closed his eyes, and the swoony bliss that you only ever see on the face of a well-fed baby engulfed him. He sighed deeply. Then I realised that he was asleep.

'He's asleep,' I said.

'Oh!' she exclaimed, and looked down at the top of his silky head, and said, 'Oh, my God, this is the – oh.'

I wasn't embarrassed because I was so interested. I compared it with the Madam Butterfly day that Jim, thinking (or at least claiming) that he was Lily's father, came to tea with his unpleasant wife. He'd wanted me to tell Lily he was her father, but I'd refused. I remembered that total lack of anything between them. No similarity, no communication, no understanding, no pleasure in each other, no blood, no link . . . I should have known then that he wasn't her father.

And look at these two. Meets his mother, and the first thing he does is curl up and sleep, as near to in her arms as is physically possible. He was five when she left – Lily's age. And they must have had love, for them to be like this now.

'He looks like he's taking up where you left off,' I said. Then kicked myself. I meant you plural, but she might hear you singular and take it as blame: 'you left'. I wasn't about to blame her. I hadn't, as the American Indians say, walked two miles in her shoes.

'This *is* where we left off,' she said. 'The night I left he fell asleep on my lap, and I carried him to bed. Sa'id was out on the river with his felucca friends. I saw them in the distance, coming in, as I crossed over to Luxor.'

I couldn't quite envisage how she had left. The English wife of the alabaster merchant, in Qurnah, in the early eighties. On the West Bank, which tourists visit for sure – to see the Valleys of the Kings and Queens, the Temple of Hatshepsut, the collossi of Memnon, one of which used to wail at dawn, until it was mended and the crack in the rock no longer sounded as it shrank in the morning sun, the statue that the Happy Prince's swallow so longed to see, and so does everybody else. But having seen, they don't on the whole stay on the West Bank, in that small and intricately connected community. She would have been known. Was she in the habit of crossing over to the city on her own at night, without her husband? Even during our comparatively short stay, five years later, Nadia and I became quickly known, greeted by name. But Sarah was there twelve years, a wife, a mother, a true attempter at the link between cultures. She couldn't have left in secret.

I couldn't ask. It wasn't my business. But I couldn't not.

'Did you want to leave?'

Hakim had let her hand drop, and she was gently, wonderingly, stroking his hair.

'I still don't know,' she said after a while, as if she wasn't thinking about it. 'I thought I did. Perhaps.'

'Then . . .'

I was thinking about what she'd said on the phone: 'I don't even know who you are!'

She made to stir herself, then didn't. 'You see that picture on the mantelpiece? The photograph? Could you pass it to me?'

It was old, faded, taken in bright sun, with the bright whited-out colours that say high summer, long ago, late seventies. In Britain these pictures are usually of people in low-slung orange crocheted bikinis, or tight brown flares and stripy scarves, squinting at the sun. This was Hakim and Sa'id, one chubby, one lean, aged say four and nine, in clean white shirts and clean white smiles, standing in front of one of the great carved pillars of the temple of Karnak, with their massive curves and scant memory of green and red, faded out and out of frame. The bleached-out colours gave it the look of a David Roberts watercolour. Behind them, and behind the pillar, half a Japanese face peered round, inquisitively.

'I sent this to my father,' she said. 'He gave it back to me when I came home.' It seemed clear to me that there was a great deal of pain here. She was still stroking Hakim.

I had got up to stand behind her to see the photograph. She balanced it carefully on her knee.

Sarah's face crumpled up.

She didn't really want to talk to me at all. I thought perhaps I should make it easier for her.

'I'll leave you two,' I said, and did.

In the car on the way home Zeinab talked about Hakim and his situation for twenty minutes without pause. She liked him, admired his courage, felt for the uncertainty of his future, was looking forward to cooking him some decent Egyptian food and having him round to talk Arabic with the boys, thought him very nice-looking and nice-mannered, wondered how devout he really was and how long that would last, and thought it would and hoped he wouldn't get into bad company ('There are some terrible Egyptians in London you know. The worst.') and wanted to know was I doing his laundry for him.

In the end Lily said: 'Zeinab, he's ours not yours, but you can play with him but you have to give him back when we ask.'

Though actually I agreed with her, I had to point out that people don't belong to other people.

'If they love each other they do,' she argued, 'and we love him so he's ours and he loves me.'

'We can all share him,' I said, hopefully, but Lily had already turned her attention to a bag of crisps that Omar had acquired somewhere along the line, so the concept of sharing had a more immediate application in her mind.

When we got home there was a package for me on the kitchen table, in white tissue. It was a box, like the one he had given his mother. A carefully lettered card said: 'Thank you for having me.' I suspected Lily had helped him. She loved the box, and that night I told her what I could remember of the story of Nut and Geb, and she jumped up to look out the window at Nut's tummy, and there it was, starless, clouded orange and purple, reflecting our sins back at us.

When she was asleep, I went to ring Harry. As I approached the phone, it rang. I left it for the machine, because I didn't want to talk to anybody else. And it was Harry. I picked it up when I heard his voice.

'I was just going to call you,' I said.

'We always were on a ley line,' he said. 'You go first.'

'No, you. It's your bill.'

'Um,' he said. Whenever Harry starts with Um I know it's something hard for him. 'I thought I might come round and cook you dinner.'

'Oh,' I said. It wasn't that surprising – he's a nice cook, tending to the oriental, the enterprising stir-fry and the coconut curry. But it was anachronistic.

'When?'

'Half an hour? An hour?'

I didn't realise he'd meant tonight. I wasn't up to talking about what I wanted to talk to him about tonight. And I didn't want to talk to him about any of the other things that were on my mind. I'd been up to my ears in people and situations all day. Two parent and child reunions in one day is too much.

He may not be her father.

Whether he is or not, it'll clear the air. If he's not, it will at least clear the space around me, and I'll just find myself true love, and true love's object can be surrogate father. I'm not traipsing through Janie's address book searching out which of her disgusting little customers it might have been.

If it was Eddie we'll never know now.

If it was Ben we don't want to know. It's not Ben. Look at her, how beautiful she is.

'Oh, Harry, I've been out all day . . .'

'All the more reason to get your dinner cooked for you,' he said.

Well we don't have to talk about it, I thought. We can just make up. I accepted graciously.

eight

Harry Cooks Dinner

He brought chicken breasts and a gnarled lump of ginger and two fresh little red chilli peppers and a fat sweet potato and four bottles of Singha beer and a plastic bag of some crispy green leafy thing that I'd never seen before, recommended, he said, by the bloke in the Thai shop. He drank, chopped, browned and sizzled ferociously for half an hour, then berated the idiocy that resulted in no noodles – his for not buying any, mine for not having any. 'Why don't you have noodles! Everybody has noodles!' The only answer I could give was bound up with the subject I wanted/didn't want to broach (Lily ate them all).

While we ate he was funny. He told me all about Tornado Tony who used to ride the Wall of Death at the Kursaal in Southend: how he had whiskers like Terry Thomas and a cravat, and to make the show more interesting he acquired a lion cub which would sit in the front of his jacket, then when it got too big for that he trained it to sit on the tank of the bike, the old Indian Chief (probably not that old in those days) that they always used because the throttle stayed open by itself, so you would be free to turn to face backwards, do somersaults, waltz with your lion cub, whatever, without having to hold your speed; then when the lion got too big for the tank he built it a sidecar, and the lion sat in the sidecar, its whiskers waxed like Terry Thomas, cravat round its neck, riding the wall of death profile to profile with the head-dressed chrome Indian Chief on the front mudguard . . . then when the lion died, he got himself a giraffe-necked woman of Borneo, who rode the handlebars and snarled at the crowd just as well as the lion used to . . . 'But where the hell did he find her! In Southend! Where did they meet! You learn every other damn thing about the story, except what the giraffe-necked woman of Borneo was doing in Southend. Strolling the front, as you do, when you're a giraffe-necked woman. Catching the Wall of Death show at the Kursaal, as the denizens of Borneo do on a Friday night . . .' Oh, he was sweet.

We were as good as made up, I suppose, but I won't rest till I manage to get it if not in writing, then at least out loud. To avoid misunderstandings.

'Hon,' I said, lounging about on the sofa in the kitchen.

'Hmm?'

'If I were to say that you were jumping to conclusions about Eddie, would you take offence?'

He thought a moment.

'No,' he said.

That wasn't enough.

'Would you believe me?'

'Yes,' he said.

That wasn't enough either.

Evidently there was more I wanted to tell him.

'Do you want to know why I was so upset?'

'I seem to remember I asked you exactly that at the time.'

'So you do?'

'Yes.'

'It was because I'd hit him over the head, and might have helped kill him.'

'I know that. I've known that longer than you.'

'Yes I know but – but you didn't do it. I did. And I only found out then. Hence shock and strange behaviour.'

'Yes,' he said.

'And . . .' I said. Before thinking quite what I was going to tell him.

'Hmm?'

'His wife has been writing to me. At least I assume it's her.'

'Ah,' he said. 'Dear old Christine. What's she got to say for herself?'

'She says I killed him.'

'Ah.'

'Fergus says she's telling everyone that they killed him . . . but they didn't, and I maybe sort of did.'

'Do you think you did?'

'If I say yes you'll have to arrest me,' I said.

'It doesn't work like that,' he said. I knew it didn't. I had no fear that the law would blame me. The law is, apart from anything else, pragmatic. I didn't blame me. I had no moral doubts at all. He jumped me, I walloped him. Serves him right. Happens everyday. Someone else wallops him a year later, he dies. Not my fault. The only murkiness is in what I did to him, unconscious. But nobody knows about that. Nobody but me. And I think I can live with it.

Looking back, my moral certainty amazes me. Actually, I didn't know if I'd contributed to killing him. What I knew, somewhere very visceral, was that I was not, repeat not, accepting any responsibility, anyway, anyhow, anywhere. The slightly less complex moral issue of whether it's all right to fuck an unconscious man who has just been trying to rape you – oh God, what am I calling less complex? OK, this was the situation: I had a life to lead and a child to bring up and I was not squandering any energy on Eddie Bates's fate or my role in it. Not at any deep level. I had decided that without it even reaching my consciousness – hell I hardly even thought about it except to go through the motions for survival. This is what we do. Cope. Don't talk to me, I'm coping. Stuff your subtleties, I'm alive, talk to me about it in five years.

'No,' I said gaily, 'of course I don't think I killed him.'

'And you didn't,' he said.

'But if she knows I walloped him?'

'Does she?'

'I don't know.'

He was quiet a moment.

'Tricky one,' he said. 'You can't ask her because, well, then she'd know and you can't ask anyone else . . . Hmm.'

'You see what I mean,' I said. 'That's what was going through my head.'

'Um,' he said. 'Um. I'll think about it.'

'And you know Eddie and I weren't . . . we didn't . . .' I couldn't quite bring myself to an outright lie.

'I know you weren't,' he said. 'And I'm glad.' There we go again. I can't tell if he's being a concerned and affectionate old lover, or basic-model patronising know-all. I can't tell. Perhaps I'll ask him. In the spirit of free communication and human connection. Worth a go. I was just gearing up to it – feeling flutes breathing a little fast in my belly – when he suddenly said: 'Can I go and look at her? Lily?'

'Of course,' I said. Surprised by his asking, by his wanting to. By his feeling that he had to ask. Oh – of course. He's being delicate.

'I just . . .' he said, and sort of smiled, and went in to her.

Then he went to the loo, and came back a moment later looking efficient.

'Have you got someone staying?' he asked.

'Yes – except he's gone away for a couple of days. Why?'

'Just saw all this shaving stuff in your bathroom. Anyone I know?'

I told him about Hakim. Chatting, friendly.

It was nice being with him, being nice. His long legs spread across the same old sofa they used to be spread across when we were young and foolish, and his familiar handsome face. Have we changed? You think so, skidding around the surface, and then the unchanging trips you up and sends you flying, and you land, winded by familiarity.

'Got to go,' he said. 'Um.'

Oh.

'What to, at eleven on a Saturday night?'

He dipped his head for a second, then looked at me.

'Well,' he said.

I seem to spend my life trying to get people to say what they want to say anyway. Am I so hard to talk to? Or is it just the nature of things?

'I'm going to pi . . . it's one reason I wanted to come round.'

'So you could go? Novel.'

'To tell you.'

I waited. I didn't like it. Niceness was receding double quick.

'I'm going to pick up my . . . well, I'm seeing someone.'

I didn't like it at all.

But it's not for me not to like. A man can have a girlfriend. What, did I think he never would, just because I turned him down over a year ago? Just because we broke up for bad reasons ten years ago?

But I didn't like it.

'Gosh,' I said. 'I didn't know.'

'No, well, you wouldn't.'

'Are you going to tell me about her?'

'Her name's Amygdala, she's a TV scriptwriter . . .'

'Amygdala! What's . . . that's part of the brain!'

'Her father's a brain surgeon. He likes the Amygdala.'

'What are her brothers and sisters called then?'

'Thomas and Daniel.'

'So he's a misogynist too.'

'What do you mean, too?'

'As well as being a sadist.'

'Angel . . .'

'What does she write then? *The Bill*?'

'Yes.'

I laughed. He looked cross. Here we go again.

Actually, he was being very civilised and I was being a bitch.

'What's she like then?' I asked, and tried to make it kind.

'Actually she's lovely.'

Of course she is. She would be. I should have known. No doubt he's about to tell me I'd like her. No doubt I would, in the normal course of things. But I couldn't help it. I hated her.

'Oh,' I said. 'Good.'

And that was it, really. Nothing to say, so I said nothing. He had to go and pick her up, so he went to pick her up.

I went into my room and looked at Lily sleeping, scratching herself.

'Sorry, babe,' I said to her. 'It's going to be a bit more complicated than I thought.' Though what I had thought I couldn't imagine.

Next morning Brigid called in on her way from Mass. Her sister had taken the children home, and she wanted to take up the opportunity of an unencumbered cup of tea. In fact what she wanted was to tell me again that I should get a boyfriend. What was I doing with my Saturday nights, she wanted to know, I was wasting away and not getting any younger and if I didn't pay attention before I knew it I'd be married to myself like she is, and she knew I wouldn't like it.

Her timing was bad. In self-defence I mentioned that Harry had come round. She began to get excited.

'To tell me about his new girlfriend,' I said.

'Oh no!' she cried.

'He's not boyfriend material anyway,' I said.

'He is just,' she replied. 'He's a very gorgeous man and I'm sorry to hear it.'

'But we've done it, Brigid, it's old stuff.'

'It's a damn shame, and you're a fool. You could've had him.'

'I don't want him,' I said. 'I've had him already.'

'Years ago,' she said. 'It's a damn shame.' I didn't agree with her. But I was incredibly bloody pissed off about the girlfriend.

'See?' she said.

'It's not that. It's Lily. She's started the Daddy thing again and if it is Harry then . . .' Brigid's husband left her and the kids six years ago, when she was pregnant with Caitlin. The Daddy thing is a bit of a subject between us. Brigid doesn't mourn John. He sends money. She's says she's well shot of him. She says it's one kid less to fuss about, and she likes her children better under 21. She's brave and tough and lets nothing touch her. 'I had true love for years and it was a pain in the neck,' she says, 'but you've not done it and you should.' I think she honestly believes this.

'You want Harry to be her dad,' she said, 'don't you.'

'I could live with it,' I said, wondering as I said it if it were true. 'Lily wants someone. She's a right to it. Harry thinks it's him. If it's true then it's true, and if it is then I couldn't stand in their way.' Stand in their way. Making a unit out of Harry and Lily. Harry and Lily. I can't even tell if she looks like him. I've seen children who look so like both their parents that they make their parents look like each other.

'And we'll certainly never find out if it's anybody else,' I said. 'And Harry's a decent man. I know him. I think we could do it . . .'

'Yes but do what, exactly?' she said.

'Be parents. Go to school open days. Ring each other up and say did she leave her pyjamas there.' The idea of Lily leaving her pyjamas at Harry's house. Oh, it's strange.

And anyway I don't know what he wants. He said a year ago that he wanted to see her. And me. Maybe he only said he wanted to see her because he wanted to see me. Or vice versa. No, he doesn't want me, so he must want to see her, genuinely. Or did then. Any way you look at it, I'm running ahead of myself here, sending her round to his for the night. His! Harry's flats have always been bachelor dives par excellence, all Horace Silver tapes and brown duvet covers. All he owns is a coffee percolator, a toolbox, and yesterday's *Independent*. Oh, and the vehicles: the Pontiac and the Ducati, both of which he had when I first met him. He's living in Kilburn now. I haven't been there.

I don't know who he is. I know he's not the man I loved years ago. I know he's not the running boy for Eddie Bates that I thought he was last year. I've got to sort this out, girlfriend or no girlfriend.

Brigid was still talking. 'But not set up home for her, with both of you?' she was saying.

'Brigid, I can't just snap my fingers and make things happen. Anyway I don't want him, for me, and anyway she's used to home with just me. She doesn't need him here.' I said this glibly, but I have thought a lot about all this. About what a child needs, and whether (and, if so, how the hell) I can give her what she needs. I'll never forget her saying to me, when the question came up during the Night of Chaos, 'You're my daddy,' and me saying, 'No I'm not,' and her reply: 'But you're not my mummy either, so it doesn't matter.'

'You could find a decent fellow and marry him and he could be father,' Brigid was saying. Ands pigs could fly and we could all go and live on the moon, I thought, but people tend to tell me I'm being defensive when I say things like that.

'I haven't found one yet, have I?' I said instead, endeavouring to be positive. 'After all these years?'

'Yes, and if you did meet a good man you wouldn't know what to do with him anyway. Anyway I say if Harry's her dad you'll have to marry him.'

'Not,' I said. 'Brigid, let's stay in the real world.'

'Funny old place, the real world,' she said.

Then it was time to go round to my mum's for lunch.

My parents live in Enfield, a fact which I find it hard to forgive. Nothing personal about Enfield, just that it's too far away on the wrong side of the city. I've got a big urge to make them move back. But you can't tell grown-ups what to do. They're only in their sixties but one day they'll be really old, and then they'll start dying, and one of them will be ringing me up in the middle of the night, or some policeman or something will, and it will all be so cold and far apart and miserable. And they've lost a daughter already.

I was thinking about all this as we drove over on Sunday morning – presumably so I wouldn't have to think about razor blades, love poems, Harry, and the fact that I was, just was, going to have to have a big talk with him. Lily was talking to her Teletubby in the back, singing with it: 'Willoughby wallaby wee! An elephant sat on me! Willoughby wallaby woo! An elephant sat on you! Willoughby wallaby wama! An elephant sat on Mama!' By the time it got to 'Willoughby wallaby winky winky! An elephant sat on Tinky Winky!' we were coming off the North Circular and I had decided to talk to them about it. Come home, was all I wanted to say. Be with us. Before you settle in to ancientness and become immovable.

So when Mum opened the door, and Lily hurtled off in

search of her grandfather, off whom she might be able to blag orange-flavoured Tictacs, I said, halfway through the conversation (in my own thoughts, if nowhere else), 'Mum, why don't you just move house? It would be so much easier and everything would just be better . . .'

'What would?' she said, unperturbed.

'All sorts of things,' I said, slightly surprised to find myself in the middle of a real conversation rather than an internal one. 'We could see you, and you could see us, and . . .'

'We're seeing each other now, aren't we?' she said, and of course we were, so that threw me. I knew I had a point but I'd lost it already. Oh yes – that it would be easier when one of them died. I didn't want to mention that, though.

I'm as bad as them. Not mentioning all over the place. Well, I learnt it from them and they learnt it from their parents and they learnt it from their parents and they learnt it from Queen Victoria.

I wondered what Sarah and Hakim were talking about, at that moment, in Brighton. If you've been separate for fifteen years, do you still not mention? The image of him asleep at her feet haunted me. Hakim sleeping at her feet, Lily sleeping in my arms. And where am I with my mother? Afraid to mention death. As if she didn't know that people die. Well she does. I know she does, like I know she's had sex. And what is, can be spoken of. I can speak. I spoke.

'It would be much easier for us to be closer as a family if we lived closer. You haven't been to my flat for about a year. And what about when you or dad die? Touch wood and all that, but. You will. And then. Um.' I found I was slightly breathless.

Mum didn't take much notice at all. 'We talked about that when we moved,' she said, 'but it didn't seem that either you or Janie were particularly settled at the time, geographically or otherwise, so we didn't think we could really take it into account.'

They'd talked about it?

'You never mentioned it,' I said.

'Well, we weren't – we're not – planning on being a burden, you know,' she said, with a little sideways smile.

'I don't think you get much control over how much of a burden you are,' I said, meaning, over how much grief is felt at your death. She took it differently: 'Well, we've got some money, and we've got the house. When one of us goes the other will stay on, and . . .'

'But you'll be alone!' I expostulated.

'People are alone, love, when their husband dies, or their wife.'

Well that shut me up. Double whammy: my company, love, existence, etc., doesn't count (nor incidentally Lily's); and well I wouldn't know, would I, because I have never had this marvellous thing, this husband/wife thing.

Evidently I was feeling particularly defensive that day.

'Surely that's when me and Lily are meant to be a comfort to you,' I said, rather sadly.

'I'm sure you will be,' she said.

I felt about six. I wanted to hug her but I didn't. Why didn't Janie's death break down all this crap? I thought. Then I said it out loud, whoosh, just like that.

'Why didn't Janie's death break down all this crap?'

I don't know what I expected. That she'd tell me off for saying crap, I suppose.

'What crap exactly?' she said. Not as if to deny there was any crap, but to know, exactly, which of the many available craps was upsetting me. I'd never heard her use the word before.

'I want to hug you but I won't because I think you might

85

not like it. I was really scared to mention death. I'm upset that you say you'll be alone when dad dies because you won't be, I'll be here, and Lily. I know it's not the same but it's not nothing. That kind of crap.' I didn't say this. Well, you don't, do you? Not if you're older than six.

Hakim will be talking to Sarah now. Who he hasn't talked to since he was five.

She was looking at me with, well, a fondness, and a sadness. For a moment I was full of hope, girding myself to speak like a raindrop on a leaf swelling before it falls. Then, 'Come to the kitchen,' she said. 'I must see about the carrots.'

What crap indeed.

I felt truly embarrassed, for her and for me. Maybe we're just not capable. Maybe she doesn't say anything about her feelings because they're too big and dangerous. Maybe she doesn't want to spend the rest of her life weeping for Janie. Maybe she thinks I've come over all Californian. It's not that she hates me. Or maybe all that applies to me not to her at all. For Mum read Angeline.

Elvis Presley was a twin, and his brother Jesse died at birth. His mother used to say to him when he was naughty: 'Jesse wouldn't have done that. Jesse wouldn't have grieved his mama so.' This was not how I felt about Janie. But the dead, you know ... They are elsewhere. There's nothing you can do about them. So we went in to see about the carrots.

Over lunch (roast chicken, carrots, potatoes, runner beans chopped into diagonal diamond shapes, stewed damsons from the tree) we talked about the rules of basketball, in which Lily and Dad were interested, and the weather, and Princess Diana's funeral (which I had hoped to avoid, and so evidently had everybody else, judging by how long the conversation lasted), and Lily's new school, and the damson crop, and as we talked I became angrier and angrier, cursing the bloody carrots and my mother and the whole thing. She was calm, giving Lily more beans. Our recent conversation didn't seem to have bothered her. Bothered me though.

I caught her eye by staring at her. She shot me the same glance, fond and sad. I felt suddenly very patronised. More so because nobody else seemed to feel that anything was going on. Such an adolescent feeling. Bursting with injustice and everybody else just handing round beans. Any minute now I'd be running to my room and throwing myself on the bed yelling, 'How could you how could you nobody understands me,' and nobody would have a clue what I was upset about.

The problem is not that I'm upset and she's not, it's that she evaded the conversation. That's what really annoyed me. She buggered off.

'No she didn't, she went to see to the carrots. The carrots were going to burn.'

It was Janie's voice, in my head. This happens sometimes. I don't like it. It makes me unsure which of us is, or was, who. It's sneaky. Particularly because it obviously isn't her. I don't know why some part of my head sends another part messages in her voice, usually messages saying very sensible things. Like this one.

It continued.

'You're so bloody impatient. Everything doesn't fall into place the moment you have an idea, you know.'

'I know it doesn't,' I said, crossly. Teenage girls doing bitchy character analysis, sniping.

I said it out loud. Mum and Dad and Lily were looking at me. I smiled like a dog that's just had an injection.

nine

Sunday Night

Lily and I were in the bath on Sunday night, porpoising about, when it occurred to me I didn't want Hakim letting himself in and witnessing this mother and child bacchanalia, which would be too much for his modesty.

'I wonder where Hakim is,' I said.

'He doesn't need us now, he's got his mummy,' she said. Well, she could be right. She often is. Actually she is the original babe and suckling out of whose mouth truth comes. But I wondered anyway.

Lily had made me put on a green clay facepack, and was now treating me as a monster. I went under water and blew whale spouts. She laughed and laughed and when I came up she was gone. I could hear her on the phone in the other room. 'Hello this is Lily who's that . . . oh. Goodbye,' and she hung up.

'Child!' I yelled.

'Coming, Mummy, don't shout at me,' she said.

'Please don't answer the phone and just hang up. It's incredibly inconvenient. Now if it rings again just leave it, OK? I would have thought you knew better.'

She looked cross.

'Well don't be surprised if I tell you off. It might've been someone I wanted to talk to. Oh bugger . . .'

I clambered out, steamy and dripping.

'Don't say bugger say bother,' she recited. 'Anyway you didn't want to talk to him.'

'How do you know?'

'It was Eddie Bates and you don't like him.'

What the

For a moment I felt the world stop. Then it lurched back to reality. The bitch. What a nasty, nasty . . . I breathed deep a few times.

'Lil,' I said, 'if the phone rings, don't answer it. Just leave it. OK?'

She started to object, but she smelt my anger and gave up easily enough. I stomped about the flat in my towel, spitting about the nastiness, the undertoad clammy nastiness of Mrs Bates's trick, the insidious invasiveness of it. I 1471ed. Number withheld, of course. Then I put Lily into bed and told her monster stories for almost an hour.

When she was asleep, I tried to let the calm of my lovely flat descend and soothe me. The calm of Sunday night. In my strange little top-corner flat, my curiously separate territory, seemingly tacked on like an eyrie to the rest of the block, it is possible to feel utterly at peace and a million miles away. Only my floor and one wall are attached to the world, the rest of it faces the wind and the sky like a clifftop nest. The A40 swells and ebbs at the cliff's feet; people and pavement are mere pebbles and beaches. Sometimes the roar of the crowd at the QPR ground comes up to me on the wind, like booming sea in a far-off ocean-bound cave. (Not often, granted. This *is* QPR, not Manchester United.) I can watch storms coming and going, see rainbows that the rest of the world misses. Once I went to Heir Island, off the very south-western tip of County Cork, and sat in an outside privy on a heather-clad hillside looking out over yellow and purple hillside to the ever-changing sea, knowing that west of me there was only America, and south only the Canaries, and Antarctica. I feel like that in my flat. West to the sea, south to the world. If you're high enough you can overlook anything.

And of course there is plenty to overlook. Plenty of cars and filth and poverty and unkindness. You'd die of grief if you stared my neighbourhood in the face every day. So I don't.

Harry does. When I think about it I'm so proud of him. Over the years he has, regularly, broken up fights, and caught murderers, and stopped people doing appalling things to each other. That's what he's for. (Don't tell me I'm being naïve. That is what the police are for. They may not all have it as their top priority but it is what we pay them for. To clear up the most disgusting crap that society produces. I won't go into detail. We all know.)

Meanwhile I rest in my eyrie at the end of the balcony, with its deck chair and plants outside and its comfort and hygiene inside, and listen to my child sleep, and count the stillness.

When I was a dancer, the most important part of the dance for me was the stillness. The moment of collection, concentration, balance. The moment held. If you can't hold the moment, it doesn't matter how much or how well you sway and shake and flick and wriggle. I told the teacher who first explained this to me Isaiah Berlin's story of the hedgehog and the fox; how the fox knows many things, but the hedgehog knows one big thing. The fox runs round and round in circles yapping at the hedgehog he wants to eat, but the hedgehog has rolled up into a ball. A motionless ball.

I've always been a bit of a fox, me. But I know about the hedgehog. I appreciate him. Admire him. I am considering becoming a hedgehog. Later. In the meantime I practise, on Sunday nights.

Lying on the sitting room floor, hedgehogging, fox stuff

came flying at me. Eddie's wife with her tricks. Razor blades. Eddie, in his coffin. The funeral, on Tuesday. Fergus, and what I am going to tell him. If anything. And Harry, and his girlfriend. And Mum and Dad. And Janie, as always, seeping through when my defences are down.

You see Janie was my best thing. My sister, ten months younger than me. My companion and collaborator. A girl of startling pride and honesty. Once when we were about twelve a man stopped us in the street. Pretending to be lost, pretending to show us a map, or an address on a piece of paper, he showed us a dirty picture that he had torn from a magazine. Janie hit him, thwack across his face. And gave him an earful, about what was right and what was wrong in behaviour to young girls. When building workers yelled at us she'd shout back. 'Oy, big tits!' they'd cry, and she'd go into a pantomime of startledness: 'Oh my God, you're right, I never noticed! Thank you *so much* for pointing them out!'

Janie was beautiful and she made good jokes. When we talked we could leave out every second sentence because we knew without saying what the next step in the conversation would be. People would wonder what the hell this gobbledegook was. We'd climb up on to the roof of our old building, where we used to live off Ladbroke Grove, in the basement flat, and we'd look out over West London and sing T Rex songs, and do harmonies to 'Hello Darkness My Old Friend' and 'Maybe The Last Time I Don't Know'. She'd fix me up with boys. I'd go shy, and she'd say 'You look lovely' as we set out for the evening. And she'd say 'You can't have that, it's not wholemeal.' We swapped clothes. At moments of crisis we climbed into each other's beds. She sent me postcards with think bubbles and speech bubbles written in over the picture. Every Friday afternoon we'd draw up an agenda, who we wanted to see, who we wouldn't be at home to, self-improvement plans to be put into operation, parties not to be missed, enemies to be insulted, friends to be supported. First item was always:

1) Make agenda.

For thirty years.

And then you find out years after her death that for years before she had been betraying you, lying to you, using you, exploiting you.

Actually, I don't believe it. I don't believe she could have done it. It must have been some other Janie.

Take this Princess Di thing. There are rumours all over the place that there was cocaine in the car, in her bag, in her bloodstream. Typical rumour stuff, but say it was true. What would her people say? The people who love her, feel for her, grieve for her, the people who have bound their teddies to crash barriers across the nation out of love of her? Joe and Josephine Ordinary Brit, lead players in the grievathon? Would they say Oh Diana, how you are besmirched, now we hate you? Would they say Oh Diana, how you are besmirched, but we forgive you? No, they would turn like Actaeon's hounds on the press and the royal family, and say How low can you sink, after everything you said, to dishonour her memory, to say such a thing, to make that up . . . They wouldn't believe it. They couldn't.

But I've seen the evidence of my sister's fall. I cannot deny what I found in that tea chest: the tapes, the proceeds. I know it is true but I cannot feel that it is true. My heart won't accept it. Because, I suppose, I don't understand it. I don't understand why she would do such a thing. Isn't that what the families always say? How could she treat us so thoughtlessly, how could she do this to me. The family's always the last to know. Etc., etc.

If I knew why she did it I could feel better.

I go over this over and over.

You know how the dance of the seven veils started. Ishtar the Babylonian goddess of fertility and chastity (yes both) went to get her dead husband Tammuz back from the underworld. She went down through the seven times seven gates and at every seventh gate she danced, and took off one of her veils and one of her jewels and gave veil and jewel to the guard, bribing and seducing. It was the dance of Shalome, as in Shalom and salaam, meaning peace and used as greeting and welcome. Salome was named after the dance when she performed it for Herod, to get Jokanaan's head.

I have longed to dance that dance. To follow Ishtar the dancer, and Demeter the mother, and Orpheus the lover, and Isis the sister-wife, and get my dead person back. My Tammuz, my Persephone, my Eurydice, my Osiris. But not in this case for love. In this case, just to find out what the hell was going on.

Someone left a pair of ballet shoes hanging from a tree outside Kensington Palace for the dead Princess, with a letter saying, 'You always wanted to be a dancer, now you can dance in heaven.' Another was from a little boy, but written down by his mother. It said that he came to put flowers for her, and on the way back he wanted a milkshake but all the McDonalds they passed were shut, then they started to talk about Princess Diana and what a wonderful person she was, and suddenly they saw a McDonalds and it was open, and they know that this was because of her, and they wanted to thank her.

We're silly about death.

But silly originally meant soulful, as in filled with soul. Sheep were silly because they were blessed, because Jesus was a lamb. Not because they were foolish. So there you go. (And as for fools – well, we all know they are the wisest of all.)

And Easter is the same word as Ishtar. Via the Nordic goddess Eostre. Rebirth, spring, cycles.

Human beings really don't like death. Never have.

Bah.

I jumped to my feet just as the telephone rang. I let the machine pick it up, and went to wash my hands, heart ticking. It was Fergus, wanting to know if I'd decided anything.

Well I have. I have decided to go to Eddie's funeral and push his wife into the grave with him.

I didn't want to tell Fergus anything about Eddie. I wanted everything to bugger off.

Lily appeared in the hall, weeping.

'I wet the bed,' she said.

I was pleased. Something easy to clear up. I cleared up.

ten

Sa'id

And then the next morning, Sa'id el Araby turned up. If I said all hell broke loose, I would be exaggerating. A bit.

I stuck my nose out the door as you do, to smell the morning air, decide how many layers of clothes to put on, that kind of thing, some time during breakfast. There he was, among the pot plants, lounging like a cobra against the wall of the balcony. There was no mistaking him. He looked just as he had done at fifteen, he looked just like Hakim, just like his father. Only, my God ... where he had been fifteen he was twenty-five, where Hakim's face was innocent, his was knowing; where his father's was noble, his was dangerous. A strong nose, a wide brow, a mouth which I don't trust myself to describe. He had loose black curls, gleaming, a little too long, alive. And one of those wiry bodies where the muscle wraps on the bone and you can see the pulse beating when you look at his wrist. I didn't look. I knew. He was gazing down at the ground, then when he looked up he had those Egyptian eyes, pale green grey like the tips of the palms at sunset in Aswan, opaque as the white sun over Cairo when the dust is up. Opaque but not blank. They knew exactly what they were looking at. Me.

'Sa'id!' I cried.

He smiled.

I slammed the door on him and hurtled into my study, slamming that door too. No no no no no. No. Oh shit.

I have a weakness. It's called sex. Sometimes it hits me. Not often. As you can surmise from the fact that I didn't fuck for three years after Lily was born. Until I . . . until the thing with Eddie.

But when it does, it does. I'm old enough to recognise it. And then . . .

A phrase from another of those ancient Egyptian poems came to me out of the blue. 'He brings a blush to my skin, for he is tall and lean.'

I was about to become putty in a man's hands. A man ten years younger than me, Hakim's brother, Lily . . . Sarah . . . Harry. Oh my God. I mustn't open the door. I sat and talked sense to myself while Lily ate her cornflakes. It seemed to work. Just because something is strong doesn't mean you have to give in to it. You don't have to roll over and wave your legs in the air. As it were.

I imagined putty waving its legs in the air, and the absurdity of my mixed metaphor gave me hope.

Twenty minutes later I peeked through the study window and the foliage outside to see if it was safe to take Lily to school. There was no one in the chair, and I couldn't see much beyond it.

I opened the door gingerly. He wasn't there. I could have wept. Then I saw the suitcase – a match for Hakim's – parked under the vine and I cursed. Lily scampered down the stairs and I followed sedately, like a respectable woman, a woman to whom sexual passion with a . . . oh God . . . is out of the question. Maybe he has a squeaky voice, I was saying to myself. Maybe he likes Whitney Huston. I had a horrid feeling it wouldn't matter.

I dropped Lily at school.

Coming home I trod slower and slower.

Up the stairs, I took a little rest on each landing.

I paused on the last but one step before the top floor, admiring the grimy concrete with its grey Rorschach splats of trodden-in chewing gum and its interestingly various texture of stone and cement. I held the iron railing, and wondered when if ever we were due for a repaint. I breathed, glad that the fresh air from the balcony dispersed the smell of piss so prevalent in enclosed parts of the estate. I girded my loins. I stepped up, and looked right, to the end of the balcony, to my doorstep and my little pretend garden. And there he was, in the chair, smoking a cigarette. The smell of it came to me on the air. It wasn't a Marlboro by a long way. I wondered whether the smoke I smelt was his exhalation; whether what I was breathing in had been inside his body.

I had to walk the length of the bloody balcony while he watched. I did my very best to keep my hips rigidly in line. No swinging. No giveaways. But I knew the worst before I got anywhere near him. He knew.

It's always the same. I couldn't feel like this about a man who didn't recognise it in me immediately. Recognition is part of the package.

Don't look him in the eyes, I told myself. I smiled at the large yucca just over his left shoulder and said: 'Sa'id, how extraordinary, do come in, Hakim's not here at the moment.'

I knew immediately that that had been the wrong thing to say. Hakim had said that Sa'id didn't know what he was doing here. That Sa'id had forbidden him to try and find his mother. Was Sa'id meant to know that Hakim had been chez moi at all? I could have kicked myself.

Well, I shall reveal nothing else. I shan't land Hakim in it. Specially not just because I've turned into a sex-crazed sponge.

I walked into the house, leaving the door open for him to follow and calling out 'Come in!' behind me. By the sense of him he is considerably more westernised than Hakim. Plenty of tourists in Luxor. Plenty of cosmopolitan life in Cairo.

No, not more westernised. But more . . . more something.

He's brought his suitcase. Think sense. And don't look at him. Not for his sake, Lord no. Not to try and make him think I'm virtuous. For my sake. If I look at him I might disintegrate.

For God's sake. I'm meant to be a grown-up.

I busied myself at the cooker. I assumed that coffee ran in the family. He still hadn't said a word. I prayed for a squeaky voice. Anything to put me off. I had the impression he was laughing at me. It didn't make me want him any the less.

Well when I'd made the damn coffee of course I had to turn and give it to him. Have you ever tried to give someone a cup of coffee without looking at them? It's like trying to eat a doughnut without licking your lips.

His eyes were full of kindness. It was almost as if he pitied me my predicament. And he was laughing at it. The scenario ran before my eyes: I sit down opposite him, he grins at me, I come out in goose pimples and within two minutes we'll be at it on the kitchen table.

I went and sat on the old sofa. The scenario ran through my mind. He comes and sits next to me and that's it.

He stirred some sugar into his coffee and said, 'Angelina, you look well. My father sends his best wishes, his compliments. He will be happy to hear that you are in good health.'

I think this is going to be worse. It's just as inevitable, but . . . worse.

His voice wasn't squeaky, by the way. Far from it.

'How is he?' I said brightly. 'Well, I hope?'

'He is very well, very well.'

Not squeaky. Light, languid, accent not so heavy as Hakim's, language more colloquial, as far as I could tell. For a moment I thought I must be wrong. He doesn't know, he can't tell. Then he laughed, and I looked at him quickly, and he gave me a fair and solid look of knowing *exactly*, before quite deliberately dropping the shutters and continuing the conversation.

This pissed me off. I don't mind being overwhelmed by animal instincts but I did not fancy being played like prey.

'So Hakim is here?' he said.

'Well he was,' I said, 'but he's gone away for a few days.'

'Where to?' he said.

I lied. Rather I obfuscated.

'To tell the truth I'm not sure. He just said he was going off, and would give me a ring. He left his stuff, though, so I dare say he'll be back soon.'

'Hmm,' he said. There was something quite unavoidably authoritative under his languidity. He cannot be as cool as he looks, I thought. He's very young. He's in a strange city. Don't overestimate him. Look at his big Luxori scarf, a white-on-white paisley weave, folded the Luxori way and wrapped round him because even glowing autumnal London is too cold for him. He's a big fish wandered far from his small pool. He's not dangerous.

I found I was gnawing the flesh of my wrist.

He has got something round his neck. I was right! It's in the genes! Not gold though. It looked like thin leather, a cord. I couldn't see what was on it.

I know Brigid and Zeinab think I need a good shag but this is not the sort of thing they had in mind.

I decided I had better lie about everything, just in case. For protection. For me, and for Hakim. And for Sarah. I wondered if she would mind her son sleeping with an older woman. I slapped myself down. This is not going to happen, and I am going to demonstrate to this boy that he was mistaken in what he saw in my eyes. Time for nice English small-talk, and aimiable Arab courtesies.

'So,' I said brightly. 'Are you here for long?'

'As long as it takes,' he said, looking me in the eye.

I looked back at him – not his eyes, but his face, looking for something wrong with it, something to cancel this out. Nothing. He looked beautiful, strong, complex, and almost unknowable.

'What?' I said. 'As long as what takes?'

'My business,' he said.

I hate it when people say 'business'. Usually it means applying for a bank loan they're never going to get to set up with someone's brother-in-law to get this brilliant thing manufactured, only they can't tell you what it is because of the patent situation, right, only it's going to be made in Spain because of the exchange rate, but there's this licensing problem . . . Or buying a five-quid deal of spliff from a man in a pub. 'Business' means you're trying to make it sound more important that it is.

But of course these rules do not apply to people whose first language is not English. And just because I don't like the idea of business doesn't mean that he doesn't have any.

'Oh, what's your business?' I said, gaily ignoring any intended off-putting.

'Import export,' he said.

Well of course.

'Alabaster?' I enquired.

I remembered him in his father's workshop. Long and skinny and dusty. A kid. I'd loved the workshop. The showroom was not so gorgeous, full as it was of over-polished ashtrays that look like browning egg white, and Tutankhamun heads with blue paint to match the We Accept Barclaycard sign. We had gone there, Nadia and I, to try to buy some raw alabaster for her – she's a sculptor, and was travelling the world to learn the tricks and qualities of different stones. She had just arranged with Abu Sa'id to hang around in the yard, the *fabrique*, to learn alabaster, when she fell ill. That's how we met them, why we stayed.

As she convalesced I lurked. My favourite place was round the back of the showroom, where the wiry brown men in their dust-covered white gallabeyas squatted under the blue sky, and carved, and bored, and sliced, and held, and burnished. They bury solid columns in the sand, wrapped in cotton like a mummy, before hollowing them out with ancient iron hooks. Raw alabaster is more like incense than like stone – it needs support. It almost crumbles in your hands. It dissolves in water. Veins and fractions seem to shatter its solidity, yet it holds shapes as round and generous as a flower. Like ice, like crystallised ginger. I used to sit about and play with shards of it, crushing it, eating it. Three colours: the white, a stone of spun sugar, or moonlight; the red, peach flesh made crystal; and the green, oily like soap, deep like seaweed, and when you scrape the oiliness with your fingernails it becomes dust. I can stare at alabaster the way other people look at clouds: spotting shapes, losing your sense of balance. At every stage and degree of polishing it changes and shifts. I see feathers and blood, the history of geometry, rivers, faces, fractal chaos. It's a stone sea to me. And that's before you hold it up to the light, or put a living, flickering candle inside it, whereupon it becomes the gates of heaven. When I'm dead I want alabaster windows, like there are in mediaeval mosques and churches.

I discussed this with Abu Sa'id once. He didn't want to talk about it. Evil eye stuff. (He also said that Princess Di shouldn't be called Princess Di, because every time anybody says it it is like a curse on her, an invocation. Princess, Di. Lady, die. So perhaps he has a point.) I wanted him to make me a tomb with alabaster windows. Or at least give me a quote. I wondered if he didn't regret the former speciality of the alabaster-maker's art, the canopic chests, in which parts of well-born ancient Egyptian corpses were preserved. You would get four chests, or one divided into four, carved as simply or as ornamentally as you like. (Tutankhamun did have that head on the stoppers of his, in gold and lapis on the white gleam of the alabaster, four heads, facing inwards, nose to nose in two pairs, staring each other out over the centuries.) In one went your lungs. In one your stomach. In one your liver. And in one your intestines. And there they stayed, while the rest of you was soaked and bound and soaked and bound and finally put away for the life hereafter, with Osiris in the West. Your kidneys and heart stay in. Over your heart a scarab of stone, engraved with a chapter of the Book of the Dead, which adjures the heart not to rise up as witness against the deceased when ibis-headed Thoth, Lord of History, inventor of writing, weighs it against the feather of truth, in the next world. Brain? Sucked out and binned. Unclean. Well, yes. You get a new one in heaven. Just as well, probably.

Which is worse, getting a new perfect body to put your Christian soul in, or getting a new brain to put in your mummified ancient Egyptian skull?

You see what digressions I send my mind on to divert from the unavoidable. Miles away and centuries ago.

Didn't change a thing. The man was still sitting there in my kitchen. Still looking the same. Saying: 'Some alabaster, yes. Different things.' Then as if he became aware that his reticence was verging on both the rude and the challenging, he stood and enquired most politely about the bathroom, and removed himself. Subject changed.

I didn't like it. Reticent young men. There seemed to be stuff going on that I didn't know about, which is fine, but not in my kitchen. Anyway, he couldn't stay here, that much was clear. I am already fulfilling my obligations. I can't actually fit two of them.

He lives in Qurnah – Thebes West Bank. Among those tombs. On that line where the green of the Nile becomes the red Sahara.

He stepped back into the kitchen. He was very quiet, a light mover. Not that tall. Shoulders broad but lean. He stepped past me most courteously, showing a delicate aware-ness of the space around me, and sat again by his coffee. His suitcase stood by the doorway like an unanswered – unasked – question.

I wanted him to leave.

He drank his coffee, taking his time.

It was a curious rerun of Hakim's arrival. How gaily I had leapt into allowing Hakim's presence here. How safe I must have been feeling to run the risk. How forgetful of the perils of the world. Other people fuck things up, Angeline.

Sa'id was perfectly at home with silence. Too much at home.

I sat.

He sat.

After while I began to feel like one of Tutankhamun's can-opic stoppers. Gazing immobile over the centuries, bound by your own silence and that of your companions. Irresistible, yet dull.

We're going to sit here forever.

Nothing will ever happen.

Well I'm not breaking it.

I have nothing to offer him, nothing to tell him. If he wants anything he can ask.

We sat.

And sat.

It could have been embarrassing but it wasn't. Neither of us were fiddling or fretting. Just sitting. My mind was wander-ing up the Nile again: if Osiris is the Nile, and his brother Set (who killed him out of jealousy) is the desert, what is alabaster? Is it of Set, or of his returned-to-life brother? Is it the bones of Osiris? (Wear it round your neck like an *aya*, or the eye of Horus, or the hand of Fatima. And there's always the testicle of Thoth. You don't know about the testicle of Thoth? Well . . .)

Just sitting.

Then after several hundred years, or about four minutes, he sighed and stood and said, 'I will sleep in Hakim's room, as he's not here.' Then he picked up his suitcase, went into Lily's room and closed the door.

I remembered something a nurse told me five years ago, when I was in traction with my recently shattered leg, and Lily was in intensive care, and Janie was newly dead, when all I wanted was to have Lily, and Dolores the nurse said 'so take her'. Her exact words were: 'Nothing succeeds like a fait accompli.'

Well there you go then.

I worked, without conviction. Sa'id went out – I gave him the spare spare keys (Hakim had the spares). Picked up Lily and Caitlin and the boys, took them to the park. When I got back there was a message from Sarah. I made some tea, and then rang her back.

'How's Hakim?' she wanted to know.

'What?'

'How's Hakim?' she repeated.

'Um – I don't know. I haven't seen him. Should I have?'

'He went back to London at lunchtime . . .'

'Oh. I . . . No, I haven't seen him. Was he coming straight here?'

'Where else would he go?'

'I don't know.'

We were silent a moment.

'What did he say?' I asked her.

'Just that he was going back, and he'd ring when he got there, and he'd be back in a day or two. I thought he'd rung you.'

'No,' I said.

'Were you in?'

'No.'

Pause.

'Well we probably don't need to worry,' she said. She wanted me to agree.

It was a bit odd. All the Egyptians I'd ever known were forever getting in touch with their families, and here's Hakim and his mobile phone not telling anybody anything. But then they aren't typical, the el Arabys.

Perhaps we should worry. Maybe not yet.

'Which train was he catching?' I asked.

'Twelve twenty,' she said. 'Gets in about one fifteen.'

It was now five something. Four hours.

'He could have gone somewhere,' she said. 'He didn't say specifically that he was going straight back to you.'

'That's probably it,' I said. 'Walk in the park or something. Shops. He wouldn't know we'd be talking to each other, so he wouldn't think we'd worry.'

'No, of course not.' She sounded relieved. It stood as a decent explanation.

I wanted to ask her how it all went, but I didn't want to invade her privacy. She wasn't my friend, Hakim was.

'OK then. Let me know if you hear anything,' I said.

'Of course,' she said.

We hung up.

I hadn't told her Sa'id was here. Now why not?

eleven

The Funeral

Lily was surprised to find yet another young man moved into her bedroom, but she took it in her stride when I said he was Hakim's brother. She liked all these relatives turning up out of nowhere. It made her think that perhaps relatives of hers might turn up too, baby sisters, daddies, that kind of thing. Interestingly she showed no signs of falling in love with Sa'id as she had with Hakim. Convenient, really. At this rate we could already end up sisters-in-law, but I really didn't fancy our being co-wives.

It was the day of the funeral.

I don't like funerals.

I didn't know if I was going to go or not.

Except that I knew I had to. Realistically I had no other way of getting hold of Mrs Bates, my charming correspondent, and though there had been nothing yesterday and, so far, nothing today, I wasn't going to let her carry on wasting her stamp money on me.

At ten, I was sitting on the side of my bed, pretending to think, 'If I leave it a little longer it'll be too late anyway, and then I won't have to decide.' But then of course I found that I was putting on my only pair of respectable trousers, and brushing my hair. I walked in and out of the kitchen six times looking for things and forgetting once I was in there what it was I'd gone in for. Finally I fixed myself bodily in the halfway and said: 'Keys. Money. Scarf. Coat.' I said it several times. I could have added, 'Brain.'

Just as I was leaving Sa'id appeared in the hall, wearing a white gallabeya, with his hair loose, tucked behind his ears, curling on to his shoulders. He looked taller, and distracted. Older than he is. He smiled kindly. 'Good morning,' he said. I tried to tell myself that he looked like an extra from *Jesus Christ Superstar* but he didn't.

I looked at his feet because I hadn't seen them before. Long and brown and clean. Shape of Bernini, colour of dark sand.

I found it very hard to leave.

Driving up to north London, taking my place as one of the metal lice encrusting the North Circular, I kept getting that horrible sense of coming to having been unconscious for the past ten minutes. It's something I've always suffered from, a kind of chronic disengagement. Since the accident, as you can imagine, it frightens me.

Sometimes I wonder why I've never had a nervous breakdown. You'd think I would have, what with everything. But I haven't.

Oh bollocks, I know perfectly well why. Lily. One, she wouldn't like it, and two, I'm too busy. And three, I love, and four, I am loved.

Pale hooded eyes.

The cemetery looked windblown, bare, a hillside above nothing. Perhaps they always do. The – what's it called – burning place. Mortuary? No. You know. Assiduary. Crematorium. That one. Well anyway – it was bleak. Institutional. Cheap benches. Blonde piano with no one to play it. There were only about ten people, including Eddie, though of course he wasn't included, he was boxed away, kept safely from us, already elsewhere, different status, don't look don't touch, he is not one of us now. He is packaged for delivery . . . elsewhere.

I was ushered down towards the front. A good dollop of me wished I hadn't come. I hid, as best I could, in my collar. An image of Eddie's neck came to me; of the tendon running down the side, and its tautness as his head lolled. And my stomach turned.

There was a tune in my mind, a wild tune.

Soon enough a man in a suit appeared and said he commended our brother Edward to the arms of the Lord, though fuck knows what the Lord was meant to do with him, and soon after that the Albinoni dirge came over the tannoy – the default soundtrack for funerals and cremations, I imagine – and then the dark, dull, nothing-looking coffin rolled off down the conveyor belt like a lost suitcase at Heathrow, and Eddie was consigned to flames. I observed a little burst, a fretwork of sparks, as the horrid little curtains drew back to let him in. Of course I remembered our first contact, when he had tried to set fire to me as I danced barefoot and bejewelled on a restaurant table in Charlotte Street. Of course I felt the irony of the moment. There was a dark gladness in me. But death requires respect. Whoever's death.

Strauss's Salome, the end when she sings to Jokanaan's head. The maddest scene of any opera. I'd seen Maria Ewing do it years ago. I heard it in my head now and my spine was lifting, straightening, as if I were going to dance. Jokanaan you should have looked at me. Jokanaan I will kiss your mouth. Exactly the opposite. He shouldn't have. I shouldn't have.

Shame's hands are still strong in my belly.

I was holding flowers but they were not for him. They were for Janie, half a mile away across this great flat open necropolis. White snapdragons. Not for any special reason.

The Albinoni faded out mid-bar and after a hypocritical

moment of silence I stood to face my duty. Turning round, I saw that the little chapel had filled up a bit. There was a group of unhealthy looking men in bad suits who I realised were the police, and Harry of course separate from them. Harry was here as the dead villain's former boy, Gary Cooper in disguise. He stood alone. I made one dim smile do for him and Fergus, and trawled the chamber for Mrs Bates. Fergus caught my eye, and nodded and gave a pointed look towards a woman in black fur and sunglasses and an astonishing pair of stilettos. A great look. Very rich widow, very Jackie O. Herodias. Unmistakably Christina.

I wished again that I hadn't come. Absurd, really. What had I come for? I couldn't remember. Oh yes, to make sure he was really dead. Well, there we go then. No one was crying, but that doesn't prove anything.

Christina Bates.

I'll get her outside.

Fergus's hand was under my elbow as I left. He's going to do it for me, I realised, to punish me.

'You could have called me,' he said, as we walked out into the nothing weather, on the nothing tarmac with its treacherous covering of damp dead leaves. I still see them with a biker's eye: damp leaves read imminent crash.

I was beginning to feel more and more depressed.

'Christina,' he said, gently, and led me firmly up to Mrs B. 'This is Evangeline Gower. She knew Eddie.' He smiled at me nastily and walked off. I assumed he'd done the obligatory exchange of mendacious platitudes with her earlier. I couldn't summon up the energy to be pissed off with him.

Ok let's get it over. I looked at her.

None of her visible face was actually her. Even not knowing her I could tell. There was lipstick and dark glasses and a mask of grief which could have sat on any face. It grimaced gently and then she took my arm and tucked it into hers, patting it, too often. 'Come and have a fag,' she said, in a gravelly and affected *ac-tress* voice. Her usual voice, I imagined.

'Only if you take off your glasses,' I said.

She stared at me – I think. I couldn't quite tell. Then she said, 'Eddie was awfully fond of you,' and took them off, and gave me a kind of smile, and then put them on again. Perhaps this was the bond between her and Eddie. He had RSC diction and profile; she spoke lines out of third-rate soaps. I found myself reminding myself that she was a human being, and wondering whether I believed it. I allowed myself to be led towards a bench and then remembered what happened last time I allowed myself to be led by a Bates while wondering what to do. Remembered his fistful of chloroform or rohypnol or whatever it was over my mouth, and the great insult of being carted off.

I wasn't frightened of her as I had been of him. And I had survived him. Beat him, if you like. Ha ha! He's dead!

I took my arm from hers and, as sympathy for her circumstances and antipathy to her played across my consciousness, walked myself to the bench, sat, and gestured to her to sit. She was crying. For a moment I feared that I wouldn't be able to challenge her. Not here, not now. I looked round rather desperately for someone I could give her to. Harry and Fergus were both in groups, talking and smoking and out of reach of me. She cried and cried. She was reaching the strangled sob stage when she started trying to talk. I couldn't prevent myself from putting my arm round her fur-clad shoulder. Dead animals, dead husband. She was saying her mum and dad wouldn't even come. I think. Anyway she was unhappy.

Then she sat up and wiped her snivelly face and took off her glasses and looked me in the eye. 'Did you kill him?' she said.

It's a hell of a question.

It wasn't that I was beginning to doubt my answer. It was just that there being no knowing, I didn't know. But I said no. Looked her in the eye and said no.

She stared a bit longer.

Or perhaps the reason why I haven't had a nervous breakdown is because I am very strong. Or stupid. Or unimaginative.

I was looking at her fiendish shoes. She caught me.

'He liked all that,' she said. 'Well – you know.'

She said it as if she were the new girlfriend and I were the old girlfriend and she had caught herself telling me something I of course would have known, and she didn't want me to think she was being, oh, patronising or idiotic. She was exhibiting deference to my position. But I had no position.

I blinked slowly, to pass the time until this should change.

'I wouldn't mind,' she said, 'if you had. No that's not true, I would mind. But not for the reasons you'd think.'

What?

All I wanted was for her to go away and leave me alone. Entirely. Now and forever. People do. Jim has. Eddie has! But he's left her behind. Of course I could go away. But I have to make her stop sending me horrible things first, stop her trick phone calls. There's no rule that says just because it's her husband's funeral and I might have helped kill him I have to sit here partaking of her mad grief, or whatever it is; but I do have to protect my life.

'Look,' she was saying, conversationally. 'I'm not myself today, but I'd very much like to see you again. Could we meet for a drink? Sometime? Soon?' It was accompanied by an 'aren't I charming how can you turn me down' smile, designed originally for casting agents I should imagine. Not sexual but using the same repertoire. Two along from the smile that says 'if you do what I suggest who knows maybe these stilettos will wave in the air for *you . . .*' It looked macabre over her tearstains. It would have looked macabre anyway.

In for a penny, I thought. Death cuts through crap. Or should do.

'Did you send me those letters?' I said bluntly.

She picked at the corner of her lipstick with her little fingernail, and looked at me sideways. 'Yes,' she said. And batted her red eyelids at me.

'Don't,' I said. 'It's very unpleasant.'

'OK,' she said. 'So will you have a drink with me?'

'No,' I said.

'Please.'

'No.'

'Why not?'

'Because you sent me anonymous letters.'

'Sorry,' she said. And smirked.

Well she would have to be a piece of work to be married to that piece of work Eddie.

'I don't give a shit if you're sorry.'

'Have a drink then?'

'No.'

'Oh why?'

'I'm nothing to do with you.'

'Please.'

'If you've something to say, say it now,' I said.

Harry was looking at us. I made a please-come-over face. He raised his hand and looked around. Fergus had disappeared.

'I don't know what to do with his ashes,' she said.

'Well I don't want them,' I said.

'I'm not offering them to you. I'm just – oh shit shit SHIT SHIT' and then she began to cry again and then to rant and rave and weep and curse, and Harry came over and we looked at her helplessly and she flung herself into my arms and I stared at Harry over her shoulder and tried not to breathe in fur, Giorgio and hysteria in equal proportions.

'Oh fuck,' he said.

'Didn't your training tell you what to do in these situations?' I asked him. Christina threw herself back down on the bench and began to kick.

'Yes,' he said wearily, and he sat beside her, pulled her up and said kindly but loudly, 'Chrissie, didn't anybody come with you today? Where are your friends?'

To which she yelled more, and tried to hit him, and jumped up and ran into the graveyard, or tried to, only her stiletto betrayed her and she fell, and lay on the tarmac like a weird great insect, fluttering in rage. I remembered sitting under one of these very trees in my wheelchair, feeling more helpless than I had ever felt in my life, nearly six years ago, unable to manoeuvre myself through the graves to solitude.

'Maybe she's hurt herself,' I said. 'Then we could call an ambulance.'

So we did.

Harry picked her up and sat her on the bench, and we sat either side propping her up, and I held her hands and whispered kind things to her, and she gurgled and shook. When she fell quiet her head sank on to Harry's shoulder like a melting candle, and then I told him that if he still wanted to do the blood test I was willing, and I'd help. He looked across at me over her tumbled dark hair, and something in his face changed a little, and I thought how old we are now, and how foolish we still are.

'Oh good,' he said.

'I know the timing isn't . . .'

'What?'

'Isn't great, I mean . . .'

'What?' he said again.

I found I didn't want to say what I had started.

'Well, with Amygdala and everything . . .'

'That doesn't matter,' he said.

I'm sorry to say my heart leapt.

'I don't mean she doesn't matter,' he said. Humiliatingly, my stomach quivered.

'She does matter,' he went on. Oh bugger. 'But the timing doesn't matter, I mean, it's just the time that it is, it's real whenever we do it, is what I'm trying to say.'

Yes. Yes, God bless him.

But I didn't like that 'She does matter'. And I didn't like not liking it. I've never liked jealousy, and inappropriate jealousy least of all.

Then the ambulance came. They wanted one of us to go with her. Harry explained the circumstances; explained that it had been her husband's funeral, explained that there was nobody of hers here, that we were not hers. As she was being lifted in she looked at me, fixed me like something from a horror film, and said loudly and clearly: 'Four abortions. Four abortions. How much can you hate a man? I'd have killed him myself. I should have. I should've done it. He wasn't yours to kill you fucking bitch and I'll have him back. I'll have his life back off you. Don't think that I won't.'

I stood back, as if hit.

I'll admit I was scared. I don't like mad violent people flinging their emotions all over me.

The paramedic was wondering if she was on anything. I'd seen a sign saying 'low cost' that morning and read it as lost cow. What kind of woman would marry Eddie Bates anyway? What kind of selfish stupid woman?

But I fucked him, so I'm not so great.

And we are all more than the sum of our faults.

Harry told them her name, and talked them out of us having to go too.

Ok, so now I had seen her, talked to her, warned her off. And now what?

'Are you all right?' he said.

'Yes.'

'Aren't you always,' he said, and I looked up quickly to see if he was being sarky, but in fact there was if anything a little resigned admiration in his attitude.

'Shall I take you home?' he asked.

I waved my flowers pathetically. 'I'm going to see Janie,' I said.

'Come on,' he said, and we walked over there with his arm over my shoulder like twelve years ago, until I detached myself because I couldn't bear it.

Jane Oriole Gower, 1964–1993
Death lies on her like an untimely frost upon the
sweetest flower

Mum had wanted the full quote because, she said, you couldn't cut Shakespeare in half. She had wanted 'like an untimely frost upon the sweetest flower of all the field'. Dad said no, because, because. I think it was because of me. Because if she was the sweetest flower of all the field, then what was I? Whereas she could be the sweetest flower without it being quite so unremitting that she was the very sweetest of all.

It could have been because Mum was his sweetest flower too.

Anyway there she was, dead, under there. I mused a little on flesh and bones and worms because I can't not. (Worms for bait in the trap.)

There was Marina Siokkos next to her, as always, with her oval black and white enamelled photograph and her writing in Greek: MAPINA. And Hubert James Smith on the other side. No room for us. Mum and Dad I think were planning to be cremated and go in with her. I don't fancy it, myself. All lying in there together, with our lies and our resentments and our unresolved deceits. Like Christmas, only worse.

So I looked at Janie, and Janie didn't look at me, and I wondered yet again what if anything I would ever be able to tell Lily about her mother. And whether it was for me to tell her, and whether it was for me to keep it from her. Brigid said to me once, 'You're the moralest person I ever saw, and don't think it's a compliment. You and your decisions and your shoulds.'

It's not just external morality. It's not some theoretical disconnected right or wrong. It's what it does to you. I should not have fucked Eddie.

Harry had gone to look for coffee. I sat on Mrs Siokkos's white marble slab and stared at nothingness and hit my head with my hands a few times to see if any clarity would be forthcoming. It wasn't. I put my fingertip in a snapdragon and let its tender white jaws bite me. Nothing. The cold was seeping through my trousers – not just cold, but graveyard death cold – by the time I saw Harry coming over the hill. I stood and went to meet him. We drank our too-hot coffee from polystyrene cups leaning against a mausoleum, our feet in dandelions and dandelion clocks, the overgrowth of summer beginning to fall apart around us.

'Do you ever bring Lily up here?' he asked.

'In theory yes, but I never have done.' Of all the moods and circles I go through and round about Janie, not one of them is right for bringing her child to her grave. Her child. Oh God, I'm even starting to resent that. Not Lily! I don't resent Lily, God no! But that she's Janie's.

Ah well, but she's not. Janie's dead and she's mine.

Four abortions.

Sometimes I wonder about children I might have had if

things had been different. Then it seems disloyal to Lily. And I might not have had them anyway. And I might have them yet. And what might have been is pointless. Anyone can hang a string of what might have been round their own neck, to adorn them, weigh them down, garotte them.

In Japan they have little cemeteries for aborted babies, where the parents can go and mourn. They seem unashamed about admitting themselves to be some kind of murderers. Here we just pretend it's not murder, as if that makes it all right.

I'm not surprised she wanted to kill him.

God but how weird.

I propped Janie's snapdragons among the tufts of long grass at the base of her stone. There's no vase. Mum brings plants in pots. They die almost as quickly, without watering.

'I suppose . . .' said Harry, then stopped himself. I looked at him but he didn't want to continue.

Later, on the way home, I realised that probably he had been about to say something about Lily visiting Janie's grave, and had thought better of it, thinking that I would not want his comments and input, as some people might term it, to start so soon after I had admitted him to the next stage of the process. He probably thought I would have snapped at him, 'God, Harry, all I said was do the blood test, I never said take over her life.'

I probably would have. I probably do make him nervous. I must try not to.

twelve

Dinner with Sa'id

Lily came out of school with a picture she'd done. 'It's our family,' she said. 'That's what we're doing at school. Our family. Miss Pengelly says can I bring in a baby picture.'

The drawing was a piece of A4, with a big wobbly cross drawn on it to divide it into four. In one box was me: long hair, big grin, legs growing straight out of my neck. In the next was Lily, wearing a crown and holding a guinea pig on a lead. In the next was Janie. I knew it was Janie because she had a halo and wings. In the fourth was a man. Just a man. She'd written who we were underneath: mummy, me, mummy, daddy.

I remembered what the dead princess said: there were three of us in the marriage. Sometimes it makes me sad that I have no role model, no pattern to follow, no one to look at and think ah, you did this before me, how did you do it?

Actually there is one. Isis's sister Nephthys, who was married to their brother Set, got Isis's husband (also their brother) Osiris drunk, and seduced him, and conceived Anubis, who she abandoned, and who Isis took in and brought up. I had completely forgotten this story but Lily was so taken with Nut and her tummy and Amun Ra's habit of putting his beloved daughter to his nose as a mark of affection, that I had looked out my Egyptian mythology books, and there it was. My role model family. The incestuous ancient Egyptian gods of five thousand years ago. Osiris, apparently, didn't realise it was Nephthys – just like Harry. So I can be Isis, left carrying the can, and Nephthys can be Janie, which makes Lily both Anubis (dog-headed god of the dead) and Horus, saviour of the world, avenger of his father Osiris – Osiris who you remember was killed by Set, out of jealousy, only Isis brought him back to life again (having seduced him *while he was dead* and conceived Horus). Unfortunately Set then killed him again, and dismembered him into thirteen parts and scattered them far and wide. Well, Isis found them all except his phallus which was eaten by a Nile crab, and the other twelve became the months of the year.

It makes me laugh. Harry being dead then alive then dead, impregnating me while dead and my sister while dead drunk, and then ending up dickless.

Actually there's a lot of single mothers in mythology. So I can find comfort. When my life seems weird, I can just look back and ask: 'How would Horus have drawn his family for Miss Pengelly?'

Over tea Lily asked me if I minded her putting a daddy in our family when we didn't actually have one yet. It was all right, she suggested, because we were going to get one soon, weren't we? I kissed the sweet parting of her sweet hair and chubbed her sweet fat cheeks, and we just melted into one of our love fests. 'You are love and attention and beautifulness and kindness,' she said, 'from your head down down down both your legs to your toes.' 'Is that what I am full of?' I said, deeply touched. 'No,' she said, 'it's what you *are*.'

What I *am*. Love and attention and beautifulness and kindness.

Well that's all right then.

And I didn't get the love hangover – am I laying too much on her, am I warping her by giving her all my love when presumably in a normal life I would be giving lots of it to some man, am I laying down guilt for her to feel when she grows up and leaves home and leaves me alone, without that love. Though I can usually dispel the hangover anyway. A few shots of 'what's normal?' and 'love isn't a cake' and 'oh for God's sake' usually sort it out. And if they don't Brigid does. 'Hitting children, starving children, putting them in armies, having sex with them: bad. Loving children: good. You great banana.'

Harry as daddy. Harry as daddy. Independence gave a warning shake of its wings on my shoulder.

Sa'id returned as I was feeding Lily, and proposed that we go out for dinner.

'Can I come?' she said.

'No,' said Sa'id. 'I will take you for lunch on Saturday instead.'

That was all right by her.

'Can we go to Tootsie's?' Tootsie's has chips, and paper tablemats that you can draw on, and chocolate ice cream.

'*La'ah, habibti*,' he said. No, my darling. 'I'll take you to Maroush.' God, he's finding his feet quickly. And stylish feet, too. Only one of the best Lebanese restaurants in London.

'Can I come?' I said, echoing Lily. Just a throwaway joke. Of course I could go, she's my daughter.

'*La'ah, habibti*,' he said, and gave me a very snaky look. It took me about half a second to work out what that was about. It worked like this: as Lily's mother it was of course my right to go anywhere and everywhere with her. Now, in courtesy, I would have to let him, if he wanted, take Lily out alone. I had squandered a degree of my position of authority for the sake of a tiny joke, and he was playing with that to see how I would respond. I was pleased. It meant he expected something of me, which I found reassuring given that I had,

I felt, already squandered and forfeited my advantages at every turn. I had told him about Hakim, I had let him stay in my flat, I had desired him. Hell, I was handing cards over to him hand over fist.

He had an air of knowing everything. He looked ancient. I had still managed to find no fault in him. Looking at him, reincarnation had begun to look like the only logical explanation. Maybe he, not Harry, is Osiris. Such a desirable name. Say it out loud. I don't suppose there is any limitation on who can be Osiris. Actually all dead ancient Egyptians (so all of them by now) were known as 'the Osiris'. Unless they were female, in which case they were 'the Isis', or 'the Hathor'. So really, I can identify whoever I want with whoever I want. I suppose.

'What a shame,' I said, turning to do something else entirely – something really important like squeezing out a J-cloth. 'Lily and I will have to go alone.'

For a moment I wasn't sure I would get away with it. Lily is getting quicker by the day: would she just say, 'What do you mean? It's my date with Sa'id!' or would she . . . She did. She immediately set up a rumpus – the right rumpus. Of course Sa'id must be allowed to come with us, she insisted. Gracefully, after some toing and froing, I conceded that he might come.

He smiled at me broadly. A wide smile, admiring my reclamation of territory. What pleasure he takes, I thought.

I keep getting these absurd double entendres. I think a phrase like that and I nearly blush. And then he looks at me as if he knows what I'm thinking.

I am fully aware of how absurd a cliché that is. Don't imagine that makes it any easier to live with.

I was also aware that it was quite a bad idea to have dinner with Sa'id. Because in order for me to go out Lily would go and stay the night with Brigid. And because of the funeral. Funerals always make people want sex. Death shall have no dominion: quick, fuck it away, out of sight, right now – yah boo, I'm alive! We're alive! Look at us!

The night was warm. The funereal weather had gone with Eddie's ashes (Where to? Who cares?) and Indian summer snuck out again, lying confusing on the London pavements like trade objects out for sale. We went to Queensway, street of a thousand nations, and sat at a pavement table outside an Egyptian café between a Greek café and a Turkish estate agent, across from the French bread shop and the Texan (Schmexan) diner. When I went to school up the road from here there were 56 nationalities among 400 children. Now there are more. Faces with cheekbones from here and colouring from there and clothes from way over yonder, muttering in languages you never heard before. West London, the world.

Sa'id ordered a *shisha* and smoked it silently and aromatically. I never order *shisha* in London although I love it. Not because I'd feel a prannit, but because I would feel surreal; to be tasting that cool taste and hearing that gentle murmur of breath through water, and not be in Egypt. He held the mouthpiece to the side of his mouth, almost vertical. You'd wonder how the smoke could get into him from that angle. He looked unbearably purely unmitigatedly other. Even here, on these streets of otherness. London had not touched him, not polished his edges, nor ruffled his sleekness.

I'd spent all day doing things that I wasn't at all sure I wanted to do, and I had achieved no satisfactory result to anything. I'm losing the plot a little, I thought. Time to straighten up. What do I want?

'What do you want?' said Sa'id, alarmingly. He was looking at the menu.

I want to kiss your mouth, I thought. I want a free mind. I want Harry to be Lily's father. I want to control what happens when he is. I want the dead to leave me be. I want everybody to be happy. Except Janie.

'Fish kebab,' I said.

He ordered *koshari* – Egyptian for complex carbohydrates. Macaroni, rice and lentils with crunchy brown caramelised onions on top, and two sauces – hot pepper and sour lemon. I was surprised. *Koshari* is common food (the word even means it). It's what bus drivers have on their way to work, off stainless steel plates in cafés with fluorescent crimson woodshavings on the floor, with a stainless steel mug of water. It is not what I would have expected Sa'id to eat with me.

He ate. I ate.

'Are you always sad?' he asked, without looking up.

Well, I was surprised.

'No,' I said.

'Only today?'

I smiled. 'I went to a funeral,' I said.

I do like a decent silence. An undemanding silence.

'Of someone I hated.'

'Ah.'

'And who I had wronged.'

Silence.

'But not as badly as he had wronged me.'

'Then you have won,' he said.

'Is it about winning?'

He looked up then. Palm tip eyes.

'You are alive, he is dead.'

'He's escaped,' I said.

'Oh. No. He is nothing. Nothing for you to worry about any more. He's out of your hands.'

'Oh?'

'It's not yours any more. Leave it. God has taken him. Leave them to it.'

God has taken him. Leave them to it.

I ate.

His eyes really shouldn't have been pale. The rest of his face was so completely Arab. Cheekbones, nostrils, brow. I want to describe him but the words turn purple. He was like leather, like a horse. He was still.

He looked at me. I looked at him. For a moment I thought 'It's now' and my belly reared up within me.

But it wasn't. He looked away and drank water and wiped his mouth, and I thought, 'I could marry *you*.'

I was quite shocked at the thought, and sent it away. I became embarrassed at even having thought it. It was a joke! I only thought it because it was unthinkable! I would never have thought it for one second if I'd thought there was the slightest possibility that I would take it seriously!

He looked kindly at me, because I was rubbing my forehead, and said, 'What?'

'Nothing,' I said. Crossly.

We passed the rest of the meal in civilised conversation. He said he liked London. Why? 'Because nobody cares what I do. Like in Berlin or Paris. Nobody knows me, nobody cares. But here I can smoke *shisha* too. I can sit with a woman in public and smoke *shisha* and nobody cares.'

As he said it a friend of Zeinab's who I knew from the park passed by, calling hello as she disappeared behind the racks of threadbare scented geraniums that protected the tables from the road. I called back to her, not in a 'come back and talk to us' kind of way, but she did come back, and I had to introduce them and I couldn't remember her name, and the waiter clocked Sa'id's name and gave him a look, and when it was all done I said: 'You see that is just because it's not your town. It's only because you don't have people here who are interested in you. It's not to do with the town itself.'

He said it wasn't just that. He said: 'London has every religion. In Egypt and every Islamic country your Islamic brothers who share your religion feel responsible for your upkeep of it. And tell you so.'

'But there are plenty of Muslims in London, quite enough to disapprove of each other if they want, surely,' I suggested.

'In Europe they are not so bold with their judgement,' he said, and we began discussing whether or not Muslims in London were, simply by virtue of being here, likely to be less strict and more open-minded, more broadly educated, and thus less judgemental than those who had remained all their lives in an Islamic society, or whether being among (and outnumbered by) members of other religions (and none) in fact made people more tenacious in their own religion. (We resolved that of course it depended on the individual.) We compared London with Paris, of which I knew next to nothing, but where he had been as a student, sharing with an accountant from Mali and two Algerian musicians in Barbes. He told of the old Barbes legal system for the Arab community – unofficial, thorough, and utterly unconnected with, and respected by, the French police. We got on to his boyhood in Luxor and Cairo, how he used to work in his school holidays on the digs; and how at the Sorbonne although his own subject was economics he had come across so many European Egyptologists keen to teach him about his own things, and teased them that he would study a little and become a Europologist and teach them to suck their own eggs. And we got on to what exactly the term 'developing country' means for an Arab state at the end of the twentieth century, and Palestine, and so on. These were good topics. Interesting in themselves, and serving to remind me of our cultural and religious differences, and unlikely to lead to sexual innuendo. Except that knowledgeable intelligence is extremely sexy. And there was the moment when he told me he'd always been half in love with Isis.

And we talked about Cairo, about Ibn Tulun (the most

beautiful mosque, and possibly the most beautiful building, even the most beautiful thing, in the world). He told me that from the top of the minaret you could look out over the Old City and weep for the damage done first by the earthquake, and then by the government, using the earthquake as an excuse. 'You look out and see the missing,' was the phrase he used. He told me that the City of the Dead was now populated as much by the living corpses of the druggies as by the actual dead and – on holidays – their living descendants, paying their respects with a picnic and chairs and some songs. Visiting the dead as they would visit the living. Deceiving death, pretending it didn't happen. Like the ancients. I used to love the City of the Dead. Such beautiful strange, empty mausoleums: Shagaratt ad Durr, Tree of Pearls, the slave queen, with her neglected mother-of-pearl mosaics. And just ordinary little houses, on blocks, on streets, but the dead have no cars, so it's quiet and the air is clear of all but dust. Though during the *khamseen* – during that sneaky spring wind anybody would want a veil . . . And we talked about Hussein Ali Mohammed, a jeweller I knew with a shop in Khan el-Khalili who was a true devotee of the dance, whom Sa'id knew too, and of course we talked about dancing, about *raqs sharki*, and some of the clubs, and comparing Cairo to London . . .

Of course I was talking in the past tense.

Of course he picked up on that.

So I told him why I didn't dance any more.

'How long ago was that?' he asked.

So I told him.

Of course he picked up on the timing.

So I told him that Lily was Janie's, and Janie was dead.

For the second time that night, death spent a moment fluttering its wings over our table.

'And can you leave her alone?' he asked.

Me leave her alone?

I was just about to say something when a small kerfuffle broke out in the café behind us: a fat young man in baggy clothes pushed past the table and ran off down towards Bayswater Road, and the waiter came out shouting and swearing after him. Something had been grabbed, something stolen. The waiter was kicking the rack of geraniums, which showered us with fragrant dust and bits of leaf like scraps of desiccated shammy-leather. He was pissed off. Sa'id watched him, with his eyebrows drawn up. I watched Sa'id. Then the waiter ceased kicking and went inside again, to call the police.

I hate it when these things happen because I like to live in my own semi-deluded world where things are nice.

Sa'id went in and paid, as the waiter was not coming out again. I went in too. The waiter was so upset.

Then we went home. I don't know why it upset us so much but it did. Which is just as well, because I was really beginning to feel quite unnerved about him and the whole thing, and anything which stopped us in our tracks and sent us home was a good thing.

On the way home he said 'And what about Lily's father?', and I said, 'We don't know who it is.' It seems I didn't want to talk about it with him.

I didn't sleep well. Sa'id was only ten feet away beyond that wall. I lay and thought in great and sculptural detail about his hands and his head and his throat and his feet and the corner of his mouth and his shoulderblades as he turned away, and the thin leather cord around his neck, and the shadow where it disappeared into his shirt. The only thing which took my mind off that was wondering where Hakim was. Neither line of thought was in the least bit soporific.

The next day he was out before I was up, which was just as well because my baser self was trying to concoct ways of walking in on him in the bathroom, which frankly would not be respectful and I knew he was not the kind of man you could do that to. He wasn't back by evening, when Harry rang. Lily was in the bath, telling me about Melanie's pink hairband, at some length, and I asked him to ring back after 8.30. He didn't sound too happy about it.

Then Sarah rang. She'd had a message on her machine from Hakim. My little flurry of excitement soon shrank down again. He said he was well, not to worry, he'd be in touch soon. But he didn't say where he was. We had a moment's unhappy silence. Then we sighed, simultaneously but not in unison. Hers was fear, mine was exasperation.

'I'm going to come up to London tomorrow,' she said. 'I'll come to you about lunchtime.' And perhaps you'll meet your other son, I thought, the one who doesn't like you.

Last week, I hadn't seen this family for ten years, I thought – well, that reluctant churlish anti-social part of me that always wishes everybody would fuck off and leave me alone thought it. That side just wanted to sit with Lily and admire the name-tags I had sewn in, to read Madeline books and hear about the playground. That side of me wanted to still my life down to nothing and live only in the sweetness of her and hers. It's a bit sick, really.

'Sarah –'

'What?' she said, suddenly, frightened.

'Sa'id is here too.'

Silence. Poor woman. Poor lucky woman. Long-lost sons coming and going like cue-balls.

'Where?' she said.

'Well . . .' I was rubbing my brow again. What was I doing with all these sons of hers? 'He's here. He's staying here.'

'Does he know where Hakim is?'

In a second I knew it, I felt it. Why? Because I knew

personally, I'd seen it before. The preferred child. The sweetest flower. She prefers Hakim.

'No. But why don't you come and ask him?' I didn't prefer Hakim, but I didn't prefer Sa'id either. Yet, look, I'm already being a sneaky protector of him who I see as unpreferred. How it never changes. Show me the unpreferred, or the assumed to be unpreferred, and I will prefer them.

I suppose the shock of Hakim appearing took the edge off the shock of Sa'id appearing so soon after. Either way she didn't seem too alarmed. I suppose once she realised she was going to have to deal with any of it, then she was halfway to dealing with all of it.

'I'll come up. Around lunchtime,' she was saying. 'Let me know if you hear anything.'

'I'll have to tell Sa'id you're coming,' I said. 'He might not be going to be in.'

'Of course,' she said, not picking up the other possibilities behind my cover-all statement. Like 'he might choose not to be in'.

Then I rang Harry back. He answered slightly coldly but I couldn't be bothered with that.

'Well,' he said. 'It's a DNA test now, and it's pretty damn accurate. The only thing is, it does need DNA from both parents, um, from me and Janie, so that could be a . . .'

I dropped the telephone.

'What?' I said. 'What?'

I was shaking, and at the back of my mind a little thought appeared: ah, here it comes. The breakdown is starting. The front of my mind had turned tornado. I was gasping and stuttering and sitting on the floor.

I thought we were going to have to dig Janie up.

There were dark wings flapping beside my eyes and I was saying 'we can't, we can't', but somewhere inside me there was a gleeful little shiny stone saying, 'Goody. Serve her right.' Stir her up, resurrect her, bring her back, get her up, and then she will do something – just like alive people do. She will have an effect and change our lives and it will be all right. She will tell us who her child's father is!

I was so happy.

But I knew it was disgusting, of course I did.

Flesh and worms.

Five years.

But I could see her again!

Harry's voice was squeaking my name from the telephone receiver on the floor.

I hadn't seen her since she climbed on the back of the Harley, in my spare helmet and her stupid shoes, which I told her to change because I wouldn't take anyone pillion if they weren't wearing proper boots. She said none of her other shoes fitted her, her feet were so swollen with pregnancy. And they were. She'd gone up to about size eight, usually she was four and a half. Size smaller than me. I gave her all my too-tight shoes, and she gave me her gone-baggy ones, which suited us fine because she got new shoes and I got old ones, and that was the right way round for us.

We were laughing about her being so huge. Pregnant all over. Could the suspension take it, could she reach round me to hold on? Absolutely not. And if she held on to the sissy bar would that not upend the bike backwards? I was instructing her to stick her arse out and lean forward, almost resting her huge belly on the seat between us. 'Just don't lean,' I said. 'Just be cool.' Hell, Janie knew how to ride pillion, she'd done it for years, but not for a while. But you don't forget that kind of thing.

She had weak fingernails and plump earlobes and she used to whistle when she was annoyed.

I hadn't seen her.

The bike landed on my leg, so I was trapped, but she had been thrown far away.

I was unconscious anyway.

Not being there for the things that change everything. Not saying goodbye to the person who was always there.

It wasn't that she left without saying goodbye. She didn't leave, you know. It was me stuck under the cylinder head, true, but it's me that has moved on, on my one good and one improving, always improving leg. She's still there on the side of the road.

What was it Sa'id said? 'God has taken him. Leave them to it.'

I remember the moment the car sideswiped us, cutting us up on the inside as we turned left. If I'd been further over there would have been enough room, or no room at all. But I was indicating. I was pretty central in the lane (no one is saying you weren't). I remember the feeling of my stomach falling, falling, falling – the same feeling you get on any little skid before you rectify it, any time your back wheel goes dancing without your permission, or the bend you are committed to turns out to have been too tight. That feeling, only it didn't stop. It was just overwhelmed. It became the undertow. I remember pain, and lights. I don't remember very often. I don't care to.

I don't remember thinking about Janie for one second. It's the moments of crisis that reveal you for what you actually are. I actually am selfish. Evidently. So I don't care to think about that either.

And the driver? Never got him, did they.

And no I never think about that either. I'm past spiralling in unalterable misery.

Dig her up.

I picked up the phone. I was not having the breakdown after all. Just as well.

'Angel?' he was saying. 'Angel, please!'

'Hello!' I said, perkily, like a children's TV presenter.

'Are you all right?'

'Do we have to dig her up?' I demanded.

'What? What are you – NO!' he shouted.

'Oh.'

Silence.

'No,' he said. 'No, no. Oh, I'm sorry. I – no, you can get it from loads of things. I'm sorry, it is a bit ... Oh.' He seemed to think it was his fault that I was upset – as if he had phrased it insensitively or something.

'I would've liked to,' I said.

'What?'

'I would've liked to. Like Old Nile.' Old Nile was our alligator that died, and we buried it, and I dug it up to see how it was.

'Angel, you mad girl,' he said, tiredly. 'You mad girl. Jesus. Only you would admit that.'

'You know what I mean, though.'

'Yes,' he said.

'Sorry,' I said, but I wasn't. I was glad, because he understood.

More silence. Our timeless silences.

'They need DNA from both parents to make a full match. I send them blood through my GP, and we can get Janie's from, well, if you have any of her hair or anything, or by getting blood from both your parents.'

'But mine is from both my parents and mine wouldn't be identical to hers.'

'The pattern's different but the ingredients are the same. Sort of. Bands and markers. I'll send you the leaflet.'

'Oh.'

I was thinking about my parents. About what they know

and what they don't know. And what I was going to have to tell them.

'Shall I?' said Harry, a little impatiently. Or perhaps it was nervously.

'Yes please,' I said. 'Yup, fine, OK. I'll speak to Mum and Dad.'

'And then . . .'

'Then you do it. Yes.'

'Yes.' he said.

I don't know if he likes me any more, I thought. Then I realised that I didn't know if Sa'id liked me either. 'Blah,' I said, and went to bed, to Lily, who likes me so much.

thirteen

Tell Your Own Mama

Sa'id didn't come back that night. When we got up in the morning there was no sign of him. This made me cross, partly because I started to imagine things about his personal life and partly because of course Lily wondered where he was and I couldn't answer her, which meant I was failing in my duty of omniscience and constant reassurance. I am meant to know everything, you know.

'No wonder you get so tired,' says Brigid.

'You can talk,' say I.

And there were no letters. So that was good. None since Saturday. If she'd been going to send anything as a direct result of our little chat I would've had it by now. Probably. So. Five days and counting. But it didn't occur to me to wonder if I'd ever be able to stop counting.

Over breakfast Lily says she wants her friend Caitlin to move in. I point out we already have two people staying. She points out that neither of them are here. I snap at her.

'Don't snap at me,' she said, 'it's not me you're cross with.'

I could not deny it.

I took her to school and revelled momentarily in the gorgeous free freedom of knowing your kid is being looked after and you're neither paying nor beholden, then I subsided a little as I picked up the day's work. I managed a couple of hours of some particularly unexciting proof-reading (I'm afraid my finances have got that bad) before Sarah arrived. (No I haven't forgotten the wads in the upholstery. But. They're not mine. They . . . they can be added to the list of things I don't think about. Shit, now I've thought of them. Yes well. All in good time.)

So Sarah arrived. Actually I was fed up with all these people arriving. My poor little doorstep. My poor exhausted welcoming smile. I took her arm and walked her downstairs with me. Yes, she left a holdall. But we were going out.

Down the scruddy stairs, past the mouldy cars, over the dogshitty lawns and on to the real streets outside the estate. The swimming pool café? The greasy spoon with wrapping paper on the walls for wallpaper? The not-so-nasty park? We went to the park.

'The thing is,' she said, 'and I wasn't sure I was going to tell you this, is that before he went off, well . . .'

We went into one of those obligatory reluctant moments. I ignored it. It wasn't Sarah I was cross with either, but I was cross. 'You can't stop the birds of sorrow from fluttering in your hair, but you don't have to let them nest,' as the ancient Chinese proverb says. Ditto birds of crossness. They were, I think, preparing to lay.

'He gave me some money.'

'Lucky you,' I said facetiously.

'No,' she said.

I looked round at her. The sun was bright but low and it shone up at her. She looked rather like an angel. A middle-aged angel. Twigs and leaves splayed out behind her.

'A thousand pounds,' she said, and looked at me enquiringly. 'It's quite a lot, isn't it?'

'Where did he get that from?' I asked, not particularly intelligently.

'I don't know,' she said.

I admired some worm casts down by my left foot, and wondered whether to walk towards the litterbin or the dog exercise area, where the dogs exercise nothing so much as their right to crap everywhere.

'You don't know. I don't know.' I was beginning to sound like Sylvester Stallone, leaning up against the bathroom door in *Rocky*. 'I dunno, y'know. Who knows?' And what is there to know anyway?

Her face took on a crumpled look, a very sad look, with fear in it. Unforgiving thoughts were in my head: you left him, you have had no idea of his welfare for fifteen years, you have another son who didn't come home last night.

'And Sa'id,' said Sarah. Oh Lord, her face.

Well yes, that probably was another reason for my crankiness.

Anyway she wept until her eyes looked like pickled eggs, and I told her everything would be all right, and tried to do so without promising my help. But when you reassure people they hear promises whether or not you make any.

'I have to make it right,' she said after a bit. 'It's my family.'

Well there's a battle cry for our times. Not so easy, Sarah. And last time you tried you ended up running away.

I wondered if when I talked to my mother about how I needed her blood so I could find out whether my ex-boyfriend was Lily's father she too would weep and scrawl in a public park.

Sarah was saying something about trust. And fear. And I remembered how I had felt when I had thought that Eddie Bates had kidnapped Lily, and though Hakim is much older and male, I could see the edge of the same maternal terror.

'I thought he'd run away from me but perhaps it's something more – Angeline do you think he could be in danger?'

'We could talk to the police,' I said. 'In fact . . .' It occurred to me that I should talk to Harry about it. (And then just as quickly – but would he think I was asking him a favour? Would I mind if he did think it? Would I mind being beholden? I laughed to myself. Get used to it, girl. You're letting him in. So let him in. My independence flapped its wings furiously but it didn't fly. Stay put, you.)

'What?' she said.

'We can ask a friend of mine,' I said. 'He's a detective.' Well he is. It sounded absurd to say it aloud, that's all.

'Oh,' she said. She looked weak and puzzled. Poor thing, I thought again. Sons coming and going, and weeping in the park with strangers who know detectives.

'I'll talk to him if you like,' I said. 'What are you going to do?'

She breathed in deep, flopped her shoulders, squinted a little.

'I'll go and see my father. I should anyway. It's possible Hakim may have been in touch with him. And I'll ... I ... can I come back and use your telephone later? I mean – I can go somewhere else, I ...'

Yeah, sure. Come and stay, with the rest of your family. Plenty of room, as they've all pissed off without notice.

'OK,' I said. She wanted to be where he had been. Where he might return. Fair enough.

'Don't ask your detective. Not yet,' she said.

'OK,' I said. 'Of course, Sa'id may be back.'

'Oh,' she said.

Oh?

I looked at her.

'You haven't even asked about him,' I said.

'Don't judge me,' she said. Not very snappily, but a bit.

'Don't snap at me,' I murmured.

She gave me a hot look.

'Sarah,' I said. 'I didn't choose to be involved in any of this.'

'Oh yes you did,' she retorted. 'You let him stay. You rang me.'

Which was true. But she said 'him' not 'them'. I was getting pissed off with her about that, but then I was pissed off with Sa'id too.

'I didn't turn up on anyone's doorstep out of the blue, and then disappear without a word,' I said, 'and two of your sons have now done that to me. I'm not sorry, I'm not angry, but I'm not prepared to . . .' I made a noise. 'I have become involved in this and sorry, but I do have opinions, and I'm wondering whether you have any interest in your other son, who didn't come home last night either.'

Her eyes skittered.

'No,' she said. 'Of course. I'll ring you later. Of course.' And off she went.

Back in the flat I tripped over her bag. Fuck it, these people.

Putting Sarah's bag on top of Hakim's things in Lily's room (which was now serving as Sa'id's), so that el Araby property was now three layers deep, I noticed that Hakim's stuff had been rearranged. Not just tidied up, but rearranged.

Well, a brother would go through his missing brother's things. No doubt I should, too. No. Sarah can, later. I don't like going through other people's things. Not since I went through Janie's.

Later, in my study (I know it sounds grand. It's eight feet by nine and has a window), I realised that my own things had been . . . not moved, not tidied or changed but just – picked up and laid down by other hands than my own. If you have a desk that no one else ever touches you will understand how I know. An angle, an air – a fingerprint of otherness. My mouth tightened and my breasts grew warm. The birds flapped. There may be intimations of intimacy, Sa'id, but this is not what's going on.

Then there was a knock at the front door – Brigid's sister Maireadh with the children. They came in and ate biscuits and drank their school milk in its little cardboard cartons (Sydney!). Maireadh and I had tea, and the enforced idleness of adults looking after lots of children having fun together. Sit and wait till you're needed to call an ambulance or provide more food. Lily took no notice of me because she had big kids to run around after. I love to see that. How she runs and flexes and tries it all out.

A long, narrow game of football was developing on the balcony when Sa'id came gliding up through the bevy of children and into the flat. He was wearing a greenish suit. Maireadh took one look at him and went rather silly about the middle of the face.

'Who's that?' she breathed. I was rather annoyed to see that his effect was universal. Some childish part of me takes some pride in liking men who other women think strange, and I didn't care to appear (if only to myself) as just fodder for some obvious sex god.

'Maireadh Brennan, Sa'id el Araby,' I grunted.

'Maireadh,' he said. 'Excuse me. Angelina. I must go away for a few days. I am sorry to abuse your hospitality. I hope you will let me return.'

'I didn't know where you were,' I said.

'I left a note,' he said. 'On the table. I'm sorry, it was sudden. Didn't you see it?'

Lily had been drawing at breakfast. I leaned to the table and retrieved her picture from among the detritus, and turned it over. His note, in beautiful small English writing that looked like Arabic. Even and flowing. He'd signed his name in Arabic.

'I hope I may return,' he said again.

'Oh yes,' I said. I felt like crying. I didn't want him to go. Should I tell him about Sarah? He was leaning into Lily's room and picking up his bag. The sight of his mother's stopped him for a moment.

'Is that Hakim's?' he asked.

'No,' I said.

No comment. He gathered his things up and as he left he took my hand for a second. Yes, the skin burned under his touch.

'Your mother was here –' I didn't say it. It wasn't just because Maireadh was there. It was deeper. His mother whom he didn't forgive. Territory beyond me. He was looking for Hakim and sorting out business that had nothing to do with her. He could deal with her later. And vice versa.

But it didn't feel good. Good as in right.

Maireadh was peering after him down the balcony. 'Ooh-er,' she said. 'I've always known you have an exciting life, it's great to see it in action.' This seemed to me fatuous, so I ignored it. Anyway Lily came in, looking tragic.

'What is it, darling?'

'Sa'id's going!' she cried. 'He patted my head but he's got his bag!'

'He'll come back,' I said. Then, 'Anyway, he doesn't live here.'

'I know!' she shouted. 'Nobody lives here except us and I think it's horrible! There aren't enough people in our house!'

I looked around at the five visitors (not counting the one leaving and bound to return, or the ones whose belongings festooned the place) littering the flat, but I knew what she meant. She only means one thing now, and everything comes back to that.

When Maireadh and the kids left, I rang my mother.

We arranged to meet at the café in the Royal Academy. I hadn't been to the Academy since I went to the exhibition of

Islamic art with Eddie and he so offensively kidnapped me. I didn't mind going there. For ten years when I was young I wouldn't go into the bathroom if my father was shaving because I'd had a bad dream about shaving – the devil had mixed thick red poison in the shaving cream. It's as well not to let these things dwell. No nesting.

Sarah called late to say she was staying at her father's and could she come by the next day. Sure.

I don't mind.

Well I don't and I do. I mind something. And I want privacy.

It is curious that although I find my father easier to talk to, and in a way I like him better, it did not occur to me to go to him about this. This was a mother thing. Mother to mother, re fatherhood. That must be pretty historically typical too. You don't imagine Leto and Europa and Daphne and everyone going to their dad and saying, 'The thing is, see, there was this shower of gold . . .' No, the women sort it out first, and then find a way of presenting it to the men.

Well, I may have seemed calm to myself on the telephone, but the first thing Mum said when we sat down with our tuna sandwiches was, 'What is it?'

For a horrible moment I thought I was going to burst into tears. But then the glass-shafted lift, so conveniently positioned almost in the middle of the café, alighted and the noise and distraction gave me a moment to compose myself. I may come out of this nakedly emotional, but I would like to go into it fully dressed.

'It's about Lily,' I said, and then quickly as Mum's eyes widened I said, 'No, she's OK. It's not a bad thing. I don't think.'

Mum just looked.

I put my hands on the table, took them off again, and gathered up my words.

'This is a bit hard, Mum, because it involves things we've never really talked about. So.'

'No reason we can't start now,' she said. Which I might have picked her up on. Like, 'Excuse me, if there's no reason then why the hell haven't we done it before ever?' But that's pointless and adolescent and we're all past that sort of thing now.

She was wearing a skinny rib sweater and a nice scarf. She looked kind. I've always been daddy's girl but she is my mother. Part of me.

'Lily wants her father,' I said.

'Oh,' said Mum.

'And there is . . .' I started to laugh. 'There's a contender. Another contender.'

'Oh my God,' said Mum.

'No, it's OK, it's OK . . .'

'But after last time – Oh Angeline, darling . . .'

'It's not like last time. Last time was only bad because it was Jim. It was Jim we hated, not the idea of a father.'

'Really?' she said, curiously. 'I thought – I rather had the impression that . . .'

'That what?'

'That you didn't . . . well that you didn't want anybody. You're very independent, you know.'

'Yes I know,' I said. 'But no. Most of that then was defence against Jim. Otherwise, I . . .'

'What?' she said.

'Mum,' I said.

'What?'

'It's Harry.'

'What's Harry?'

'The contender.'

She was silent a moment. Confused.

'Your Harry?'

This was no time to be pedantic. 'Yes.'

'But Harry was your boyfriend, not Janie's.'

'Yes.'

Having to say it to my mum made me suddenly very very angry about it. Fucking bloody Janie. My fucking boyfriend. I felt myself going red and my lip was trembling.

'But,' she said.

'It was after we'd split up,' I said. Who was I trying to excuse?

'Oh,' she said. 'Oh dear oh dear.'

I gave her a little time. And myself.

Then: 'But do you see, Mum, that's it's not such a bad thing.'

She looked at me.

'He's a lovely man.'

'Oh,' she said. Poor Mum.

Her sandwich sat there like a pile of paving stones. She stared at it. It's curious how we have to comfort other people through our own difficulties. Difficulties which are more ours than theirs, say.

'Is that why you don't like Janie any more?' said my mother. 'Tell me.'

How did she know that?

Schoolteacher. Teachers have eyes in the backs of their heads. They're paying attention when it looks as if they're not. My mother was a very good teacher.

'Something's changed. In the past year or so. You two used to be so . . . but you don't like her any more. Something has happened since she died. Is it this? Is it Harry?'

'Yes,' I said. Clutching at straws. I tried to look very upset about Janie and Harry. Though I had been, only moments before, I couldn't summon it up again. I had moved on, taken

up residence in my acceptance of it, for the purpose of giving Lily a good dad and not giving my mother too much
pain.

'But you just said it wasn't such a bad thing. You don't
mind about it so much. You just said so.'

'I mind and I don't mind, Mum. There's no point minding.
He'd be a good father, and if he is her father we must let
him be. You know, truth and all that.'

'But you don't know if he's her father. And you still don't
like Janie. You like him but not her. So it's something else.'

I said nothing.

Sitting there as the lift went up and down and the sandwiches sat and all around us people came and went, talking
of Damien Hirst. Sitting there, silent.

'Tell me,' she said.

'It's bad,' I said.

Oh fuck, I've admitted there is something.

That means I'm going to tell her.

'Tell me.' As she said it the angle of the tip of her left
eyebrow reminded me of Janie. To whom I always told
everything.

'She was a whore,' I said. Cold cold stomach.

Oh God. I've said it.

'Oh Angeline,' said my mother. It was a little scold, she
was disappointed in me, how could I just produce low abuse
at a time like this.

'No,' I said. 'A real one. A prostitute.'

Need I tell her any more? Need I tell her about the immediate and intimate treachery? That through our physical similarity and the uniform of my profession she had whored me?
That she pretended to be me, and fucked men from my audi-
ences who had wanted me? That she let Eddie Bates think he
was fucking me and give her – me – that bloody little Mercedes she was so proud of and we all rode around in?

'I know,' she said.

For a moment I thought she was saying 'I know' to the thought in my head.

But she wasn't.

'What do you know?' I demanded

'That Janie was a prostitute.'

Ahh.

And we sat and stared at each other. Your daughter, my sister. Our dead girl. So we stared. Dry-eyed. Dry-mouthed, in my case.

It's a watershed. Down which side of the mountain are we going to flow? The same side? Different sides?

We hovered. Suspended. Waters swaying, heavily, the impulse, gathering weight. Big heavy waters.

'How do you know?' I asked.

'How do you know?' she asked.

'Mum there's a lot . . .'

The chairs were not comfortable enough. I wanted comfortable chairs if we were to have an uncomfortable conversation.

'How did you find out?' she said.

And the waters began to lap over the edge, and trickles began to run down.

'From stuff in that tea-chest. The one that was in the attic.'

'What was in it?'

'How did you find out?'

We stared at each other. I wasn't going first. I was willing to tell her the truth, but as little of it as possible. There is pain I am not willing to be the bearer of.

Her face was still, her mouth drawn down at the sides as if pinned for stability. Holding her face together.

I don't want her to know why I hate Janie.

Trickle, trickle.

'She told me,' she said.

Oh my God I was jealous. She told her. Janie told Mum.
Didn't tell me. Now that is against the laws of nature.

'When?'

'The summer when you were sixteen – no, she was sixteen.
You were seventeen.'

My stomach started cramping. Cramping away, gently but
irresistibly. Sixteen?

'I had no idea,' I said.

'Of what?'

'I . . .'

'But you said . . . but you know. You told me.'

'*Then* what?'

'What?'

'What happened? Tell me what happened.'

She gave me a straight look. I think she decided I was more
upset than her. She told me.

'It was the summer. Nearly autumn. She came home with
a leather jacket. Elegant. She said she got it from the Oxfam
shop and I didn't believe her. She did that cross bluffing thing
she does, and said a hundred different things, and then she
said someone gave it to her, and that seemed true, so I asked
why, and she said why shouldn't her friends give her presents,
and, oh, you can imagine. She pretended to think I was
undermining her, you know, saying she wasn't worth such a
present. As if. As if.'

I remembered the jacket. Azzedine Aliah, if I remember
rightly. Beautiful. She told me Gina Goulandris had given it
to her. It was quite possible. Unwanted Christmas present,
that kind of thing. Mum wouldn't have been able to conceive
of it.

Sixteen.

The detail she was giving, it sounded as if this was an
isolated thing Mum was talking about.

Oh dear.

'She told me the Greek girl had given it her but she was lying. I rang her mother, God help me. And so I challenged her, and she said it was someone else, and it . . . and in the end she said it was a man. And I wanted to know why. I was going to warn against men bearing gifts. Expensive gifts. Warn my poor innocent.'

Poor Mum.

'So she lost her temper and it all came out.' Mum raised her hands involuntarily, turned her face slightly away, as if to ward it off.

She doesn't know the scale of it. She doesn't know.

'It was one man. She'd met him, and he'd . . . propositioned her, and he . . . Oh, I don't know the details. She never would tell me. She had some kind of loyalty to him. She said he wasn't old. Perhaps she said that to make me feel better, or to stop me going after him . . . I should have. Should have gone further. But she promised. She said leave it at this and I'll never do it again. She said she'd run away with him if I . . . And she cried and promised. So he was off the hook.'

There was shame on her face. Shame that she'd let him go, not been able to deal with it. The good teacher, failed. Browbeaten by her young daughter.

'Mum? Where was I? When all this was going on?'

It's a curious thing to feel jealous of being left out of, but I did. Oh, I did. This was my family. Fifteen, eighteen years ago. This is clearing nothing up – this is opening new expanses of web, casting shafts of half-light on to shadows I didn't even know were there. Though I was there when it happened.

'You were out belly dancing. Or so I found out later.' Her face had taken on a primness. Oh. Both her daughters lied. Both her little teenage daughters going out and being sexy in the world and lying to her. But I wasn't doing wrong. Oh fuck.

'I know I should have told you earlier, Mum, but I . . . it

didn't seem important. It was never the right moment. It was every reason and excuse you ever heard. Do you know I didn't think you'd be interested?'

Even as I said it I bit my tongue. Indictment. Daughter didn't think mother would be interested. If Lily ever said that to me, about *anything* she did, let alone take up a career in an ambiguous world, at sixteen, or grow an interest and passion like mine for the dance, and not tell me because she didn't think I'd be interested . . . I might as well have slapped my mother's face.

But she's not like that. No doubt that's why I am.

'Of course I would have been interested,' she said. But she wasn't hurt. She didn't mind my thinking that she mightn't have been interested. Ho hum.

No doubt that's why she didn't notice when I started staying out late every Friday night dancing. Because she was occupied with Janie's new career.

Sixteen! And promised her mother never again. Ha bloody ha.

'What did Dad say?'

She gave me a look. 'He doesn't know,' she said.

Well that floored me. Eighteen years. My God, but marriage is incomprehensible.

'You didn't tell him.'

'No.'

'You didn't tell me.'

'No.'

'Why not?'

For a moment she looked as if she had never asked herself the question. As if it had never crossed her mind. Then she laughed.

'She didn't want me to. She was so ashamed. She minded more about your knowing than about your father . . .'

Ha. Ha ha ha.

I turned to attend to my coffee. It was cold.

'This isn't what we came here to talk about,' I said.

'One thing leads to another,' she said. 'How did that lead to this? I can't remember.'

'Never mind,' said I, remembering all too well. I wanted to take off before she wanted my version. I'd told her about Harry, I didn't want to say more. Not now, pray God not ever.

'Now listen. Harry thinks he may be Lily's father. He wants to make sure. I'm with him. I think we should just find out the truth and I hope it is him because he is a good man and I can bear him being part of our lives and I would be very happy to have it cleared up once and for all. And Lily really wants a daddy. So,' I found I was breathing rather fast, 'he is going to do what we think of as the blood test; in fact it's a DNA test and because they need DNA from both parents, and because Janie is dead, that means we need a blood sample from you and Dad. Blood samples.' They aren't the same person, after all. Not a unit.

'We,' said Mum.

'What?'

'You said "we".'

'Yes.'

'So it's all set.'

'Yes. There's no other way.'

'Well, I – and if it's not Harry? Have you thought about this? Because if it's not Harry, how many other *contenders* are going to crawl out of the – oh my God. Oh my God. Oh Angeline no. No. No.'

She wailed.

She started swaying. Realisation knocked her sideways, swept her feet from under her. I was round the table and holding her in my arms and stroking her head like I stroke Lily's after a nightmare. But this was not after.

Unbelievably sad. Cradling your mother's head while she weeps like a baby. Eyes closed, rocking, rocking, holding, rocking.

After a few moments the café man came, and coughed gently.

'May I . . . ? Is there anything . . . ?' he said. There were tears in his eyes. I think he thought it was widowhood.

'Glass of water?' I said.

A glass of water is not actually necessary at these times. But it is necessary to honour the human urge to help, by giving it something to do. Perhaps he had a widowed mother. Perhaps he had a dead sister the extent of whose prostitution was just coming to light in the family.

Mum soon straightened up. She is an Englishwoman, after all. She didn't want to stay in the café where she'd made a spectacle of herself, but I didn't think she was up to moving immediately. A little girl scampered past, wearing a pink sparkly fairy dress, clutching postcards from the Victorian Fairy Painting exhibition. Oh my Lily.

'So she carried on,' said Mum.

'Yes,' I said.

'And you hate her for it.'

'Because she never told me.' Well, it's one of the reasons.

'And because it leaves this question mark over Lily.'

'No. Anything's better than Jim.'

'Ah. Yes . . . and she was up till the end?'

'Presumably not while she was pregnant . . .' And it was my turn to feel sick, and gag, and start to sway. Lily. Lily, inside a whoring body. Tiny Lily, unborn Lily, being sprayed with the septic semen of God knows who . . .

Yes, but come on. Lily is the fruit of *something*. And never was there anything more innocent and beautiful than Lily.

'So it would be good to ascertain if Harry . . . don't you . . . ?'

'Oh yes,' said Mum. 'Yes. I see what you mean.'

She was pale as a fungus. I went back to Enfield with her on the tube. We didn't talk about it much on the journey, but we did decide not to speak to Dad about any of it for now, and I held her hand all the way.

fourteen

Chrissie, Get Out of My Bath

The city is becoming turgid. Getting through it is like wading in concrete. Concrete, pain and the past. It takes all day to get from west to central, deconstruct your family and break your mother's heart, then go east, and back west in time for the end of school. But in some small way, thank God for it. Sitting on the tube for about two hours I could let what else Janie did settle in my mind, let it all separate, so the dead leaves could rot and sink and the clean rainwater rise to the surface. Except, like in the bogs at Glastonbury, the layers of shit seemed to be reaching a higher level every time I looked.

It seems every time I poke her memory some other nasty worm comes crawling out.

That's enough disgusting metaphors.

The fact was that by the time I arrived at the school gates that Friday afternoon my mind was clear and my feelings were under control because that's how it is. They have to be. Many are the things Lily will have to come to terms with and many are the ways I will have to help her, but for now, while she's so small, my main jobs are protection and the rationing of chocolate. And I can do them.

Sometimes I feel like some kind of psychological pelican, pre-digesting all the knowledge that my child will ultimately need to consume, so that she can digest it more easily in the end. Pray God let me not sick it up before the right moment.

Enough disgusting metaphors, I said.

Sarah arrived soon after us. Within moments she was drinking coffee and reading an Arabic newspaper. I had to laugh.

As soon as Lily was asleep the protective rings of good humour and patience that rise to protect the mothership and her young sank down again, and so it was in slightly depleted mood that I rang Harry. Not there. Left a message. Declined to call office, or mobile, or send a fax, or bleep him. I can't believe he has a mobile *and* a bleep. People so desperate to be got in touch with, and then when you do you can't communicate anyway because everyone's humanity is soul-deep in assumptions and second-guessing and desires we can't admit. I just said call me. I seemed to be developing a cough. Brigid has a rhyme: Get bronchitis, get pneumonia, then for sure the boys won't phone ya.

Sarah suggested that she cook some dinner. It's a great way to invite yourself.

'Are you staying?' I asked.

'No – I mean – I can go to my friend in Clapham, I . . .'

'Whatever you like,' I said. 'That's the el Araby dorm. And yeah, cook. Please.'

She looked so depleted herself. I was sorry I had been so cross and mean earlier. After all, my child is safe abed, and hers are out wandering among the dangers that face young men. Which are not few. But I did not want company. I wanted a serious session on the hedgehog. Janie was pulling my hair, Sa'id was running his fingers down my spine.

Oh God, if only.

I'm sorry, I'll rephrase that. Thank God he's not, actually.

I tried to smile at her. I didn't mean to be sarky. We should have things in common. English women who have loved Egypt. Then I got the telephone and pulled it on its special long extension cord into the bathroom, and from the depths of the suds I rang my mum, who was small-voiced and calm, and Brigid, who was knackered, and Zeinab, who had five people from the World Service coming to dinner to moan about the BBC's management, and there was, still, an automatic urge to ring Janie. As I was ringing the girls, you know, doing the rounds. There was her number, right there in my memory. In my fingertip. No address book of mine ever had her number in. I always knew each one. If anyone had tried to arrange my funeral from my address book, like they did the dead princess's, they wouldn't have got hold of those I loved the best. They're not in there, they're in my heart.

She didn't tell me because she was ashamed. She made Mum promise not to tell me.

Well, it's nice to have something from the dead that I didn't have before. To know something of how she felt.

I was so so sad that she felt she had to keep secrets from me.

I was crying in the bath when the doorbell went.

Sarah answered it. Cheeky cow.

Female voices. Sarah's and another, loud and raucous. And upset.

Oh, for God's sake, what now?

I put my head under water and started to sing.

The bathroom door burst open.

It was some kind of mer-harpy that rose out of the bath in a fury. I didn't care that I was wet or that I was naked, all I cared was that there was a child in my bed, a weepy mother in my kitchen, two runaways on my mind and God knows who and what messing with it from beyond the grave. I did not consider it reasonable that my very bathroom should be invaded.

'Get out!' I yelled, sheets of water slip sliding up and over the edge. 'Get out of my bloody bathroom!'

'Not until I get some – some –'

It was Chrissie Bates. She seemed to have forgotten why she had come.

'Excuse me,' I said, only a modicum more quietly. 'Excuse me, but would you mind fucking off?'

She slipped on the bathmat. Whether she was lunging for me I don't know. Anyway she seemed to have cracked her head, so I stepped over her as best I could in the minute room, and wrapped my towel around me, and yelled to Sarah.

'You let her in, would you mind getting rid of her?'

'Who is she?'

Sarah looked scared. Terrified, in fact. Of course she usually leads the quiet life of a provincial academic. She's not used to this.

'She's the widow of a psychotic gangster who used to have a crush on me. And I think she's drunk.' I prodded her with my toe. Gently.

'Oh bugger,' I said.

'Yes,' said Sarah. 'Sorry.'

'What did she say?'

'She said she was a friend of yours. Sorry. I didn't think.'

'Yeah. Well.'

Poor Chrissie. Pathetic sight.

'Is she all right?' said Sarah.

'Shouldn't think so,' I said, and went to put some clothes on. I hate getting dressed too soon after a bath. You're not properly dry, and your bra straps stick to you. I hadn't been intending to get dressed again anyway. I had been going to put on some comfortable yet slinky black velvet underwear and an ancient gallabeya and my Turkish dressing gown. This is what I like to wear when I am on my own quietly at home in bed trying to escape from/think quietly about things that are trying to do my head in. I don't know what I like to wear for throwing out hysterical yet comatose widows.

I pulled on a pair of jeans and some jumper, and felt very cross about having to do so. Damned if I'm putting shoes on, though.

Back in the bathroom Sarah, ungainly in the doorway, was cradling Chrissie's head, and Chrissie was coming round. It was drink more than anything.

'She might be sick,' I said unhelpfully.

Sarah looked up at me aghast. At my heartlessness, I think, rather than the imminence of vomit.

I reached under the bath and pulled out a basin, and folded a towel to go under her head. 'Put her in the recovery position,' I said. 'She'll come on out when she needs a cup of tea.'

Sarah apparently didn't know the recovery position. So I did it. The amount of Giorgio Chrissie was wearing, I nearly passed out too. From the kitchen came a waft of garlic veering from caramelising to burning.

The thing is, once you're a mother you're used to doing everything. So I turned down the garlic, threw in the chopped onions (which annoyed me, because I prefer them sliced in moon-pale rainbows – chopped onions to me look amateurish, lumpen, English). Then I made tea, and sighed, and picked up the paper I hadn't got round to reading and the post that hadn't arrived when I went out that morning. Two bills, a suggestion that I might have won five trillion pounds from *Reader's Digest*, and a handwritten envelope postmarked from the West Midlands that filled me with dread. Same envelope, different handwriting, different postmark, same . . . smell. Thank you, Chrissie. Marvellous. What a multi-media experience you are tonight.

Inside was a letter from Eddie. His mad, tight, black handwriting. His idiosyncratic way with words.

My Darling Girl,

It seems to me that the thing to do is for us to go away; I imagine that you imagine you can't, because of the dear child and so on, but there is really no reason why everything can't be arranged. You may have thought that I had forgotten you but I can't really believe that you would think that. I'm just writing to say Don't you worry. Don't you worry. I'll let you know as soon as I can what the arrangements are, as soon as we have these little legal details sorted out. I'm afraid I can't tell you where yet either in case you do something silly like show this to my little scoundrel Harry. But rest in peace, all will come out in the end!

I do miss you, you lovely thing.

See you soon, all my love, EB

I stared at it blankly for quite a while.

'What is it?' asked Sarah.

'My past come back to haunt me,' I said. 'Either it's a letter from a dead man, or it's a very old letter that has taken eighteen months to get here, or it's a letter that a widow finds amusing to send on posthumously. It's not funny, either way. Any way.'

I stared at it a little more. No date. Postmark date was yesterday.

Chrissie must have found it somewhere and sent it, a charming follow-up to the phone call.

Bitch. I had still, after all, been half prepared to be not entirely unsympathetic towards her, but no longer.

At that moment the gurgling noises in the bathroom took on new energy, and in a moment Chrissie appeared in the doorway like the ghost of Medusa in Chrissie Hind's make-up. Sure enough we turned to stone.

She collapsed on the sofa and burst into tears again.

'You,' she said. 'You . . . You . . . You.'

I waited.

'You just ... you wait. You can't ... You won't get away with it.'

Ah!

'You know ... but you can't have it. You can't fuckin' have it. I need it and You Can't Fuckin' Havit.'

'Go away,' I said.

'Fucking ...'

'Chrissie, shall I call you a cab?' I said politely. ('You're a cab!' went the joke in the back of my mind. I couldn't stop it. Pathetic.)

'Fuckin ...' she replied.

I didn't want Lily waking up to this.

'Sarah, would you be so kind? The number's on the wall by the phone, I don't want to leave her ... thank you.' Sarah crept to do my bidding.

Chrissie wept a bit more.

'And stop sending me these,' I hissed.

She looked up at the the letter. Squinted at it.

'Never,' she said, shaking her head. It seemed to mean 'I never sent it' rather than 'I will never stop sending them'.

'What?' I asked, just to be clear.

'I never,' she gurgled. 'I ... that's Eddie's writing! You fucking –' and she was off again, and grabbed the letter off me, and read it, and shrieked her indignation, and was carrying on like some kind of banshee when Sarah slipped back in and said a cab was coming. She didn't look very convinced. She went and sat down by Chrissie, and offered her a cup of tea.

'Yes please,' said Chrissie surprisingly. Her mascara was everywhere; her face completely out of focus. Every now and then she would droop forwards, then nod violently, nearly knocking herself off the sofa with the force of it.

Sarah gave her her tea with a look of absolute pity and

only a dusting of disgust. Chrissie tried to take the tea without giving up the letter, either to the floor or the table or to any person. She sighed.

'Put it down, no one's going to nick it,' I said.

She looked up at me, scared.

'Drink your tea, there's a cab coming for you.'

'You and me have got to talk,' she said. 'We have. Yes.'

'I think not,' I said.

'Yes we have. It's not legal and you can't keep it. So you've got to give it to me. It's mine.'

'I don't know what you're talking about,' I said. 'Go home.'

'This doesn't – wossit say?'

'What?'

'Wossit say?' She was moving her eyes over the surface of the letter but nothing seemed to be sinking in. Her eyebrows took on the angle of puzzlement. 'I don't know,' she said pathetically. 'I don't know.'

I think she may have truly believed that she hadn't sent it. But if so, it was only because she was completely barking.

'Chrissie,' I said. 'I don't know what you're talking about. Go home. Go down and wait for your cab. Go on.'

'It's coming?' she said.

'The driver won't come up to the door because this is a horrible council estate in a big dangerous city,' I explained, as if it weren't completely bloody obvious, 'and I won't come down with you because my kid is asleep here. So please. Go. Wash your face, go.'

Sarah went with her to wash her face. Then collected her handbag and steered her to the lift. Then went down with her, and found the cab, and came back up looking knackered.

'Thanks,' I said. The worst and most immediate fears had left with Chrissie, but there were plenty left. I can't have her making a habit of this.

Damn.

'What was all that about?' Sarah asked.

'I don't know,' I said, and wondered about purification rituals, whether I should get someone in to burn a native American smudge stick for my flat's aura, or to put rose quartz crystals on my passageways.

'Angeline?' said Sarah. I looked up at her. Her concern seemed completely genuine, completely normal, completely kind. But I was in no mood for concern.

'I'm going to bed,' I said. 'It's been a long day.'

'I'll get a cab,' said Sarah. I didn't stop her.

After she left I picked up my letter from beyond the grave and put it on my desk, half brushing at my fingers to get the dust of it off me. Then I washed my hands. And went to bed. Sa'id's fingers were already trailing the back of my neck as I got in, but Lily woke, chasing him away, and kissed me all over my face. 'It's a heart of kisses,' she said. 'Could you tell the shape? I kissed you a heart of kisses.'

Actually I don't think she was awake.

First thing on Saturday morning the telephone rang. I grabbed it to stop it from waking Lily who lay like a miracle with her feet in my belly and her head half under the pillow. But sleeping. That was the miracle.

It was Harry. He was sounding disgustingly efficient for what couldn't be more than eight in the morning. Had I spoken to my parents? I told him about my conversation with my mother. Not about the extra chapters of Janie's history, or about how churned up yet unsurprised I was by them, nor about the strange comfort that I felt at having had something, whatever, back from the dead. The knowledge that she was ashamed. Nor that Chrissie had been round. No, I just told him that Mum was talking to Dad and no doubt they would soon be ready to go ahead with getting the blood samples and, er, that seemed to be it. It was curiously dry and unemotional. Early morning. 'OK then, great,' he said. And that was it. We might have been travel agents, confirming a booking. If we hadn't been I might have mentioned Chrissie's visit, and the latest letter. But I didn't.

A surge of want-not-want came over me. I want this to be emotional, I don't want this to be emotional. What do I want? It does help to know.

To kiss Sa'id.

fifteen

Sunday Night Coming Down Again

It was a quiet weekend. I quietly thought about Janie. I rang my mum and we talked for a long time about nothing much. Sarah rang saying she was going back to Brighton, saying she'd ring, telling me to ring her, desperate to communicate when there was nothing to say. There was nothing I could do but wait.

So Lily and I went to Kew and had a picnic under a willow tree, fighting off geese and watching the slant of sun on water. Then we came back to Shepherds Bush and wandered down the market, buying parsley and fresh hot popcorn and falafel sandwiches – really nice ones, the falafel sizzling and lumpy like they should be – and we stopped in to see Charlie the parrot in the pet shop, and Lily was given a livid green and scarlet feather. And we got some dangerously hot little fried Brazilian doughnuts, and a three-pack of knickers for Lily. And we went to the Syrian supermarket and bought five varieties of baklava for tea, along with stuffed vine-leaves and olives and livid crimson sausages with pine nuts and chilli, and a small forest of broccoli. It looked like green clouds, like I would imagine a rain forest looks from above. We greeted the Ghanaian barber and the Egyptian fishmonger and the Armenian deli-man (so we bought some rye bread, and Lily got a piece of turkish delight) and the Indian sweet-shop lady, and we laughed when a Scandinavian asked one of the Syrians for red pesto and the Syrian said what, Bisto? At least I laughed. Lily didn't get the joke. She only gets one joke. What's the fastest cake in the world? Scone.

The sky was blue and London was beautiful and so was everything in it.

And when we got home the flat was ours. I opened all the windows and Lily got out her Bananas in Pyjamas colouring-in book and I put on Summer Breeze by the Isley Brothers very loud, because although it wasn't summer and there wasn't really jasmine in my mind, we were doing a pretty good pretence of it. Then we changed the sheets on her bed as the sun paraded a glorious old-testament sunset across the western skies, complete with shining light shafts and purple cumulus, nicely set off by the deep green OXFORD AND THE WEST signposts, and the almost empty Saturday evening A40. Those who had left town had left; those who were coming had come. We who stay are here. And then we ate baklava and broccoli in the bath with candles, which was very beautifully sticky and funny, and then she fell asleep in her own bed and I put on my gallabeya and velvet knickers and Turkish dressing gown and a Bach cello suite, and I lay in the middle of my own floor and sang along. Because I felt like it.

On Sunday night, with Lily sleeping, I listened to my answerphone for the first time since Friday. Two from Sarah, saying nothing. One was Mum, how was I. Zeinab, did we want to go to the park. Then Sa'id: 'I was going to take Lily out. I am so sorry. I'll ring you again.'

He has such beautiful manners.

I wished he'd left a number. There's something about ringing someone back, making that connection, yes I want to talk to you too, I'm not just accepting your attentions, I'm paying my own.

I couldn't ring him, so I rang Harry.

Harry was a bit chilly.

This was the third time running Harry has been a bit chilly.

Fuck him.

I went to bed. I love going to bed.

Thank God the post the next day didn't arrive till after I'd taken Lily to school. There was a letter from a lawyer I'd never heard of. I've learnt to dread letters from lawyers I've never heard of. This one was a corker. Blah blah, legalistic waffle, effect of which was, here is a letter for you from Eddie Bates, written and left by him to be delivered to you should he kick the bucket.

This is all very well, I found myself thinking. This is all very bloody well. I held the enclosed letter – dangling, by the corner. Same type of envelope. Same handwriting.

So why post one directly, and have one sent via a lawyer? Depending of course who posted the other. I stared at the envelope, and found that my shoulders were bunched high around my neck, and that I was cold.

I stepped on to the balcony, and leaned over, and gazed out at the road west, the envelope dangling still.

The dead won't leave me alone.

I opened the envelope.

My darling girl.

You will not read this until after I am gone, and not unless my life has been a failure in at least one – and not the least – way. I hope you will never need to read it. But perhaps I have failed, and you have grown old without me, and stand now old and in need of help from one who always – but you know.

So. My darling. I know you too. I know you are proud. I would not for the world offend you. But this is for –

because, you know, I know you know, because I told you. It is for Lily. Don't be proud. It is not for you to interfere here. You cannot come between a child and her father. Don't squawk! I saw the integrity in your soul when you battled to accept what you hated but believed to be the truth – that Jim Guest was her father. And I saw you fight Jim off. If you read this, I have never tried to prove my claim. I don't want her, I never wanted her. I wanted you. And she is your Achilles heel, my dear, isn't she? Persephone to your Demeter? So for your sake I honour her. And because it might have been me, and for your lovely sister's sake, and just because it becomes a man to look after women, there's £100,000 for her in an account in your name at the Banque Misr, Nile Hilton branch, in Cairo. It's all quite clean and legal. You are safe. Go and get it.

Oh, my darling girl. Perhaps it would have been worse any other way. I know that what I wanted you for were the very things you would have had to have given up in order to be with me. Thank god I never lost faith in you, and you never lost your understanding.

Ever your EB.

By the way. Mr Stephens is under instructions to donate £100,000 to the British National Party within six weeks of the date of my death unless he hears from the bank that you have collected the money. In person!

It was almost familiar by now. The surge of fury, humiliation, outrage, incomprehension. The heat under the skin, the tightness of the teeth. The words – he's mad. Fuck him. He can't do this. He's done it.

I never used to be manipulated. Gossip, machinations, bitchery, small group politics. It didn't work on me. Nobody knew what mattered to me. I rose above, and laughed. I was the queen of transcendence, and I hardly even knew it.

But Eddie!

Here he is, dead, and he's running rings round me.

I am only a delicate little human being. I only want to be left alone. I am fed up with being tormented by dead people.

Actually . . .

Now I come to mention it.

I am not quite so tormented by Janie.

Well, I'm not. Since Mum told me of her shame. Her shame has comforted me. Brought me pity. Compassion. Compassion? Maybe.

£100,000 to the British National Party. He is such a bastard. Such a clever bastard. How could he know so well what I could not accept?

He didn't know me. He didn't. He saw me dance, and his . . . feelings for me were based on that. We had half a dozen conversations. I danced for him, and fought with him, and he told me what Janie had been, and his role in it, and he drugged me and kidnapped me and jumped me and I knocked him out with a poker and fucked him while he lay unconscious. Where was there time for him to get to know me?

And did I know him? Knew enough to know I didn't want to know more, that was all.

Yet.

Admit it. If you don't admit it how can you ever deal with it?

A tiny, narrow, fine, thin thread of fascination, needling through the right and proper reaction to such a man. A sharp wire which made me hate and fear and mistrust all the more. A vulnerability to him.

Anyway he's dead.

I decided to ring the lawyer, because perhaps it was all nonsense.

When I got through to him it went like this:

'Mr Stephens? My name is Evangeline Gower . . .'

'Ah yes, Miss Gower, I've been expecting to hear from you. You will have received our communication . . .'

'Mr Stephens, did you read the letter from Mr Bates to me?'

'No, that was a private communication which we simply sent on as a matter of routine after Mr Bates's demise . . .'

'Have you sent me any other letters on his behalf?'

'Well no, Miss Gower, though . . .'

'Though what?'

'Well as you may know, as I assume the letter will have explained, though perhaps . . .'

'Mr Stephens, please don't attempt to be discreet. My letter said that he has put £100,000 in a bank account in Cairo for my daughter, and that if I don't give you proof that I have collected the money by a certain time you are under instructions to donate a sum to the BNP. Is that true?'

'Well yes it is.' I could feel him not commenting. Of course he wouldn't comment. Lawyers don't. They don't say, 'Yeah. My client was a flaming loony, wasn't he?'

'Mr Stephens,' I said. Sighed. 'Mr Stephens, what would you accept as evidence?'

'The bank is under instructions to let us know when the transaction has been completed.'

'Mr Stephens.' ('That's ma name! Don't wear it out!' cried the inappropriate comedian in the back of my head, in a Grand Ole Opry voice.) 'Mr Stephens. I don't want the money.'

He was silent for a moment. 'The legacy – the sum of money – is not in your name. It belongs to the child.'

'She doesn't accept it.'

'She is a minor, isn't she?'

'Yes. Five.'

'An interesting question,' he said. 'And a complex situation.

But my responsibility as a trustee of Mr Bates's estate is to fulfil his instructions. If the legacy is not collected within the time stipulated, I must make the other payment.'

'It's blackmail,' I said.

'What an interesting point,' he said. Just the kind of thing Eddie would have said. Oh shit, what kind of lawyer would an old gangster like him use anyway? Why am I appealing for a let-out from the man representing my enemy?

'Thank you, Mr Stephens,' I said, and I hung up, and I recalled what I had been saying to myself about answers. Well, I had one. I knew now what Chrissie had been going on about. So I can go and get the money and give it to her. Simple. Spit Eddie in his dead eye, too, by doing what he wanted, then doing what I want, thus squishing his plans in the dirt. Dead men can't win.

And if I give her the money maybe she'll leave me alone.

I screamed, quite loudly. One good thing about my neighbourhood is that you can do that, and nobody bothers about it.

The phone rang. My voice was still a bit out of control from the scream, and I answered it sounding funny. It was Sa'id. I gasped his name like a young wife waiting for news from the front, like a lost traveller. But squeaky, too. He wasn't sure it was me. Then there was a knock on the door, and another, which rapidly became an actual knocking, and so before I could speak to him I had to go and placate it. It was Mrs Krickic from next door.

'What's the matter!' she shouted. 'Why you screaming!'

So much for the neighbourhood. I placated her.

Out of this foolish chaos I came back to the phone.

'Sa'id?'

'Angeline?'

'Where are you?'

'Edgware Road. Can you come?'

'Can't you come here?'

He was silent a moment.

'OK. I must collect things too. *Meshi*?'

'*Meshi*.' OK.

'Now?'

'Half an hour.'

'OK.'

It felt like a lovers' tryst. But it wasn't. I was going to get some facts out of him. It is not unreasonable to want to know what the hell is going on. And anyway, what's so sacred about reason? I want to know. Do I need a reason?

Being a rational kind of gal, I am not convinced by this line of argument – of reasoning, I was going to say. But there *are* more things, Horatio. There are.

I changed from crap baggy clothes to fit-for-the-outer-world almost slinky clothes. From ancient black trousers to the bootcut ones. From an old sweatshirt of Zeinab's husband's to a little Agnès B sweater that I bought when my book was published. And I put on some mascara. Well yes I did. Oooh, missus.

Then the door went again.

Harry.

'Hi,' he said.

'Hi,' I said, surprised.

'I was a bit chilly yesterday,' he said.

'Were you?'

'Yeah,' he said. 'Sorry.'

'Oh. All right.'

A silence.

'I was passing,' he said.

'Anything else?' I said.

'Cup of tea?' he said.

Why not? I let him in, and went through to the kitchen. Actually there were things I kind of wanted to talk to him about. But didn't. Like missing persons, and letters from dead people.

He didn't seem to have much to say. He looked tired and sad.

'Yeah?' he said. He thought I'd said something. So I did.

'How can you tell if someone is missing?' I only said it because I wanted to get back on good terms with him. Wanted to unfreeze the chill which I seemed to be contributing to. I just wanted to say something, and that was what popped out, because it was on my mind, and because I had been thinking of talking to him about it. Out it popped.

'Because they're not where they should be,' he said. 'What's it about?'

So I told him.

'You remember the Egyptian boy who was staying with me? Who wanted to find his mother? Well we found her, and he went to stay with her and . . .' I could see the freeze settling back in. A cold seeping from him, across the floor and up my leg.

'What?' I said, accusingly.

'What do you mean what?'

'What's the matter?'

And another of our little silences.

'What's the matter,' he said, slightly bitterly, as if considering an academic question. 'What's the matter.'

'Yes,' I said. I knew this tone of voice. It precedes anger, and is often symptomatic of conclusion-jumping. It is his worst habit.

'Angel,' he said. I knew what he was going to say: 'I'm not a fool'. Before going off in as foolish a direction as ever man took. 'Angel, I saw him. Please.'

'You saw him! Where? How d'you – but you never met him, did you? Did you meet him? How did you recognise him?'

He was silent.

'Harry! What!'

'I saw you and him together,' he said. He sounded embarrassedly aware how like a line from a country and western song that ends in murder this was. 'I saw you outside that café in Queensway. So drop it.'

'Drop what?' I said, automatically continuing bolshie and defensive, while underneath trying to make sense of what he was saying.

'I saw you with your Egyptian friend. In Queensway. So stop pretending that he's some kid that you've lost, some little orphan. Please.'

Oh. He thinks Sa'id is Hakim (or vice versa). He saw me with big handsome grown-up Sa'id and he's jealous. Ha ha ha! And he thinks I was lying. Oh very bloody ha ha ha.

'That was his brother,' I said coldly.

'What?'

'That was Hakim's brother Sa'id. There's more than one Egyptian in the world.'

'Why's his brother here? I thought they lived in Egypt.'

'People travel, you know,' I said. Sarkiness just gets me sometimes. For example when I feel put upon.

'Oh,' he said. He sounded sad.

'I don't lie to you, Harry,' I said.

'That's why I minded,' he said.

Oh fuck it. I started laughing, and then I started to hum: 'We can't go on together, with suspicious minds . . .' And he started laughing too, and then he said, 'You know I called in the security videos from the café . . .'

'You what?'

He sounded sheepish. 'I called in the video. I didn't want to look at you when we were passing . . .' I didn't ask who 'we' was. No nose-rubbing. 'So I got the video in the next day. Silly really.' He offered this as a reconciliation object. A confidence shared, a foolish secret for us to bond over.

'You got the video from the security camera so you could spy on me,' I said.

'Ah –' he replied.

'For fuck's sake, Harry,' I said.

'Oh,' he said.

The thing is, I was delighted that he was jealous, but I was utterly undelighted to be spied on. Anyway it's wrong. Just because he's police, and he can. It's an abuse. I don't like that. I don't like him doing it. I looked at him, sitting in his grown-up clothes, his older face, his familiar shoulders, his unchanging slouch.

'You shouldn't do crap things,' I said.

He looked back, under his eyelashes. A pause.

'Oh?' he said.

When he says 'oh?' in that way, that slow, challenging, lazy, insolent way.

This is why chairs get thrown out of windows.

God but the baggage piles up around us, wherever we sit. If we sit still for three minutes it come swooshing in on the tide and gathers round our feet, and one bit spins away as another bit spins closer, and gradually it all settles in around us again. Flotsam, jetsam and the kitchen sink.

I wasn't going to make a headmaster speech about how it damages him as much as it damages me. I didn't care to hear his opinion on what I had done that was crap. I didn't want him here when Sa'id came.

'I've got to go out,' I said. 'No doubt we'll speak later.'

And then there was the knock on the door, and then the rattle of the key in the lock as Sa'id got no answer and let himself in. Harry didn't take his eyes off me.

Sa'id walked in, pale.

He and Harry sneered at each other.

'At least I told you,' Harry said, and stood and left. Spitting. Part of me grabbed his arm and shouted, 'He's not my fucking lover! Ask him!' Not the physical part of me though. Not any part that anyone would notice.

Sa'id ignored the drama. Just glanced at Harry as he left, then settled himself at the kitchen table and asked me for coffee. I was about to snap at him to make it himself. Hovering on the knife-edge where courtesy and feminism battle it out, cheered on by cultural habit. Courtesy and cultural habit (his) won this time. As I made the coffee he inquired after my health, told me I was looking well, *alhamdulillah*, and so on round the calvacade of courtesies.

I wanted to ask him if he'd found out anything about Hakim, but I sat, and accepted the cavalcade, because there is nothing you can do till it has run its elegant course.

'I am sorry I have not been able to return to your home before,' he said, as it started to draw to a close.

'Sa'id, please don't stand on ceremony,' I replied. 'My home is your home.' A fairly naïve thing to say, though it didn't occur to me at the time.

'Yes,' he said, thoughtfully, not being by any stretch a naïf man. 'But not, also.'

I looked a question. He didn't follow up on the more complex notions of how at home, if at all, a foreigner can feel in another land, or a man in the women's quarters, or a Muslim in a house of Christian extraction, if not actually Christian, or any of the other things that didn't cross my mind. He applied himself more immediately and locally.

'You have noticed,' he said, 'of course, that there are some things happening, and you are wondering what and why. And you want to know, because you are human, and female, and you feel an interest.'

'And because I may be able to help.'

He looked at me slowly.

'But you know, Sa'id . . .'

He smiled at me.

'I am living in a state,' I found myself saying. 'I am surrounded by mysteries and confusions, and I want some order, and some knowledge, and I don't know where to start.' It is surprisingly easy to say such things to foreigners, things you wouldn't say to an English person. Perhaps because we are all constantly living in fear of the judgement of our peers. 'So,' I continued, 'I have decided to start with the giving of knowledge.' I didn't know I had, until I said it. 'I am telling what I know, in hope that others will then tell me what they know.'

'Sympathetic magic,' he said. 'You make, and what is made comes to you. You imitate, and it becomes real. Give and it shall be given.'

'Yeah,' I said.

He was still smiling.

'So what do you have for me?' he said.

He didn't think that I had anything very much. He didn't know that I was about to leap straight into the heart of territory that he didn't even know I knew he had. I was about to gatecrash, to overwhelm my natural urge to respect privacy. I was about to connect. I was scared, a little. Did I think he would bite me? Was I afraid that he wouldn't?

'Your mother,' I said softly.

His smile just wasn't, any more. I don't know where it went. It was like the Cheshire Cat in reverse.

I am in no man's land until he responds. I started to map it. For myself, and for him.

'Hakim came here to find her,' I said, 'and he did find her. I helped him. She's been here. She's very worried about him. He knew that you and your father wouldn't like his plan so he didn't tell you. That's all.'

He was silent. Silent like ancientness. Silent like a sphinx or a desert dawn. Like a million picturesque things.

Then he stood up.

'You helped?' he said.

'Yes.'

'It was not your business.'

'He was living in my house.'

'He is a child.'

'He was here, staying with me. Of course I looked after him.'

'It is not your business.'

'Please don't accuse me, Sa'id. How could I keep a child from his mother?'

When I looked there were tears in his eyes.

'I told her you were here,' I said.

'What did she say?'

Oh shit.

I couldn't say it.

I couldn't lie.

'She wondered if you knew where Hakim was.'

He started to laugh, and then he left the room and went into the el Araby dorm. He left the door open and I went and sat on the floor in the passageway outside, like a servant, my back to the wall and my knees drawn up, and I sat there till both my good and my not-so-good leg ached. After about twenty minutes he came out and took my hands and pulled me up, and as I came level with him he kissed my face, and he carefully wiped the lipstick from my mouth with his fingers and I took hold of one of them – the middle one, strong, brown, clean – with my teeth as it passed and then his hands ran into my hair and my hands ran into his and the blood began to shimmer and the breath to fall.

One kiss and I am flying, flying over the cliff. The kiss is it.

I broke away and looked at him. His eyes were there, full on mine. Those pale eyes. But it wasn't the lust, the immediate fire. It wasn't what I had wanted from the moment I opened the door. It was something . . . else. More. Other. Bigger? Different. To do with the known him, not the unknown him.

He kissed me again. And again. Just a kiss. Just a flight over the –

My breath was gone and my words with it.

He put his hand on my waist, just settled on the curve like a butterfly on blossom. 'May I?' he said.

I couldn't speak. But I assented.

Deep, deep, melting, strong.

And he took me to my own bed under my own window, and laid me down, and as my clothes came off he said, 'I'm not doing this because of my mother, I'm doing it because of you. It's just timing. The two are not conflated.' And as he started in a part of me was wondering at an Arab man who uses a word like conflate, and at such a moment, and the rest of me was screaming out the naked strength of joy. Flesh to flesh, cock to cunt. The rest is history.

Afterwards we slept. Of course. I was electrified and knocked out, simultaneously. This was my first sex since Eddie, a year and a half ago; my first real sex for five, six years. By real I mean consensual. And wasn't it just. At some stage we half woke and did it again.

Even as I slept I couldn't imagine why I didn't spend every hour God had given me fucking. I could not conceive any more glorious pastime, any nobler activity. Feeling my limbs slipping back into place, my not-so-good leg forgetting itself, my heart swelling and relaxing, my blood flowing clearly for the first time in years. Feeling the life and youth and immediacy of this man who had seemed so ancient and mysterious. After the poeticals comes the body.

I know virginities don't grow back, but something was blown away that afternoon.

It occurred to me that he'd produced, used and disposed of a condom – two – and I had hardly noticed. I think I love him.

No, that was a joke.

It was a *hejeb* on his leather cord. An amulet: verses of the book, bound in leather and hung by three small loops. For protection. Worn smooth and dark by the years next to his skin.

sixteen

'You are dearer than my days, you are more beautiful than my dreams'

It must have been nearly four when I was woken by the rattle of the door. Opening, then closing, and Maireadh's voice in the background calling out, and I was out of bed grabbing my Turkish gown, then Lily was running in, and grinning, and saying, 'What's Sa'id doing in your bed, Mummy, and why haven't you got any clothes on?'

So the first time I let myself go, the first time I *do it*, what happens but the very thing that I feared, that was half the reason why I didn't do it for so long.

There's a moment before things fall into place when they are suspended, when they could fall anywhere: into the right place, the wrong place, a place that will do, just about. Or all over the floor in pieces, crashed and burned, mendable or not. During that moment you are powerless. You cannot nudge. No levers respond, nothing has any effect. You watch, in slow motion, as pieces fall.

Lily was grinning. That seemed to be all right. Sa'id was rising up from among the cumulus of white duvet, sleepy, smiling, looking clean and for once young. Beautiful naked torso. I was watching, watching. There was no time even to consider what I wanted.

'Hallo, *habibti*,' he said. 'Can you make coffee?'

'Of course not. I'm five,' she said. But she was flattered.

'Can you make a glass of water?'

'Of course I can.'

'Will you, please?'

'Of course.'

And off she ran.

I think that's all right.

Yes, that seems all right. For now.

He held out his hand, and I went to the side of the bed, and sat, and took it. I didn't know what to say. I kissed his fingers quickly to show friendliness, and ran after Lily. She'd made Maireadh put the kettle on. Maireadh was grinning too. Laughing at me. She and Brigid have just the same laugh. Silent, superior, very good-humoured and benevolent. I began to hit my forehead with my hand, and sat at the kitchen table, and began to laugh too. Lily came and sat on me. I hugged her, and hugged her, and realised that it was only me who was worried.

'You smell funny,' said Lily.

My first reaction was to shriek and push her off me, but I didn't. She doesn't know what I smell of. She doesn't need to know. For a moment I had been careless with protecting her, but no damage seems to have been done, so I don't need to punish myself. Not yet, anyway. We'll see.

Maireadh was positively sniggering.

'Hello darling,' I said to Lily.

'You *are* funny,' she said. 'You smell funny and you are funny. Can I have HobNobs?'

'After your proper tea,' I said. (Why do anarchists drink camomile? Because proper tea is theft.)

'I must go,' said Maireadh, covering her mouth with her hand. 'I've left the kids with Reuben.'

'No tea?' I said. She laughed at me again.

'You've enough on your plate,' she said. She's going to tell Brigid all about this, and it's going to become one of those myths, like the time Caitlin and Lily tied themselves together at the wrists and nobody noticed all afternoon. She left, carrying the story with her like a bag of particularly nice buns to share.

I made an omelette for Lily, and coffee for Sa'id, and he emerged in a gallabeya to drink it. It was one of those curious moments; perfect yet skew-whiff. Man woman and child, sitting and eating. But we're eating breakfast though it's tea-time, he's my lover but not her father (Is he my lover? And to be technically nice, I'm not her mother). I should be just looking after my child but in fact I am fainting with desire. It looks normal. But it's not. But then again, it is. Because it is normal not to be normal. On some levels.

I felt quite perfectly divided. Here is my child. Object of my total love and loyalty, number one candidate for attention. She may just have had a bit of a shock. Or perhaps not – I can't tell yet. And here is the man who was just in my bed, for the first time. 'Normally' he would be object number one under such circumstances.

God, even his feet are beautiful. The long parabolic struts of his instep, the arch of his toes. Dark honey to my milk white.

Thank God it's nearly Lily's bedtime.

I was torn. They were perfectly happy. Chatting to each other. It's only me who feels weird.

The happy families scenario lasted for about an hour. Then the question arose: which bed was I going to put Lily in? I started thinking about this as soon as she was sitting down in front of her omelette – my mind moving on, as always, to the next stage. I became conscious, for the first time, of how crowded my flat was with other people living there. Not in the way it had been with Hakim and Sarah, or even with

Sa'id before. It wasn't a physical issue, an issue of space. It was emotional. Before, they had retreated to Lily's room. Now he didn't. I was pleased. But. If he was not using her room as his territory, this could mean he was already moving out of it, in his mind. And into where? Well, my room. I liked this and I didn't like it. Well, I liked it but I felt . . . threatened? Unconsulted?

Ach, I was leaping ahead. He wasn't moving out of Lily's room. He just hadn't been in there. And anyway, he had, to get his gallabeya. So perhaps I should stop panicking, and worry about what I wanted, not what he wanted. Let him sort that out.

Everything is becoming fraught with meaning. Stop it. Stop it right now. You're not seventeen, to decide what everybody else is thinking.

Lily was playing with her egg, chasing it up the knife with the fork, then dividing it into little piles and putting them together in gangs.

'If Sa'id wants to be in your bed can I be in mine again?' she said.

A toad appeared in my belly. Why, I didn't know.

Five years of protecting your child from adult sexuality and now, over tea, by chance, without discussion, a man seems to be moving in with me.

I looked at him.

He looked at me. His eyes said yes, yes. But he doesn't know what I have at stake here. He doesn't see that great bird at my back; he doesn't know the slow-moving dance I have been doing round Harry. He doesn't know the great reluctance in me to have a man too close.

I am not imagining that if he sleeps in my bed tonight and tomorrow he will move in and stay forever, marrying me and controlling me and taking over my child and forbidding me things. Even in the European way, let alone the Arab. But if he sleeps in my bed tonight Lily will start to know about things that I didn't want her to know yet. Adult sexuality. Which I didn't want her to see until, unless, it was . . . well, until it was as I chose to represent it, i.e. perfect. Nuclear. Come on, be honest – until it was husband and wife forever domestic with the little child and all that. Until it was what I grew up with. What my parents gave me. Or the nearest facsimile I could manage. Which I couldn't, so, nothing.

In other words I'm being a controlling illusionist, suspending my child miles from reality in a frozen fantasy of my own. Using her as an excuse, not a reason, to lock myself away. If I can't have my girlish dream of mutually independent domestic bliss, then I'll have nothing.

Angeline, get over yourself. Perfection does not march fully formed into your life and lie down on a plate waving its legs in the air. And if it does, it's only perfection in one area – and there he is. Sexual perfection. Human perfection. The lover. Don't throw him out because he is not domestic perfection, forever perfection. And anyway how do you know what he is? What he will be? Or even what he thinks – what this means to him?

'*Aiwa*?' I said to him.

'*Aiwa*,' he said to me.

'I know what that means, that means yes,' said Lily.

'*Aiwa*,' I said to her.

'Can I get down?' she said, as she slipped from the table and ran to her room, where she started to rearrange dolls on the bed. I kissed Sa'id hard, burnt up like one of those amaretti papers that float to the ceiling, then went to change the sheets, my knees giving way.

As I put Lily to bed I lay beside her, murmuring that I loved her, in case she should feel the emotions in the flat, and miss me.

'I know you love me, Mummy, you don't have to go on about it,' she said.

'Are you getting enough attention from me?' I asked.

'Give me lots now and that'll do till morning,' she said, holding out her arms, so I piled her arms up with attention until she said it was too heavy and could I put it under the bed so she could get it when she wanted it. I lay with her till she slept, then went to Sa'id, and lay with him. Divided? Yes and no.

Later Sarah rang. I wasn't going to answer the phone, but I heard her voice from the other room as I lay counting the hairs on her son's chest (seventeen). I tensed a little.

'Who is that?' he said. Which he hadn't said before, to other disembodied voices floating down the hall.

I was silent for a moment.

'Your mother,' I said.

For a moment I heard reality flooding up the balcony and crashing up against the door. Tendrils of it snuck into the flat. One seeped as far as the bedroom, and tapped on the foot of the bed.

Sa'id shifted, turning his head, moving his arm. He didn't turn his back on me.

He said nothing. Sarah was still talking but I couldn't tell if he was listening. I was. Hakim, when, tomorrow, okay. I couldn't really make it out. But the tone wasn't happy. She wasn't calling with good news.

Hakim.

'Sa'id,' I said. Tentative. 'Please don't . . .'

He turned his face to me, then extended his neck back a little as if to get me in focus.

'Please,' he said. 'No more opinions about my family.'

'She's worried about Hakim,' I said. 'So am I. Aren't you?'

'No,' he said.

'Why not?

'Why should I be?'

I stared at him. A cold streak of alienation flowed down my bed.

'What?'

'He's OK,' said Sa'id. 'More or less. What's the problem?' He looked a little surprised at my reaction.

'Where is he?'

'I sent him back to Cairo.'

I stared at him.

'What's the matter?' he said.

'We didn't know where he was,' I said.

'He'd finished his work here. He didn't do it very well, so –'

'What work?'

'The samples he had brought over, the people he was to see. Why he came. You know. The business.'

'Samples?'

'He brought over some of the things we make, and some other things, for some new – potential new – business partners. And he made some payments, and collected some, and paid some compliments and so on. That's why he came.'

'And why did you come?'

I felt like a cross child, squeaking for explanation to a patient adult.

'Because he hadn't come back,' Sa'id said. 'And because when I was speaking to people on the telephone from Luxor it became apparent he was not doing what he had been told, and he wasn't returning my calls, and he wasn't at the hotel, and you know I've mentioned these people in Cairo he's going round with . . . So I came and sent him home.'

I thought of the ball of lapis and the beautiful Nut boxes. And the thousand pounds he'd given his mother.

'Well for God's sake,' I said. 'For . . . Sa'id, why didn't you tell me?'

'I didn't know you needed to know.'

It is such a shock when a person who has so far understood everything suddenly demonstrates total lack of understanding.

'He's my friend, Sa'id. He stayed here. Lily loves him. I helped him. I was worried about him. Jesus. I'm going to ring Sarah.'

'Wait,' he said. 'Wait.'

So I waited. Naked beside him, sitting up as he lay, surrounded by the detritus of passion. Our clothes embracing each other in cast-aside piles on the floor. He didn't sit up. Even as I sat, his complexity and his authority remained, horizontal, silent but unavoidable.

'Come back down,' he said. 'Come back to me.'

So I did. He pulled me on top of him, arms around my waist, breast to breast, face to face, and he stared me in the eye.

'I'm sorry,' he said. 'I didn't know you were worried. You didn't show that you cared for him. I should have known.' I stared him back, and kissed him. I could hardly take my mouth from his face. I couldn't move away but he was still talking so I just put my face against his neck, under his ear, and held on to him. I remembered when he might have told me, and when instead I had told him Sarah was here, and we had become . . . distracted.

'But Angeline,' he said. 'Angeline. Do not think to bring my mother and I to each other. Do not waste your kindness on this.'

'I wasn't going to,' I said. He turned and craned his head to look at me again.

'Yes you were,' he said.

It occurred to me he might be right.

I thought about it for bit.

Then: 'But I must tell her Hakim is safe.'

'Why must you?' he said.

'Because she is in pain.'

'I don't care about her pain,' he said. And for a moment I understood, and I sat with him in that separate land of his self-protection, cushioned by decisons he made years ago about how to feel, and more precisely how not to feel, about his mother and the pain she had given him.

'Yes you do,' I said. 'You didn't use to, because you couldn't, because it hurt too much. But you do now, because you are a kind man, and you can afford to. Now is your chance.'

He raised an eyebrow at me.

'You believe in forgiveness,' I said. 'So forgive her.'

He just looked at me.

'You'll like it,' I said.

And looked.

I didn't know for sure that I wasn't just digging a deeper and deeper hole for myself. But I knew that if I couldn't say things like that to him then there was no point.

I wondered whether to tell him too that I minded her pain. Hugely. That she was a mother fearing for her child, and that I knew something about that, and I wouldn't wish it on my worst enemy. But I left it for now.

He pulled me back to him and our bodies started in again. I couldn't tell if this was in agreement, or part of a process of mutual persuasion, or just a retreat to an area where we had no disagreement.

Later, when he was sleeping, I rang Sarah.

'He's back in Egypt,' I said. 'Sa'id says he's fine.'

'Egypt,' she said.

'Yes.'

'But . . . why did he go? I mean . . . we were just . . . Oh fucking fuck,' she said, which surprised me.

'What?' I said.

'Why didn't he tell me?'

'Hakim or Sa'id?' I said.

'Hakim of course. He should have – oh . . . Oh. I'm so pleased he's not in trouble. God,' and she started crying. I made the kind noises.

'But he's gone back,' she said.

'Yes.'

'But we . . . I'd better go out there then.'

That did surprise me.

'Why?' I asked.

'Because I want him – it's not over, it's just starting. We can't just let it cut off in the middle. Why did he go?'

'I don't know,' I said, semi-truthfully.

'And Sa'id,' she said. It was strange to my ears to hear his name in her voice now. 'Sa'id. Is he still here?'

'Yes,' I said.

There was silence down the line.

Am I meant to tell her I'm having an affair with her son? I didn't. I knew I wouldn't. I hadn't told anybody. Didn't want to. It was private. But reality is at the door, three foot high and rising. Tomorrow perhaps I'll let it in.

'Blast him,' she said.

'Don't,' I said.

'What?'

'Don't say that. He's your son.'

'Excuse me,' she said, about to start in on the 'it's none of your business' line again. Maybe that's hereditary, too.

I interrupted her. 'Sarah,' I said, 'look, my sister died, and we had about three tons of unfinished business, and I'm still dragging it around with me. Life's too short, Sarah, or too long, or something. He's your boy. Be good to him. That's all.'

She started trying to say something, but I wasn't in the mood to listen. 'I'm going to bed,' I said. 'I'll talk to you tomorrow.' And I went back to Sa'id, who was lying splayed like a crucifixion in my bed, and traced the many beauties of his body until he woke enough to fuck me again.

Later I asked him why, of all the doorsteps of all his acquaintances in all of London, he pitched up on mine.

'For this,' he said. 'For you.' But he didn't elaborate.

seventeen

I Wish I Was in Egypt

I told Sa'id about my conversation with Sarah. Mum was picking Lily up from school and taking her back to Enfield. We had till Sunday. I couldn't not tell him. No clouds over our free time, our dream time. These are our things, take them on. I was not happy at this go-between role between my lover and his mother, but I couldn't see any way out of it now. So I told him just that I had told her Hakim was safe in Egypt, and that she intended to go there herself.

We were in the kitchen; he reached out and got my shoulder, and pulled me to him, and rested on me.

I find it so lovely beginning to come to know somebody. Knowing, for example, that when he feels weak he holds on to me. Knowing that though relaxed, he is always very much in control, and doesn't much like not being, and that at the same time as he resents me stirring things up, he looks to me for support through them, and holding on to me is his literal support. And that though he would not admit to insecurity in words, his actions are transparent, and he doesn't mind that.

'Then I must go too,' he said.

I almost laughed. Fair enough. Five years off, three days on, I thought. It couldn't have worked anyway. I didn't want it to. I just wanted . . . well, I hadn't had time to think about what I wanted. I had wanted to kiss him. And I started to get to know him. And I felt for him.

We hadn't even mentioned the future. Or our practical difficulties. Our different nationalities and religions and cultures. Let alone where we live, and our responsibilities, and our families and work. Now it will never have a chance, because the romance is over. This is the flood. Reality washing everything away.

I was very sorry. Not surprised. Goodbye.

'Will you come?' he said.

Ha ha ha ha ha.

I actually sat down on the kitchen floor and laughed. Laughed and laughed. Of course he didn't think I was mocking him. Of course he understood that I was not laughing because it was an absurd idea. It wasn't an absurd idea at all. All he'd said was would I come.

I went and sat across his lap and wrapped my legs around his waist and laid my head on his chest. I could go and get Eddie's money. I could have a holiday. We could make love twenty-four hours a day. I could try perhaps to help with their el Araby soap opera. I could visit Abu Sa'id. And Orlando. I could lie on the roof of Ibn Tulun and watch the doves glint in the sunshine; I could go to the clubs and let the beat of the tabla rock my blood. Then I could come home, either broken-hearted, or having seen the light, or bringing him with me, or whatever. Who knows. *Che sará sará*. The future's not ours to see, we're going to Wemberley.

And if I was away maybe Chrissie would lose interest . . . no, nobody ever notices if you go away.

Well, I was going. It felt like an old part of myself waking up. The part that does things, whether or not they're wise. The dancing girl, the biker, the poet and the fool. Protected by God – well, I always had been. There had been so much protection for Lily. It wasn't that we hadn't needed it. We had. But perhaps we didn't any more. You need some security if you're going to take risks. It seems that I felt I had it. I felt young. I felt safe. Safe enough to be dangerous. Even when a bunch of lilies arrived, smelling to high heaven, with a card saying 'I always get what I want' in florist handwriting. I just laughed at it. Rang Fergus, got Chrissie's home number, left her a message saying, 'Fuck off. You can have your money. But fuck off.' Then I dropped the flowers off the balcony and didn't even watch as they spun slowly like helicopters and landed splat on the road.

Sa'id didn't see them. I didn't want to lie to him. I really didn't.

We spent the weekend in bed. He cooked for me, I danced for him – I did, I danced! He kissed my feet, and learned the difference between my good leg and my not so good one. By Saturday we were black and blue. I love my child but I loved her absence.

I was to meet Mum and Lily in St James's Park on Sunday afternoon for the handover. Was Sa'id going to come? I didn't want to introduce him to my mother. Nothing public. But I didn't want him to be away from me. Six days now he had been by my side. My hands moved of their own accord to hold on to him.

'*La'ah, habibti,*' he said. 'I'm going to walk. Is there water I can walk by?' I directed him to Hammersmith, to the tow-paths and the muddy Thames, so like and so unlike the Nile. Planes for palms, pigeons for egrets, mud for obsidian. I didn't want to let him go. I was so happy that I didn't want to let him go, that I let him go easily.

I found Lily and Mum by the pond, admiring flamingoes. How full I felt to walk from one love to another. (I'm not saying I loved him. But I was in love. At least, there was love there, and I was in the middle of it.)

It was a very London day. October. When the days are starting to be shorter and you feel good for claiming the daylight when you can. When light is golden yet chill and gleams on pavements like slate; and sadness lurks behind bus-stops. I've lived in this town all my life. They say you're never more than twenty yards from a rat in London; I'm never more than quarter of a mile from a personal landmark. St James's Park? It's where I used to come to meet David Barowski when I was seventeen, and he was at school round the corner, and we'd hide in the undergrowth and smoke joints and snog, then go to Gino's Italian Café and Restaurant and giggle over sandwiches. And up there is the Ritz, where I once got into an embarrassing situation in a suite, after a Saudi wedding I had danced at. (I'd never seen inside the Ritz. Of course I wanted to go.) And now there's New Scotland Yard, down the road there, where Harry sits, detecting. And the café where he told me Eddie was dead.

And there's my mother and my child. Well, my heart was full.

Lily had a sticking plaster inside her elbow. She showed it to me, proud. 'I'm plastered!' she yelled, which made me laugh.

'What is it?' I asked.

'It's the blood test,' said Mum.

For a moment I couldn't think what she was talking about. Then I remembered.

Well, I know why I was so upset. I felt left out.

'Oh,' I said.

'Grandma's got one too!' cried Lily, pulling up my mum's sleeve, or trying to, from two foot shorter. Jumping about, anyway. 'And grandpa! We all went together and the doctor took all our bloods and put it in bottles like when you go to blood donors but not so much! I didn't cry! I got a sticker, look!' She did. A teddy bear with 'I was good at the doctor's today'. 'Really it was yesterday but Grandma said I could still wear it so it's OK isn't it Mummy?'

And Harry will have had his and they're doing it. They're doing it. Without me.

I know it was childish but I minded. I really minded. I wasn't there when she was conceived and now I'm not to be here when she is . . . identified. Patronised. Fathered.

Surely they needed my permission to take her blood? Though actually no, because my parents have parental responsibility for her too, so they could give permission.

So I felt otiose.

'Why didn't you tell me, Mum?' I said. I wanted it not to sound cold, but it did.

'I did tell you,' she said.

'No you didn't,' I cried.

'Yes I did. Last week. When we were arranging the weekend. I said "And I'll take her to the doctors and have them take the blood."'

'I have no memory of you saying that,' I said. I felt as if I were picking a fight. I didn't want a fight.

'Well I did,' she said. Firm but gentle. Fair but tough.

And no doubt she did. Last week, after all, I hadn't exactly been concentrating. At least on anything much beyond Sa'id's earlobes.

'I'd have wanted to come,' I said. 'It is quite a big thing.'

'I was surprised when you didn't suggest it,' said Mum, but she was smiling.

'What?' I said crossly.

'Who is he then? Sa'id?'

Lily grinned at me.

'He's not my daddy, is he? You said he wasn't. But if he's your boyfriend does he have to be my daddy? I was just wondering because I don't know if there's room for a boyfriend and a daddy. I don't know where they would all go. Grandma said he must be your boyfriend but I wasn't sure, I said I'd ask you. Is he? Sa'id I mean? Because if he is and the daddy wants to be your boyfriend what do we do then?'

Mum was, as near as a respectable woman can, pissing herself. I was dumbstruck by the realisation of how different my life is now to my previous experience of romancing. My mum and my daughter have been gossiping about me. My five-year-old is taking a responsible attitude where I am hiding my head under the duvet. And she doesn't seem worried. Not hurt. Not insecure. Not damaged. Just interested, and responsible.

'Yes, he's my boyfriend,' I said. Addressing Lily. I squawked silently within at the admission. Boyfriend. I haven't had one for years. (Part of me thinks Harry is my boyfriend still.) I tried the words on. Oh dear. 'He is. And no, boyfriend and a daddy aren't always the same thing. Some boyfriends are daddies and some daddies are boyfriends. Some are husbands.'

'What kind is my daddy?' she asked.

'Don't know yet, love. Probably the not boyfriend, not husband type.'

'My blood will help tell. I'm helping to find him. My blood will help us to recognise him when we meet him,' she said.

Well, at least that's pretty much how I would have explained it to her myself. Had I been given the opportunity. Or had I not been too taken up with my louche pleasures to take up the opportunity.

My mother had an expression on her face like a great benevolent sad rock. I knelt to give Lily a hug but she ran away. She'd seen a squirrel.

My mum never interferes. Other people moan about their

mothers getting involved, but mine never does. Sometimes I wish she would. Sometimes I think she doesn't care.

'Harry said . . .' she said, but I cut in.

'Have you been talking to him?' I asked shortly.

'Of course,' she said. 'Organising all this.'

God, I was pissed off.

'Great,' I said. I had been about to ask her if she and Dad could take Lily for half term, while I went to Egypt. Now I felt disinclined. They'd do everything without me and I wouldn't be needed ever again. Them and Harry. Bloody Harry.

But I wanted to go. God how I wanted to go. Sun. Sa'id. Holiday. Sleep. Omali. A quiet *shisha* on a tiled floor in the shade. A drowsy felucca. The Sufi dancers at al-Ghouri, whose movements echo the patterns of the hangings on the walls – if you laid the cloths on the floor I swear their feet would follow every blue and white arabesque and swirl. The movement of light. The Nile. Skeins of desirable things that awaited me in Cairo strung across my eyes and heart. I wanted to go. South.

I ran after Lily, and caught her. 'Would you like to spend a week with Grandma and Grandpa? Shall we ask them? For half term, you know, when you don't have to go to school?' Now I couldn't remember if I'd ever explained to her about holidays. They didn't really have them at nursery. Did she know she would get these great gaps, when she didn't go to school? Did she know there was one coming up?

'YEAH!' she shrieked, and raced to Mum, and asked her. It's great how they do your dirty work for you.

Mum was looking up questioningly at me across the stretch of grass. I nodded. She bent back to Lily and they were agreeing. So that was sorted.

I am not the only person in the world, I told myself. I am not the only person in her life. If she is to have a father, I am going to have to make room. So start moving over now, and stop being such a childish controlling paranoid.

And that way you can go to Cairo.

'There's one other thing,' said Mum.

Lily was after the squirrel again. I looked up.

'About Janie.'

I'd sort of forgotten. In that superficial way you can when you're doing something else. Sort of. Mum looked as if she recognised that, and was slightly sorry for bringing it up. As if she thought I *might* bite. I wasn't going to. As Harry wouldn't say, it's good to talk.

'Mmm?' I said.

'When you were teenagers, she was jealous of you.'

I tried to think why, what of. My mind clouded – I couldn't make sense of it.

'I think, looking back, it was the dancing. All the attention you must have had. I don't know.'

Of course she didn't know. For years I had kept the dancing from my parents. Fear of disapproval and prohibition at first, then habit and reluctance to admit the deception. So Mum was on guessing ground. Surmising.

Was Janie jealous of me? Of that? Of the sequins and the leering, of the money and the fun, of my having something that was mine?

I made a soft, understanding little snort, but I didn't understand.

That night Harry rang. I was reading with Lily, and Sa'id answered. We both knew that the days of leaving the machine to bulge were over. We were into a new stage. We were going to have to learn to operate vertical as well as horizontal. It was happy families time. Sort of. We knew too that this stage wasn't going to last. Do you think I would have let him answer my phone if we hadn't been going to be leaving the country almost immediately? I think not.

He didn't bat an eyelid at Harry. Didn't ask who it was, just called me and passed it over. I had had a lurking fear that he might be a jealous man, possessive as Europeans always expect Arabs to be, but he wasn't. Not a jot.

Harry, on the other hand, said: 'Was that him?'

'Yeah,' I said.

'Oh.'

'Well,' I said.

'Yeah.'

So you see we were doing well.

'Anyway,' he said, pulling himself together. 'Just wanted to tell you about the blood tests and stuff, keep you posted, you know . . .'

'Yes I do know,' I said. 'Mum told me. And listen . . .' I didn't want it to sound cross. But I had to say it. 'Please – um – when you're doing things, like that, I mean – could you let me know?'

'I am letting you know,' he said.

'Before?' I said. 'I felt quite odd, to think that it had happened and I hadn't been there, and I didn't know. I need to be included, that's all.'

'Then you should listen to your messages, and ring people back,' said Harry. 'Get out of bed and pay some bloody attention.'

Get out of bed?

Oh. Yes. My mind flew back twelve years. My first week with Harry. In that absurd squat in Clerkenwell where the sun shone in all day, and we tracked its movements across the bedroom ceiling and the walls, and when the square of butter-yellow light was over the electricity point we'd get up and go to the pub for an hour or so before going back. To bed. 'Sun's over the powerpoint,' he'd say in a comical naval buffer voice. 'Time for a chota peg.' Leathers and boots all over the blue-painted floorboards; crash helmets procreating in the corner, dancing costumes hung up behind a cloth. His Ducati and my Harley parked outside, worth twice as much as anything within. I could hear his bike thundering up five minutes before he arrived, the unmistakable crack and judder of a big Italian V-twin. I could hear it from Holborn. He and some mates were running a despatch company down there: the Holborn Globetrotters. Harry and me, when we were young.

'Sorry,' I said.

'What for?' he said, slightly bitterly.

'Blaming you when it was my fault. Sorry. I've been . . .' Damn, I didn't mean to say this. 'Busy.'

'Yeah,' he said.

Oh bugger.

'But listen,' I said, trying to change the subject. 'You know, when the next stage comes up, I mean – talk to me. We have to keep talking. Don't we.'

'Yeah,' he said.

'Well?'

'Yeah,' he said.

I'm not playing this game. I don't know if it was punishment because of Sa'id or what. But it was a bore.

'Yeah,' he said again. 'So you start.'

'Ummm . . .'

'Tell me stuff.'

'I'll call you later,' I said. 'This is silly.'

'No – no, wait,' he said. 'Sorry. Sorry. But Angel – look. Umm.' His preparation for saying something difficult noise. I waited for the short pause. It came, it passed. 'When I started seeing Amygdala,' he said, 'I came round specially to tell you, because I thought it mattered, and that under the circumstances you had a right to know, and now you've got this bloke and it's like I'm some kind of . . . oh, I don't know, just for wanting to know. Wanting you to have the grace to tell me. So when you start saying "we've got to talk" like some BT advert, it's just sounds a little bit absurd, if you see what I mean. Ironic, I think might be the term.'

So he was right again.

'So tell me about him,' he said.

So I had to. Insofar as I knew. But 'I can't now, hon,' I said. 'He's here . . .'

'Is he living with you, then?'

'Sort of. By default. He was staying here anyway. You know.'

'Yeah.'

'Well, so there's that. And, um . . .' I wanted to give him something. To show willing. 'Well, I'm going to go to Cairo with him in a week or so, at half term, and . . .'

The line went funny. Not in itself, but with the strength of feeling at the other end.

'You're what?'

'Going to Cairo. With Sa'id. At half term . . .'

I could hear him thinking. I could feel his brain racing. I could taste the intensity of his reaction.

'Don't go,' he said.

'What do you mean don't go? I'm going.' I was irritated. Every time we get on to a sensible level one of us does or says something stupid. 'Who are you to tell me not to go?'

'Oh shit shit,' he was saying. He wasn't listening to me. He sounded distressed. Genuinely.

'Harry, what is it?'

'Can you come out? Now? Come and meet me?'

'No,' I said. 'Lily's only just come back and it's school tomorrow. I need to put her to bed.'

'Later? Please. Please. Your man can babysit. Please.'

I didn't want to go out. I didn't want to ask Sa'id to babysit while I went off to see another man. He wouldn't like it either. I didn't like the thought that with Sa'id here Harry couldn't – as it seemed – just come round. I didn't like to think that his presence in my life was already constraining it.

'Come here,' I said, just to get it out in the open.

'No,' he said. 'It's private.'

If he won't say it in front of Sa'id, if he's making the point of not meeting him (which I don't blame him for – I wouldn't want to meet Amygdala) then it must be about Sa'id. So went my logic. My sympathetic ear went too.

'Well then sorry,' I said.

He breathed for a while. And thought.

'Meet me tomorrow? Please? I'll come up to the Winfield. What time is good for you?'

Daytime. Lily will be at school; Sa'id if inclined to be suspicious will be less suspicious. God, this all bodes well for the harmony and relaxation of our future lives, doesn't it? Time for a civilised modern dinner party, I think, of me and Sa'id and Harry and Amygdala.

We arranged to meet at noon. Harry was jumping about at the urgency. I didn't like it.

'Was that your friend?' said Sa'id, as I came back into the kitchen. He was stirring onions, adding ground and chopped up little bits of I'm not quite sure what, that he'd bought at the Syrian supermarket.

'Yes,' I said.

'Tell me,' he said, quite kindly.

So after I had put Lily to bed, I told him some more of my secrets, of what I had not told him before. That Harry might be Lily's father, that he had been my boyfriend, that he had slept with Janie, that we were just now trying to prove one way or the other, and when we did, well . . . we would have to find a way to live.

'He slept with your sister,' said Sa'id with a little snort.

'It was after we'd broken up,' I said.

'Sweet,' said Sa'id, musingly. 'You protect him and yourself. What about her?'

'It's between her and God,' I said. 'I don't hate her so much any more.'

He smiled into the aromatic haze rising from the hot oil.

'Your complicated life,' he said. 'Are you sure you have room for me?'

'Oh God yes,' I said. 'God yes. Yes.' Without thinking.

He didn't seem to mind.

'So are we spending this week in bed too?' he asked. 'Or shall we go back to work? I have things to do before we leave.'

It was sad. Kissing goodbye to our first stage. Sad but realistic.

eighteen

What Harry Knows

Next morning's post brought a letter postmarked Taunton, containing a large piece of white paper with my name written on it in inaccurate phonetic Arabic, covered with lipstick kisses, and 'Sorry!' across the bottom in fluorescent pink.

I wondered if the stalking law they've been going on about had been brought in yet. There must be something I can do to stop this bloody woman.

Sa'id looked at it. 'What's that about?' he asked.

'Oh –' I didn't want to talk about it. Didn't want to get into Eddie, in any detail. I told him in next to no detail. Wife of the dead man, had been rude at the funeral, silly, nothing really. He looked at me cool and slow. He knew perfectly well there was more to it. He let me know he knew. I looked at him, let him know I knew he knew. He said nothing, but held me in his gaze, kindly, gently. I swear my heart grew warmer inside me.

I held that warmth when I went to the Winfield, edgy about Harry. At noon it was still, or already, reassuringly dark and smoky. Already a few diehards were playing snooker in the vast back room, wreathed in nicotine and low lighting. Harry was at the bar, where Liam, who has been a good friend to me over the years as only a barman can, was ignoring him.

Harry was drinking a vodka and tonic. I was surprised. Ordered a coffee.

'What's that about,' I said, indicating the drink, as we retreated to a quiet and distant corner.

'Nerves,' he said.

Well, that had to be a lie. I've never seen Harry nervous of anything.

'Why?' I said.

'Sit down,' was his reply. I sat.

He drank. Almost emptied the glass.

'You said I shouldn't do crap things,' he said. 'Well. I'm about to do something and I don't know if it's crap or not. I mean it not to be. I think you'll understand. But. I am about to. Oh shit.'

He was shaking. Almost.

'What,' I said, gently. Observing.

'Please don't go to Egypt,' he said.

'Why not?' I asked. If he could give me a reason why he was acting so strangely then I could consider it. But not without.

'For me, because I ask you?'

He knew that was hopeless.

'OK then,' he said. 'Do you remember when I asked you to stop seeing Eddie Bates, and you wouldn't?'

'Yes,' I said, warily. I couldn't see where this was leading.

'Did you think I was jealous?'

'No,' I said. 'But I knew you would think I thought so. I only saw him at all because Cooper had stitched me up. I wasn't interested in him.'

Harry gave a little snort.

'Do you think I'm jealous now?'

'It had crossed my mind,' I said delicately.

'If I could convince you that it's not that, would you agree not to go?'

'No,' said I.

'Oh shit oh shit,' he said. Somehow more resignedly now. Then he took a breath and regrouped.

'Why are you going?'

'Because I love Cairo, I haven't been there for years, Sa'id has invited me, I . . . OK, I'm Emma Woodhousing a bit for his family. Their mother is going out and I feel a bit responsible and a bit interested, you know, having helped Hakim find her and everything. And,' I said. It occurred to me that I hadn't told him about Eddie's little legacy.

'And?' he said.

I sort of laughed. 'This curious thing has happened. I was going to talk to you about it actually. You know Chrissie, and those letters . . .'

'I thought they'd stopped after the funeral,' he said. Very short.

'No. Why have you gone white?'

'Carry on,' he said.

'Well to start with they weren't too bad, then I got one with a razor blade in, and some with poetry, and stuff. I told her to stop sending them. She came round after the funeral, drunk as a skunk and yelling. Then I got this letter from a lawyer. I thought you knew most of this.'

'Some,' he said.

'Saying, well. It enclosed a letter from Eddie, saying, if you please, that he's put £100,000 in a bank in Cairo for Lily, just in case *he's* her father, don't you know, and if I don't fetch it before a certain date he's set up another £100,000 to go to the BNP. Clever fucker, eh?' Even as I recited it I felt sick.

Harry had gone green.

'Oh sweetheart,' he said. 'Oh sweetheart.'

'What?' I demanded. 'OK, what?'

He shut his eyes for a moment and dipped his head like a pigeon.

'What I am about to say,' he said, 'I'm saying purely to save your life. Don't ever tell a fucking soul. Ever. I'm putting . . .' he laughed '. . . my job on the line here. And quite a few other things.'

I goggled.

'If I ever deceived you about anything, and I know I did, I'm making up for it now. Angeline,' he said. 'Angeline, keep this to yourself. I'm trusting you. Trust me. We're talking here, oh yes. Angeline.'

He had taken my hands in his, and started to play gently on my knuckles as if they were a xylophone.

'He's not dead, angel,' he said. 'He's not dead.'

Well, I didn't need to ask who. There's only one person who should be dead.

'He's living in the Middle East. I believe Egypt, though I haven't been told. I wouldn't be at all surprised if it were Cairo.'

I sat. Shocked.

'Well then I'd better kill him,' I thought. Immediately.

Everything I ever hear about him fills me with fear. The toad in my belly and the bird on my back. I had a flash of his face from years ago: in the flames, the very first time he tried to hurt me. Fear when he was alive, fear when he died, fear from his letter, fear now, oh my God yes.

'Why is he alive?' I asked. Very quiet. Vey controlled.

Harry watched me carefully, as if to estimate my capacity to take on information. Was I losing it, as I had so very recently when told the bastard was dead? No, I was holding on to it.

'Witness protection,' Harry murmured at last. 'The people he grassed up, you wouldn't believe. Interpol adore him. He's the CIA's favourite valentine. Various Colombians are a little pissed off, but . . . Don't go, Angel. Don't go.'

Witness protection.

'So he just gets a new life?' I whispered. 'Somewhere else?'

'Yes.'

I sat. Silent.

Then: 'Fucker!'

Then: 'Thank you for telling me.'

Then: 'I can see why you couldn't before.'

'I didn't know before,' he said. 'I didn't know when I told you he was dead.' He looked a little relieved. Probably he thought I would be furious with him. I was – well, I would be, but my mind was otherwise occupied. I'd think about that later.

I thought about the letters. How much simpler it was, that he had sent them. The ones from him, at least. How it fell into place. The flowers: 'I always get what I want.' The phone call, my God.

'The thing is though,' I said, 'that I am still in danger from him,' and I realised I was shaking.

Harry started to speak but I hushed him.

'He sends me this love poetry. Invitations. Blackmailing manipulations. Expectations that I will run away and join him. If I hadn't burnt them I would show them to you. Actually I had one this morning . . . I thought it was from Chrissie . . . I thought she was sending them . . .' It was in my pocket where I had thrust it. I offered it to Harry.

'Oh dear oh dear,' he said, sounding for the first time a bit like a plod-style policeman.

'And Chrissie is sending stuff too . . . I don't know what is who. And he's joking about thinking he's Lily's father – at least I think he's joking. I can't live like this, Harry.'

'No,' he said.

'And if he's officially dead there's nothing you can do for me either.'

'No,' he said.

'If you kill someone who's officially dead, can you get done for it?'

'Interesting point,' he said. 'I'll look into it.'

Then I started crying.

Harry stroked me inefficiently, then gave up and took me in his arms.

Liam looked across disapprovingly.

Later, Harry said, 'I'm sorry you can't go.'

I laughed. 'Oh but I am going,' I said.

He looked at me.

'If I don't go there now, I can never go anywhere ever again. Do you see? I fucking am going.'

nineteen

The Madness Sets In

The last time I had faced a crisis with Eddie, a madness had come upon me. A wild energy. It was something to do with fucking him, and something to do with violence, something to do with winning, and something to do with escaping. It had lasted through that chaotic day, the day when Jim crashed and burned, when Lily reverted to me, when Harry told me about him and Janie, when Ben Cooper was carried off by the long arm of the law. It had taken me a while to burn it off. I felt something of the echo of it today.

Eddie was alive. My enemy lives. My enemy is tormenting me not from beyond the grave but merely from Cairo. My enemy will regret the day he was born.

The thing is, I'd had enough.

Sa'id almost sniffed at me when I came in.

'What's happened?' he said.

It's not that I didn't want to tell him. But I couldn't. Or could I? He didn't know who Eddie was. I could give him another name, another story . . . but I would be lying, and he would be able to tell. But if I don't tell him, I am still lying, and he will certainly be able to tell.

So. Literal truth or emotional truth?

And if I tell him, aren't I walking straight out and betraying Harry? The way things have been round me lately it wouldn't be surprising if Sa'id turned out to be either a major Cairene gangster, who has sought me out specifically to track Eddie down, or the chief of the Egyptian secret police, or God knows what.

God, that would explain why they suddenly turned up out of the blue. On my doorstep when they must have others they could go to. Why didn't they go to a hotel?

Do I really think that?

It would be no weirder than a lot of what's happened.

I went through to the kitchen and looked at him.

'Sa'id, why did you come to my house?'

He knew I wasn't talking about the romantic reason he had given me before.

'To find Hakim,' he said.

'Why did he come here?'

He paused a moment. 'For help to find his mother.'

Well. Yeah. That sounded all right.

'How did you know he was with us?'

He smiled. 'He sent us a postcard. Saying he had seen you.'

I liked the way he didn't mind my questions.

'Are you a policeman, Sa'id?'

He fixed me with the pale eyes.

'No,' he said.

'Are you a criminal?'

'No,' he said. 'Are you?'

'But you're not surprised that I ask.'

'I see that you have a mystery in hand, and you can't tell me.'

'Do you mind me not telling you?'

'Tell me if you are in danger.'

'Maybe.'

'Maybe you are, or maybe you will tell me?'

'Maybe I am.'

'Will the danger be in Cairo?'

I have no reason not to trust him. Except he did search my desk.

'Why did you search my desk?'

'I was looking for anything about Hakim. I should have asked but you weren't here. I'm sorry. I didn't know you had noticed. Do you think I am the danger?'

'No.' And I didn't. But it's not just me involved here.

It was unsatisfactory. He didn't know enough about my past to hear the whole story. And I couldn't tell him. There was so much behind it. I didn't want to go over it all, and there were things I didn't want to tell him anyway, even if I could do so without compromising Harry. Things like how I had killed Eddie (the first time). That sort of thing. Because if he knew he might not love me any more. It's that simple. Luckily I didn't have to think about that, or about whether he loved me anyway, because I couldn't betray Harry and that was that.

Haha! I hadn't killed Eddie! Well that was a comfort. In a way.

I went to call Harry.

'Does Chrissie know?' I asked. He was on his mobile, in a cab.

'Nobody knows,' he said.

'So how do you know?'

'I'll tell you later.'

'Why don't you ride the Duke any more?'

He laughed. 'Why d'you think? The electrics are fucked. I'm sorting it out.'

'When?'

'Spare time, girl, as if I had any.'

'Where?'

'Kitchen table, of course.'

'OK,' I said.

I went back to Sa'id.

'Still coming to Cairo?' he said.

'Yes,' I said. 'That's not what this is about. I mean, it's not about him.'

'OK.'

'You'll have to help me,' I said.

'Of course,' he said. Then: 'If there is danger for you in Cairo, you must tell me. I respect you. Your reasons. But I can protect you. Don't prevent me from doing so. Don't shame me.'

When I came in with Lily after school the phone was ringing and Sa'id was answering it. Lily went into the kitchen for milk.

'Eddie,' he said, passing it over. I took it, frozen, and held it in mid-air. Four hours ago I would have thought it a trick of Chrissie's. I didn't know what to do.

His voice came from a series of distances.

'Evangeline!' he was crying, with high enthusiasm. 'There you are! My little honeybunch! Let me hear your voice!'

Frozen.

'Now who's the dago? You don't need to wipe your arse on that kind of thing. Speak to me darling. Are you coming? Are you coming? Or shall I come and get you?'

I hung up slowly.

Sa'id's clear eyes were on me.

I unplugged the answering machine after that, and didn't answer the phone. Every time it stopped ringing I 1471ed. Sometimes it was the 'unobtainable' of a foreign number.

He knows I know he's alive. He doesn't care that I know. He thinks I will come and get that money, knowing that he will be around. He's acting like we're going on holiday together. After everything.

Sa'id was superb. I couldn't tell him. He knew, and didn't

make me. Just held me, in his arms, in his gaze. And they say only Allah is perfect.

Harry came round on Thursday. It was my idea. He and Sa'id shook hands, then Harry and I went back to the Winfield and yes, Sa'id babysat. It was OK. I liked it.

We sat in the same darkened corner, darkened further by Liam's disapproval. I had to go and have a word with him. 'Liam,' I said, 'Harry's a nice man. You don't need to worry.'

He laughed hollowly. Ever since he had sent his copper friend round to Eddie's to check on me, and Harry had been there, he's had a bigger down on Harry and a bigger air of concerned disapproval for me. The thing being, Liam thinks Harry is a villain. Most people do. Because he sort of used to be. That's his cover. Very good cover too.

Liam drank a glass of milk, and told me affectionately to sod off back to him then and not blame him if it all came to a terrible end. I promised I wouldn't.

'Talk me through it,' I said to Harry. 'Tell me everything.'

'What are you going to do?' he asked.

'I don't know yet. You must help me.'

'Don't go,' he said.

'Talk me through it.'

He told me that it was very simple. He told me that in the course of his interrogations Eddie had offered to deal, and that the powers that be, having satisfied themselves as to the quality of what he was offering, had agreed to it; that he had been tried and convicted and imprisoned by a system which had no idea of what was going on behind the scenes; that the 'illness' had been a preparation for his 'death'; the clout by the old enemy a mere handy coincidence. He told me he didn't know that much about it. He said he wasn't meant to know about it, but that he had a mentor on the RQZ, or PST, or something (half police business seems to be in acronyms; it's impossible to follow) to whom he had spoken about me, and my experience of Eddie, and this mentor had told him what had happened. Because the mentor, personally, had some doubts about dealing with Eddie of all people in this way, and that Harry, as a significant officer in the case, had a right to know, and particularly because of me. I was gratified. To know that someone somewhere gave a fuck.

'Do you think it was a wise thing to do?' I asked him.

'What?'

'Deal with Eddie that way.'

'No,' he said. 'I think it was mad. But nobody cares what I think. And anyway, officially I don't know. And if anybody knew I knew then I'd get' – here he gestured a silence – 'into trouble. And blow the project.'

'But the project's aim is to protect Eddie,' I observed.

'Yes.'

'And you don't give a shit about Eddie. You'd happily see him rot.'

'Yes.'

'So why protect the project?'

He was silent a moment.

'It's my job,' he said, then before I could pull his hair out he said, 'No, listen. I have to respect my job. I have to keep my cover, and ours, and my colleagues'. Don't I?'

This was a macho boy teamwork thing – all the stuff I don't get. But I know it exists, and there's not much you can do about it. For some people it matters. I hadn't thought Harry was one. Had him down as more the maverick.

'It's just loyalty, Angel,' he said.

'So why does anybody else want to protect Eddie?'

'He's their investment.'

I didn't see that.

'You don't grass your grass, because then nobody will ever grass to you again.'

'But nobody even knows he's alive! How would any potential future top villain witness protection scheme candidates ever know what had happened? It's ridiculous, Harry, the whole thing. They should just have killed him anyway.'

'That's not allowed, sweetheart.'

No. It's not.

Silence sat on us for a while.

'So how can I do it, Harry?'

'Do what?'

'You know.'

'Get him?'

'Yeah. Get him.' Get him. Win.

Stop him. That's all.

'I don't know,' he said.

'Well think of something. Talk me through it.'

In the end I talked him through it. I'd go and pick up the money. He'd find me.

'Is he allowed back in Britain?' I asked.

'No,' he said. 'Not that that would necessarily stop him.'

True.

'Don't go,' said Harry. 'What can you do? It's what he wants you to do. You're letting him win, reacting to his blackmail.'

'No,' I said. 'I'm doing what I would be doing anyway. I wouldn't go just to get the money . . .' As I said it I knew I would. The BNP, with their disgusting little stickers and their disgusting little minds, could do a lot with £100,000. Thinking of my neighbourhood and my friends, of peeling off and scrubbing out the ignorance and hatred that appears from time to time – not too often, they know our soil is not fertile for them here – on our walls and bus-stops. Thinking of Stephen Lawrence, and the war. Thinking not just of the pain and damage they cause to Blacks and Jews, but the outrage they cause to me, and to any halfway decent person, simply by being, and being so pathetic and poisonous . . . No, Eddie had me there. Having the power to stop them getting money, I would. So he wins that one. But he won't win in the end because I am going to. I just don't know how.

'Why do you have to win, Angel?'

He knew why.

'Because I'm proud,' I said.

'Not enough,' he replied.

'Because he's threatening me.'

'Ignore it. It might go away. If not reconsider, deal with it later.'

'Because he knows my weaknesses.'

He looked a query.

'Because he started in about Lily. Saying he might be her father. It was bad enough posthumously, but what if he makes anything of that now?'

'Legally he doesn't exist,' said Harry. 'He won't exactly be applying for parental responsibility. Dead men don't get custody.'

'I'm not in the least bit worried about anything legal he might do. Legal isn't really the problem here, is it?'

'Nope.'

He sighed. He felt guilty. Poor sod.

'I'll have a word with . . .' He paused. I supposed he meant the mentor. He couldn't even tell me the guy's name. 'You never know.'

'Never know what?'

'I don't know,' he said.

'Nor do I.'

'Don't go,' he said.

But I had to. It didn't matter about anybody else. I knew that I had to get him. It was just between him and me, really. I was more scared of him than of anything in my life, but I wasn't scared, too. Or either.

twenty

Cairo

Our flight was on Friday morning, changing at Athens. It was another beautiful golden eternal Indian summer day. Every time you thought winter drab might finally set in, it dispersed again and that old and melting October sun came on through again. Seemed like autumn would never end.

We left for the airport in shiny early morning silence, astounded by the secret life of the city, the clean quiet calm of 5.30 a.m. We seemed to be 'we'. How had that happened, I wondered. Turn your back for two seconds and the habits of a lifetime curdle. Sharing reactions. Except that there I was, suddenly, hurtlingly lonely for Lily, and Sa'id was not. And suddenly nervous. Scared, even. Not of Eddie – not yet. Of being apart from my beloved. No small hands. No ridiculously charming comments. No being patted absent-mindedly. None of the little love representations to which I was so accustomed.

The plane was called Neoptolemus. The journey was long. All that time to be doing nothing; suspended in inability to affect or move on or do anything. The very voyage was like traction; like those weeks in hospital with my shattered leg up and pinned, immobilised, on drugs, in pain, plotting how to make sure we kept Lily. Heathrow, check-in, wonder, coffee, boarding, waiting, sitting, dozing, eating, landing, waiting, air-conditioning, musak, coffee, transfer, boarding, welcome aboard, seat belt, no smoking, sitting, crunching joints, sleeping, waking. Absolutely nothing you can do. Sometimes I find it relaxing.

Sa'id was quiet. I watched his face as he dozed. Watched as he happily took his copy of *Al Ahram* on the plane. This is an Arab man returning to his homeland, where he will be different to how he has been with me, in mine. So then I had another sudden flurry of fear. Not for him, nor of him, but of Egypt. What do I know about this country I am so attached to? It's been what, eight, nine years? What am I doing? Who is this man and where is my child?

But I know the answers to all this. What I don't know is what is going to happen.

I had booked myself into the Hussein, a hotel whose small-scale faded grandeur and balconies made it an English-woman's dream. Also it was well away from Downtown, where Eddie would be waiting for me. Also it was in the gate to Khan el-Khalili, where I could get lost like nowhere else in the world. Sa'id was not booked in with me. He was to stay at his aunt's in Garden City, officially, though of course he would not. He didn't want me to stay at the Hussein – said there were fleas, it was too old and dirty. I wondered if it was now. In my day it had had bell boys in clean darned uniforms, soft with age, all of whom would arrive together to change a light bulb, and an old old man who would fold the towels into a different shape every day: Monday a lotus, Tuesday an ibis, Wednesday a papyrus flower, Thursday a palm. Sa'id wanted me to go to the Sheraton or the Nile Hilton. I could understand why, up to a point, but it had made me sad, because I had grown accustomed to his understanding everything, including things he had no business understanding. Woman things. English things. Then I said, 'Why do you want me to stay at the Hilton?' and he looked a little puzzled for a second, and then he laughed and said, 'I don't. It is automatic. What we say to visitors. I am just saying what my aunts used to say.' So I was happy with him again. Though a little sad to be a visitor. But then I am. So.

When we finally spewed out into the air terminal there was the sign saying that drug smugglers were liable to death by hanging over and above a fine of 500,000 Egyptian pounds. Which I read as hanging over and above a fire ... which I thought, in the second before I self-corrected, was going it a bit. And there was the bit saying they hoped this warning will be needed, or heeded, and someone had added in a not, because the top of the h's downstroke had been worn off (or was it an n all along?)

And we were there, and it all unfolded out over me, and I was so pleased to breathe that air and sense that city that I nearly hugged Sa'id, before remembering that actually, no, I shouldn't. Because now we are in another land. This other land. So other, and yet so familiar.

The other travellers were greeted by relatives and small children and bunches of slightly dilapidated gladioli; we were not. The el Arabys are not like other families. I wasn't sorry. Others had family cars waiting; we found a black and white Cairo taxi, fake fur dash and Hassan el Asmar blaring on the stereo. There were so many things I had forgotten about Cairo. Not the smell – or at least I thought I hadn't, but when it came over me, fragrant with apple and honey and shimmered through with dust, I realised I hadn't remembered it at all.

Midan el Hussein. The sparse palms of the wide and formal square, looking pristine today like an illustration from a Babar book; the clean walls of the mosque of the prophet's grandson, for whom the square is named; the inlaid tambourines hanging from the shop ceilings, the outside ceilings, because what is inside and what is out is different here. Those damn beige leather toy camels. The neon green gleaming through the lattices on the minarets. Remembering how scared I was the first time I arrived here, and spent two days on the balcony watching a tiny girl I nicknamed the Princess, in a grimy garnet-coloured satin frock, with a frill, and grey track-suit trousers underneath, playing with a plastic bag while her mother sold paper handkerchiefs. First it was a hat (which worried me), then it was a doll, then a football, then a balloon, then home to two small stones, then a sledge (which gained her a companion, who pulled and was pulled), then forgotten as a young boy with a pink football appeared. I looked for her now. She must be fourteen, and probably long gone from here. Though where would she go?

I had what might have been the same room, and I sat on what might have been the same balcony smoking a Cleopatra (I had forgotten that I smoked in Cairo) and looked out over what might have been the same soap opera: a biggish boy with a piece of rope is hitting out at a smaller boy, who lies down in the middle of the street and yells, making a huge drama and bellowing. No one takes any notice. The bigger boy hides the rope, just in case. The smaller boy jumps up and runs and gets it, chases the bigger boy up Sharia el Moski. A few minutes later the bigger boy reappears, having won the rope back. The smaller boy, frustrated, steals a glass from a café table and stalks Bigger Boy. They circle each other, just two figures in the milling crowd, Smaller Boy (a coward) using a large lady in purple as a shield. A prosperous man in a silver suit remonstrates. Plump lady takes no notice whatso-ever. Café man requires the glass back, and after a little scuffling Bigger Boy (though something of a psycho) gives it back. The glass breaks; as Café Man chases Psycho across to the garden a passer-by picks up the shards of broken glass and puts them on a café table. A waiter appears and takes them in. Coward festoons himself across the wheels of the cigarette seller's small wagon, protected by the man's desire to protect his stock. Psycho glares from across the way and slowly, slowly, through the milling crowd, inches his way towards him.

A small girl who could well have been the princess is chasing a football; she is knocked down by a man in a white gallabeya and turban, riding a bicycle. Six or eight people gather; an orange-shirted one-legged man sitting on a skateboard swoops her up, cuddles her and crab-propels her on his board back to her mother, trapped under a baby and her wares on the kerbside. She sits with him, protected, as a policeman with a Kalashnikov tells off the cyclist, who proceeds on foot, pushing his bike, chastened.

A scampy girl of about seven, in ankle-length black and antimony, is stroking the Psycho, trying to get him to play. He is now five feet from the Coward, staring at him. The cigarette man takes no notice, though the coward is lying almost entangled in the paraphernalia of his wagon, his livelihood.

The princess substitute jumps up and runs to play; she kicks the ball under an otiose green railing that wanders across the square. A young policeman kicks it back. She is pleased, and passes it again and again to see if he will do it again. He does. It hits a fat man's belly. He ignores it. Princess chases it. Another man heads it. A beggar in blue with writing in a white patch on his back wanders, whirling, very very slowly, then suddenly picks up, focuses, touches four people for money in three minutes then disappears, presumably to get his dinner. A herd of fat-tailed sheep pass by, followed by a lime-green Mercedes. The cowardly boy gives the psycho money. Is he paying him off? Or had he stolen it in the first place?

What had I forgotten? I hadn't forgotten a damn thing. I felt the dust settle into my hair, and began to laugh when the evening muezzins started up from both al-Hussein and al-Azhar just across the main road, rivals as ever with the most beautiful voices. I hadn't forgotten the names of the times of day when you pray: *Fajr Sobh Zohr. . . A'sr. . . Maghrib* and *Isha*. I hadn't forgotten the period during which an appallingly tuneless muezzin had arrived at al-Hussein, and everybody said he was someone's son-in-law and couldn't be sacked . . . but he was, in the end. I hadn't forgotten Ahmed el Gentil who ran the el Halwagy coffee shop round the corner, so called because he was kind to everybody, so he said, and who claimed to know everything in the whole world. I hadn't forgotten how your snot goes black within hours of arrival, how the last of the mameluks leapt from the walls of the citadel on his horse. Nor the constant encouragement from young men in the street that you should 'walk like an Egyptian' – directly through the wild and gloriously sociable traffic. Beep beep. I'm coming through beep beep no you're not beep beep oh yes I am beep beep oh OK then beep beep *shukran* thank you beep beep *afwan* you're welcome beep beep what? Oh nothing I'm just beeping along to the music on my radio. Beep.

Nor had I forgotten what I was here for.

That first night I just wanted to go out. I wanted to get the city inside me, soak up some dust, some heat, start to merge. Newness in town is visible. But soon the dust (not fluffy dust, soft flakes of old human skin – we're talking grains of desert, hard, fine, creeping, insidious and insinuating) settles into your skin and you no longer look shiny and new, and you no longer get the scampy behaviour that tourists find so irritating, or overwhelming, or just odd. People talking to you, that kind of thing. And if you do, you can take it on to another level of playfulness. So we unpacked and showered and fucked and ate felafel sandwiches, then about one in the morning set off under the burnt orange night to the Paradise, on the Pyramids Road. This was where I was first showered with rose petals while I danced, so I have a soft spot for it. The odd visitor who finds it thinks the vases of half dead roses on the tables are a sign of it being a third-rate dump (which it is, in a way, but that's not why), but that is because *they don't understand*. The roses are half dead because they are all going to end up scattered over the dance floor, along with little waxy jasmine flowers pulled from garlands, and cash, of course. And let me tell you it is a glorious feeling when those ten and twenty pound notes flutter over your head and settle momentarily on your shoulders, your damp bare arms, swirling round you like doves at harvest time before the pick-up man dives in to grab them and stuff them in the box to be shared with the musicians after the gig.

I almost cried when we walked in. Same bilious green carpeting on the walls, same star-shaped mirrors and burgundy table cloths, with no doubt the same cigarette burn-holes in them. Same boxes of paper handkerchiefs with the handkerchiefs carefully taken out and folded into triangles and tucked back in in a fan-shape, interleaved with withering rose-buds. Same men in suits doing the high-stepping straight-backed stampy dance, with the arms punching upwards and forwards, rolling kind of like a cowboy with a lasso, the unmistakable and delicious dance of Cairene nightclub man, audience variety. Same long boat-shaped fruit plates, covered in silver foil which tweaked up grandly at each end like Cleopatra's barge – the barge she sat in was of aluminium foil. Same fug of *shisha*, same green-jacketed waiters (far too many), same withered parsley under the kofta that we used to swear went round every table in turn and came out again the next night. Same Saudi, sitting on his own, gobbling with his eyes. Same girls in shiny shiny tights and tiny tiny skirts. Same waddling boilers on stage, not even dancing, not even pretending to, just shuffling inelegantly in four-inch heels, malfitting underwear and skin-tight stretch emerald and puce latex velveteen, with matching anklet, with diamante bow. They come free with the male singers – the worse he is, the more of them he feels obliged to lay on.

But they soon went off, and evidently we were just about late enough because the next act was better – a girl in a tight baladi dress seemingly based on Tutankhamun (gold and turquoise, with a lot of cutaways), who had a lot of personality if not much in the way of moves, and four crap boy dancers in high-waisted trousers and pink lurex boleros. I've never understood about the boy dancers. Four of them prance about, often enough counting under their breath – *wahid, itnein, telata, arbah* – and never letting one movement flow into another. They have a kind of facile elegance, but they never stretch, never burn. They should all be sent to see the Sufis at al-Ghouri, then sent home to weep for twenty years.

Then came an excellent band – four tablas, two violins, *oudh, ney, quanoun*, three tambours of various kinds, saxophone, accordion and *no electric keyboard*. They played mainly that wild Sudanese rhythm which just kills me – boomboom, boom boom BAH – oh God, it doesn't translate. But it got me, as it always did. Fuck the leg. I was up there soon enough on stage (this is normal, it's what happens at Egyptian nightclubs. Everyone gets up and joins in the show. Don't think I was being really embarrassing). Boomboom, boom boom FLICK, boomboom, boom boom TOSS, boomboom boom boom THWACK. Sa'id, God bless him, was charitable. I think. The audience were – oh lord, an Egyptian audience. As always. Up on stage joining in, calling the singer over for a chat, taking over the mike to sing. A new voice came on while I was dancing, halfway through a song I adore – I never knew who wrote it, but everybody used to sing it, just another haunting love song, *habibi* this and *habibi* that, gorgeous. I looked up from my entranced state and saw Sa'id, my own *habibi*, mike in his long brown hand, eyelids lowered and singing like a fucking angel. His mouth moving round the words of his own language, his other hand, cigarette between his fingers, making the formalised little rolling, beckoning movements that singers in that language so often make. The men. Sa'id doing it. Doing it well. They wouldn't have let him have the mike if they didn't know he could. He must be a regular or something. When I used to dance here he was fifteen.

His hands fall from his wrists like lilies. The veins, the strength. If a lily could smoke suggestively, that's what my baby's like.

I shimmied over to the table, and took the heads off all our roses, and shredded them, and poured them over his head like love. He laughed through his song and didn't miss a beat, and later putting down the mike he found his wallet and took out a pile of notes and, standing up beside me now on the stage, flicked them over me. Swiftly, neatly, compactly. Some men throw them on the floor – huzzah! Some hurl them in the air. Some try to stick them down your clothing. He showered them on me like kisses down my spine. They hovered around us a moment, fluttering in slow motion in the shifting shafts of red and yellow light, and the dusty drifting *shisha* smoke. And we stood there, covered in money and love and roses, just before dawn, under the revolving disco mirror ball, suspended, sacred, blessed, surrounded by whores and fools and musicians, for all of twenty seconds before the pick-up boy swooped in.

Around six we left, under the low burning ball of the risen sun, and slung back into town, picking up some *belila* (*omali* with wheat instead of bread – same effect) from the stall on Sharia Faisel, passing the lions that could be cousins to the ones in Trafalgar Square on the Kasr el Nil bridge, humming

Sudanese melodies. The boys were already throwing down water against the dust of the new day. Stands were rattling and the wild dogs were running back to the desert. Then he sang 'Enta 'Omri' – You are My Life, an Umm Kalthoum song. You are my life; its morning began with your light. Before you my heart saw no joy, no taste in the world but the taste of wounds . . . I have only now started to love my life, only now started to fear that life will hurry on. In the light of your eyes, each joy my imagination had desired has met my heart and my mind . . . A song of redemption through love. He knew all the words. The muezzin started up the *sobh* as we flew up on to the flyover leading down on to Sharia al Azhar and the old city, and the minarets glowed gold in the dawn just for us. And the *hillel* moon was up and gleaming silver in the west, and it was too fucking perfect for words.

I woke at midday to a note saying he'd gone to see about some things; he'd see me at Fishawy's at four. That was fine, because even without last night's excesses I wanted to clear my head. This was a crazy idea. Cairo is not a head-clearing city. Reaching a different plane, maybe. But not clearing your head as it is generally understood.

I decided I would go to Ibn Tulun, and I would climb the minaret, and I would walk round and round its stone topknot in my bare feet, smoking cigarettes, until some resolution to my situation emerged. So I did.

Except I didn't smoke. Because you can't, really, at a mosque.

First the taxi driver didn't want to take me, saying I would prefer to go to the Pyramids, Giza, Memphis and Saqqara on a day trip, very good price; then he asked for twenty pounds, then he took me all round the houses, then he wanted to wait for me and take me on to another half-dozen places I didn't want to go to. Then the young boy in charge of the key to

the door that led to the minaret told me he went to Qur'anic
school, asked did I want him to sing the call to prayer and
the Qur'an to me (What, all of it? I was tempted), told me I
shouldn't wear lipstick, asked for one caramella, one face
cream from my bag for his sister and then wanted to kiss me,
offering various parts of himself: lips, cheek, forehead, chin,
hand, nose, and finally neck.

'Go away,' I said. 'This is a holy place.' He leapt. My
respect for the mosque meant his disrespect for me had been
much worse. He was embarrassed.

These things used to happen to me in my first week here;
not since. And not at a mosque, anyway! Things have
changed, evidently. And evidently I was not dusted through,
not quite invisible yet. But soon enough the boys crying 'welcome' on every street corner would start to cry 'I know, you
live here, don't want T-shirt' instead.

So I sent him away, and trod the great external staircase
which encircles the minaret like a helter skelter, up to the
topknot, where I started my circles up in the sky, sun hot on
my back, stone cool beneath my feet in the shade, hot in the
glare, pigeons glinting in the cloud-latticed sky just like I
knew they would, the dome of the fountain huge and solid
at the centre of the great wide courtyard way below me, wide
enough for Ibn Tulun to keep his armies in, and the arcades
shady and mysterious around the edge. And I walked, and I
walked, and I didn't smoke, and I walked, and I looked across
at the great ugly Turkish-looking mosque of Muhammed Ali
up on the citadel hill, with the sandy ridges of the desert
behind, every ridge echoing the shape and angles of a sphinx's
head, and looked away towards the Cities of the Dead, and
over to the domes and minarets of the mosques of Sheiku,
and Sultan Hassan, and Ar-Rif'ai and Aqsunqur, and as far
as the great gate Bab Zuweila (the Fab Bab, Nadia used to
call it). And yes, as Sa'id had told me, some of them were

missing. I tried to recall what was then, what was now; to picture this fabulous skyline then. I saw the loss, but the specifics were not with me. My mind addled trying to make it out, and I looked down to soothe myself, down on to the roofs filled with rubbish, satellite dishes, broken ladders, from biblical mud-walled terrace to biblical mud-walled terrace, skinny dust-coloured cats negotiating narrow dust-coloured walls, and way over in the distance I could see the great pyramid at Giza black and mysterious compared to the endless sand-and-dust colours of the city, and beneath my feet I saw the ancient, smooth, cracked and settled, smoothed and worn, earthquake-surviving eleven-hundred-year-old stones, and way off below I saw the crenellations of the wide dusty pink roof of the arcades of Ibn Tulun, like a row of soldiers, of cut-out paper men carved in stone, holding hands eternally all round the playground of the roof. I wasn't going to go and look at them any closer. Patterns against patterns: you move, the distant objects visible through the ranks of men move, the ranks are still but the patterns shift against each other. That which should be motionless doesn't seem to be. Everything double, all the time. And down inside the mosque itself, you can sit for days watching how the light falls through the windows, how it shifts, what it casts, how the patterns lie, and creep, and change. You can. People do. The sunlight by day and the moonlight by night. It can make you nervous. This is why today I had chosen the top of the minaret, way above all mysteries, crowning them.

And I circled, and I circled, and I circled, and I saw no solution except killing him. And as I was not going to do that, I was fucked.

So there is no avoiding the next thing. Collecting the money. Which I don't want to do yet. Because then he will know I am here, and whatever is to happen will start to happen. And I don't want it to, because I am scared.

So I am still in traction. Not physical traction, not voyage traction. Mental traction. Fear traction.

So get out of it. Get over it. You're not here on holiday. You're not going to Aswan to float about in a felucca under mimosa trees. You're here for this.

I met Sa'id at Fishawy's on the edge of the great market Khan el-Khalili. He was there before me, trying to keep English time for me; I was assuming he'd be running on Egyptian time. He sat in the narrow alley among the wooden screens and ancient freckled mirrors, while the posh end of the bazaar carried on around him. It was still pretty hot and the mediaeval shade of the high walls of the old city's narrow alleys was welcome. For a moment I wondered whether I should go to any well-known place, any place where Europeans go. Perhaps I should bury myself in . . . no. I'm here to do it.

I watched him for a while before joining him; just admiring, you know. He was wearing his enormous white scarf, and smoking *shisha*. His skin had picked up already, as southern skin does on home ground. It was darker, richer. Polished or burnished or something like that. When he turned to look for me and saw me, his pale turquoise eyes appearing from the shadow of dark wood and latticed stone, his curling mouth unsmiling in civilised ancient shadows, his lean back straight among the looping shapes of the *shishas*, for a moment I was amazed to think this man and I even knew each other. Other. We are other. But then we are all other.

It was just a little shock of how exactly at home he was, and I wasn't, despite the old days.

We exchanged all the small courtesies required when you try to sit in a space where there are already four long-legged skinny metal tables, four men, three *shishas*, a waiter, a boy with a ladle of hot charcoal and long tongs, and a huge palm in a brass pot. *Malesh, esfa, malesh, shukran*, as you step on their feet and knock their drinks over. Patches of afternoon sun fell through the gaps in the awning, the *shishas* bubbled gently around us, a soft and constant bubbling mingling with the burble of the market, conversations in French and English and Arabic, the sound of the *oud* and the *ney* from someone's radio a little way away. Walking in this city it is impossible not to dance. There's always a rhythm seeping out from some-where. This week I kept hearing Khaled, the Algerian who used to be Cheb Khaled, but Cheb means Young Man and he's not so young any more. The song was 'Aïcha', in Arabic and French, a love song to a girl in the street, comparing her to the Queen of Sheba. Reine de Sabaa. A perfect song.

We ordered coffee, thick and black and rich. We both take it *ariha*: on the smell. Just the scent of sugar. Sweet, but not too sweet.

'Like you,' he said. And cracked up laughing.

'You tourist boy,' I said. 'You flirt.'

He curled his tongue up to his upper lip and grinned at me. 'Why,' he said. 'Do you want to visit my shop?'

'Do you have a shop?'

'Of course,' he said. 'Every Egyptian has a shop. Or a brother with a shop. I can take you to Uncle Sharif's shop. You know what Sharif means? Noble. So you see we will make you a very nice price.'

'Nice price for you or nice price for me?'

'Nice for you is nice for me, you tell your friends and everybody will come to Uncle Sharif's shop . . .'

It was very disconcerting to see him play the salesman, the trader trying to call you, to sell you Tutankhamun T-shirts and little models of the sphinx set in clear plastic pyramids. Everybody does it: the men with their trollies of gas canisters, rattling them with sticks; the shoe cleaners, the loofah men. You make your noise to get your business. Rattle your adver-tising.

He was teasing me, but I didn't like it.

'Do you do this?' I asked. 'I mean, is this what you do?'

'No. I have boys to do it for me. But if I am on the street and the girl is beautiful. Sorry, was. Then I would. Of course.'

Suddenly in this context we were something else. 'Don't,' I said. 'It's making us sound like some . . . we're not some pick-up romance. Just because I'm . . . and you're . . .'

'*Elli shuftu abl ma teshoufak enaya,*' he said. What I saw before my eyes saw you. A line from 'Enta 'Omri'.

Then 'Do you mind?' he said.

'Mind what?'

'That I am an Arab man and you are an Englishwoman?'

'No,' I said. 'I am enchanted by it.'

'Ah,' he said. 'Enchanted.'

'Yes,' I said, fully aware of how Europe has always been enchanted by the East, and how it has invented its own East to be enchanted by, and pinned it down, invaded it, exploited it, colonised it, declared superiority over it, patronised it.

'Tell me,' he said, reading my mind again. 'Have you read Edward Sa'id?'

I knew he was talking about *Orientalism*.

'Yes,' I said.

'I thought you would have,' he murmured.

'Is that a problem? Do you think I am orientalising you?'

'No,' he said. 'I just wondered.'

'Anyway,' I said. 'You're English as well.'

He just laughed. 'No I'm not,' he said.

The patterns on patterns were closing in around me again. Everything about the man and the city fills me with desire and I am not permitted to touch him. I hated the idea that someone looking at us might think we were anything other than pure and perfect lovers. I who don't give a shit what other people think of me. Perhaps it was that I didn't want them thinking it (what?) of him. I didn't want them thinking he was a street boy who'd struck lucky. Or that he was with some old white sex tourist. (I am older than him.) Or that there was any kind of orientalising going on.

Oh really. Send those thoughts away.

'Have you seen Hakim?' I asked. Just to move on. I did realise that I had one great big subject to broach with him. Eddie. I didn't know what to say to him about it. I didn't know where to start. I knew I must. Didn't know how to say it. So I continued to cancel that drama with another.

'He is here,' said Sa'id. 'With the mother. I don't know where she is staying. My father is very upset – angry because Hakim is being very stupid, not so much because of her. He was stupid in London, now he is being stupid here. He is testing his strength, you know. Young man behaviour. Little brother. He wants to lock his horns with everybody and be his own man, but he has no judgement. He won't listen.'

'Have you talked to him?'

'He knows better. He knows best. Knows everything. He has these new friends here and wants to make his own business. So this is what he must do. I told my father, let him do it, let him make his mistakes. But my father is upset too about the mother, but puts it all in the same hat and doesn't know which thing is upsetting him ... and how are you, *habibti*?'

'Poor Abu Sa'id,' I murmured, but, 'No, poor Angelina,' he said, and took my hand, and held it very carefully for a moment before giving it back. But I still didn't tell him.

'Angelina,' he said.

No names, no details, I thought. I am alone here.

'*Habibti*?'

'The thing is this,' I said to him. He didn't take his eyes off me. 'There is someone here, in Cairo.'

I found myself almost gagging. Where is the madness?

Where is my courage? Where is my heart? 'My enemy. He means me harm.'

He turned to concentrate on the *shisha*, stirring up the coals. When he had it glowing again he turned to me, looking at me over the mouthpiece. It is an unbearably thoughtful attitude.

'It's the one – he came back from the dead. The one who was dead. Isn't.' I now had to think on my feet, sort my truths from my half-truths. Sa'id just carried on smoking. 'You spoke to him on the phone. He let me think he was dead. One of his tricks. He plays tricks. Once he kidnapped me. He has threatened me.'

Still no reaction.

'He threatens me with love. He thinks I should be his – he believes that I am, and only my own bad judgement is keeping us from eternal happiness.' I think that's it. Something like that. He wants to fuck me and fuck me over; I want to kill him. That's about right.

'Egyptian man?' he said.

'English.'

'Living in Cairo?'

'Yes.'

'Since when?'

'Only a month or so.'

'His name?'

I couldn't tell him. I couldn't. Before, I couldn't because it would be betraying Harry. Now, I didn't know.

'Not mine to reveal,' I said. Hurting inside at what he must be thinking, that I don't trust him.

'What do you mean?'

'I don't know,' I said. 'I mean – I don't know his name. He had a different name when I knew him before.' It was true. Harry hadn't been able to tell me the new name – he didn't know it himself. He would, he had said, try to find out. He hadn't held out much hope. I suspected that he would much have preferred to get me picked up and deported for my own safety. Or guarded, or followed. Perhaps Interpol are watching as we speak. I suspected that he thought I would hate him, hate him if he tried to stop me. Perhaps I wished he had risked that.

'Eddie,' said Sa'id. 'I wondered.' Of course he hadn't forgotten. Then, 'You are asking a lot of trust,' he said, and I was, and I wasn't giving him any.

'I know,' I said. 'I know.'

But he still didn't push it. How long can I rest on his patience? It seems endless.

'Tomorrow,' I said, 'it will begin. Tomorrow I am going to set it off. He will know tomorrow that I am here. I am to go to Banque Misr at the Nile Hilton to pick something up and . . .'

He raised one of his elegant eyebrows.

'Money,' I said. Oh fuck. 'Lots of money.'

He raised the other.

'Oh. Oh.' I put my knuckle on my forehead and prayed for grace. 'He said, if I didn't pick up this lots of money he would give it to a bunch of fascist, racist – you know. Far right bastards. Murder immigrants, beat up refugees, those people. You know.'

He knew. He laughed. For a moment I was afraid. But it was only admiration.

'Clever man,' he said. 'Very clever.'

'Yes,' I said.

'Eh,' said Sa'id, with a kind of shrug. 'Brains versus virtue. Good fight.'

'Sa'id,' I murmured. 'Please.' We were talking quietly anyway but our voices grew lower and lower.

'It is good to know what you are fighting,' he said. And of course that's true too.

'But his brain is – what we might loosely call mad. He

continues to trust me and expect things from me though I hate him, I've told him so, I've hit him over the head with a poker . . .'

'Why?' said Sa'id.

'He was trying to . . .' My stop was abrupt. Not a nice girl not wanting to utter words of shame, but a girl all too aware of her own shortcomings. I don't want to talk about this because I don't want to lie about it and I cannot tell the whole truth. I can't tell Sa'id that. For all our deep pure and human sexual communion; for all the curious things we've cried to each other at moments of intensity. I don't want him to know I did that.

But he thought he understood, and muttered something deeply admiring in Arabic, to do no doubt with virtue and honour and a good woman being above rubies, or some such, and I felt filthy. Looked in his beautiful eyes and felt filthy. Because of the lie. Because of not trusting him to understand, not giving him the choice, not not not.

But if I don't give him the opportunity to . . . this is not going anywhere if I don't.

Look what happened with Harry, when we didn't tell each other.

I could tell Sa'id about how my designated driver had left me alone and drunk in the car, in the middle of traffic, because that was not my fault. I could tell him how seeking to avoid incrimination (because of the upcoming custody case with Jim) I had ended up beholden to Ben Cooper, who had set me to spy on Eddie, because although I did wrong I did it for the best of reasons. I could tell him about Janie. I wanted to tell him all that, fill in for him all the gaps in his knowledge of my sorrows and dramas. And I would tell him. But I cannot tell him that I fucked Eddie, because I don't forgive myself that, and I cannot imagine anyone else forgiving me.

And I can't say anything that might betray Harry, because

if Harry and I can't trust each other by now, after all the crap we've been through, what's the point? Well, Harry and I do trust each other. I know that.

And if Sa'id and I can't trust each other?

Oh God, not now. We are here now and this immediate problem must be dealt with now. And later I will see where that leaves us.

'So you want men to be with you,' Sa'id was saying. 'Invisible men. All the time.'

'No,' I started to say, and then thought better of it and said, 'Yes.' Because I realised at that moment that he could arrange this. And I was glad. Oh yes I fucking was. He plucked a mobile phone out of his side pocket and dialled, and spoke – fast and guttural and quiet, I couldn't follow – and said, '*Tammam.*' OK. Done.

'Gosh,' I said, though it wasn't quite as sinister and impressive as it would be at home, because here any man of any stature has a number of other men who will do things for him. Ask someone for a light and he'll send a small boy to buy you a lighter. So it was just like that. Only a bit more so.

He made a small hands open and shoulder shrug gesture. The least you would do, under the circumstances. OK.

'Are you a big man, then, Sa'id?' I asked. I couldn't not. What with the singing last night, and now this – I want to know who my lover is, and who he is in relation to this city. 'Are you a big man?'

'Don't you know?' he said, with an exceptionally naughty grin, at which an image of the body wrapped up inside his scarf and his Arab dignity brought heat to my skin again. Never mind covering up the beautiful woman because of the chaos she causes to men, what about the chaos the beautiful men cause to us? Even covered?

He saw it, and it pleased him, and he accepted it with an

indulgent sideways look, and a murmured '*malesh*', never mind, and took me back to business.

'And then what?' he said.

Ah yes. That again.

I shook my unclear head. 'We'll see,' I said.

'You just take the money and go home?'

'Maybe,' I said.

A tiny and immutable silence sat between us for a second; a moment in which we might have started to talk about what happens afterwards – but we didn't. Later.

'Then next time he thinks of another trick,' continued Sa'id, as if the silence had never been.

'Maybe,' I said.

'And?'

'He's threatened Lily,' I said, and my heart returned to me. A phrase from the Book of the Dead spun across my mind: 'May my heart be with me in the house of hearts.' And something about my mouth, and my two legs that I may walk therewith, and my arms and hands that I might overthrow my foe. I saw myself like a Pharaoh on a temple wall, smiting Eddie, holding bunches of tiny enemies by the hair and smiting them. I knew it wouldn't be like that. And I said, 'Let's go and fetch it now, shall we?' And I was ready to.

He looked at me, and I swear there was love in his eyes. I've seen it once or twice and I know what it looks like.

'One moment,' he said, stopping me, sounding for a moment for all the world like the trader again. 'Where does he live?'

'I don't know. I thought maybe he would be at the Nile Hilton because he doesn't know when or if I am coming, so perhaps he would need to be near. Anyway, more likely downtown than round here.' Though why do I think that? What do I know about how that mad fool's brain works?

'What does he look like?'

'Mid-fifties. Handsome. Posh. Grey hair. Though what do I know, perhaps he looks completely different now.'

'Does he speak Arabic?'

'I don't know. I wouldn't put it past him.'

For once Sa'id failed to understand an English expression. I tried to explain it. Then a ferocious-looking gipsy woman in black appeared with a censer of burning frankincense which she proceeded to whirl in wild circles round first Sa'id's head (he bent it acceptingly) and then mine, jerking it shortly and viciously also towards my belly. No, I told her. Not belly. Heart. I gestured my heart to make it clear. She narrowed her eyes and relocated her blessing, or whatever it was. No doubt she thought I wanted a lover not a baby; I just wanted my heart to know I was glad it was back. I wasn't going to lose it again. It is easy to be lost in a land where there are no pictures of things, only patterns based on them. A land of interlocking patterns. I thanked her and gave her *baksheesh*, whereupon two small girls (one the antimony child from last night) appeared trying to sell me paper handkerchiefs, and we decided to leave.

Another phrase rose from the depths of my memory: 'In Egypt one does things on impulse, because there is no rain to make one reflect.'

We ambled on up towards the hotel, both thinking I think of having the last shag of peaceful times before we moved into the next stage, dealing with Eddie, and then, only then, dealing with ourselves and what we were going to be to each other. But even as we stepped up to the threshold, before we even entered the dark shabby hall, even over the Khan el-Khalili smells of felafel frying, and coffee, and perfume oils, and *shisha*, came the unmistakable death-sweet scent of tuberoses.

I hissed to Sa'id: 'Walk on. You don't know me. Stay near.' And cursed the fact that this street debouched into the square, with no alleys off before getting there. Should I go right down Sharia al-Muski? Or risk the open square and across on to the main road, and trust the crowd? I went right. I could hear Sa'id whistling behind me. 'Enta 'Omri'. God bless him. I dived down al-Muizz l'din Allah, then right again at the olive man and again at the packets of braid to trim your gallabeyas with (avoiding the oil drum and the family of scrawny cats) into the little network leading to Mahmoud's Fancy Dresses shop, everything for the belly dancer, which I hadn't visited since 1989 and wasn't going to visit now, but it was a part of the labyrinth with which I was familiar, and that was good enough for me.

Sa'id caught up with me in a dark piss-smelling corner under a piece of rope-bound wooden scaffolding holding up a crumbling wall.

'What?' he said.

'The flowers.'

I held on to him.

'What?'

'I smelt tuberoses. Did you smell them?'

He put me back from him a little and looked at me, holding my head carefully, a hand on each cheek.

'The hall of the hotel was full of tuberoses. That is the kind of thing he does. Just to . . . tweak my chain. Tell me how clever he is. He thinks it's romantic. Or claims to think so. He . . . ach.'

'So he knows where you stay.'

'Where I was staying,' I said.

We stood in silence a moment, a fool and her lover, hiding in the middle of the bloody bazaar.

'So we go somewhere else.'

'Yes.'

How the hell did he find me? He's only been here a month and already it seems he has picked up the oriental habit of omniscience. He's probably been handing out pictures. Probably half the musicians are in his pay. Fool to have gone to Paradise last night. I hadn't thought he'd be so . . . more fool me.

twenty-one

Family Life

Then Sa'id and I had a row, because I wanted to go and hide somewhere in the market, over towards Bab Zuweila where I knew a seamstress who had never spoken to a man who was not an immediate family member, and in whose house I felt I would therefore be pretty discreet and safe, and he thought I would be utterly and completely visible if I went down there, the whole neighbourhood would be chatting about it if an Englishwoman suddenly appeared, and I should go somewhere like his other aunt in Maadi (which is kind of like Putney – where you go when you're well-off, you get married at 28 and you aren't intending to be very interesting ever again). Too many ex-pats, I said. You'll blend right in, he said. Fuck that, I said. He didn't like me swearing. I just looked at him and he saw what I feared – that he was becoming more foreign, more other to me, and so was I to him, and that we would no longer be able to operate together.

'Don't worry,' he said.

And he looked at me, and he looked over his shoulder, drew me further into the doorway, wrapped his cloth around us, drew up my dress and quickly, impossibly, invisibly, fucked me. Even as I realised what he was doing, I yelled out. Couldn't not. And gasped and clenched my teeth and came on his second thrust, and he on my contraction. And I quivered, and our clothing fell back into place and we were laughing, and shaking, and he looked at me as if to say, OK? A woman with a bundle on her head scurried by. Someone hawked, a donkey brayed. He brushed the dust from the back of my head and my arse where he had pushed me against the wall. My fears were dispelled. It had taken forty seconds, which is a long time in Khan el-Khalili and he was a damn fool.

'Thank you,' I said. He knew what I was thanking him for.

'*Afwan*,' he replied. Then 'Don't go to Maadi. Come to this aunt's. Separate rooms. Very sexy. We will have to do it like this all the time.'

I laughed.

'No, it's a good idea,' he said. 'Don't do this fantasy mystery in the old city. It won't work. I can't help you down there. There is a diplomat living in my aunt's block, so plenty of police around all the time, on the entrance, you know. It's a nice big flat. A bit – well. You'll see. Come. She has already invited you.'

'What if the danger follows me there?' I couldn't bear it if my presence would bring harm.

'Police,' he said. 'Me. Invisible men.'

It was tempting. Very tempting. Handing over half the problem. But I couldn't. Couldn't do it.

'No,' I said. 'I can't. It's my thing, I must do it alone, I must stay alone.'

'Angelina,' he said.

'What?'

'You are not alone.'

I looked a query at him.

'*Sah*?' he said. Isn't that right? 'You are not alone. I am here.'

Yes. He was here.

I started to say something but he cut in.

'Fact,' he said. 'Not in dispute. Not under your control. At the moment.'

Oh.

Well . . .

I couldn't fault it, actually. I didn't want to get rid of him, so yes, I was not alone.

Oh.

'OK,' I said.

He made a little obeisance with his head. To my understanding.

'So let us go to Garden City.'

I thought a moment.

'Give me the phone,' I said, and I rang the Hussein. Karim the manager came on. Ah yes, madame. What can he do? Was there any message? Yes, madame, big flowers come for you. My heart sank that it was true, and rose again that I had been right – *cleverer than him*. Sadly Karim does not read English. I want to see the note.

'Karim,' I say. 'Who brought the flowers?'

A boy. Oh well.

'Karim,' I say. 'You are the best hotelier in Cairo and you are my friend and my brother.' (I like to lay it on thick.) 'But sadly I must leave the hotel because I am to go tonight to Upper Egypt. Yes, I'm sorry, such short notice. Can Shakira pack up my things for me and I will send for them? Yes, I'm sorry. Thank you. What is my bill? Please send it. Put in my passport too, and the note from the flowers. Thank you. No, please keep them. Put them in the restaurant. Of course. Yes I will be back soon, *ensh'Allah*. I am so sorry. *Malesh*, thank you. Thank you. *Masalaamah*.'

'OK?' I said to Sa'id.

He looked thoughtful.

'OK,' he said.

We took the back streets down towards Bab al-Futuh,

clambering through the market, over goats, past the café accoutrements section where *shisha* cords hung in bundles like dead snakes, past piles of enormous tin trays, lanterns and funnels, coffee pots and some of the most beautiful mosques in the city. There was a football match on; Zamalek v el-Ahli, and every shop had its television. Every tailor in his hole in the mediaeval wall ironing in front of the football, every café crowded, every child scurrying with a tray of glasses of tea. The horses and donkeys were grazing off the backs of their wagons, the green neon strips coming on on the minarets, the dust of the day settling, the young men throwing down water for the last time, deftly missing our legs as they flung it. At Bab al-Futuh we sat for a while in the dusk under its nine-hundred-year-old arch. The northern City of the Dead stretched out to the east, dim and frightening. The living who live in the shadows among the tombs were watching the football too.

After a while a taxi appeared, and we took it. Sa'id made a phone call, arranging for someone to fetch my things. I sat low in the back, 'Enta 'Omri' running through my head. Before you was darkness ... I have started to dream my reality in the light of your eyes. And we headed downtown.

Actually I felt better out of the old city. It's inebriating down there. Intoxicating. Like an unfocused pattern when you look too close, which from further away would fade into stripes of light and dark. You can go mad just noticing how many ways a dome can be made to fit on to a square. And the sinuous streets, the shifting shadows, the doorways and darkened windows, the ninth century waiting to get you. The ancient buildings down there are never in the same place twice: they move when you're not looking. Cats and children and dust and ancient murders. Pickles your head. Holes for boiling oil to pour through, tunnels you can't see but you know are there. Tattered dusty canvas hangings, faded patterns of interlocking flowers and arabesques (tracks of Sufi feet), once red and green and white, now dust, flapping, over ancient stone and wooden scaffolding bound together with rope. People moving like the ants negotiating the worn pile of the carpet in the Barsey mosque, following the channels of warp and weft, breaking out over the faded crimson thread but constantly frustrated by a strong green cord that they could not surmount, which became the limit of their world. Jasmine flowers just sitting there. Kufic inscriptions carved in stone, floriate and foliate. Roofs covered in rubbish. Lazy shifting in the wind. Static and mobile; is it alive? Is it a mouse, or is it a scrap? Or is it a feather? Or – oh. It's nothing. It's not there.

Once a shopkeeper called to me. 'Madame, what do you want?' 'Nothing, thanks,' I called back, being civil. 'Oh, I have nothing,' he said. 'Very good nothing. Best quality. Come and look.' So of course I did. He showed it to me, cradling it carefully in his empty hands. 'Oh it is beautiful,' I agreed. 'For you I make special price,' he said. 'For you, is *cadeau*.' 'Oh, that's too much,' I said, 'I can't pay you that much.' 'OK OK madame,' he said. 'No problem. You take two, same price.' 'Oh,' I said. 'What can I say. That's a good price. *Mabrouk*,' I said, congratulations on a good sale. '*Mabrouk*,' he said. 'You are good customer.' 'Don't bother to wrap it,' I said, and we neither of us laughed, we just looked at each other gleefully and I went my way.

But I can't be doing with that kind of thing now. My enemy is English.

The aunt – Amina – lived in Garden City, which is not how its name sounds. The building was tall, like a transplanted block from a prosperous French boulevard. Sa'id and the police greeted each other without fuss. The hall was high and grey, gloomy. The lift worked. No door. The number of each floor was painted on the yellow wall between landings. The 7th was ours. I like 7.

She was out when we arrived. Maid let us in. It was, as he had said, large. And dim, and cavernous. Cool bare floors, heavy rugs, heavy furniture in the tasteful end of the Louis Faroukh style: rococo legs, gold and white, striped silk coverings. Massive mirrors, freckled like the ones at Fishawy. This was some old money. Sa'id and I sat like guests on a settee, and the maid brought 7 Up.

'She's not Abu Sa'id's sister . . .' I asked. This couldn't be the same family as the house in Qurnah, so white and blue, so workmanlike. It didn't connect.

'My father's brother's wife,' he said. 'My uncle died after they were married. Young. Cancer. This aunt's family is – as you see. This was her father's flat, and she came back after her husband died.'

'Did they have children?'

'No time,' he said.

'But you all stayed in touch, still family. That's good.'

He smiled a little. 'She and my father don't speak. Nobody speaks to him.'

'Why?'

'Because . . . the mother, and . . .' He did the rolling, beckoning movement with his hand, which in these circumstances means: and there's more, always more, but you know that, and we can talk forever on this, but we're not going to talk of it now . . . the bodily equivalent of dot dot dot.

I sank in the settee, as best I could, and wanted to sleep. It must have been eight or nine by now.

'Go and wash,' he said. 'Come . . .'

First he showed me his room. His room! Where he always stays in Cairo. It was bare. A narrow bed, tightly made; a dark wooden table, a carved wardrobe. A light switch that had been painted over a dozen times, but not since 1954 by

the look of it. A newspaper on the desk – *Al Ahram*. His
bags from London in the corner, clean laundry folded in a
pile on the foot of the bed.

Then mine. Similar, even emptier. Perfect. And the bathroom. Suite in Cairo bathroom blue. Whoever did those huge
blue sinks must have made a killing, back in 1954. He brought
me two towels. Rough and white. And he kissed me, as he
went off. 'Your bags will be here soon,' he said. 'We can stay
in tonight and tomorrow we will do it. Don't go out without
me.'

Did I feel reassured? Or what?

Did I feel hemmed in and taken over?

Did I mind?

It was the same as with Harry. Am I being cared for or am
I being bossed?

Oh fuck.

'*Habibi*,' I said. 'You can tell me what to do, but I won't
necessarily do it. You know that, don't you. English woman,
you know.'

He knew.

'Yes *habibi*,' he said. Not *habibti*, for a female. *Habibi*, for
a man. Teasing me.

I heard him talking to the maid as he left. A quicker, more
guttural Arabic. Too Arabic for my ear. I wonder if he spoke
harmoniously for me on purpose, so that I could follow easily.

I was rising up from deep in the huge, cornelian-stained
bathtub, where I had been marvelling at the hollow clanking
and growling of the plumbing and the height of the ceiling
above my wet head, when I heard voices. Talking English.
Walking past the door. Fuck me.

'Sarah!' I called out.

'What!?' Her surprise was total. 'What? Who's that?'

'It's Angeline. I'm in the bath,' I called.

'What are you – hello!' she cried, through the door.

'What are you doing here?' I called. 'Hang on. Wait. I'll be out in a moment.'

'Oh,' she said. 'Sorry, I'm confused.'

'Don't worry. I won't be a mo. Is Hakim with you?'

'Yes,' she said, and her happiness at the fact flowed straight through the door. I was glad.

But Sa'id said the aunt didn't speak to Abu Sa'id because of Sarah. Oh. Just when you think you understand it all changes again. Oh.

I met up with her ten minutes later, damp but dressed (alas in my dusty all-day circling Ibn Tulun and shagging in the Khan clothes again) in the drawing room. The maid smiled and had mint tea for me. I thanked her nicely and was sweeter with her than I had been when Sa'id was there. I don't know why. It's a girl thing. I don't know why. Can't deal very well with more than one person at a time. Maybe that's it.

Sarah didn't look entirely pleased to see me. Not not pleased either. Confused.

'What on earth are you doing here?' she asked, as well she might.

'I had to come,' I said. 'On business.' (Ha!) 'Madame Amina invited me to stay. Family friend,' I went on, as she was looking at me with some confusion still. I called the aunt Madame in case Sarah felt I was . . . occupying her territory, or something. Or over familiar. And after all, I still hadn't met the woman. But Sarah doesn't know that. Yet.

I don't want to tell her about Sa'id.

'What business?' she said and for a moment I was lost without a lie, but then she carried on. 'Actually I'm glad you're here. You – I – I'm glad. Hakim will be pleased, too.'

'Where is he?' I asked.

'Out. Coming back.'

'And how's it going?' I asked, friendly. It occurred to me

that she might be ill at ease in this house, rather than with me. Well she might.

'How long have you been here?' I asked, just as she asked me the same thing.

'I just arrived,' I said, as she said, 'Since I arrived – four days.'

'And . . .' I said. I wanted her to tell me how it was, what the balance was, who was what. Like had she seen Sa'id? Did she know he was here? But I was awkward. Don't be.

'And what's been happening?'

She laughed. 'Hakim has been making Amina make up with me. It's good.'

I wasn't going to mention Sa'id. I wasn't going to.

'She tells me Sa'id is coming,' she said.

So I didn't have to.

'Ah,' I said.

Then 'How do you feel about that?'

'What do you mean?' she said.

'Well,' I said, thinking to be polite, and gentle, and not liking the fact that I was lying by default. 'Well, Hakim came to find you . . .'

'And Sa'id didn't.'

'Yes.'

'Different folks,' she said, after a moment. I had the impression she was scared. I didn't blame her. He was a little frightening – do I mean frightening? Around that subject. I wanted to help her. Her firstborn.

'I remember what you said about your sister,' she said. 'I want you to know that I understand that, but it is not simple.'

'Of course.'

'And he was always . . . not like Hakim. Hakim was always cuddly. Always loving. Sa'id is hard to please. Was. Is. Have you talked to him about me? When you were in London?'

I realised she had been dying to ask this, and was kicking

herself in her pride, at having let the question out. Well, I was glad to see her showing interest.

'Yes,' I said.

She looked at me.

'As you say,' I said. 'Proud.'

'Did I say that?'

'In so many words.'

'Proud about me?'

'About himself in regard to you. He wouldn't talk about you. I felt he was . . . he felt betrayed. But that's hearsay, you know. Inadmissible. I told him to forgive you.'

'Thank you,' she said. Sarcastically. Prickly. Yeah, proud.

'I'd say it to anyone,' I said. I am not going to be defensive here. I thought of my mother, of Dad, and Harry, and Lily. And Harry again. When I go home I am going to be a heavenly relative. Let her be Harry's. Please please God, let her be Harry's. And let us live happily somehow.

Soon after that the aunt returned, and then Hakim, and it became a little party. The aunt was older, sixtyish, quiet, courteous. Elegant. One of her eyes was slightly milky. She asked me quiet questions, but she was not very interested in the answers. I didn't mind that at all. She evidently doted on Hakim. Even the milky eye lit up when he arrived. And when he saw me, and fell on me with delight, and told her at length that I was his darling, his beloved English aunt, she and Sarah exchanged looks that I felt were quite possibly to do with earlier conversations about how hard it is for a boy to lose half his national identity, and how natural that he should need to seek it out. I didn't of course bring up with Hakim any of the things Sa'id had been saying, and he was so pleased to see me and apologised so sweetly for having left without saying goodbye, and asked after Lily with such affection, and told his aunt at such length how beautiful she was, and how clever, and begged me so prettily to take out my photo of her to show, that I relaxed into it being a sweet family reunion, undercurrents at ebb, and affectionate sociability in flood.

Then Sa'id came back. The aunt went out when she heard his voice in the hall, and spoke to him. Her voice came through urgent. He didn't come in. Amina returned and looked at Sarah, patted Hakim, and said to me, 'He would like to speak to you.'

I went out to him. Heart lowered again. He knew what I wanted; I knew I couldn't make him want it. I wanted to, though. I wanted to knock his head together.

He was sitting on an elegant hard chair in the hall, his hands clasped in front of his knees, his head low. He looked up and said, 'Did you know?'

'I knew she was coming to Cairo. I didn't know she would be here.'

His head swayed a little. He looked so sad.

'Don't ask me, darling,' I said. 'You know what I think.'

He beckoned me to him without looking up. I stroked his head. Beautiful curls. Cradled his brain in his handsome skull and sent love through my fingertips to him.

'It was very hard when she went,' he said.

'I think she thought it would be harder if she stayed,' I said.

He sighed.

And again. I waited it out.

Finally: 'Come,' he said. 'Let's go out and smoke. Let's go to the Grillon and find some intellectuals to talk nonsense with. Let's go and sing to the moon. Let's go to Aswan. Come.'

'OK,' I said. 'I'll get my shoes.'

I went back in to the others. It's not my own tragedy so I cannot dispense with manners.

'He wants to go out,' I said. 'Goodnight, Madame Amina, Hakim. Sarah.'

I'm not a practised deceiver. And she is not a fool. Her look was calm, understanding, collective. I looked her in the eye, and gave her a small nod. Just to let her know that she was right, to let her not be bothered by doubt when she had better things to be bothered with. I think her face hardened a little. Her eyes changed. A little. I couldn't tell what from or what to.

Well at least it's done. As it would have to be.

I went out the other door, towards the bedroom. I was in my room, picking up my shoes and my fags before I realised she had followed me.

'Well?' she said.

Strange the ways these things happen.

I almost asked if she minded. It's nothing to me if she minds. But there's something.

'A few weeks,' I said. 'And yes. Insofar as we can tell.' Love, I meant. Though I couldn't say it.

'Oh.' She was disarmed. She knew I didn't care. Knew she was badly placed to have an opinion. But as the thought ticked through her eyes I realised that she was making it her fault, or her – hers, anyway. She was making it a mother thing, because I am older. And I minded that. I nearly said: 'It's nothing to do with you,' meaning, 'It's nothing to do with the fact that you deserted him and he needs a mother,' but realised in time how it could sound: 'It's none of your business.' I said neither. Nothing. For a moment. Then I said, 'Yes, I would like you to make up, but it's not for me to . . . and I am not playing any part in that. No direct part. Just in case you were thinking anything of it.' Like that I might, or that you might like me to.

'Well,' she said, with a little bitterness. 'I seem to have forfeited my role rather.' Which made me angry.

'Don't insult me,' I said, quite gently. 'And don't insult yourself. You're his mother, it's your job to look after him.

Forever. That's all. What I am is between him and me.'

She gave me a narrow look from under the hand that was fretfully wandering her forehead. 'Yeah. Right,' she said.

'I'll see you later,' I said, and gave her a straight look until she acknowledged me.

'Goodnight,' she said. And I went, and Sa'id and I drove round and round the city in the dark, and ended up back at the City of the Dead, sitting up on the steps of someone's mausoleum, drawing patterns with our toes in the dust by the light of the high golden moon, till he fell asleep in my lap. Much later I woke him, and we drove home. He didn't say much, and I held his hand all the way except when he was changing gear.

When we got in my bags were in my room and a great fan of tuberoses stood on the hall table. Shit. They'd sent them on.

The note was on top of the bag. We sat on the floor in the corridor to read it.

My darling girl how unspeakably happy I am that you have arrived. Dinner tomorrow? The Semiramis has a great show on, but if you're tired we could go somewhere quiet like Justine or Arabesque. I'll call you. Bring your friend! I cover you with rose petals – ever yours.

Shit.

We stood and for ten minutes Sa'id held me and I listened to his heart, then we went to our separate beds. As I went in he said: 'That phrase, "tweak your chain".'

'Yes?' I said. 'What about it?'

'You are the dog on the chain, he tweaks it to see you jump?'

'Pretty much.'

He was silent a moment. (Remember Lily counting out a moment. One to four, five to eight, with a tiny pause at four.

That's how long a moment is. Whenever I say I'll be a moment she counts it out to make sure I'm not too long.)

'So should the dog not take off the chain?'

I was quiet for two and a half moments.

'Yes,' I said.

It was the first night I had slept without him since we started, but there was only an hour or so left of it. I wanted him very badly.

By the time I emerged the next morning Sarah had gone out. Madame Amina was playing patience in her little sitting room, which was apparently what she liked to do. Hakim was prowling round my breakfast, waiting for Sa'id to appear, spoiling for something.

'What are those flowers?' he demanded.

'Someone sent them,' I said.

'They weren't here yesterday.'

'Sit down,' I said. 'You're curdling my coffee.'

'What?'

'I'm having breakfast,' I said. 'Be calm.'

He sat. Disgruntled. Shifted in his seat.

Then: 'I want them to . . .' he said. 'It's not so much to ask. He'd like her if . . . it's his duty. He must to do it. He must. *Sah?*'

'*Aiwa,*' I said. Yes. 'Give them time. We can't do it for them.'

He was so pleased at the idea that they might do it at all that the idea of giving them time to do it was most acceptable. 'You think it will be all right?'

'Has to be,' I said. 'He likes happiness. So it has to be. More or less.'

He ruminated, then sat down and ate three eggs and two mangoes and drank three cups of coffee.

I smiled at him blankly, and ruffled his head as I finished up and went to my room to think about my heart.

Sa'id came in half an hour later: or rather knocked, as propriety required, and called me out.

'Are you ready?'

'As I'll ever be,' I murmured.

twenty-two

Let's Go to the Bank

We drove down. Parked right on Midan el Tahrir, by the back entrance to the hotel. Back entrance indeed – the block rose huge and rich above us, with its gardens and terraces, gazing out over the breadth of the square, where crazy lanes of traffic entangle themselves in arabesques, and pedestrians fear to tread. Where you know for sure that Cairo traffic police have the lowest sperm count and the highest levels of lead in their blood. The Egyptian Museum, pink and colonial, the colour of a British colonel's neck in the tropics, sat to the right, calm and protected, like the Hilton, from the everyday mayhem going on outside.

By the time we got back the car would probably have been rolled somewhere else by a pettish taxi driver, but when I suggested to Sa'id he put the handbrake on he didn't agree. 'We have an invisible man waiting in an invisible car as well,' he said. 'Not to worry.'

We sauntered up the wide steps as calm as you like. Sa'id in his greenish suit, me in string-coloured linen and sunglasses, like any foreign lady. It was hot – of course it was hot. My eyes were sandy with lack of sleep; my head soft. Cairo head. Nobody could tell that inside my soft head I was running through what Eddie knew I knew, and what I might have to dissemble about to protect Harry. Eddie knows I know he's alive. At least I don't have to fake amazement to save my skin, or Harry's.

Past the palms and curious stone busts on pedestals, past the tables of the Ali Baba coffee house where the prosperous young people smoked and drank domestic Stella. It was just after noon. Hot. Calm.

'Where is the bank?' I asked again.

'Through the entrance, left off the hall and second on the left. Where it always was.'

Yes.

I don't know what I expected Eddie to do. Jump out and ... Oh God.

Through the hall, second on the left after the boutique full of embroidered caftans and appliquéd leather-work cushions. Banque Misr. OK.

In we went. Clerk was free. 'Evangeline Gower,' I said, 'come to make a collection.' Gave him my passport. Sa'id stood back, against the wall. Waiting. Looking, if I may say so, deeply cool.

Ah yes, said the clerk, and went away, and came back, with another man – manager? Who looked at the passport, and me, and said ah yes, and then there was a form to fill in (I lied about all that I could – like where I was staying. Put Hotel el Hussein) and then another, and I was to sign something but it was in Arabic. I read it as best I could, and called Sa'id over and he read it for me. The manager couldn't keep his eyes off me. Fascinated to see who it was.

I was just waiting for his voice to come bouncing in, for the 'Angeline, darling!', or the gunfire, or whatever he was going to use to amuse me today.

The manager spoke to Sa'id, assuming I didn't speak Arabic. 'Nice-looking babe,' he said, or words to that effect. Sa'id said to me – in Arabic – 'Hey, Angeline, this gentlemen thinks you're a nice-looking babe.' 'Really?' I replied – in

Arabic. 'Tell him I think he's a nice-looking gentleman.' The manager flushed purple. I put my hand out to pat his arm. 'Don't worry,' I said. 'Don't worry. I don't mind people thinking I'm a nice-looking babe. Really I don't.' He was so relieved. The exchange cheered me. Made me feel strong, beautiful and clever.

'Now why are you calling the bank manger *habibi*? I can't leave you alone for a second, can I? You naughty old thing . . .'

Sa'id had his hand over mine. Otherwise I might have lost it. But I didn't. I stood. I breathed. I waited. Half a moment, including the little pause at four. Turned round.

And there he was. Eddie Bates.

'Hello Eddie,' I said.

'Tschh,' he said, crossly, sucking his teeth.

'What?'

He recovered himself.

'François du Berry,' he said. Holding out his hand. Taking mine. Little bow as if to kiss, but not. '*Enchanté*.'

'French!' I said. His accent was OK, but really. 'Oh no. They'd never take you for a Frenchman. Crap choice. Really.' Oh my God, I've gone straight into the banter. I can still do it. Great. Good.

'Don't be so sure,' he said. He was doing the accent in English too. Just a leetle. Actually it *was* good. 'I can be very convincing. I just don't need to be in present company. Absurd, isn't it? Now won't you introduce me to – Sa'id, isn't it?'

'François du Barry, Sa'id el Araby,' I said, giving it full guttural Arabic pronunciation and hoping Eddie wouldn't pick it up, which was pointless because he obviously knew already, but I had to do something.

'Hello,' said Sa'id, giving that full Arabic pronunciation too. Ah. He was going to pretend not to speak English. What a good idea. Now does Eddie speak Arabic, that's the next thing. Anyone can spot *habibi* in a sentence. Doesn't mean a thing.

'Come and have lunch,' said Eddie. 'So much to talk about. The restaurant here is not bad. Or we could go out. Which would you like?' He was smiling radiantly. He is unbefucking-lievable. Swanky silverish prosperous-fellow suit, new hair-cut, same patrician face, noble nose. A little tanned, in an expensive-looking way. It suited him. Newish scar on his forehead. Whoops.

François my arse.

'Something to pick up first, Eddie,' I said, smiling archly.

'*Chèrie*,' he said, lightly, warningly. Of course – I'm not to call him Eddie. This is farcical. 'You can fetch it later – too heavy. You know what these primitive currencies are like. You'll have to hire a bearer. Oh but you already have.' He beamed at Sa'id, who smiled politely back, as you would if you hadn't understood but could see that a joke was being made.

'No, now,' I said. 'Come come. I've come all this way.' I was glad I had. Seeing him, my heart flooded back to me. Hearing him. Racist cunt. I've decided I don't mind that word used as an insult any more. I'm just unmanning him. Unmanning him with femininity. That's all. Actually cunt could be the great female insult.

Even so, Egyptian pounds. It was going to make a hell of a package.

Eddie made flirty little moue. 'Oh all right,' he said. 'You can give the lady her money, Mahmoud. Count it out.'

'Don't bother,' I said, but the first clerk was already at the machine, which was whipping through notes at a rate of knots, rattling as it flicked and fanned them through. It was made of bilious green metal, dimply, with a rubber belt. I watched. And watched. It was getting quite a groovy little rhythm going.

'He's jolly handsome, isn't he darling?' Eddie didn't even bother to sidle up to my ear, just announced it straight out. 'Such good taste. Except for Harry of course. Does Harry know about this one? And does this one know about me? Oh dear oh dear. You're lucky I'm so very fond of you. Thousands of men would mind, you know. But I'm just so very pleased to see you that I really don't. But he doesn't *have* to come to lunch, does he? Send him off with the money instead. Then at least if he steals it we'll never be bothered with him again. Actually that's rather a good idea. Cheap at the price! I'll stop the counting now, we could send him off with what we've got to so far and then there would still be plenty for the lovely Lily. How is the lovely Lily?'

'Dead,' I said. I don't know where it came from. But it suddenly seemed a good idea that he should think she was dead. Then he wouldn't bother her.

'My sweetheart!' he cried. 'No!'

'She was knocked down by a car,' I said. 'Three months ago. Didn't you hear?' Now as I filled the story out I couldn't bear to do it. The words stuck in my throat, as if saying them would make it happen. Like magic words. Which were of course invented right here on the Nile. By Thoth. I desperately tried to conjure up antidotes to any bad luck I was bringing down. Thoth, *habibi*, I don't mean it, I don't mean it. Banish the image even as I say the words. The overall effect was to make me seem strangled and miserable, so from that point of view it was good.

Once again Eddie was demonstrating his . . . his complete detachment from the human race. I'd just told him my daughter was dead, and I think he believed me, and he claimed this grand emotional connection to me, and this is what he said.

'That must have been terrible. Now do let's finish this off, and go to lunch.' The money was ready. Five hundred and forty-seven thousand Egyptian pounds, plus change, in a

cardboard box. The bank staff were very worried. One of
them was standing by the door, which was now closed, and
he wasn't letting anybody in. I didn't like that. Eddie didn't
seem in the least perturbed. I dared not look at Sa'id.

I stared at the box. What the fuck is this. This is mad. 'The
money was for Lily, Eddie,' I said.

'François,' he snapped.

'So she can't have it.'

'I'm sure she would have left it to you in her will,' he
replied, already halfway out of the bank, ignoring the box.
He genuinely didn't care about it. This is great – he doesn't
care about it, I don't care about it, yet here we are, him using
it and me being manipulated by it. I glanced back to Sa'id.
He caught my eye as he handed his holdall to the clerk, and
asked him to put the money in it, and, while it was being
transferred, he held my eye as I had held his head last night.
Eye beams twisted. His strength flooded down the beams,
and mine leapt up to meet it. So far so good.

The bank men didn't want us to leave, fussing and whoosh-
ing and making a big irritating business about us just walking
out with the cash. As we insisted, they gradually fell back,
eyes huge, disbelieving, amazed. Sa'id picked up the holdall,
took my arm, and led me to the door. It was open again.
Eddie was outside in the marble corridor, waiting for us. So
far so good.

'We can't have lunch, I'm afraid,' I said. 'It's been lovely
to see you but we've got to get on, so if you've . . .'

He cut straight in. 'Go away,' he said to Sa'id. Sa'id didn't.
I wasn't scared. We were in the middle of the Nile Hilton
surrounded by white marble and bell boys and well-dressed
Germans. The square outside was crawling with tourist
police. I wasn't scared of this. I was scared of the long run;
of next time.

Eddie took my arm and led me to a sofa. I considered

resisting, but didn't. There used to be a prison down in the old city where the prisoners' hands grab at the bars of the windows, down by your feet. Dirty skinny hands, bitten nails, gnawed knuckles. Hopeless hands. I always made a point of avoiding it, when I could remember where it was. I intend to mix with the Egyptian justice system even less than with the British, as far as I possibly can.

Sa'id walked alongside me, silent, carrying the money. We sat. Sa'id stood in front of us, unabashed. 'Go away,' said Eddie. '*Imshi*.' This is what you say to an annoying child who pesters you at the pyramids. It is not what you say to a grown-up. I was glad that Sa'id seemed to have that Egyptian gene that enables them to ignore rude ignorant foreigners.

Eddie turned to me and flung his arms around my neck on the sofa. 'Darling,' he said. 'Make him go away. I want to talk to you. I don't want to have to knock you on the head or slip drugs in your tea. It's so childish. And it just leads to misunderstandings. We must have a new beginnning here and your friend is getting right up my nose.'

'I don't think he'll want to go, you know. If I were you I'd just ignore him.'

'Oh don't be silly,' he said. 'How can I fuck you with him there? Though actually . . .' and his eyes lit a up a little, and wandered down Sa'id's long and elegant body, and up again. Sa'id still betrayed nothing. He was just standing, waiting, cool as you like, not bothered. I was beginning to think maybe he *didn't* understand English. It was me who wanted to punch Eddie for looking that way at my darling.

Sit on it. It's just a tweak on the chain.

'Come upstairs,' he urged.

'No,' I said.

'Why not?'

'Because we have what we came for and now we must be off.'

'What, you're just going to take my money and go?'

'It's my money now,' I said. Not that I gave a shit about having the money. I just knew who I didn't want to have it. 'But you can have it if you like. I don't care.'

'So why did you come?'

He knew why.

'You know why.'

He shouted with laughter. 'Yes and it worked, didn't it! But Angeline,' he said. 'You know what it's about. Angeline, I have to. It's not fair. I tell you; just once. Just once. Don't I deserve it? I could have forced you, I never did. Just come upstairs with me now, and let me fuck you and that's it. He can come too if you like. But just let me do it. It's only fair. You fucked me. Didn't you? Eh? You did, didn't you? Cheeky bitch. So you owe me one. Don't you!'

The fact that he's right means nothing. There is no debt here. He did me wronger than I did him.

'But you know our tragedy, darling, don't you,' he murmured. 'Of course you do. The girl I want is the girl who wouldn't let me. That's why I want you. Let me and I won't love you any more. Promise. Because you know I'm not going to be so picky forever. Don't make me rape you,' he whispered. 'Don't make me. I don't want to. It won't satisfy me. I'll only come bothering you again. You know it. And you know I'm going to do it anyway. If not now, tomorrow. Or the next day. Or next year. You know I can. So let me. Make it easy. Let me fuck you. Let me fuck you. Let me fuck you . . .' His voice was growing quieter, he was leaning in to me, repeating and repeating the words, murmuring. To an onlooker, he might have been commenting on a passer-by's outfit. I could smell him. Eau Sauvage? – no, Blenheim Bouquet. Beautiful cool cedarwood smell. The world continued around us. I couldn't move.

And so we stayed.

Sa'id leant across, leaning one arm on the wall behind us. The other moved in front of Eddie's face. Sa'id spoke softly, in Arabic. Eddie ignored him, then flinched suddenly. Sa'id spoke again. English. 'Mr Bates, you are new here, and I am not. Nobody here cares anything about you.'

Eddie looked up at him. Which is when I saw the curve of sharp steel at his throat. Sa'id's hand was steady, his face dark and calm, his eyes ancient. As Eddie raised his head he seemed to be baring his throat to the blade, almost, almost on purpose. There was something sacrificial in the movement.

The world hung still.

Then Eddie raised his head that little bit further, and kissed Sa'id full on the mouth.

The world hung.

Sa'id smiled. His most dangerous, beautiful smile.

Straightened.

Folded away the knife. Picked up the bag.

Gave me his hand.

'*Masalaamah*,' he said. Goodbye.

We left.

As we passed through the garden I started to run; Sa'id reached out his long arm and stopped me.

Down the wide steps.

Taxi, madam? Taxi?

Our car had indeed been moved, and blocked in by cabs. I waited while it was liberated. It was like one of those puzzles: move this bit to make way for that bit and you've blocked the bit you first thought of. I didn't look back the way we had come. Got in the car. Head on the dashboard. Sa'id got in and drove; round the square, on to the October Bridge. Driving. After a while I stopped him and got out and was sick against a dusty wall by the pharmaceutical research station. A skinny dog came and sniffed and I was sick again.

Sa'id passed me a bottle of Baraka and I washed my mouth and poured half the rest over my head. He drank. I lay along his body, holding on to his strength and fragility as he leant on the side of the car. Held him. Took water in my hand and washed his face, his beautiful mouth, and rubbed it and washed it again.

The dog scurried away. A child came out and looked at us, and then went away, probably to get his friends to come and look too.

We sat on a low dingy wall, in a bit of tattered shade beside the road.

'Sorry,' he said.

'Why!'

'Raising the stakes,' he said.

I thought about it. 'I don't think you did,' I said. 'They're high anyway. I think you just showed him that we have a hand. Showed him one card.'

'Maybe,' he said. 'But – sorry.'

'No, I think it was good.'

He grunted.

I breathed for a little while. Checking myself: brain: still there; hands: still here. Heart: beating. Eyes: clear. Belly: steady. Then I checked Sa'id. His eyes were shut. He seemed unscathed. But.

'Sorry,' I said.

He opened one eye.

'The kiss.'

He made a bitter little face. 'I'd rather he kissed me than you,' he said. And laughed.

'I'd rather he didn't kiss either of us,' I said.

'Of course.' He stood up and started to prowl around. 'Come on. Let's go and put this shit somewhere.'

'What?'

'The money. The five times as much as I make in a year that you have in that bag.'

Oh. I hadn't thought that he would have strong feelings about money. But then he's a merchant. He has money, and you don't get it if you don't have strong feelings about it. Unless you're me, and it keeps landing on your head and you can't use it. And this is a country that knows poverty. This money may be a curse and an irrelevance to me, but it's still a fuck of a lot of money.

'Would you like it?' I asked.

He put his head on one side and looked down at me. 'No,' he said. 'You idiot. Get in the car.' And we got in the car and after five minutes or so we started laughing, and laughing, and had to pull over again. Relief. For the time being.

twenty-three

Give Me Your Hands

Back at Madame Amina's, over coffee, behind green shutters, under the slowly flapping fan, Sa'id began to tell me what he thought about Eddie. But then his mother walked in.

I nearly laughed. She was wearing a greenish suit. A woman's suit, made out of some soft cloth, a baggy elegant suit, but still a greenish suit. Just the same shade. But I didn't laugh.

Sa'id was looking up at her. She was standing in the middle of the room, stock still at the place she'd reached at the moment she'd realised we were there.

I jumped up and muttered something about coffee and tried to get away, but Sa'id was annoyed at that and gestured me to sit still and shut up. So I did.

He continued to stare at her. And she at him. And I at each of them in turn. How do they look to each other after so long? I tried to imagine not seeing Lily for ten years. Tried to remember not having seen Harry for ten years. How could Sarah not take her handsome son in her arms? How can they keep this up?

Then he stood and, speaking in Arabic, said to her, 'The coffee is fresh. Have some.' And left the room.

She sat where he had been sitting. Drank the coffee I had poured for him.

'Is he coming back?' she said.

'I don't know.'

She flung her head against the back of the couch and sighed, long and hard. I felt for her, but there was nothing I could say, so I didn't say it. Instead I went to his room where he was lying on his bed, and I sat on the end and didn't say anything there either.

After a while he got up and locked the door, and pulled me down with him on the bed, and we lay there together, on our backs, tucked tight, and after a while we fell asleep, and after a while I got up again and went to my room and slept there, till dusk. The tuberoses were still in the hall and the smell seeped through.

Sarah woke me. She had a note for me from Hakim who, she said, had been in and out like a whirlwind.

'He left you this,' she said. 'I don't know what it's about. Wouldn't let me wake you till he'd gone.'

'Gone where?' I said, dopey with daytime sleep.

'I don't know,' she said. 'He was upset.'

I took the note, scribbled in Arabic. Couldn't really read it. I could only make out one word, written in English letters. François.

What the fuck?

'What does it say?' I said, tearing off my nightshirt and flinging on all-purpose dust-coloured baggy trousers and long shirt, for travelling in hot dusty places.

'It says that François has further plans, knows you have left the Hotel el Hussein but does not know you are here, and that you should stay put, he is going to see him and sort it out.'

What the fucking fuck?

'What's it about?' she asked. Smelling my adrenalin.

'A mad cunt with tuberoses,' I said. What plans? Sort out what?

Hakim.

Businessman teaching him things.

Shit.

What plans?

I went to wake Sa'id. He was up, showering. He came out from the bathroom wet and beautiful in a gallabeya the colour of unpolished lapis. There is a word: *tarab*. It means, roughly, the way music makes you feel. It comes to mind. Even now. There is probably a word in Arabic for the feeling in the small of your back inspired by the sight of your lover's wet hair.

'We have to go out,' I said.

'Why?'

I showed him the note. His hair dripped on it as he read it.

'Well?' he said.

'I don't know. But I thought – the new business contacts, the people you don't like . . . If he's working with Eddie then . . .'

'Of course.' Of course he said of course. Of course he takes it all in and is a step or two beyond. 'But now what?'

'Find him?' I said.

'Why?'

'Eddie –' I said.

'What do you fear?' he said. Calmly.

'That Eddie will hurt Hakim if Hakim turns against him.'

'*Aiwa*,' he said. 'But he will hurt you more. And we don't know where they are. So?'

Good point. We hadn't a clue.

'Eddie mentioned some places. The Semiramis, Justine, Arabesque . . .'

'Do you want to tour Cairo in case he is in one of these places?'

I thought about it. 'Yes,' I said. 'It's stupid, but we can't leave it. It's all we have.' I can't leave Hakim in my danger.

He looked at me quizzically. 'You want to go where Eddie is?'

'Not in the least,' I said. 'But if Hakim . . .'

'He was *very* upset,' said Sarah.

Sa'id ignored her.

'Sort it out,' said Sa'id. 'Oh God, the little brother's idea of sorting things out. OK, we'll go and find him.'

'I'm coming,' said Sarah.

'Neither of you are coming,' said Sa'id.

'Yes we are,' I said. 'I'll stay in the car, I'll go in disguise, but I'm coming.'

'So am I,' said Sarah.

'She should come,' I said. 'She can ask things that you can't without arousing suspicion. Eddie won't recognise her. She can play the dumb tourist.'

'English women,' said Sa'id, and laughed. Bitterly. He went to get dressed.

I thought about disguise and though it seemed stupid it also seemed sensible. Perhaps Madame Amina would have a *burka* or something. She still moves like a woman who expects to be wearing a scarf, even though she isn't. She never extends her left arm; it's still holding some piece of cloth in place next to her body, the habit (ha!) of a lifetime.

For God's sake, I can't wear a *burka* to a nightclub. A *burka* could make me look like any woman from further east and a little more devout than Egypt, but not like someone who would be let into the Semiramis. I shall just put on something long and wrap a scarf round myself.

I thought about the scarves I had brought. (Of course I had scarves. You don't not have, in Cairo.) They weren't big enough – of course I had scarves, but small, or fine, or easy scarves. I *am* European.

I went to Sa'id's room. 'Lend me your white scarf,' I said.

Years ago in Morocco I had accepted the loan of a man's scarf on a chilly night and he had taken it as a sexual acceptance. Oh well.

He passed it to me, the scarf within which we had fucked, and wrapped it round my head and shoulders like a cage. I let it hold me, knowing it could grant me invisibility, freedom. I wanted him to kiss me but he didn't.

First we went to the Nile Hilton. Sarah enquired at the desk for Monsieur du Berry; no, monsieur was no longer staying in the hotel. Sa'id called a few other swanky hotels, the Sheraton, Intercontinental, the Ramses Hilton. At the Semiramis he wondered if M. du Berry's booking for tonight at the nightclub could be increased to a table for eight. Bingo! Increased it was. So that was one thing we knew.

Then we went to Arabesque, and on to Justine and Aubergine in Zamalek, to all the places we could think of where an Eddie might go. At each place Sarah went in to look. It was stupid. We would have to wait. So we parked up outside the Semiramis and sat. Sa'id and Sarah had still not addressed each other directly. Like it or lump it I was in the middle. Just sitting in the car in the warm night, it became ridiculous. But I couldn't say anything.

Sa'id sent a small boy for a *shisha*, and had it brought to the car. Two tourist police in their white uniforms eyed him. Sarah went and smiled at them. They asked her if she spoke Arabic. *Shwoyya shwoyya*, she said, just a little, which is what a tourist would say, not what the academic English Arabist would say. She was playing her role. They smiled at her and said Welcome Cairo. *Shukran*, she said. *Afwan*, they said. Where you from. And all that.

Time passed slowly. And we didn't know where Hakim was. Sa'id rang home. No sign of him, said Madame Amina, and why is everybody behaving oddly tonight? Who? said

Sa'id. Coming and going at all hours, she complained, and she thought Hakim had a girlfriend. Where, said Sa'id. Zamalek, she said, of all places. He was forever getting her driver to take him down there. What address? She didn't know. Ali would know. Could she get him? No, he had gone home for the evening. Where did he live? Way out God knows where. What was his number? He didn't have one, you have to ring the tea-house. What was the tea-house number? She went and got it. He called, and somewhere out in the middle of nowhere a tea-house child was sent to fetch Ali the driver to the phone, and an address was revealed. Not a street I knew. Sa'id did. 'Swanky,' he said. One of my words.

So we went round there. I sat silent in the back, Sarah attempted to look prosperous and respectable in the front as we passed the languorous policemen on each corner. The house had its own garden, a drive going round, locked gates. I could see lights on in the house; shifting and moving through the foliage in the garden. We sat.

Crickets chirped.

Smell of jasmine and warm lawns watered at dusk.

We sat.

Sa'id's phone rang.

'Hallo?' he said. He spoke in Arabic, answering questions, and asking them. *La'ah*, he said, a lot. No. Then got to *meshi* – OK. Then he passed the phone to me. 'Hakim,' he said.

'Where are you?' I said. We spoke Arabic.

'At Monsieur François's house,' he said. 'Tell me one thing –'

'What.'

'He says you are his wife. To be his wife. That you are waiting to be together.'

'It's not true.'

'Then why does he say it?'

'He wishes it were true.'

There was a silence; a full silence. Crickets on the line and crickets in the garden.

'He says you are going to be married. He says you are going to Upper Egypt on honeymoon. I have booked rooms for you at the Winter Palace Hotel. He has been planning it for weeks but he just wasn't sure what day you were coming. He said you just had a tiff, but he is seeing you tonight and you are leaving on the *wagon lits* and you will marry there.'

I had a sudden weird image of Eddie and I in morning suit and full white meringue, side by side in the billiard room of the Winter Palace, among the stuffed animals and leather furniture and orientalist prints of Nubian boatmen at places now drowned beneath the great lake, and I snorted. This is great. White slavery in the east with Eddie as the Sheik of Araby, carrying me off into the desert. And a pair of actual Arabys protecting me. Eh. Except I'm not sure Hakim is protecting me.

'He is a mad fuck who lives in a dream world, and Hakim, he is dangerous.'

Sa'id was making wanting-the-phone faces. I ignored him.

'No. Not so. He is kind and good. Of course you must not marry if you – but he is kind and good. He loves you. I was so pleased when I realised it was you.'

'What?'

'All these plans and things. He was saying his fiancée is just very shy and new to Cairo, that she wouldn't be going out much. But when I saw the flowers I knew, because I took them to the Hotel el Hussein. So I was surprised when it was you because you are not new or shy, but I was pleased for you to be marrying such a man.'

'Hakim, have you told him where I am staying?'

'Of course! He knows where I live. I told him you are old friend of my family, that I stay with you in London, that you stay with me.'

'Listen, Hakim, please . . .'

Sa'id grabbed the phone off me and started a big brother thing. I grabbed it back and said: 'Hakim, this is more important to me than you can imagine. Let me tell you. I have known this man – François is not his name – I have known him for two years. You have known him for what, two weeks, a month. Trust me. Leave him. Leave his house as soon as you can. If you like I will tell you everything that has passed between him and me but believe me he is a bad man. Do not tell him anything about me. Hakim?'

The silence was there. Then: 'What has passed between you and him?'

I didn't want to tell him. I didn't want to heighten the pressure, to raise the stakes. I only wanted to show a card, to show I had a hand. Which card? Threatening Lily? Telling me he'd kidnapped her? Kidnapping me? Drugging me and trying to rape me? Prostituting my sister? Trying to set fire to me, all those years ago in Charlotte Street, when I was dancing on the table and he poured brandy at my feet and expressed his admiration by setting it alight?

'Hakim,' I said. 'Believe me.'

'I don't know why you would lie.'

'I'm not lying. I'm not lying. Believe me he has done me wrong.'

Hakim was silent.

'We must get off the line, Hakim. Listen, he kidnapped me once before, OK? Please. Just come away.' I didn't know the word for kidnap so I used the English.

'That's true, actually. If she's saying what I think, it's true. She was being recalcitrant and wouldn't come. Silly girl. I must say you've a nice accent, darling.'

FUCK.

'Eddie's on the line,' I hissed to Sa'id.

'Now sweetheart. Has Hakim told you all my plans? Oh

bother, I so wanted it to be a surprise. Never mind. Come along tonight to the Semiramis and we'll talk it all over. Hakim will come too, probably. If he's good. Will you be good, Hakim?'

'Yes,' he said, faintly, on the extension. Crackly.

'I'm annoyed with you, Hakim,' he said.

'Yes,' said the boy.

'What's happening?' said Sarah.

'I'll be there,' I said.

twenty-four

Semiramis

'We're fucked,' I said.

'How so?' said Sarah.

'Eddie was on the line. He probably didn't understand much but he got the gist, that Hakim and I know each other and I was warning him off. Hakim says Eddie has plans to take me up the Nile and marry me.'

'Get the police,' said Sarah. 'Really. If this man has been making threats . . .'

'It's not so simple,' I said. I looked at them. How much could I say? We had to get through tonight and get Hakim back, but then life continues, and I wasn't going to betray Harry. I wasn't. I was pretty sure that Eddie didn't know Harry was police; and then there was the system of loyalties, the police stuff, that Harry had betrayed by telling me. I didn't understand that, but it didn't matter. For me it was simply between us. I do not betray Harry.

I wished he was here. But he'd be a fat lot of good, really. In Zamalek. But even so.

'The thing is, Sarah,' I was saying, 'that as I said I know this bloke of old, he did once kidnap me, I didn't press charges for a lot of very complicated reasons, and he has come back to haunt me, and all I want is to get him off my back. Now it turns out . . .'

'Oh dear,' she said. Faintly.

Sa'id was thinking. I could tell because he was holding my hand.

'Enta 'Omri' again. Give me your hands, so my hands can rest in their touch. (Give me your eyes, so my eyes can roam free in their world.)

'Are you the only thing he wants?' he said.

'I suppose.'

'What he was saying today, one fuck and he leaves you alone, do you believe him?'

'No. And anyway I'm not doing it.' Why is he asking that? Does he think I would? Is he testing me?

'I know you wouldn't. And I wouldn't let you.'

If there's one kind of phrase that riles me, it's anything involving 'not', 'let' and 'you'.

'But *habibti*,' he said. The female again. Bossed and protected.

'Yes?'

'You know his mentality.'

'Insofar as it's knowable.'

'So what do you think?'

'I don't want to go tonight. I'm not going where he is. But we must get Hakim because, what he was saying . . . he was saying if I come to the club Hakim will come to the club. It's a trade. Hakim for me. One way or another. He did that before with Lily.'

'With Lily?' he said. He looked shocked.

'He said he'd kidnapped her, blackmailed me with it. He hadn't, but I didn't know that. She was just late back from tea. Every mother's nightmare.' Oh gosh yes you can look back and laugh. Hollowly.

'But Hakim is with him,' said Sarah. 'We know that.' She looked a little green under the neon street lights.

'He's a big boy,' I said. Not meaning it.

'He's not that big,' she said. 'And he's silly. And Lily wasn't even kidnapped anyway.'

'It's not a competition, Sarah,' I said. 'Any of us are in danger, Hakim most so at the moment. Chill.'

'Sorry,' she said.

'*Malesh*,' I said.

She and Sa'id still hadn't addressed each other. Still carrying round all the crap that needed to be cut through.

We stayed outside Eddie's a little longer, then went on to the Semiramis because Sa'id thought it would be a good idea to choose our table. Backs to the wall. That kind of thing.

It was about one when we got there. How long since I was last here? Eight years or so. It's pretty much like the Paradise, only better nick all round, better quality, higher prices. Two fairly superior babes in stretch velvet were actually singing along, and a singer who seemed to be Lebanese was having a go. The band were OK. I recognised the tabla player from somewhere a long time ago. Plenty of them, but two electric pianos which I hate. They were finishing up. Eddie wasn't there yet. Our dinner started to arrive: masses of it. Dish after dish of tabbouleh and houmous and babaghanouk and tahina and chicken liver and felafel and God knows what. I wanted a drink, but there's something about these hotels that stops me from ordering. Not just the prices.

Then the band changed, a bunch of guys in satin waistcoats started up a rocking rhythm and a dancer came on, in a full length black and gold beaded encrustation, with body stocking, and gave it her all. Which was not bad at all, except that she had shoes on and I just don't hold with that. But it was all right. It was all right when she came back in a skin-tight baladi dress with a pantomime horse in a carnival outfit; it was all right when the horse started working the tables and came nibbling my neck with its huge pantomime nose. It was almost all right when the girl came round and danced to me, until I realised she was Eddie's sex toy from London, the Turkish one from Marouche, the night he drugged me. It wasn't all right when she wanted to pull me on stage. Eddie hadn't come in yet as far as I could see, but I bet he was there and I bet he had fixed this.

'She belongs to Eddie,' I hissed to Sa'id, as I resisted. It is very hard to resist a dancer who is trying to get you up. I know, I've been one. But I really don't like being pushed around.

'No,' I said to her. 'Fuck off.'

She understood. Everybody does. She made some inexpressibly rude Turkish gesture and moved on. Sa'id went to the loo, telling me to – well, motioning through the noise – that I was to stay put and everything would be OK.

The next thing was absolutely not all right. Back she went on the stage, and announced to the assembled mob that as a special favour to her Egyptian friends Hakim and Sa'id el Araby and for the pleasure of her loyal Egyptian fans the lovely dancer Angelina, Amira Amar, who has not danced in Cairo for eight years, has agreed to make an appearance. Gratifyingly, there was some applause. Unfortunately, I was too angry to notice.

I pushed back my chair, pulled Sa'id's scarf around me and walked swiftly to the door. The cloth seemed to fill; I felt like a ship in full sail, and suddenly mouth-witheringly aware of the dirty pictures Janie had made, combining the dancing and the veils and the porn. Made and sold through Eddie.

Go up on stage for him? Dance for that fucker? Last time I danced for him I spat vodka in his face. And on his dick.

'Where is he then?' I said. 'Where is he?' The doorman was nonplussed, but soon steered me round to the back of the club, to an alcove. Where sat Eddie, two girls, a big lug in a bad shirt and Hakim, looking green even in the dim light, blocked in by the lug.

'I want a word with you,' I said, and grabbed Eddie's arm, and hoicked him to the door. 'Outside,' I said. Luckily everybody thought it was funny – a woman pushing a man, a joke, obviously. No one followed. The lug offered to, but Eddie gestured him to stay with Hakim.

I would have thought it was funny, too. This is what it comes down to: 'Oy you – outside.'

In the corridor, nightclub lit, I pushed him up against the wall and looked him in the eye. He didn't struggle. He was loving it.

I can't do this wrapped in Sayeed's cloth. I stood back from him and lifted the mass of fine white wool up over my head, pulling it and casting it aside, and I stood there in my long shift and my bare arms again, my free woman visible woman clothes. My me clothes. He should have knocked me down or left, or something, but he didn't. He watched. He wasn't alarmed by my anger at all. He liked it. Girl disrobing. In a public place too. Mmm!

I put one hand against the wall and leaned in towards him. I'd always assumed I was shorter than him but I wasn't. I looked down at his throat: the throat I'd bitten in my lust, the throat I'd pictured as I'd thought his dead body burned, the throat to which Sa'id had held his blade. I leaned on my good leg and I thought of strangulation. As I breathed out he breathed in and I realised he was taking in my breath, savouring it, watching me. And I breathed in his breath, and I looked him in the eye.

'Leave me alone,' I said. 'Leave me alone, leave my friends alone, leave my family alone. I don't love you, I'm not going anywhere with you, I don't care who or what you threaten. This is stopping right here. Here and now.'

He didn't love that. Well he did, because it upped the stakes a little. But he never gave me the respect necessary for the stakes to go really high. He wasn't scared of me. He only wanted the shag, he didn't need it – he could live without it. I was nothing to him. He didn't even bother to bring his lug out of the club. He was just winding up the sexual energy, artificially, so that he could have a sweeter and more pornographic orgasm at the end of it. Ain't that just like a bloke. He doesn't give a shit.

But the only way he would stop tweaking my chain was if I took the fucking collar off. So I did.

He carried on breathing me.

'But you owe me,' he said quietly.

'No I don't.'

'One fuck.'

'God, you're like some fucking street boy! One fuck, madam. You owe me, mate. You owe me my sister, my reputation and my peace of fucking mind. I would like to kill you and I might yet.'

'I'd like that,' he said, with a little smile. 'Way to go.'

So this was how he was going to end. Knifed by a rent boy, some street creature with a pretty arse who wanted an extra ten quid.

And for a second I lost my concentration. And in that second he tripped me, grabbed me and pushed me round the corner. Some service corner. Dark.

'It'll have to be rape then,' he said. 'What a waste.'

Whereupon I kicked and screamed, and no one came, whereupon I was cursing my bad stars and stupid temper and punching him in the mouth, as far as I could reach, whereupon a dark figure came up the corridor like a shark and leapt on him, and pulled him, and began to punch him, rhythmically, hypnotically, whereupon there flashed a gleam of silver and I cried out, 'No! Stop it!' and pulled my rescuer off my enemy.

Fuck.

Protecting Eddie Bates.

Fuck.

Of course the lug appeared. Then the hotel security – this is Five-Star, after all. Eddie was rapt, shocked, with blood on his mouth. And the shark? It was Hakim. I went to him and took the knife, and kissed his cheek, and held his head, comforting him and holding him in, holding him still, holding him down. Grateful to him and angry with him. A thought skittered across my mind: Thank God Lily is a girl.

I pulled the scarf to us, hid us in it. It smelled of Sa'id: leather, sandalwood, cleanliness.

The guard was pushed aside by a more important guard, then he was pushed aside by the nightclub manager, then he was pushed aside by the manager of the hotel.

I tried to look demure, or shameful. Or shamed. Or something. 'This man attacked me,' I said, in Arabic, gesturing Eddie, clutching the white cloth. 'This man defended me.' Gesturing to Hakim.

'This woman attacked me,' said, Eddie, but he said it in English, and anyway ... women don't attack men in nightclubs. Specially not women with veils. Even if the veil has slipped.

'This man is my brother,' I said. 'This other man I don't care about. Please don't tell my husband. I must return to him. Please. This foreign man is just a fool. He is nothing.'

And the parlaying began, and my husband was sent for. And out he came. Purple with fury. Spitting his Arabic like a fishwife. What the fuck had I been doing? What the fuck was going on? He leaves me for two minutes and look. He thanked the guards. He took Hakim by the scruff of the neck; he looked at Eddie, and he didn't spit at him. But he might have.

The manager was confused.

'Home,' Sa'id said to me.

Ther trouble was, I didn't know if he meant this anger. Or what he meant by it. Who he was angry with.

The guard wanted to know should they call the police. Nobody had seen the knife.

'Of course,' said Sa'id. 'But my wife will not speak to them.'

And you see nothing happened. Eddie was saying nothing. Sa'id was taking me away. And there was only one witness – me. Who was, anyway, involved. And anyway I had no say – I was some bint in a cage. I was off scot-free.

Sa'id gave his name and address. One of the managers seemed to know him. Hakim gave his. I didn't have one to give. I was Mrs Sa'id. Property of, like it says on the back of the biker girls' jackets.

As I turned to leave, Eddie said, 'Did you just save me?' I looked at him under the shadow, and said nothing.

'Quits then,' he said.

Sa'id looked at me.

'*Aiwa*,' I said.

And left. Free as a fucking bird.

twenty-five

God, when he created the world, put a great sea between the Muslims and the Christians, 'for a reason'

Sarah in her relief was very angry with us all. We ignored it. Hakim was chastened. I was chastened. Sa'id, despite the fact that he'd been on his arse on the bog at the moment of crisis, was the only one who seemed to hold his head up.

We drove back to Amina's, a funny edgy bundle of people, emotions ricocheting around the car. Sa'id opened the door for Sarah and Hakim, and said to them both, 'Go to bed.' Sarah looked at him, and said, 'Sa'id.'

For the first time he looked at her. I swear it was the first time.

'Later,' he said.

'Sa'id,' she said again.

He closed his eyes.

'Later,' he said. More gently.

She looked at him for a full minute, her face dramatic in the dim light and shadow of the night. He said nothing more; just stood, eyes shut. But something changed.

She went towards the lift; not obediently, but carrying her expectation like a parcel under her arm. To be unpacked. Later.

Hakim refused, and said he wanted coffee.

'Go to your mother, Hakim,' Sa'id said brusquely. The policemen at the gate raised their heads. One was smoking.

They looked unbearably weary. Hakim risked an unruly look, then went after Sarah.

Me, he told to stay in the car. Exact words. 'Stay in the car.' I was beginning to get annoyed with him.

We drove off again.

'Where are we going?' I said.

'We are going where young couples in this damn city have to go if they want to talk in private. We are going to the Corniche el Nil, to promenade. And to talk.' He was angry. I didn't like it. It didn't suit him. His straight nose got even straighter and looked narrow and pinched.

So we arrived on the Corniche, and he parked and took my hand and practically pulled me across the eight lanes of intersecting suicide traffic that invented new lanes as and when it wanted, even at two in the morning, and we stood by the river and looked out. Tonight it was black, with neon stripes of green and orange, waving, like a baladi dress in chiffon and interweave.

We leaned against the balustrade, and for a while we said nothing.

I felt sad, actually, because I realised that I liked him being authoritative with other people; or when it suited me, but not now. I felt we were about to come up against it.

'So what happened?' he said. 'How come you were out in the corridor with the man you didn't want to go anywhere near?'

So I told him. About the dancer's announcement, and my flash of temper, and my realisation about the chain. About being tweaked. 'It's what you said,' I told him. I told him I felt safe, in public. I told him I just had to tell Eddie.

There was some silence.

'It's not your fault Hakim was working for him,' he said.

'No,' I said.

'Nor that Hakim felt so strongly to defend you.'

'I'm glad he did.'

'I'm not. He could have been hurt.'

'Sa'id, Hakim had a knife. It wasn't him who was going to get hurt.'

His beautiful eyes opened a little wider. It changed the effect of the light on his cheekbones. They go back so far – to his ears. Such a strange face.

'Then he could have been arrested.'

'Yes. But he wasn't.'

'Yes. Because you were quick-witted.'

'Yes.'

He sighed.

'So are you happy now?' he asked.

'No.'

'Why not?'

'Because you aren't.'

He smiled.

'I'll talk to my mother,' he said.

'I don't give a shit about your mother.'

It wasn't true. I just didn't then. I was feeling too much else. I felt the ground opening up beneath my feet. I felt love lurching.

'Now that you have sorted it out,' he said, '– have you sorted it out?'

'I think so,' I replied. 'I think – he said quits. I think he means it. I think – yes. From what I know of him. His mentality.' I used Sa'id's word on purpose. His word in my mouth to bring us closer again.

'Well, I must go back to work,' he said. Then, 'Tell me one thing.'

I knew what it was. Knew it couldn't have passed him by. Knew I wouldn't be so lucky.

'Yes, I did,' I said. Why waste time.

'He said. Let me get this right. He said you did and he didn't.'

'Yes.'

'How?'

I didn't want to say it. I was ashamed. I didn't want to tell him. In a way this was the moment when I started to cry, the crying that didn't stop for weeks.

But I did say it. I took him close to me and felt the warmth of his cheek, as close as a razor, and I whispered it in his ear, into his black curls, breathing their familiar scent, and I held his head to my mouth, and whispered as if he wasn't there, as if I was just practising saying words, words I found difficult. When I finished talking my tongue brought one of his curls between my teeth, where I held it for a moment, afraid to let go.

I thought it quite likely that he might hate me now.

We weren't on the same side any more. We had been for so long.

'Sa'id, you're not on my side any more.' I said it out loud, breaking the silence that followed my confession. The silence while the words did their damage.

'It's not that,' he said finally. 'It's just we've come a little further.'

I was silent. I didn't know if I believed him. I hitched myself up on the balustrade to sit. He reached his hand out to steady me. At least he wasn't tipping me in the Nile. I lit a fag. And waited.

'So I must go back to Luxor,' he said. 'There is lots of work to be done.'

Oh not like that, Sa'id. Please not like that, after everything.

'You know my father made our business but he never liked it. I like it. And I'm good at it. So I must go and do it.'

And?

'It's what I do.'

And?

I smoked. If I looked back at an angle I could see the

reflection of my cigarette glowing deep in the deep water.
Glowing brighter, and dimmer.

He looked so young. He should be along here with a 23-year-old Egyptian virgin, not with me.

'Sa'id, please. Please.' I wasn't crying.

'You saved Hakim tonight. You caused his danger – you did, you made him want to protect you – and you saved him. You are doing the same to me.'

'Sorry,' I said, foolishly.

'Shut up,' he said.

I turned away so that I could watch the river better. All the lights on in Giza across the way. Pyramids down there. This ancient Nile. He leaned beside me. Facing in to the city.

'Why are you so angry with me?' I could think of a thousand and one reasons, but I wanted to know which was his.

He was silent for a several moments. I counted.

'Because you put yourself in danger. You did it without me.'

'But it was my . . . danger. It was mine.'

'Yours and that man's.'

'Are you jealous of that?'

'Yes, but that is not . . .'

'What?'

'You didn't let me . . . you prevented me,' he said. I knew what he meant but he kept talking. 'Your anger took you. You were not with me – not because I wasn't there physically. But inside, you were alone. Because you wanted to be alone. You are by nature alone.'

I knew what he meant. He meant that when it came down to it I didn't need or want a man because I am that kind of Englishwoman. I wasn't going to let him say it, because it could never be taken back, and it wasn't true.

'I am what I am, but that doesn't mean I can't love,' I said.

Dammit he is meant to love me *for* my character, not despite it.

The silence sat. Floated on the water. Drifted away downstream towards the delta, and the sea.

'Come with me,' he said, 'and we won't talk about it for a few days.'

Can you do that? Can you get away with it once the subject has been raised?

His eyes had gone dark as the river.

The only other option is to jump in and swim home.

That night separate beds, the next day he was out, doing things, finishing off business. I wanted nothing but to sleep until I could take him in my arms again and make it all right. I couldn't understand why it wasn't. But it wasn't. There was a story in the back of my mind that I read years ago, about a northern woman on the beach at Alexandria, married to her Egyptian love, losing him, pinioned on the edge of each world by her love for their child, watching the surf which licked Europe lick Africa. Something about how the beach knows nothing of the desert, and the surf knows nothing of the depths of the sea. Written by an Egyptian woman, Ahdaf Soueif. I do believe that east and west can meet, that north and south can live. I do believe it.

Hakim was curdling my coffee again over breakfast. He wanted to go over everything. He wanted blame, redemption, love and demonstrations that we had not lost faith in him. Well, I could understand that. He wanted to apologise; he still wanted to kill Eddie. Last night he had personified the collapse of a stout party; today he was almost raring to go again.

'It's over,' I said.

For moments during the night I had wondered, could I really believe that? Just because he had called it quits? Why wasn't I afraid that his wildness would just skip over that promise the moment it felt like it, and put me back where I had been before? Why did I trust him? Well, I didn't trust him. I trusted myself. To deal with him, any time, any way. I'd rather not have to, but I could and I would. I'd done it before, and I could do it again.

'For you maybe, not for me,' he said. And that was true. I didn't know for sure that Eddie would leave Hakim alone. Or Sa'id. I thought he would. But there's always a but.

'Hakim,' I said, gathering myself to consider him in the midst of my own travails, preparing to matronise. And realising in time that it wouldn't do any good. And still I couldn't tell the truth about our enemy. But I had to make sure Hakim would not go poking about in Eddie's embers, stirring things up.

'Hakim, it's over. If you have any more argument with Eddie – François – he may come back for me. Don't do that to me. Forget your argument with him, for my sake. He didn't know you knew me.'

Or did he?

Hakkim was bullocking: swaying his head in obstinate male youth, thinking *bollocks*.

Did Eddie know?

'When did you meet him, Hakim?' I asked.

'A few months ago,' he said.

Oh. Oh oh oh.

'Why did you come to my house?' The danger may be over but . . . did I know what it had been?

'Because you were nice before. Just because you were kind. I wanted you to help. You did help,' he said, and smiled. For a moment he looked like his brother.

'He didn't send you?'

Realisation hit him slowly, like speeded up film of a flower unfurling.

'No no no no,' he said. 'Absolutely just no. No. He didn't know – he didn't even know I was in your house. He just thought I was in a hotel. He gave me my mobile phone, you know, so he could ring me all the time. That was him! I was going to tell him I had been in the hotel but save the money. I gave it to my mother! I was just doing my work for him and my work for Sa'id. No connnection was made. No con-nection.'

'What was your work for him?' What difference did it make? Did I care now?

'I went round the place and posted some things for him and . . .'

My curdled coffee spluttered from my mouth.

'Posted? Posted what?'

'I don't know. You know I don't read English.' He was peeved that I had brought up the subject. I was picturing us at that breakfast table, me naturally assuming that the anonymous letters were something to do with him. Not that they were from him . . .

Ha bloody ha.

I couldn't blame Hakim. I don't suppose he had even looked at the envelopes.

Ha bloody ha.

'Hakim, *habibi*,' I said. 'He's promised me to leave you alone. Leave him alone too? Please? Because if you don't my life won't be worth living. Promise me. Hakim – we're human beings. All we are is how we are to each other. Promise me.'

I called Sarah in. She witnessed the promise. Wanted to know what it was. Never to go near that man again, I said. I'll drink to that, she said. I would have felt a surge of pity for her if I had any feelings to spare.

'What are you doing now?' I asked her.

'Giving up any hope of anybody explaining to me what

has been going on around here,' she said. I told her that Hakim would tell her. He knew enough for public consumption. His could become the official version.

'I want Sa'id,' she said. This sulkiness was unbecoming. If understandable.

'Give him time,' I suggested.

'Oh, yeah,' she said. 'Yeah.'

She was waiting for 'later'. She would spend her days in the Egyptian Museum, admiring canopic jars, she said, until he deigned to talk to her. Yes, I like them too, I said. The alabaster ones, and the tiny little gold and lapis coffins that go inside each one.

Looking at her, and her strange position here, I thought we might have been friends. I think she did too, because she sighed and wondered would I like to go with her. No, I said, I'm going to Luxor. With Sa'id.

She looked at me as older women must have looked at younger women for generation on generation. With incomprehension at how we were going to repeat their mistakes, even though they had made them, and shown us and told us how pointless the exercise was. Well sorry, darling. We do what we do. All of us. Over and over.

I did want to know her story. I did. I just . . .

Maybe later.

'Well,' she said. 'That's that then.'

'Sarah,' I said, not pleading, but with a touch of . . . something.

She looked at me.

'It was very, very difficult,' she said.

Yes.

Perhaps I'll ring her in five years and ask.

'Will you go and see him?' I asked her. I meant Abu Sa'id. She knew I did.

'What for?'

I had no answer. For your babies, I might have said, but her babies are grown.

We took the night train, with the money between us on the seat. And in Luxor he changed again. Going over to the West Bank in the early early morning after arriving he took a friend's felucca and sailed us, though it would take twice as long as a motor launch. 'Enough of engines,' he said, and instead we had the creak and silence of the dawn, lined with reeds and egrets. Mist encircled us, and the sunrise seeped crimson and gold through it. He gave me his scarf again, against the chill. Invisible in the mist loomed the grandest ruins in the world: Karnak and Luxor, the temples and the tombs, the sacred lakes, the avenues of sphinxes, Ozymandias, King of Kings; the colossi and obelisks, the pylons and stelae, the kiosks and pavilions and hypostyle halls, the sanctuaries and Nileometers and the giant scarabs and the endless ranks of statues of Ramses the Great. Hatshepsut, Medinat Habu, the Ramesseum. The red granite, the white marble, the limestone. Thousands of years worth of the glory of the ancestors, thousands of years old. Invisible in the mist.

The river was like wet concrete stained with watery blood. Eau de Nil is a great many colours. If a mafioso had buried his enemy here, this is how the evidence would creep out. And once again Sa'id's eyes matched the river, bloodshot with the sleepless night on the train, sitting up as mile upon mile of Egypt was consumed beneath us. Tea at Esna, bread at Edfu. Traction again, though it shouldn't have been because the only business I had was with the man next to me. It's just we weren't dealing with our business. Hiding in our own mist.

He steered with his foot, like the Nile boatmen do, manipulating the great sail and the wide pale boat as Nile boatmen do. Why wouldn't he? He is a Nile boatman. He was born here. He couldn't have been a boy here and not learned to do that. There is practically no wind but he knows where he is taking us. He could negotiate the first cataract against the wind; he can sing. He could make me stay here. His linen is pristine though he has been on a train all night. He eats bananas half the fruit at a time, and smokes his *shisha* out of the side of his mouth, his top lip hardly touching. This is what he is.

I remembered what he said: 'Do you mind, that I am an Arab and you are an Englishwoman?'

'Enchanted,' I had said.

Even through the blood, his eyes were exactly the colour of the palm tips, now I had the opportunity to check. Aswan at dusk, Luxor at dawn. Apart from Lily, I don't think I had ever loved anyone so much.

Abu Sa'id met us at the dusty landing stage on the West Bank. Thebes. My past self was so happy to see him but my present was too bound up to notice. I can't even remember how he was with me. Mariam was at the house. She brought coffee. *Ariha*. A little sweet. Not very.

Sa'id went into the shop and worked all day. I went and took him to lunch.

That evening we walked up on to the hills behind, on the scrubby lunar land between the Valley of the Kings and the Temple of Hatshepsut at Deir al-Bahri, and we looked down on to its great terraces and ramps, and told each other all the bits we knew of what she had written on the walls there, and on the great obelisk across the river, about her voyage to the land of Punt in search of myrrh, about her fake beard and her insistence on Amun Ra being her father, so that she could rule even though she was a woman, and how her nephew had chipped away every picture of her on her own temple, because he had grown to hate her, waiting so long to inherit. We walked for hours in the dark. He held my hand and the sand bit my ankles with tiny nips. We fucked in the sand, wrapped in his gallabeya and his big scarf, under the moon, no longer crescent, lying on its back in its southern way. Orion – Osiris – above us, and the empty tombs below. It was not comfortable but it was magical. Hatshepsut, he said, was an Englishwoman.

The next day he worked in the morning, and I sat upstairs at the workshop, poking through boxes of antiquities, or fake antiquities, or antique fakes stone-baked in faience. Little dark figurines, tiny Anubises, Sekmet and Bastet. Thoth, heavy and dusty. Weird things.

'They are fake, made for tourists in the nineteenth century,' he said, drifting up behind me like a ghost. 'So they are now genuine, valuable fakes.'

'Are they valuable?' I wondered.

'Depends to who,' he said.

Later that I day I watched him selling a couple of unpolished vases to a German couple. He knew I was watching. He was good. Of course he was.

'But how much does it cost?' the girl kept demanding, sitting on the leather sofa in the shop, as if a price were a lump or a measurement, an absolute truth. As if he were tricking her by keeping some genuine concrete price secret from her. She just wanted to know where she stood. Sa'id was sweet with her. 'It costs something between what you will pay and what I will accept,' he said. She didn't get it. In the end they paid . . . a good price. She wanted a camel too. Sa'id said he could get one for her.

'Can you?' I asked later.

'For her, no. She doesn't want one.'

After that I went and sat in the yard and watched the transformation of alabaster, and thought about Nadia, and the nature of stone, and the nature of other less tangible things, about the past, and about the future, and about Lily. There is something fantastically long about the past in this neck of the woods. Of the desert. I felt I was sitting on Set's lap, Set god of the desert. The vicious stripe of green by the river, then the dust, the clean dust and the thousands of winds, and the hidden mysteries beneath it. The tombs they're still uncovering.

Then Sa'id came and we went out for lunch, so we could be away from the population of the workshop, and he told me about the tomb of the Sons of Ramses, only uncovered in 1995, full and promising. Maybe 50 sons in there. He had a friend who was working on it. I don't know. Maybe he was offering me things to keep me interested. As if I wasn't interested. As if that were the problem.

We sat in the dusty garden of a cheap hotel within spitting distance of the colossi of Memnon, the statues that don't sing any more. Where the friends of Oscar Wilde's swallow are waiting for him, where he should be, instead of distributing bits of gold leaf to starving children and sick artists, torn from a heartbroken statue in the middle of winter. October. It's a good time to go south.

I told him I wanted him to give Eddie's money to a charity in Cairo. Something for children. Not too religious, if possible, but it didn't really matter. Really I wanted to go the top of the minaret at Ibn Tulun and scatter it like rose petals, like shreds of gold leaf, over the city. Fluttering like the waters of heaven on the beauty and the pain. But I knew I wouldn't. So – the sensible equivalent.

'You want me to do it?' he said, under a green vine.

'Yes.'

'You won't?'

There was pause.

A melamine table, a tin ashtray, a cricket scritching.

'No,' I said.

It wasn't entirely clear what he was asking; what I was saying no to.

But I said no.

twenty-six

The End, and the Beginning

I cried all the way back to London. All the fucking way,
wrapped in his scarf that he wrapped round me on the river
bank. On the boat, on the train, in the cab, at the airport,
on the plane, in Athens, on the next plane. 'Enta 'Omri'
running through my head: '*Elli shuftu, elli shuftu, abl ma
teshoufak enaya . . .*' What I saw before my eyes saw you.
The way Umm Kalthoum sings it, the length and beauty of
her phrases, makes the melody sound how written Arabic
looks. The artistic elongations, the arabesques, the stretching.
And the release, the compression, the fitting of the language
into a separate form, for its own beauty. Floriate, foliate.
Like Hakim's Qur'anic *aya*, tear drop from his neck.

This is how I felt. Elongated into a beautiful form.

He didn't ask why I was leaving him, or try to stop me.
He'd expected it. It was me who hadn't. I'm not talking about
the end of half term.

The *hejeb* on his throat.

I had a lot of imaginary conversations through my tears.
Continuations of our conversation on the Corniche el Nil. In
my version he called me *habibi*, told me I hadn't let him help,
let him love me, and do his duty as a lover, and if I hadn't then,
I never would; and I told him that that was his pride, that my
problem was solved so why did it matter how, that anyway

he had helped, hugely, comprehensively, that I couldn't have done anything without him. It made no difference.

I was silently, semi-consciously aware that I was weeping for more than him.

After a while it was for Janie: for her, not for myself about her. Because she was ashamed and jealous, and now she's dead and unforgiven, and she never knew her child.

I lingered on unforgiven. Whether it was the right word. Remembered what Sa'id had said about the dead: 'God has taken him, leave them to it.' And asked me something like 'could I leave her alone'. We didn't finish that conversation either.

Another line from 'Enta 'Omri': 'Through you, I have reconciled with my days, Through you, I have forgiven my past.'

Unforgiven. Maybe not.

Sa'id, how could you think you didn't help me?

And I cried for Mum.

For Lily.

For my leg and the imminence of death. For loneliness and loss.

Several times I found myself turning to him for comfort, and he wasn't there. I knew he was turning too, and nor was I.

Harry and Lily met me at the airport. I didn't have the energy to be surprised. He carried my bags to the Pontiac.

I cried even more.

'Was Egypt really horrible?' Lily asked. No, I said.

Then she said she liked it when I cried, because she could be specially nice to me. I hugged her to me as if she were the last child on earth, and cried more.

'You left him there, then?' said Harry.

I looked at him through my pall of tears and said, 'Well spotted.'

'And the rest?'

'I'll tell you when I've stopped crying,' I said.

'Ah, you're going to stop?'

'I hope to,' I said.

It didn't seem that he was being unkind, but I don't think I would have noticed either way.

'Did you find my daddy there?' Lily wanted to know. 'Did you bring him back?'

There was an enormous billboard on the Uxbridge Road: it said, 'I wish I was in Egypt.' Pictures of temples and sphinxes and stuff.

I cried all night.

I was still crying when Harry came round the next morning. Crying at my little pretend garden, my view over the fucking A40, at my kitchen, empty and untouched for a week. It was finally cold and wet.

Lily wanted to know why I was crying. Not surprisingly. I told her. Told her Sa'id had had to stay in Egypt and I had to come home and I was sad. But that I wouldn't be forever. Which I knew I wouldn't be, because you're not – hell I even got over Harry – and because I prefer in my soul to be happy, so I would be. Because it's that simple. Somewhere. I had just lost the way.

Lily was very kind to me. Interested. She brought me handkerchiefs a lot and was pleased to be useful. I tried not to suffocate her in desperate embraces; tried not to clutch her too tight. It's not fair to make a child bear all its parent's love.

Harry came the next morning too. On the Ducati. I heard the crack of the exhaust coming like a figment from the past. He made my coffee for me and said my mother wanted to talk to me and said could I ring her, or answer the phone. I agreed I probably would. Soon. Ish.

Also he wanted to talk to me. I must have lit up. Certainly I felt my heart lurch.

'No,' he said, 'we haven't heard yet.'

'But due soon?' I asked.

'Next few days.'

Oh boy.

When it was time to take Lily to school he walked along with us. I wondered if he was practising. When I looked at him sideways he didn't look back at me. We are awaiting the outcome and till then we could do nothing. Nothing. I understood that.

On the way back the tarmac had a dull glow to it, and the sky sat on our heads. Dead leaves waiting to fall. Ten past nine, Tuesday morning. Reality biting at my heels again. Imaginary birds flapping round my head.

'Have you stopped crying?' he said.

I wondered whether I had, and thought probably not. It struck me that he is very patient with me.

'For the time being,' I said, gingerly.

He suggested a cup of coffee. We ambled along through the wetness to the Serbian café. Hatchet-faced young men sat in groups, wearing anoraks and talking about football. Men with faces which said they had stories, stories they would never tell. We settled in a corner.

'So what happened with Eddie?' he asked.

One of those little questions. One of those innocent, simple questions. Like 'how are you?' As if I had a clue about any of what had happened with Eddie, since the first moment that he impinged on my life, trying to kill me. One day, maybe, if I achieve great wisdom and understanding, I will realise that along the way I have learnt something of what happened with Eddie.

But in the meantime, for now, I could give it an innocent simple answer.

'All done,' I said. Saying it made me feel better. Hell, it was all done. I believed it really was. Not all understood, but all done.

'What did you do?'

'Told him to fuck off and leave me alone.'

He smiled. I was glad he did.

'Was that all it took?' he asked.

'It was quite a lot, actually.'

Yes, wasn't it. The focusing of fury, the discovery of one of his rare human spots. And how did I discover it? It wasn't so clever of me. It was fluke. No, it was ... emotion. My anger and my sense of honour found it. Nothing to do with me – with the me that I control. My poor over-valued head. As with the last time I hit on one of his rogue specks of humanity, when he first told me about Janie being a whore. He had become utterly, humanly sympathetic, just for a moment. Real, and kind, for a count of eight in the middle of his madness. Because of my pain. My uninfluenceable pain. So it was the liberation of emotion from the deadweight of intellect that did it.

But he wasn't a fellow you would trust to react to the same thing twice in the same way. But that's OK, because I didn't trust him an inch anyway. It was me, me, with the chain taken off, that I trusted. My capacity to deal with stuff.

Take Chrissie for example. There had been hang-ups on the phone and it hadn't occurred to me to 1471. I'd binned three alien envelopes waiting for me on my return, without thinking. There's a lot to be said for not thinking. Later I might want to give her a ring. Take her for that drink. Or I might not. It did occur to me that I had given Sa'id the money which she may still want. Well, fuck her. Let her try, if she's hard enough. The threats are theirs, but the fear is mine, and if I choose to cast it from the minarets then there it goes. Gone.

And the fact that my instinct was to save his life proves that my heart and honour are bigger than my fear anyway.

'I was told there had been a disturbance with a woman in a nightclub . . .' said Harry.

'That was me.'

'I thought so,' he said.

He wanted something more about all this. He wanted the full story. I felt I would give it to him, one day. He deserved it.

What am I saying? Will I tell him about fucking Eddie? About protecting him?

I looked at Harry, looking at me as I mused and digested. Our balance was off. It was as if we didn't both quite fit in the space available to us. Shifting around, budging up against each other, causing things to spill. Curdling . . . maybe.

'And Sa'id?' he asked. Unembarrassed.

I found my tears were still there. Not that far away.

'He's very like you in some ways,' I said, out of nowhere.

'I know,' he said.

'I got rid of him too,' I said.

'I wonder what you mean by that,' he said. His voice was a little tight.

'So do I,' I said.

'Well,' said Harry. Carefully. As if he were not at all certain that what he was saying was what he ought to say. 'He was more dangerous than Eddie, wasn't he?'

Now what does he mean by that?

'Well, you know. On a day to day level. If you . . . let me put this right . . . if you were going to be in love with a man, and I think you were – are – I don't know, but if you were to be in love, not racing off to Cairo but just like day to day, being with him, then you would have had to . . . change. Wouldn't you? Make room in your sock drawer. Move house or something. Compromise. Not your specialty, really. So if you ditch him, romantically, you don't have to think about it and you can carry on in cloud-cuckoo land. I mean, where would he have put his shoes? Quite apart from everything else. And,' he said, anticipating my reaction and putting his hand on my arm to hold me still, not looking me in the eye, not looking at me at all, and speaking quicker, as if to get the words out before he stopped himself, 'forgive me but since Janie died it seems you're happy for everything to die, except Lily, of course; it seems you want to kill things. Because of . . . whatever, how you feel about that. About Janie.'

I told him to fuck off.

'I'll be precise,' he said. 'Your career. Dancing. Your old friendships. Your parents, at times of . . . delicacy. This romance with Sa'id. Me, when I approach you. The world. You don't want it. Since she died. Since you might have died. Since you started hating her.'

'I don't hate her.'

'Good,' he said.

'Look at me,' I said.

He looked.

I left the café.

Back at the flat I tried to make it nice again. Straighten it out. Standards had slipped while I was away and life seemed to have seeped out of my home while I was otherwise engaged. Neglect it and it dies. I washed up and made beds and hung laundry and tried to increase the levels of comfort and hygiene, to make it human, warm. Home. My heart wasn't in it but superficially it helped.

Happy for everything to die. Fuck him. I took out my anger on the pillows and the kitchen floor. Shaking out the chair in the kitchen I lifted Janie's box from its depths, and put it on the kitchen table.

'I don't hate you,' I said. It was the one thing I did that morning that was either convincing or convinced.

Then the news came on the radio saying that 62 people had been murdered at the Temple of Hatshepsut in Luxor, and I cried for another two days.

When I took Lily to school the billboard on the Uxbridge Road had been papered over in white. I rang Cairo and Sarah said that Sa'id looked as if he was going to die. I wrote him a letter saying I would always love him, but I didn't send it.

A week later I was reading Lily her bedtime story – about Emily, a guinea pig who loves to travel – when Harry pitched up.

'Hello,' he said. There was brightness in his eye, and intensity.

'Hello,' I said, and let him in.

'When you've finished, can we have a chat?'

'Of course,' I said.

I went back to Lily's room and finished the story, and read another one, about a princess. The sun prince had fallen in love with her and she laid three ruby red eggs, and sent him a message via a snow-white crow, but the crow got distracted and never delivered the message.

Then Lily wanted Harry to come and say goodnight. He sat on her bed and even though my tattered sanity was still floating in a high wind I could tell that he was her father and that he had come to tell me so.

I stood in the hallway eavesdropping. They were sweet together. Then he came out and she wanted me again. I lay beside her and kissed her and hugged her and stroked her and hugged her and kissed her and she told me to get off.

I went out into the hallway where he was waiting and said to him: 'Tell me it's good.'

'What's good for you?' he asked. We hadn't spoken since I had walked out on him.

'You are,' I said. I bit my lip as I said it. It didn't come out quite as I meant. I meant, you as the father. Not you, as you, for me. I was annoyed with myself.

'Me? You remember me?' he said.

Did I?

I opened the cover, swiftly, briefly, over the deep well of him, him and the past. Glimpsed love, pain, pride and mis-understanding writhing like a garland of snakes. Gleaming unbearably on the surface was the knowledge that what he had said about me in the café was true.

'Yes,' I said.

'Who am I then?'

'Some bloke I used to know.' I couldn't not be hard here. I didn't want to be hard but I was terrified. Terrified.

He smiled.

'Some bloke who knows you,' he said.

He was standing in the landing just where I had been when Sa'id first kissed me. Sa'id would just – oh fuck. Sa'id is not. Sa'id –

Why do I feel that I'm giving up? That I'm abstaining, losing, conceding, copping out, betraying? Some part of me expects to be tarred and feathered for this. For not being in Egypt right now, for letting Harry in, for giving up something. For compromising, for making the best of it.

Well exactly.

'What happens now, Harry?'

'I tell you the result.'

'I already know.'

'Are you happy?' he said. He could see that I wasn't. He wasn't either.

'No,' I said. 'I'm fucking terrified.'

His eyes filled with something – no of course I couldn't tell what, I'm no judge. He wanted to say something. Couldn't think what. Perhaps emotional incompetence was what filled his eyes. Or sympathy. Or his own fear. Or amazement and tenderness that I admitted mine. Could have been any of those.

I just prayed he wasn't going to ask me to . . . marry him, or be with him, or . . . however they phrase it these days, just because of Lily.

'Last time we reached this point I said it was too convenient,' I said. Jumping the gun.

'So you did,' he said. 'You.' He started to laugh. 'Convenient. You're about as convenient as a train crash.'

So I laughed.

And he laughed.

But it wasn't all right.

After a while he said: 'I'm still me.' His throat was tight. 'Yes.'

We stood like that for several moments. Backs to the wall. But not faces.

'Mu-um,' came the cry. Oh my God, saved by the Lil.

'Coming,' I called, and went in. Brushing past him.

'What are you talking about?' she asked.

'Not sure, really,' I asked.

Harry came in too. He was standing beside me, beside the bed. Oh my God. Like a million nursery book illustrations. My backbone wriggled. I turned to look at him – checking it was him, wondering what on earth he was doing there. In the grander, metaphysical way. He caught my eye and said 'Shall I?' with his eyebrows. Just like a dad, checking with the mum before saying something. And I acceded, did that 'OK darling' mother-agreeing movement of the head.

Oh my God. It's as if it's genetic.

I don't know if I want to be a mother with a father around. I don't know how to do it. Fuck.

Ugh.

Suddenly we're – whatever it is we are. Janet and John's mummy and daddy. I saw us as a line drawing. I was wearing an apron; he was in a casual suit with knife-edge pleats (steamed and pressed by me) and smug expression. I was going to cook some time-saving recipe from *Good House-keeping*, with a can of mushroom soup in it. I wanted to run away screaming.

But I had agreed to this. To something. Promised her, and nodded to him.

Remember your heart and your honour are bigger than your fear.

It's Harry. It's only Harry.

'We were talking about your father,' he said. He was white as a sheet. Glowing in the dimness of her bedroom.

'That's interesting,' she said. 'Is it you?'

He was calm, and strong, and pale. Nice. As I would have wanted him to be. She was round and wakeful and interested. She just wanted to know. I wasn't worried about her. She was made for this. She'd been waiting for this all her life.

Her life. My life. This is my life.

I'm not losing a daughter . . . she's not losing a mother. Not.

'Yes,' he said, and as he said it the set of his shoulders changed a little, and something shifted inside him.

She just stared at him. Stared.

Didn't look at me.

Then climbed out of bed and into my arms, still staring at him. He smiled. Sort of. Put his shoulders back slightly, in a proud way. Something of his loucheness was slipping away before my eyes.

She put her face in my neck and whispered. 'Should I cry?' she asked me. Her tiny body full of emotion. Heavy with it.

'No,' I said, and felt fear running off me like water.

* * *

I lay down with her and after a while she went to sleep, having said no more. When I emerged an hour later he was in the kitchen, sitting. He looked up as I came in and said, 'Well?'

'Fine,' I said. 'I think.'

After some silence he said he was sorry.

'What for?'

'In the café,' he said.

'But you're right,' I said. If he takes it back I will be so angry.

'I know,' he said, 'but I wasn't gentle.'

'But you were right,' I said.

'Don't rub it in,' he said.

'It's OK,' I said. 'I don't need to do it any more.'

He smiled. Gave me a glass of whisky.

'Harry,' I said. 'You have a child.'

'We have a child.'

It was, in its truth, astounding.

'How the hell did we manage that?' I asked.

'By the strangest and most roundabout route,' he said.

There was an idea floating around the room that this was where we had always been meant to end up anyway. I don't know whose idea it was. It was just there.

When I looked up from my glass he was looking at me.

'I've been thinking about this,' he said. 'As you might imagine, and I've worked out what I want to say. Right.'

He stared at me.

'Go on then,' I said.

Later he told me what he had been going to say. He had been going to say, 'I've always respected you and I always will, and I'm your child's father, and I'm certain that there is a way we can work this out and be good parents and be happy, and that's what I want to do so how about it.' And he had been going to say something about wanting to be there but not wanting to invade, and something about money, if he could think of a way to say it without offending me. And he had been going to mention that Amygdala had told him that he was clearly emotionally unavailable what with this paternity thing, and left him. And he had wanted to say something about how much he had loved me, but then the tense seemed wrong.

But he didn't. He said 'oh fuck', vehemently, and stood, and I caught his eye, and we hung there like moments on a chain.

'Oh fuck?' I said. With a tiny echo of a laugh.

'Oh yes,' he said.

It was suddenly both emotionally transparent and very dirty. We stared at each other.

'How about now?' he said. 'It would save so much time . . .' Which was pretty much what he had said to me within two minutes of our first meeting, twelve years ago.

I knew what I would be saying yes to. Part of me wanted to say yes.

I could only manage 'maybe'.